Praise for
Finn O'Malley and
AWAKENING OF LIGHT

"*Awakening of Light* is a fun and inspiring read. I thoroughly enjoyed the motivational aspects woven throughout the book, especially the core messages that address the many ways we limit ourselves and restrict our inner power when we don't dare to take risks. I came out of this book with the message that life is too short not to get out of your rut, take risks, seek adventure, and truly *live*. As a suburban wife and mother, I would like to visit another realm every once in a while, and this book took me to one. I can't wait for book two!"

—Sarah Finkelstein Waters
Author, *Soul Custody*

"*Awakening of Light* is an elemental masterpiece! This book had all the ingredients to weave me inside the pages and transport me into another realm filled with magic and mystery. Jax the cat had me rolling on the floor with his dry, cat-like humor. The character development was brilliant. In fact, I am waiting for Aislynn to knock on my door wearing skinny jeans, with coffees in tow, so we can catch up. O'Malley led me on such an emotional journey that by the last page, I caught myself staring out my bedroom window, looking at things differently and wondering what magic is waiting for me."

—Tina Kay
Cohost of *Dare to Rise* Podcast

"Wow! Such an adventure. This was something that started slowly, building up to a wonderful magical adventure. I just couldn't put it down. Well-written characters. O'Malley is great at seeing into the mind and dragging you there too. Very enjoyable read."

—Patricia Harris

"I was sucked in from the first page! Imagination and creativity join with forces beyond this world to create an epic one-of-a-kind story that you won't want to put down. A must read!"

—Sarah Secrist

"Absolutely fabulous! O'Malley is a five-star author. She captivates at the first word and keeps you enthralled until the very end. Then she leaves you yearning for more, and Aislynn is a heroine to love! Brave and cunning, magical and practical, stunning! She's supported by the ultimate heart stop, the breathtaking Rowan. This is a must read . . . over and over and over again!"

—Natalie Matthews

"Finn O'Malley is a master of magical adventure. She has created an enchanting world ruled by elemental magic and peopled with unforgettable characters, like a smart-ass cat who may be more than he seems. O'Malley's Aislynn, both relatable and powerful, is a heroine you will want to follow through the Realms."

—Amy Fenster

Awakening
of Light

Awakening of Light

Book One of the Keeper of Elements Series

Finn O'Malley

Clearfield, UT

Cover Design by Jayelle at Dream Saver Covers
Editing by Hannah Lyon at Castle Lyon Editing
Formatting by TNT Editing
Author photo by Transparency with Meagan

ISBN: 978-1-7341135-2-5
Library of Congress Control Number: 2020925612
25   24   23   22   21   1   2   3   4   5

To Tristan and Riley

Anything is possible when you follow your heart.

*Now, more than ever, we must
remember the magic that resides in
each of us.*

PROLOGUE

Thousands of years ago

The three stood cloaked in the darkness of night, aglow in a circle of magic.

"We must protect this from ever occurring again." Aliro, the Keeper of Air, spoke in a hushed tone.

"How do you suppose we do that?" The Keeper of Earth asked from beneath the folded layers of his deep emerald velvet cloak.

"He must be punished." Air's fists clenched under her own thick cloak as swirls of yellow golden light emanated from behind her small frame.

"I agree, but what punishment is enough?" Earth's voice was soothing to Air's anger.

"No punishment will stop him. He will persevere no matter our choices," the Keeper of Fire finally spoke in a quiet tone.

"But we must try! It is our duty." The torment alive within Air's eyes reflected through the dim light.

"I have seen what is to come," Fire said as flames danced around the circle. She knew, no matter the spell, Water would find a way to create chaos across the realms.

"Air is right; we must try. Perhaps with time, our brother will see the error in his ways," Earth relented. Silence saturated the forest, waiting. The future depended on this moment.

Fire acquiesced, raising her arms to continue, and the three Keepers weaved a spell to protect the realms from magic.

1

February 16

My lips rolled over my teeth in annoyance as I weaved around a slow walker in pristine white tennis shoes. The boots and high heels of those around me resounded in steady clicks through the glass walkway hanging between the buildings of the downtown Minneapolis skyway system. Our very own indoor rat maze, with everyone scurrying to their next destination and stopping for cheese along the way.

Mind you, if the skyway system didn't exist, we were likely to freeze to death, as this was the time of year the wind chill factors sucked your life essence the moment you tried to breathe. Living in the Midwest in January and February became a nonstop meme haven for ridiculous laughter, and I lived here. *Willingly.*

I was surprised my brain was capable of these chaotic, albeit cohesive, thoughts this morning as sleep didn't come until after two. Problems with a design layout of my department's current project led to a plethora of swearing and caffeine until I forced my computer genius upon them. Darting around more suits and gymers (my nickname for the insane humans who found it exhilarating to work out at five in the morning), my annoyance built. *All different kinds of rats, I suppose.*

Finally, the green glow of my personal savior: Starbucks.

Of course, there was a line. I wasn't the only one addicted. Pulling out my phone, I tried to ignore the two chatty females in front of me talking of early morning deposition. *Lawyers.*

Gag me. I couldn't tolerate the essence of "Professional Barbie" playing out before me. They were a stereotypical display of perfect hair paired with dull gray suits, complemented by black stiletto heels and shoulder bags filled with laptops, paperwork, and case files.

The smirk crossed my lips before I could stop it; I existed as the precise opposite of that image. My foot bounced up and down impatiently, and the metal clips of my favorite knee-high boots clanked against the zippers. No courtroom appearances for me; much to my mother's disappointment, I had not followed in my dad's footsteps.

Contrary to the acceptance in the general public, in the professional world I still held stereotypes—even in the Advertising / Graphic Design world—with my nose piercing and tattoos showing at my wrists. The long wool coat I purchased at the thrift store didn't fit the style, either, but it fought the soul-sucking cold.

As orders were taken, I stepped forward in line. *That's right. Move these puppies along. It's coffee, not rocket science, people.* From rats to puppies? What was the deal with my mind this morning? I supposed my crankiness derived from the fact I expected today to be an utter nightmare. My cubie neighbor would nag at me all day to finish my layout when she hadn't finished hers, which would result in my finishing hers as well. *I hate deadlines.*

Finally, it was my turn. "Shot in the dark, Margo."

Margo existed as my personal god. Well, Monday through Friday, anyway. A true saint. Her eyes brightened as she laughed, sending wild red ringlets wiggling around her face. I tapped my card against the countertop.

"That bad, huh?" she inquired as she punched my order into the computer.

"Deadlines." I handed her my card with rolled eyes.

"Well, I have some good news for you . . ." She waited half a second. "I got the internship!" Margo's face lit up with a squeal, holding my card in the air.

"Really?" For the first time this morning a smile crossed my mouth, and my heart lifted. Weeks had passed since I helped her apply for several internships at local firms. Friday happiness vibes infiltrated my morning irritation. "That's awesome!"

"Yes! Thanks to you and your amazing letter of recommendation. Seriously, thank you, Aislynn. I would have never got the job without your help."

"Of course! Your work is amazing. You deserve it." I smiled, glad that I'd been able to help. *Maybe today won't be so bad after all.*

"Could we make that two, please?" A soft, singing voice interrupted.

Or not.

"Excuse me," I snipped, turning to glare at the man behind me. "Your turn is next, I promise."

Well. I had yet to consume my coffee like some addicted neurotic caffeine junkie. Here I was again, this time arguing with myself. This needed to stop. I scowled at the over-eager-order-placer with irritation: *a suit. Figures.*

He caught me off guard, though, as his blue eyes pierced mine, not looking at me, but into me. Oddly, I found I couldn't break the stare until his gaze shifted back to Margo.

"Yes, well, if it would please you, I would like to, ah . . . feed into your addiction today." His voice, slightly accented, drifted through the air.

Margo, like a traitor, shrugged. She made the adjustment with comments regarding his kindness as he handed her the appropriate bills to cover both drinks. He didn't receive the same smile from me, only a steely glare from the corner of my eye. *I don't need anyone to buy me coffee,* I thought as I shoved my card back in my wallet.

"Fine. Thank you."

See? I can be nice, I thought as we moved aside. I attempted to mindlessly scroll through my social media apps, but instead found myself examining my Addiction Feeder. His suit looked expensive; however, upon closer inspection, he didn't fit into my "suit" category.

There was something unruly about him as he tugged at his tie, making me think he was trying to fit in. A masculine attractiveness combined with overnight stubble made many in the coffee shop look twice, because he seemed to have a somewhat dangerous side to him. I was certain he had broken his nose at least once, its shape giving an allure of interest to his face. Again, I found myself peering at those startling eyes. Something peculiar made me stare longer than I should have, and he caught my gaze. I tried to distract myself with my phone.

Our two coffees were placed on the counter, and mine was already in my hands as he reached for his. I gave a small toast as thanks with a flat ungrateful smile. Unfortunately, he didn't understand the gesture as I could feel him behind me. Although a few steps ahead, he quickly caught up. *Damn!* Being short cursed me again. *Great.* A morning stalker. Just what I needed today.

"I am Rowan," he said, sipping his coffee and grimacing at the extra kick of espresso.

"And if you didn't recognize the gesture of thanks, I am leaving now." My agitation shined through like a beacon while I tried to quicken my steps, but it didn't seem to bother his already long stride.

"Oh, I recognized it. They told me you might be . . . difficult." He said this more to himself than me, taking another sip.

"Yeah, that's generally what they say." My irritation bubbled over into pure sarcasm. Amy or Carie probably put him up to this; they always insisted I needed to date more. I repeatedly told them I was on a permanent hiatus from men, still recovering from my last relationship . . . or what I liked to refer to as my twenty-seven-month prison sentence in emotional hell.

"Are you always this chaotic?" From his tone, I could tell he implied he meant more than my walking. Creepy music drifted in my head.

"Most days," I grinned, tugging the new bangs I'd decided to cut last weekend behind my ear. "Do you always follow people?"

"Most days."

"You're a riot." At least he was entertaining. Most people gave up on a conversation with me at this point. Yet, still there, he walked beside me, never missing a beat. Not normally this snarky, I pondered my grumbly attitude. Perhaps the cloudy skies and impending snowstorms hovering over the Twin Cities contributed to my mood.

"That is not my intention." His clear, steady eyes glanced my direction.

"Yeah, well if you knew me, it is mine." *Now beat it, mister.*

"So I was told."

Ooh, mysterious! The skyway seemed outrageously long today, almost like time had slowed. *Why me? Why do I always attract the weirdos?* Even if they are attractive, obviously this one was nuts.

Ah, at last, I reached my destination in the rat maze. My building. As Starbucks was my heaven, this building was my very own hell.

"Well, this is where we say adieu my friend." Again, I gave a quick toast with my coffee as thanks. He stopped, nodding my cheers with an irritating smile. Stepping into the elevator, I pushed my floor, holding my coffee to my lips as he stared. I could still feel his scrutinizing eyes after the doors closed.

I didn't give my mysterious morning stalker much thought once I succumbed to the entrapment of my cubicle. By the end of the day, my eyes nagged at me as I shut down my computer. I didn't accomplish everything I intended, but at least Melissa's layout was finished. *Thanks to me.* "Formatting problem," my ass; I called it a lazy problem. Pulling the various hot pink post-its off the edge of the screen, I tossed them in the trash under my desk. As I popped my head up, Carie's blue eyes peered over my cubicle. The edges of her blonde bob rested on the flimsy wall between us.

"Leaving?" I asked, pulling my messenger bag out of the drawer. "I'll walk out with you."

"Yes, finally! Eight hours of mind-numbing work . . ." She came around the corner of my desk wrapping her caramel cashmere scarf around her neck and, at the sight of my thin leggings, shivered. "I hope you brought a coat. It's snowing."

"Huh?" *Snow, freaking great.* I secretly hoped the storm would've held off until tonight . . . or forever. My weather app lied to me.

Carie, of course, was all smiles. She loved the snow. She and her fiancée snowboarded. I wondered if anyone told them Minnesota lacked the small aspect of mountains. We were lucky we had hills, if they could be called that. I should have sympathy for her as it was her first winter here.

The third storm this week had stirred my loathing of Minnesota winters. I was filled with hatred for each evil flake that fell, but at least I didn't have to shovel or drive in it. Those were the moments when I cherished my purposeful choice of downtown apartment living—including an almost perfect walk through the skyway system. I didn't need to walk on snowy streets or deal with rush hour traffic on the surrounding highways.

#winning

I grabbed my wool coat from under my desk and considered the painter's cap sitting in the bottom of my drawer. Instead I grabbed the thin hairband at my wrist and looped it through the top section of my short messy bob. In the elevator bank, we waited several minutes for an empty ride. Every time one arrived, the doors revealed human bodies crammed beyond capacity, trying to escape the building.

Eventually, Carie and I separated to different elevators with quick goodbyes. The doors closed in front of me as coworkers and fellow building rats talked about the storm, reporting from their phones about the roads and accidents. *Suckers,* I thought as I stepped out of the elevator. Crossing the Crystal Court, I peered up at the giant glass block ceiling above as I took the escalator up to the skyway level. Clouds the color of muddy gray threatened a heavy snowfall. *One thing the weather app* didn't *lie about.* A perfect night for streaming my favorite show and a glass of wine. My soul whimpered with impending jubilee. I glanced back down watching my step off the escalator. Suddenly, as if appearing from nowhere, my Addiction Feeder was at my side. I tried to believe it was annoyance that made me tremble, but he didn't seem to notice.

This is a coincidence. Just ill-fated luck of bad timing. He must work in my building.

"Hello again," he said. "Busy day?"

"And you care because . . . ?" Together we joined the throngs of people walking through the skyway.

"I suppose I don't. Is it not common courtesy to ask such things?" His words were thoughtful, as if he didn't understand my lack of an answer to the common conversation starter. Bizarre.

"Awkward much?" I chided. From the corner of my eye I could see him tug on his purple paisley tie again. "This might be the oddest interaction I've ever had. You aren't going to kill me, are you?" My eyebrows locked together, considering the chances of coincidence over intentional stalking.

"No. That would defeat my purpose of being here," he answered.

My hand gripped the buttery leather strap of my bag tighter, adrenaline ticking up a notch with concern. *Did he think that was an option?*

"Of course it would. What might that purpose be, anyway?" My sarcasm was thick and dripping, a defense mechanism hoping to push him to find someone else to bother.

My internal stress didn't disturb him. "I have many purposes, but at this specific moment it would entail you."

"Me?" I gulped. Maybe he really was a psychopathic killer. Serendipitous path crossing likelihood catastrophically exploded at my feet. *There goes that theory.*

"Yes. You, Aislynn."

When he said my name, I tried to not be surprised. Instead, I returned to my "Amy or Carie put him up to this" theory.

"And what do you want to do with me?" My voice was coy. I switched my antics. Why not play along?

"Well, it is not something you will take kindly to, I do not think." He gave me a sideways glance as I swerved around two slow-paced women.

"Uh-huh . . . is this some sort of bondage experiment or something?" I said as we veered together again. Perhaps I could shock him. Maybe then he would go away.

"Excuse me?" An amused smirk crossed his lips, and the lady we passed gave me a dirty scowl.

"It's Rogan, right?"

"Rowan."

"Whatever. I dunno who put you up to this. It's amusing, but I am going to go home now. It's been real." I refused to lead him straight to my apartment; my mom had taught me the big, bad city was teeming with plenty of crazy people.

"You do not understand. I have not made myself clear."

"You haven't made anything clear!" My voice hitched. We crossed the skyway over Marquette Avenue, and I glanced down at the snow accumulating on the streets. I found myself making a quick decision to return back to street level, veering toward the next escalator. Maybe it would be easier to ditch him.

"Aislynn, I was sent for you. From Hallervania. There are many who believe you might be in danger. I have come to convince you that you are needed. You and your gifts." Rowan stepped on the escalator.

"Whoa, whoa . . . my gifts?" As if that was the most bizarre thing he'd mentioned. Something he said flickered in my brain, like old memories trying to resurface, or a fuzzy picture refusing to become clear. I turned back forward to watch my steps, giving him a few more moments to consider his reply.

"Yes. Gifts. Powers. Ailianna believes you are quite powerful," he said ordinarily, as if this was something commonly discussed in everyday conversations.

My eyes widened, and a burst of laughter escaped in a sharp huff. Was this a joke? "Uh-huh. Are you insane?" I shoved the thick swoop of bang that escaped my hairband behind my ear with irritation. *Why did I decide to cut my bangs?*

Oh yes, tequila told me to do it. "Obviously, you are . . . unwell. Do you need medical help? A doctor? Medication?"

His eyes blinked in rapid motion as if somehow tracking my internal dialogue. *Weird.* Maybe he escaped from the behavioral center? Only I would attract such a person. Shaking my head in bewilderment, I glanced back at him while I pushed open the door to the street.

He smiled; the seriousness evaporated. "I know this may all be hard to believe, but unfortunately, there is not much time. Otherwise, I might have gone about this differently."

"Sure. Not enough time," I agreed with my head bobbing. "I see." Seriously I added, "Is it the aliens?" Standing half in and half out of the door to the street, the snow began to blow back inside across the tile.

"Aislynn, please close the door. It's cold," Rowan said, and for a strange reason I didn't quite understand, I obliged. Moving from the entrance and the constant stream of people in and out of the doors, I crossed my arms in defense. This entire conversation exceeded past Fun Land.

"So, what are you talking about? Forgive me, I am not quite following." Why was I still standing here? Why was I still listening to this man? Even as the questions poured into my head, something locked me into place. The freezing air nipped in sharp bites through my coat as people bustled through the doors.

"Hallervania has been waiting for you," Rowan explained, "for you to come into your gifts. Ailianna believed there was plenty of time. Time for you to slowly come into your . . . destiny, for lack of a better word."

"I think you are confused. I've never heard of Hallervania. I think you have the wrong person," I insisted firmly.

"Unfortunately, that is impossible."

"Oookay. Anyway, Rowan, it's late and I want to go home. You can understand . . ." I turned, walking out the door. Before I could form another thought, Rowan stood in front of me. My mouth popped open in shock as I whipped my head behind me to where he had been a moment ago. My brain tried to process what had just occurred.

"Aislynn, you do not understand. I cannot allow you out of my sight." His words were firm.

"I . . . uh . . ." Stuttering in shock, I started again. "Well, that is called stalking and it is illegal." My voice was harsh at my simple explanation of the law, if only to distract me from his disappearing/reappearing act.

"Yes, well it would be too dangerous to leave you alone. There are others after you, and they do not want to help you."

"And you do?" The pitch of my voice cracked at the absurdity.

"Yes. Of course. It is my job."

"And you, are nuts!" I said, throwing up my hands and walking around him.

"How about I give you a history lesson as we walk?" Rowan suggested as he turned to follow me again.

I groaned pressing my fingers to the bridge of my nose. "How about you seek professional help?"

"Aislynn, haven't you ever believed there was more to your life than this? Nine hours or more a day at an advertising firm in front of your computer, day after day? A bigger purpose?" He gestured up, toward the buildings towering around us.

"Yeah, sure. I would much rather be traveling the

world eating bonbons on my own plane, but I haven't won my millions in the lottery yet."

"I mean beyond that."

"Uh-huh. Sure. Well, as nice as that would be, without a job, that is called being homeless. Not so appealing, my friend."

"How can Hallervania's future be held in such a difficult person's hands?" Rowan murmured to himself. I thought it was rather rude, as I heard him perfectly.

"Hallervania's future? What is Hallervania?" I dared to ask.

"Not what, but where; it is a place. Beyond this realm." He looked past me as he said this, past the street, the buildings. Beyond everything.

Oh my God. This guy is *nuts.*

"Let me try again," Rowan continued. "Your gifts. Haven't you ever wanted something, and then it happened?" We stopped at the crosswalk, waiting for the light to change. White delicate flakes collected on my shoulders contrasting the black wool of my coat. This was why I walked inside the skyway, instead I was contemplating how to ditch crazy boy.

"For example," he said, and pointed to the light across the street. "Wanting a light to turn from red to green at the very moment you thought it?" Before he finished his sentence, the light changed to green and we began walking. "Even simple things."

I thought for a moment, trying to follow his madness. "Okay, let me see if I follow you here. You are implying I have powers or 'gifts,' as you call them. Meaning I can make things happen." We reached another block, and another red light. "Like make a light turn green." Before I articulated the *n* in *green*, the light changed. My mouth became an immediate smirk.

"Precisely," he confirmed.

"I didn't do that."

"Of course you did."

"So you believe." I didn't believe it. Impossible. Sure, everyone at one time or another believed or wished such things were possible. But we all grow up. Childhood fantasies and dreams were whisked away with reality. Things like jobs, bills, and adulting came with the realization that such "gifts" were impossible. Life was ordinary. Being human was ordinary.

"Lights change pretty often here. I'm certain I had nothing to do with it." My boots slid through the sludge of wet snow accumulating on the sidewalk, bringing awareness to the slippery slope of my current predicament.

"I told you it was not something you would take to."

"Uh-huh." I still hadn't figured out where I was walking; I couldn't just walk home, not with my friendly neighborhood psychopath by my side. Snow pelted my face and created a bone deep chill pecking at my resolve, sending full body shivers through me.

"Why don't we grab a bite to eat? That should ease your thoughts of leading a psychopath to your home."

I snapped my head up. It was as if he had plucked the words right from my thoughts. Before I could disagree, I found myself grumbling, "fine."

2

Soon enough we were sitting across from each other in a diner some city-goers found unique. It was one of my personal favorites because they served breakfast all day. I pushed my bag next to me, checking my phone out of habit. Banners flashed warnings of the impending snow totals. And a text from Amy. *Maybe I should ask her about Rowan.*

Hey, planning on stopping by this weekend to drop off your book.

The waitress interrupted my quick scroll to take our drink orders, and my phone dinged again.

This storm is gross and making me twitchy. Why do we live here? We should go somewhere warm. And GREEN.

Dismissing Amy's ramblings, I considered Rowan in front of me. After this, I was going to go home and sink into a glass of wine. I'd earned it after a week of deadlines and crazy guy. I leaned back in the booth, shoving my phone in my bag. I would text Amy back later.

"I only agreed to this because you are slightly intriguing," I clarified. "I don't think it's fair to feed into your delusions, but hey. It's been a dull week for me." My hands softly slapped at the table.

"I understand," he said, glancing out the window, watching the snow fall in heavy thick flakes.

"So, your accent . . . I can't place it. It sounds Irish, but not quite anything I have ever heard before." I had always been good at accents and it annoyed me I couldn't place Rowan's. The waitress returned, placing my coffee and Rowan's water on the table.

"It's Hallervanian."

"Oh yeah," I replied swiftly. "That's right by Transylvania, right?"

This he found humorous. A full smile broke across his face, his perfect white teeth shining through. Maybe he wasn't completely lost. There was hope yet: maybe he was only half-deluded.

"As I said before, it is not of this realm."

"Right," I agreed, dramatically drawing out the word. I waved my spoon, stirring loads of sugar into my coffee. "Realms," I pondered, sipping from my cup.

"I am here for you, Aislynn. I am hoping that if you will come with me, at least you will be safe."

"To Hallervania? Not of this realm?" I set the mug on the table.

"Yes," he said.

"And there are others after me." I paused, and Rowan nodded. "And they are bad, but you are not?"

"No, of course not. I wish to bring you no harm. Although Ailianna believes Daragon does and will. Which is why we need to make our move."

"Ailianna? Who is she?" I picked up my coffee again.

His brilliant, not of this realm blue eyes narrowed, pausing for the slightest moment before speaking. "She is of Faerie descent and is gifted with sight. She knows what is to happen."

"Faerie descent?" I laughed, managing to swallow my coffee before I spat in his face.

"Yes."

My head shook with gentle shock. "What about you? Do you have gifts?"

"Of course. My gifts are various, but not on the same scale as yours." He took a sip of his water, pushing the straw aside.

"And what exactly are my gifts?"

He paused, thoughtful before answering. "Well, your potential, some believe, is extraordinary. Perhaps beyond what we have seen before."

At this, my eyebrow shot upward.

"It is believed," Rowan continued. "You would call it . . . telekinesis. But it is more than that, combined with your family magic."

I burst into laughter, almost spilling my coffee. "Family magic?" My hand held my temple, trying to process the information. "Now I know you are crazy. My parents live in Eden Prairie. They are about as boring as it gets. Magic? That would be out of their realm."

"Well, your parents aren't exactly what I meant," he said.

"I don't have much family. I'm an only child, you know," I said, taking another sip.

"That you are aware of."

"You are rather cryptic."

If by cue or magic, the waitress set our order on the table, smiling widely at Rowan. He didn't notice, mesmerized by the food before him and began to eat in silence. Not a word of faeries, magic, or distant realms.

I, however, did not enjoy my food to its fullest potential. My mind was otherwise occupied. I wanted to believe in my Amy or Carie theory, but the thought lost steam as soon as it entered my head. I couldn't deny Rowan hit a nerve when he mentioned my pitiful existence. I always believed there had to be more to this life than what the average human made of it.

Somewhere in the deep core of my being sat an awareness of a deeper purpose, and this was not it. Nowhere near.

Then, "magic."

As I thought more on the word, the concept, there were facts that arose in me that I'd denied my whole life. For instance, that green light did not shock me like it should have; it had happened before, countless times. But I ignored it and other small mysteries because they didn't fit the average human theory.

To fit in with society, even with awkwardness, I couldn't go around claiming I could do things that were not easily explained. Suppression came easy after a while. I didn't deny the wonder in these things, but I didn't broadcast them either. Especially not to my friendly psychopath.

Which led me to my next thought: *Can he be real? Can I believe the things he was proposing to me?* Anything was possible. I always believed in that one thing.

"Have you come to a conclusion yet?" Rowan's voice disrupted my thoughts.

"Hmm?" Shaking myself from my internal dialogue, I

realized I would need to decide what to do with them and Rowan.

"Your thoughts. It seems you are reaching some sort of decision." He tilted his head to one side, curious eyes watching me. Water droplets from melted snow dripped off the edges of his dark hair.

"I . . . uh . . . I thought Ailianna was the one gifted with sight," I said, smiling.

"She is. My gifts are not in the same vicinity as hers. I have impressions of ones' thoughts. Sometimes clearer than others; in your case, your mind is like a flower, opening and closing in the likes of the sun. I could sense you were coming to a conclusion, about what to make of this and me." He took a sip of water.

"Interesting. Your gift, I mean. And yes, I suppose I was." Somehow, we met with a kind of understanding without sharing our thoughts. *Weird.*

Rowan pushed his empty plate aside, placing the silverware carefully across the plate. I hardly touched my food but found I had more than enough to stomach and pushed mine to the side as well. Folding his hands in front of him on the table, he waited.

"You are not as disbelieving as you led on to be."

The smirk crossed my lips before I could stop it. "No. I suppose I am not. Mind you, other realms? That really is beyond me."

"It is sad that children of your world are told fairy tales, with their young minds believing anything is possible, only to have it taken away because you must grow up. Surely, these possibilities are now impossible."

Again, my thoughts were plucked right from my own mind.

"So, I must revert to childhood and believe in fairy tales?" I questioned.

"No, but know this: if you had never stopped believing this conversation would have been quite simpler."

"Touché." I couldn't argue his well-made point. "So, we go to your realm, then?"

"In such a hurry?" he teased, angling his head.

I didn't like that he was receiving impressions from my mind. It was intrusive. Rowan's head snapped back to center as if I had slapped him.

"Ah, you learn quickly."

"What do you mean?"

"You are blocking me again, this time by choice."

Had I? Could I block him from my thoughts only because I thought it? This was too much. "I . . . I . . ." I didn't know what to say.

"It is okay. It does not hurt much." A warm smile touched his lips. "Ailianna said my coming here, being near you, might increase your gifts. Make them . . . blossom. The magic of Hallervania is strong and having a connection, even through me, makes your gifts more . . . available to you."

"I see." I really didn't, but I could understand.

Suddenly, the comfort between us snapped. Like lightning, alertness filled Rowan's eyes and shifted into pure vigilance.

"They know I have come for you." Seriousness filled his voice. I observed the transformation before me: the smiling man vanished and, in his place, was a fierce warrior.

"What? Who?" I questioned, glancing around the restaurant.

"Daragon. The ones I told you about. Those who wish you harm. We must leave, now." He reached in his suit jacket, placing bills, almost double what the ticket could've been, on the table. He ushered me toward the back of the diner where the restrooms were located.

"Rowan! There isn't a door this way," I hissed.

"Just go!" In the hallway, the men's and women's doors stood to our right and left.

I raised my hands in confusion. "Now what?"

Those clear blue eyes met mine.

"Now, Aislynn, you must trust me." And for the first time, he touched me, grabbing my hand before I could protest.

"What do . . . ?" Before finishing my thought, the hallway, the doors, and the diner, disappeared.

And then we were standing in my apartment.

I couldn't breathe or form a thought. As I gasped for breath, my throat tightened. Air. I needed air. My brain committed to hyper-fragging complete dysfunction. Sensory control blasted responses through my body, pinging my nervous system in repetitive alert signals. Everything was spinning faster than my mind could control.

"Just sit." Rowan pushed me down into my overstuffed reading chair. "Breathe, Aislynn." He forced my head between my legs.

Gradually, air began to fill my lungs as they remembered how to function, moving air in and out. Oxygen began to circulate throughout my body once again. My fingertips tingled, my nerve impulses trying to function. The room took shape before it fully disappeared, and I passed out into oblivion.

"I am sorry. The first time is a bit . . . overwhelming." Sincerity trickled in his voice through the fierceness.

I watched through a dizzy haze as he opened my closet, reaching for a duffel bag I kept on the top shelf. It occurred to me that I shouldn't be surprised he knew where to look. He snatched clothes, randomly leaving empty hangers swaying in their place.

"What . . . are . . . you doing?" I struggled to talk as the room began to still. The air felt as though it had been sucked from my body as if my body didn't exist, and then everything came back again. My mind was catching up with my body, making me feel ill. I ran to the bathroom, vomiting what little food I had eaten at the diner.

My breath uneven, I rested my forehead on my arm draped across the toilet seat. My stomach heaved, and I tried to take slow, even breaths. Standing with caution, I reached out for the doorway, my hands grasping each side for balance.

"What the hell was that?" My voice was uneven as a wave of nausea threatened again. Rowan barely gave me a glance.

"I am sorry to have done that to you. Without the expectation of what I was doing, well, obviously . . ." His face was remorseful as he swarmed around my apartment faster than my brain could comprehend, shoving my personal things in the bag. "Magic affects the body differently for everyone."

"Did we just teleport?" I whispered. Believing something might be possible and actually doing something I knew was entirely unbelievable shocked my system.

Rowan stopped moving for the first time. He looked at me and nodded. "You would call it that, yes."

"But . . . I didn't . . . that's . . ."

"Didn't believe it was possible?"

Teleportation? Being in one spot, then disappearing, to reappear at another location. *No. It can't be possible.* My brain would not comprehend the concept. As wispy as I was at times, I tended to be a logical person. Teleportation defied any type of logic and reason.

"Aislynn."

My name brought me back, although my thoughts continued to torment my mind. My eyes refused to focus as I tried to contemplate what happened and what teleporting meant.

"I . . ." Stuttering, I walked to my bed and sat with my hands limp in my lap. In that moment, everything changed. My soul beckoned me, and everything Rowan said, though impossible, was all true. A part of me, a small hidden piece of me, resonated with him.

Rowan knelt before me. "Aislynn, we need to go. I thought there would be more time to prepare you, but this is not the case. Please, if you can help me get your things in order."

Order? Where will we go? I noticed for the first time my cat, Jax, swirling his sleek black body around Rowan's legs. I found the humor in the situation as Jax, held nothing but disdain for everyone he had ever met.

But I supposed this was different; Rowan wasn't of this realm, was he? Jax jumped on my lap, piercing me with his sapphire blue eyes. An assurance settled in his face, almost like a conversation.

"Yes. He speaks to you," Rowan spoke up. "He always has, but now you choose to listen."

I tried not to be irritated with Rowan as he jumped on my thought train. With one long stroke, he swiped his hand down Jax's body and continued to move around the apartment.

"Okay," I said. Not only to Rowan, but to myself as an

affirmation of everything that occurred in the last hour. "Just please tell me we don't need to teleport again because I am not a fan."

Rowan smiled, but regret filled his eyes. "Ah, well . . . next time should be easier."

"Easier? Like next time, I won't vomit my brains out?" Running my tongue over my gritty teeth, I desperately wanted mouthwash.

"Ah, there you are," he replied as relief saturated his face. "I thought I lost you."

After a quick brush of my teeth, I began adding things to the two duffel bags Rowan had collected, while unpacking things I didn't need. Grabbing my messenger bag, I organized my must-haves: my laptop, my sketch book and pencil bag, and cell phone. I wondered if the damn thing would even work, and without hesitation wrapped up the chargers, adding them as well.

When I found myself in front of my jewelry box, my bag slipped through my hands and landed with a soft thump on the bed. Carefully pulling the delicate drawer open, I retrieved something I could never leave without: a small wooden box with ornate carvings etched into the top. I traced my thumb over the box as a bright, powerful memory flooded back to me.

When I was seven or eight years old, I spent the summers with my grandmother. At bedtime, she would tell me fantastic stories. They carried the same thread of three young women from another world; "another realm" were the words she used. The three young women fought Light versus Dark to save their world from being destroyed. Each of the women were bestowed different gifts and powers.

The story came rushing back and I remembered she would start it the same every night:

One of them was blessed with the gift of sight, the second a powerful witch, and the third given many gifts, one of which was the ability to control things with only her mind. She filled my head with stories of elemental magic and magical beings. One particular night when my grandma finished the story, she looked down at me, brushing my hair over my ears.

"Aislynn. My dear, sweet Aislynn, I have something for you. It is very special and extremely important."

I remembered being utterly absorbed in her story, then she opened her aged hand, showing me a small box.

"Now, dear, this is a gift from me, but you must promise me something first." She brushed another stray hair behind my ear.

"Okay, Grandmamma, I promise."

"But dear! You don't know what you are promising!" She tapped me on the nose with her finger as I giggled. "This box is very powerful. You mustn't open it. Not until it is time."

"But, Grandmamma, how will I know when I can open it?"

"My dear child, you will know when the time comes. You will be older and wiser. You will remember this moment, you will get the box, and it will open for you. Do you promise not to open the box till then?"

I was a serious child when it came to my grandmother, and I was passionate about her beautiful stories, which I wholeheartedly believed. "Yes, Grandmamma. I promise."

"Alright, my dear Aislynn. With all the magic of the Hallervanian Realm, I give this to you for love, protection, and understanding of the things you must do." I giggled as my grandmother tended to stay in character when it came to her stories.

Opening my hand, she placed the box in my palm, placing hers over the top. "So mote it be." She kissed me on my nose and turned off the light. I remembered holding the box the entire night in my little hands and everywhere I went the entire summer.

Returning to the present, the memory left an aching hole in my heart. *Hallervania.* The parallels between Rowan's truths and my grandmother's stories were exact. A pulse of adrenaline spiked, and my heart pounded in my chest. *Everything was true. Magic. Other Realms. Teleporting.*

My ears buzzed as the beautiful wood gleamed in my palm, as it had all those years ago. A subtle shimmer began to glow at the edges of the box. Certain this was the moment my grandmother had meant, I reached to open the lid.

"Aislynn!" Rowan shouted. "Nooo!"

Turning, I saw Rowan stumbling over the bags trying to reach me.

"Aislynn, not yet." His eyes penetrated mine as he shook his head. He held his hands over mine, keeping the box securely closed.

"But . . ."

"Yes." He nodded with intensity. "But not yet. Not here." He folded my hand over the box as the shimmering began to glow a steady white light. "Bring it and keep it close as you always have. Our time has ended. We must go."

Nodding, I pushed the box into my messenger bag.

"Right then, Aislynn. I promise this will not be like last

time. We will go to a place where we can prepare for our travels to Hallervania. There, we will have more time."

I pulled my bag across my body, joining Rowan in the living room. With the two duffel bags on each side of me, I stepped in, creating a circle. Jax jumped over the bag and sat squarely in the center. I smiled. Of course he would be coming.

"Aislynn, I want you to close your eyes and breathe."

I closed my eyes with hesitation.

"Relax . . . let your mind fall away."

Peeking through a slit of my right eye, I watched power shimmer in waves of iridescent greens around Rowan.

"The things you perceive are not as solid as you believe. Let everything fall away and breathe." Rowan's voice was hypnotic, and my eyes closed as my body relaxed.

"Okay, Aislynn. Open your eyes."

My eyelashes fluttered open to a brilliantly wooded clearing.

"Oh . . ." I stared at my new surroundings. This was nothing like before. One minute I stood in one place, and with a blink of an eye, I was somewhere else.

"Thank God I don't need to throw up." I almost laughed.

"Better, yes?" Rowan traced a circle through the space, speaking softly under his breath.

"We're not in Kansas anymore, Toto." I looked down at Jax, who meowuffed at me.

"Do not compare me to that little annoying dog!" Jax haughtily turned and meandered toward Rowan, who hid his own snicker.

"Excuse me?" My eyes widened. "Did my cat just speak to me?"

His mouth hadn't moved the way ours did. Instead, I had heard his words in my head or both of our heads. Talk about confusing.

"It seems so." Rowan's eyes held laughter, and I forced a snarled smile at him.

"You have some explaining to do, sir. Like, for example, where are we?" I asked.

Obviously, this wasn't Minneapolis, as everything there was covered in six inches of snow. Here, thick trees with velvety rich bark were covered in moss and surrounded by bright, colorful wildflowers.

The space radiated warmth and light. A deep, earthy smell penetrated my nose, reminding me of spring. The opening of trees appeared natural, but the circle of fresh earth exposed seemed too perfect.

"This place is between your Realm and mine, known as the Astraea Portal. It is safe, given of Light and protected for all those who come here."

"That's rather cryptic," I said. The bright light of the clearing gave me pause. When we left my apartment, the evening winter light saturated the sky, but here in the clearing I saw a sunny midafternoon sky. "Hey, how is it so light here?"

"It is rather simple, really," Rowan replied over his shoulder. "When you travel in your realm, whether by ground or sky, depending on your destination, you go forward or backward hours in time, yes? Well, it is the same concept. When you travel through Realms, the same thing happens; depending on where you are and where you are going, a certain amount of time passes."

I sat on one of the nearby stones, waiting for Rowan. Meanwhile, memes of exploding heads passed through my thoughts. My senses were in overdrive as the wind rustled the leaves. Rowan's steps were soft on the ground as he finished whatever he'd been doing and sat beside me.

"Daragon sent his searchers for you. I am sure they found your apartment and are aware of what transpired there." He glanced at my bag still hanging on my shoulder. "They cannot follow us further, for now."

"And the box?" I asked, leaning forward on my knees.

"It is safe here. Between the Realms in this place, no one can reach us. Not with Dark or Light magic."

"What would've happened? If I had opened it back there?" I asked. "You were pretty insistent."

"It could have been cataclysmic," Rowan replied, his face serious. "I am certain your Realm is not ready for the power within that box. I would rather not think of it. From what I've been told, it is important." A tightness around his eyes made me realize there was much I didn't understand.

"Oookay, so, I had this box all this time and I could've destroyed my Realm? What in the hell? What if I would have opened it?" Bits of anger raced through me. What had my grandmother been thinking when she gave an eight-year-old a box with powers not of this Realm?

"Do not blame her. She knew what she was doing. From what I understand, she was truly remarkable. The box was held safe for many years." Rowan's gaze shifted to me while stroking Jax.

"What if it had been stolen? What if I'd sold it? Or given it away?" My voice edged higher with each question.

"Impossible. That would not have happened. Do not worry so much over these what-ifs as they make no difference here."

Glancing around the open space, I tried to let my

worried thoughts go. I didn't bother being annoyed that he knew my thoughts before I spoke.

"And my cat? I can talk to my cat now?" I slid back to the conversation earlier when I thought Rowan was crazy. Now I felt like I was crazy. Animals talking? Boxes with powers? My hands slid over my face as if trying to wipe away the madness.

"The more time you are with me and as we move closer to Hallervania, your gifts will only become stronger. It is best this happens slowly as a sudden surge of power... well, you said you aren't a fan of the vomiting." His warm smile returned.

"Ha ha," I snapped insincerely as I pet Jax, who had temporarily forgiven me calling him Toto.

He rubbed his body against my legs, and I thought about the day I found him. Two or so years ago, tiny mews interrupted my walk home from work, not long after my breakup. At first, I thought I had imagined the sound coming from one of the alleys between buildings. I paused, listening when a little black kitten crawled from underneath decrepit, wet cardboard. Bending down, I had held out my hand, trying not to scare him.

"Hey, little guy." The kitten sat in front of my hand, mewing with fierceness. Careful, I extended my fingers, trying to pet him. He mewed again.

"What are you doing out here all alone?" I glanced around, trying to find the mama cat or maybe litter mates, but nothing. Just him, all alone. His eyes, still kitten blue, watched me search underneath the trash and cardboard, mewing.

"Where's your mama, huh?" I crouched down in front of him.

"I can't have a cat," I tried to reason with the kitten as he grazed himself against my legs. Then taking his two front paws he dug tiny claws into my pants, mewing louder.

"I know. I know, apartment rules. They are asshats. I can barely handle myself, let alone you."

After another meow, he crawled up my leg and sat on top of my thigh. I didn't want a cat nor could I own animals in my building. He blinked, meowing mercilessly as if to convince me of his horrible circumstance. With one finger I stroked under his chin and my defenses broke.

"One night! Then I need to find you a home." With a small meow, he crawled up my jacket.

"Hey! Hey! Little guy! Those claws are sharp." Stretching his tiny body, he brushed the top of his head against my chin, making me smile. I ran a hand down his back. That was probably the first time I had smiled in months. He nosed his way into the opening of my jacket, pushing his way inside.

That was the moment I was doomed. The tiny fluff ball curled against me, looking up with clear eyes, purring. We discussed on the walk home the importance of silence upon entering my building, and the small kitten never made a peep. After he devoured a can of tuna, I went to Target to pick up kitty supplies. That night he slept on my pillow and I slept through the night, a rare occurrence for me.

After that, I owned a cat. He was one thing that pulled me from the depression I lulled myself into by the berating of inner demons. Together we concocted a secret plan to hide his existence in my apartment building.

Jax pushed his body against my hand, forcing me into more petting as I shook off the old memories.

"Who is this Daragon guy?" I asked Rowan. "And why does he care about me?"

"It is not you as much as the box. Although I am sure he wouldn't mind destroying you if he had the chance."

"Oh, thanks." My sarcasm brought an uneven smile.

Rowan shrugged. "Hallervania is made of Light and Darkness, and at different times throughout history, it has been controlled by one or the other. Thankfully, Darkness has not had control for several hundred years now. Daragon would like that to change. Many years ago, it was foreseen there would be three children born under the years of the Third Sun marked by the Goddess of Light. These three children would grow, becoming influential forces for Light."

I listened to Rowan with familiarity as memories of my grandmother's bedtime tales once again flooded me. There seemed to be key aspects of the story that were missing, but I couldn't make the pieces fit together.

"We were told it was of the utmost importance to keep these three safe until the time came for them to fulfill their destinies," Rowan explained further. "If the three did not survive to adulthood, Darkness would gain access to Hallervania and what had been for hundreds of years would change. So, the time came when the three children were born with the markings of our Goddess. The third came with an even greater gift. But Darkness was aware of the prophecy with their own Seers and began to plot to destroy the three." Rowan's voice was a soft singing beside me.

"Your grandmother became involved at some point and ingeniously hid you and this gift in the Earth Realm, something never done in the history of Hallervania. Our people were told you were gone, that you had not survived. This gave Darkness hope. She did this knowing it would only keep you safe during your childhood years; the time would come for you to return to Hallervania. Chaos had been foreseen if you were to be raised in my Realm and she wanted normalcy for you." A soft smile crossed his lips before continuing.

"For a while, things were somewhat normal until Daragon came into power. He did not believe you were gone and ruthlessly searched for you. As Ailianna came into her gifts, he was able to penetrate her visions; as she saw you in the earthly realm, he did as well. Ailianna saw he was close to finding you, which is why I was sent. Daragon must have been closer than Ailianna realized or someone is following me, which led them straight to you."

I tugged on the delicate gold chain I wore at the hollow of my neck, a bad habit that occurred when I stressed over things, moving the emerald pendant back and forth. These events started long ago without my knowledge or control and questions bombarded my mind.

What about my parents? How were they involved? Had I been kidnapped? A rampant barrage of questions poured into my mind, as I wondered the unknown truths of my identity. I assumed Rowan wouldn't have the answers; my only hope was the answers would come before my patience ran out.

Instead of allowing myself to freak out, I switched directions. "But if he wants the box, now that it's here, can't we take it back and it would be safe?" In my heart, I knew things were much more difficult, but I asked anyway. *Distractions.*

"No, Aislynn. The box is nothing without you. Only you can control the contents, which is why the Goddess gave it to you." Rowan ran a hand through his thick dark curls, roughing up any professional appearance he held in my Realm.

"But I didn't ask for this." I didn't intend for my words to sound sharp.

Rowan let out his breath, turning his attention to the clearing or magical Aster-whatever portal space. "We usually don't. Our destinies are usually thrust upon us."

"Once we get to Hallervania, will we be safe?" I glanced over at him, watching his intense scan of our surroundings.

"Unfortunately, Aislynn, this is only the beginning," Rowan answered. "Now that Daragon knows you are with us, he will stop at nothing to destroy you and the box. This is their chance of stealing power for Dark."

4

A stillness radiated through the clearing and I tried to digest everything Rowan told me. Birds sang and chattered their songs, making me wonder if they were stuck in limbo or if they could travel freely where they pleased. The wind rustled through the leaves, creating a cool dampness under the canopy of trees.

"Aislynn," Rowan began, "I know much of this—"

A flash of light and loud crack sounded through the air. Rowan jumped to his feet.

"What in the hell was that?" I yelped while standing and looking for the source of the sound. Rowan walked the perimeter of the circle, dragging his hand through the air.

"Daragon. Or his searchers, rather; they are testing us." He peered over his shoulder in my direction.

"But I thought you said they couldn't reach us here?" I took tentative steps toward him.

"They cannot." He shook his head gently. "But that does not mean they will not try."

He reached out to the open space again with his hand,

speaking quietly in a language I did not understand. I watched a visible shimmer around the edge as Rowan walked, the light trailing behind him. My mouth fell open as I watched, mesmerized, until another loud crack and flash of ebony light sliced through the air. Flinching unconsciously, my own girlish scream escaped my mouth.

"God dammit!" I swore. I didn't particularly enjoy being frightened by unseen enemies. The shimmering of light within the circle was still visible, but now in my annoyance and fear, I could *feel* the shimmer as well. A strange sensation tickled my senses as the tips of my fingers zinged with vibration.

Enamored by the sensation, I closed my eyes. As if threads were attached to my fingers, I was able to pull and manipulate the vibration. Like pushing my hand under water, a current of power began to thrum in my hands.

I realized the threads were not from the fringes of the circle, but from everywhere. The dampened earth below my feet, the rocks, trees, and even the air around me. When I moved my fingertips, the strands of energy connected me to all of those things. My anger allowed me to connect with these threads, and now my wonderment helped gather it all.

"Uh . . . Aislynn . . ." Rowan's voice was distant and muffled. I was too aware of my senses to be bothered by his words.

"Aislynn." His voice was firmer as he touched my shoulder, bringing me out of my trance.

"Huh?" I stared blankly. *Wow.* What was that? Instead of just seeing the clearing, I could *feel* it. It was a living, breathing entity, pulsing with me as one connected energy.

"Um . . . would you be careful? You do not want to draw too much too quickly. Do not let them bother you.

They cannot harm us, only annoy." His words and strong gaze pulled me from my reverie.

"But . . . ?" A sly grin slid over my mouth as my eyes brightened. "Can't I be annoying back?" I arched one of my eyebrows at him.

For a moment, I thought Rowan was going to say no, explaining the dangers or whatever else he wanted to go on about. Instead, he gave me a half shrug. He folded his arms with a snickering smile, implying, *Go for it.*

My eyes glittered with excitement.

I brought my attention to the imaginary border in front of me, and this time it was more difficult because of the absence of anger. Taking a breath, I closed my eyes and reached for the shimmer of power around me. The trees and the earth beneath me became visible in my mind's eye, and the light tickle of a breeze caressed my skin. It gathered easier this time; the energy came simply as if waiting for me to call upon its presence.

As it began to spin within my fingertips, I noticed a warm tingling collecting to my demand. Concentrating on bringing my hands together and opening my eyes, I found a beautiful ball of light swirling in my hands.

A small sound of shock escaped my mouth as I moved the lustrous silver light from one hand to the other. Awe emanating from me, vaguely aware of Rowan taking a few steps back, I focused on the wall of power in front of us. Rowan had created a bubble around us in his strange whispered language, a sphere of protection, I imagined. I thought of his bubble as semipermeable, keeping things out, but if I chose to leave I could, as would my little ball of light.

I made a quick decision to throw it, and several things happened at once: a lovely crack sounded as my ball flew through the circle and I flew backward several feet, landing on my ass.

"That was . . . exhilarating!" I pushed myself up on my elbows and Rowan smiled, offering his hand for help. I brushed off the dirt and debris stuck to my leggings.

"Pretty impressive as well. Your sister was right. You are—"

"My *what?*"

5

Rowan took a step back from me with his hands up. "Aislynn, please let me explain."

"Nice job, Rowan. You knew you were not to tell her. She isn't ready." Jax apparently had a lot to say now that I could hear him.

"Jax, please," Rowan said.

"What do you mean, my sister?" My words were sharp, my eyes wide and demanding as the edges of my reality crumbled. A part of me knew. I had been hanging on to the smallest thread of hope that all of this was not real, that I was in a dream, going along for the ride. However, my grandmother's stories slammed into me, connecting with something deeper. They were not stories as I had once believed, but truths disguised as such.

I was one of the three. And as Rowan had just so nicely let slip, the other two were my sisters.

The three were marked by the Goddess of Whatever. *Why me? I didn't ask for this.* Frantically, I looked for an escape. I wanted a path, a window, anything that would take me back to the bone cold of downtown Minneapolis and my shitty little apartment.

Ailianna was my sister. But what kind of sister? For twenty-seven years, I'd believed I was an only child. *I don't want a sister.* Who was the third? Not one, but two sisters.

Bile rose up the back of my throat. The moment I acknowledged these small truths, a spark lit within me and something shifted. Instead of being aware of just myself, I could feel Ailianna and my other sister. Hers was a name I had not known before, but now it was clear to me as my own: Aila.

Blood pounded in my ears, and I clenched my teeth to calm the thoughts flooding through me. I leaned over, thinking about vomiting, *again.*

"Yes, they are waiting for you. They have always been there." Rowan hesitantly touched my shoulder, as I sunk back to the stone.

Visions overwhelmed me as I saw them through childhood, growing up in a world so different from my own. Pushing my palms into my eyes, I rocked forward, my elbows digging in my knees as images pummeled me. Their gifts and powers were being embraced and cherished, to flourish beyond my imagination. Shame sauntered through me as I realized how inept and unprepared I was in comparison.

"So much . . ." I mumbled out the words almost incoherently as the frenzy of emotions took over. Running my hands over my face in frustration, I glanced up at Rowan.

"I can't do this." I winced again. Then a strange thing happened: a brand-new voice sounded in my head:

"Do not be sad, little sister. We have much to be thankful for."

Ailianna's voice. The intrusion was foreign and awkward. This was too much.

"I think I have to vomit again." My hand flew to my mouth as I fell forward on my knees. My body retaliated against the sudden surge of power filling me, something else I wasn't prepared to handle.

I had family, people I didn't know, and an entire Realm existing without me. Blackness crept in at the corners of my vision and I forced my fingers to my mouth, trying to focus on staying conscious.

"Breathe." Rowan's voice was soft as he ran his hand down my back.

A stream of heat flooded through my body, followed by a tingling throughout my skin. I concentrated on my breath. As the warm air filled my lungs, it gave me stability and evened the swirling going on in my head.

I pressed my palms into the material of my pants, breathing out with intention. From the edge of my vision, Rowan reached into his pocket, pulling out a small vial of blue liquid. I didn't dare ask.

"Drink this, Aislynn. It will help." He offered the bottle to me.

At that point, I was desperate. For a quick second, I thought of the blue pill / red pill in *The Matrix*. Shaking my head, I put the vial to my lips and swallowed its contents.

❧

Strange images filled my mind as awareness trickled into my body. I felt the emotions of memories from my childhood and my grandmother. Voices impinged into my brain, but not normal voices, because technically I wasn't hearing them: they were in my head. My thoughts were heavy and fuzzy. I tried to remember, then realization struck.

Shit.

This wasn't a dream. The more aware I became, including the lumpy dirt beneath me, I found myself in the middle of the clearing with Rowan's suit jacket haphazardly draped across my body. Rowan and Jax's voices continued their barrage through my head:

"She will be waking soon."

"Yes, I know. The potion did not last as long as we needed. She did too much."

"You shouldn't have let her gather her powers to antagonize Daragon."

"Yes, I know that now."

"After, she was not capable of handling a truth of our Realm. Her sisters could have waited."

"I know. I know."

There was agony alive in Rowan's voice.

"This is my purpose, Rowan. This is why I have been with her all this time, to know when she will be prepared for these things."

"Do you think she can handle travel?"

"I hope so. We haven't much time left here."

I pulled on my memories of drinking the vial and realized it had knocked me unconscious. *God dammit. A girl gets a little nauseous after finding out her entire world gets flipped inside out, so let's just dope her with sleepy juice.*

Jax's laughter interrupted my internal grumbling. *"Sleepy juice! That's a first!"* Jax hooted, and upon opening my eyes, I half expected him to be rolling on the ground in ferocious laughter.

"Glad I could be of entertainment." Finally, I sat up, giving them both steely glares.

"Welcome back, Aislynn. Do you feel better?" Rowan asked.

"I feel drugged, dammit! Was that really necessary?" I stood slowly, shaking off Rowan's jacket.

"Unfortunately, yes. Your body could not handle much more. The potion's purpose was not to drug you, but to help your body absorb the changes that are occurring. Without it you would have passed out and been very ill."

"So, I should say thank you?" I arched an eyebrow with my mouth a firm line.

"No thanks necessary. As your protector, it is my duty."

I rolled my eyes; apparently, he didn't sense my sarcasm. "What does that mean, anyway?" I pushed my hair out of my face.

"What?"

"The protector business?" I asked, waving my hand in the air.

"Well, my magical line is one of protection," Rowan explained. "Those who carry this particular thread of magic are trained and guided by the Council of Magic to protect unique magical objects, and/or beings who have important roles in the magical destiny of Light. I am extremely good at what I do, and they use me when it is of the greatest importance." A sideways grin crossed his mouth.

"So, only the best for me, huh?" I gave him the same smile.

It became apparent, even though I was completely clueless about everything magical, for Rowan this was his existence and livelihood. *Perhaps I shouldn't be so hard on him.*

"Are we leaving soon?" I asked as I hung his jacket over my arms.

"Eager, are we?"

"Well, all this talk of destinies needing to be filled . . ." My words felt hollow; traveling through otherworldly realms scared the shit out of me, but I didn't want them to know. "Hey, you changed," I added.

Rowan's expensive suit was gone and in its place were clothes, well, not of this Realm. He wore pants the color of broken tortilla chips, made of a sturdy material that would withstand being worn often. The shirt was a deep basil color, lightweight and moved freely around his body. This was his normal gear, hardy and rugged.

"Yes, the suit, though a necessity at the time, was quite uncomfortable," he said.

"You know, Rowan, I've always thought the same thing," I laughed as I tossed the jacket to him. Glancing down at my own clothes, I felt I had been wearing them for days.

"Yes, that is probably a good idea." Rowan folded up the jacket.

I dug through my bag for a pair of jeans and pulled out a simple black t-shirt. I searched for a place to change, and instead Rowan and Jax dutifully turned their backs. I wondered for the first time what Hallervania would be like and how different it would be from my world.

"Well, it certainly isn't Kansas."

"Very funny, Jax." I swore if the cat could've grinned a Cheshire smile, he would have. Getting used to your cat talking was one thing; him having an unwavering sarcastic wit was entirely another thing.

"You will get used to it," Rowan said as he pushed the suit jacket into my bag, pulling the zipper closed.

He walked to the north point of the clearing. Ahead of

him was densely wooded forest, but as he spoke softly in his native language, the trees transformed before us, becoming a clear path from the circle.

Dense, dark soil six feet across led out into the forest as sunlight trickled through the trees, creating patches of sun on the path. The shimmer of power now encompassed the path before us.

"Come, Aislynn." Rowan gestured at me.

I twisted my lips in my teeth and pulled my messenger bag over my shoulder. Jax trotted down the path away from us, and my eyes darted to Rowan with concern. For the first time since being in Minneapolis, I stared into a new pair of eyes. The blue intensified into a clear, crystallized blue, dazzling in the sunlight.

I found myself taking several steps toward him to gaze further at how they were beautiful and unlike anything I had ever seen before. If his eyes had been this striking in downtown, people would've freaked out. Okay, *I* would have freaked out.

"It is quite alright, Aislynn. You are safer here than ever before." He tried to reassure me, mistaking my awkward staring for fear. With the path enveloped in magic, Rowan watched me. Aware that he sensed my thoughts, I shook my head, focusing back on my current predicament.

Traveling to another Realm.

"Magic is within us. Of course, there are parts of the earth which are more powerful, but we are always connected to magic through our mind and consciousness. It moves with us," he said, trying to explain. The sun cast odd shadows across his face, glinting across his hair and the dark curls at the nape of his neck.

"You will soon learn how to embrace your gifts and not feel so overwhelmed by magic. It will only take a little time."

Something within me pounded to be freed, the magic I meticulously kept hidden swirling its way to the surface. My steps felt heavy. Pieces of my grandmother's stories slipped in and out of my mind, begging me to remember slivers of my childhood.

We walked for some distance before Jax stopped. He sat in the center of the path, though nothing significant appeared to stop in this particular area; it looked much the same. The space in front of him began to transform. Branches moved, crisscrossing from each side of the path connecting in layers of wood.

Green ribbons of moss hung to the ground as a curtain or doorway, impossible to see through. Visually confusing the eyes, the world of solid structured things disintegrated as everything became an illusion.

"Aislynn, are you ready to return home to your destiny?" Rowan asked in a husky whisper.

"I didn't think I had a choice." My eyes flashed to his.

"You always have a choice. This door will lead you to Hallervania, or just as easily take you to your apartment in Minneapolis. The choice is, and always will be, yours."

For the smallest moment, I didn't know what to think. Up until this point I didn't believe there were options. My eyes jumped from Jax and Rowan's faces, both waiting for me and my decision. Looking back to the mossy doorway, the air breathing around me, the sisters I hadn't met, the forest waiting, I knew there wasn't a decision to be made.

I would not deny the internal knowing flooding through me; I needed to figure out what my grandma wanted me to find. Blowing out the breath I held, I glanced at each of them.

"I'm ready."

"Never had a doubt," Jax said as he disappeared through the moss. Rowan rolled his eyes, motioning me to follow.

6

Moss tendrils tickled my neck as I crossed into Hallervania for the first time. Blinking rapidly at the open field before me, vivid emerald grass reached past my knees, accompanied by dots of wildflowers in vibrant colors. I shielded my eyes from the sudden transition to the bright landscape. The field stretched into rolling hills with layering mountains in the distance, contrasting the almost turquoise sky glistening above.

Rowan appeared behind me, the mossy doorway invisible from this side. A popping sound escaped my mouth as he appeared from nowhere. The new world around me moved and breathed as if alive and one singular entity. A gentle breeze cut across the grass in waves, shifting the colors from emerald to bright kelly green like a kaleidoscope in motion.

Jax moved ahead of us, his inky black tail swishing the long green threads of grass, engulfing his body. With a light touch, Rowan's hand caressed the small of my back, encouraging me forward with a smile.

Unsure, I turned to see Jax dart through the grass and in a small leap bounded to the top of a crumbling rock wall. After a second glance in Rowan's direction, I followed my cat down a small path nestled next to a shallow river. Every step forward left me more speechless and my mouth opened and closed like a half-dead fish.

A village took shape in the distance and a knot formed in my belly, fearing as we traveled Realms we had traveled back in time. My insides turned at the thought of having no running water, electricity, or my other first world amenities.

"Not quite. Your thinking is too linear. Just because we are not in your Realm, we must be moving forward or backward in time. This is untrue. We are in the same time, only a different place. Things are different, but not medieval," Rowan explained. "Although I do not know how partial you are to your transportation system." A smirk crossed his mouth.

"Transportation system?" Finally, I managed words.

He nodded. "The vehicles you use?"

"Cars?"

"Yes." His eyes flashed with laughter. "We do not have those here."

"But . . . ?" my dark eyes questioned.

"How do we travel?" A smile formed. "Your favorite way: teleportation." He laughed as I shivered at the thought, even though the second time wasn't as bad.

"We use magic to transport ourselves, as well as the things we need and use. There is no need for these cars or the oil used to make them go."

"You are missing out. Windows down, sunroof open, music blaring—might be one of my favorite things," I said, holding onto my modern-world joys. I pondered how different our world would be if we simply didn't need cars, and I realized how easily teleportation would be abused. I cringed at the idea.

"Magic, as I said, is everywhere, and plentiful," Rowan commented as we walked. "It can be called up for Light or Dark. It is up to the user of how it is manifested. Do not worry; the people of Hallervania understand the ramifications of abusing the powers we are given." A line appeared between his brows, and I questioned the truth of his words.

"Our gifts are treated with respect. Your realm is capable of much the same . . . if they surpassed the needs of greed and wealth, and instead focused on the inner powers rather than trying to gain them from an outside source. You would live in a different world."

His idealistic thinking brought me hope, and a deep collaboration of community. That point of evolution perhaps when people chose to come together and live harmoniously with each other was something my Realm was light years away from.

We weaved on the path through a grove of aspen trees, the stark white contrasted against the warm cinnamon lines within the bark. The concept of living this way seemed too hippy-dippy and the cynical side of me gave into fear, recognizing my Realm would abuse such an existence. I had limited faith in my side of humanity and an unexpected carnal protection emerged within me to protect this place I didn't know.

Rowan didn't seem to notice my thoughts and awareness settled into me to use more control. With practice, maybe I could know when to allow and when to block him.

"What about money?" I asked, changing the subject before he caught on to my rampant internal mind-melt.

"Unneeded. People live peacefully together for and with one another. Surviving on their own would be difficult, so with a mutual understanding for the betterment of our society, we support each other."

I scoffed at the ridiculousness of his words. Hippy-dippy indeed. Maybe they did LSD, too.

Rowan swept around a tree, dropping a few feet to the landing below. "Bartering and trading are key elements within our society. Every soul has a gift, and these can be exchanged." He offered a hand to help my landing, and my eyes were wary with doubt.

"You know, that sounds ridiculous and too good to be true." I stifled a half laugh with jaded eyes. My thoughts sauntered back to the evolution idea: is anything possible?

Then I realized how ridiculous my thoughts sounded. It was easy for me to accept the concept of other Realms, but those Realms not needing money or cars was baffling and unrealistic. *Is it possible that my Realm paradigms are so deeply ingrained I can't see any other possibilities?*

Talk about disturbing.

"The small things are forgotten when someone like Daragon comes into our lives," Rowan was saying, bringing me back to the present. "The people of Hallervania do not want to lose the peace we have enjoyed for so many years. This has been threatened and torn at by Daragon and Darkness."

I pondered this strange lifestyle. From the outside, it appeared idyllic and a hell of a lot simpler than my world.

We cut off the path in the woods, arriving on a road of sorts, and I noticed cottages scattered over the landscape. The homes weren't the modern design I was accustomed to, but upon closer inspection, they weren't medieval either.

Built of bricks and stones much like at home, but more noticeable were the beautiful gardens surrounding the cottages.

Yards adorned with flowers, herbs, and an endless variety of vegetables filled every open space. Children played outside, running through the grasses, not neatly kept with mowers but left to be wild. I watched two young blonde girls giggle as they threw not a regular ball, but a bright glittering light ball. The beautiful mass of energy changed colors from a deep magenta to a crystal pink as it floated between them.

Okay . . . not much like my home at all.

Rowan veered to the right, down a narrower path, the trees becoming thicker and the houses less visible. The bubbling of water over rocks soothed me, distracting me from otherworldly thoughts and obsessions. Ahead, a small bridge led over the river to a home separate from the others. Stumbling a bit, I paused, looking up. I tried to decipher what was different about this place. Perhaps it only *felt* different.

Crossing the worn wood planks of the bridge, a warm light filled me. The path's edges overflowed with flowers that I didn't recognize. Yellow and pink petals overlapped, bulging from every direction.

The dark walnut door pushed open, revealing tiny bare feet and folds of velvet in the deepest turquoise, reminding me of the ocean. A woman stepped out, and thick, long blonde hair fell in front of her face as she closed the door behind her.

"Aislynn," she began as she pushed hair around her ears, exposing angelic, faerie-like features. But it was her eyes which captured my attention. The same stunning turquoise as her dress, they shimmered in the similar crystallized appearance of Rowan's.

"Aislynn, your sister, Ailianna." Rowan formally introduced us, which seemed ludicrous.

"Hi," my voice squeaked as she hugged me.

"You must be exhausted." She pulled back, scrutinizing me in a delicate manner, making me uncomfortable.

"I . . ." That moment screeched to the number one spot on my list of most bizarre encounters of my life. "Uh . . ."

Ailianna disregarded my uneasiness. "It is so good to see you."

Her words caught me off guard, as she implied we had met before. A warm smile filled her mouth and a dimple dotted her right cheek. Anxiety began a slow creep into my chest, a tightening restricting my breath. The idea of a sister and the looming question of *how* we were related rattled in my head.

Someone came around the corner of the house, and Ailianna's arm wrapped around my waist, leaving me torn between comfort and the angst building in my heart.

"Rowan, Jax." Aila's voice was a song as she acknowledged them, and I tried to comprehend how I knew this was Aila.

Shorter than Ailianna, she was dressed in the same type of pants Rowan wore, complimented by a loose shirt in the lightest lavender color.

With a half a glance at me, she removed the leather satchel of arrows draped across her chest.

Arrows? The fear of traveling back in time registered again.

"I thought I felt you." Aila tugged on her chestnut braid as her crystallized emerald eyes evaluated me.

"Yes, they have just arrived," Ailianna spoke, and I could tell she was ignoring the obvious tension between me and Aila. "Aislynn, you must be starved. Traveling and magic takes its toll, as you are aware." With a gentle kindness, she eased me into the house.

"What am I? Chopped liver?" Aila spouted as she dropped her bow at the door and came in behind Rowan and Jax.

My heart skipped in apprehension as I walked into their strange home, in an odd place with people I didn't know. The spacious entryway gave way to high ceilings and an open floor plan. On my left, a fireplace lined the entire wall, deeply inset. Several Dutch ovens sat in the fire and other smaller pots hung on iron bars built into the walls.

The oddest part was the lights. Light didn't come from candles, windows, or the fire, but from bright white energy balls scattered about the room. Some sat low while others floated higher toward the ceiling.

Rowan took my backpack and set it on my other bags. *Where did those come from?* Jax jumped on the massive polished wood table dominating the room and Rowan pulled out one of the benches, his eyes meeting mine in question.

Unease kept me locked in place, observing the normality of these women in their home while feeling completely out of place. The simplicity of comfy chairs and endless bookshelves strewn with crystals and potted plants tucked here and there offered warmth and coziness, but I felt like an alien. An impostor.

I don't belong here.

Ailianna encouraged me from the table, offering me a plate. Rowan and Aila didn't hesitate and filled their plates with food, some recognizable and some not.

Finally, I brought myself to sit, scooping a mixture of rice, beans, and vegetables on my plate through overlapping conversations. Rowan and Aila bantered along Jax's snide comments while Ailianna flitted about, adding a bowl of sweet rolls in front of me. Hesitant and awkward with my movements, I slowly grabbed a roll. My stomach declared its own opinions, growling in fury.

The explosion of flavor in my mouth distracted me from the worry and discomfort. Instead, I reveled in the simple enjoyment of tastes and textures, almost magical. Halfway through my plate, a bizarre awareness filled me, as if the food was working harmoniously with my body, making every part of me, physical and magical, work more efficiently.

My fork paused in return to my mouth, tentative to eat another bite. It was creepy to receive a high from food, wasn't it?

"It is the way we grow the food. With intention, love, and light," Ailianna smiled. "This way it provides more than nutrients for our bodies; it also gives our whole being nourishment." She handed me more bread, her eyes glittering.

Trying to decide if it was irritating to have my mind connected with someone—or multiple someones—swallowing hard, I set down my fork. I decided I was finished with creepy magical food.

"You get used to it, or it just makes you crazy," Aila said. A seriousness to her voice told me she wasn't trying to be funny but implying I *would* go crazy.

"Aila! I don't think she needs more today," Rowan chided as he narrowed his gaze.

"Only being honest! On that note, thanks, Sis, for the grub. I have to finish my rituals." Aila gave Ailianna a half hug before reaching over her to snag another sweet roll.

A strange sensation ran through me.

"Jax, are you coming? I could use your help."

"I suppose I've had enough to eat."

Until this moment, when I heard voices in my head, it was because I was talking about them or with them. This, however, was different. My eyes shot to Aila and Jax as they shut the door behind them as I tried to comprehend the difference.

"She decided to share her light with you, a big decision for her," Ailianna said, interrupting my thoughts. "Having you here and such a crucial part of our destinies goes against her nature; she sometimes thinks she can solve everything herself."

Very distinctly, Aila's voice trotted in my head:

"I do not."

I assumed Ailianna heard her as well, as her lips turned upward.

"She is stubborn, that one. But I think we all are in our own ways."

"What do you mean 'share her light'?"

"Well, even though magic surrounds us, we still have control over our own magic. We can decide who and when we share it. Because the three of us are connected, it is harder to push each other away than let each other in. This is her way of accepting her destiny, much in the same way you have." She stood as she spoke and began collecting the plates.

Controlling magic. Memories forcefully pushed themselves into my mind, and I tried to resist the onslaught. Images of middle school and lightbulbs shattering above my head in riot with my moody hormonal outbursts. I slammed the door on the images before Rowan or Ailianna trailed onto my thoughts.

I need to be more careful.

The overwhelming sensation pummeled me as I thought of everything I needed to learn. My thoughts trickled back to the two little girls playing with the energy ball; even they were more advanced. Magic was an integral part of their lives, and I knew nothing.

No. That is wrong. I had spent years suppressing unexplainable events I couldn't control.

"It will come. Your sisters will help," Rowan assured me, and patted my arm. Agitation grated through me. His riddles and pacifying comments were not helpful. The word "sisters" felt like an explosive detonator.

"Yeah, but I should already know this if I had been here learning instead of being oblivious somewhere else!" I cried out. "Sisters? What does that even mean? How are we sisters? Sisters by blood? Sisters by magic? I need answers!"

My questions were violent demands. Spikes of anger flared under my skin, threatening to seep out. *Just like in eighth grade during gym class when the showers burst on, spraying water everywhere, sending girls shrieking from the locker room.*

"You will." Rowan's nonchalant response became my last straw. The memories of my teenage years layering with the current events playing out before me melded together as one. Frustration rolled through me and words stuck in my throat. The glass in my hand disintegrated in my grasp. A garbled noise escaped my mouth as the glasses across the table suddenly shattered one after another. Shards exploded across the room, landing throughout the remaining food.

"Oh my god," I stammered. My lack of control frightened me and sent me scrambling back from the table. "I'm . . . I am so sorry." My hands shot to my mouth in horror.

I focused on blocking the brain link between Rowan and Ailianna. Being here, with magic everywhere and *available*, I couldn't contain myself. The control I worked so hard to maintain since childhood was something they didn't understand. Fear and shame burst through, and I slammed the doors shut on the memories trying to clamber to the surface.

I can't allow this. What am I thinking? My hands shook, and I clenched them tightly, desperately trying to hold on.

"Aislynn . . . it's okay." Ailianna took a step toward me, but I knew she saw my control disintegrating, and stopped.

I wanted to turn and run.

"Go." Her voice faltered, and eyes filled with concern.

I *needed* to get out of here, to process everything that happened since that morning, afternoon . . . it felt like days. In reality, it had only been a few hours. Panic rose through my chest, spreading like wildfire. Ailianna's voice echoed quietly in my head:

"Go. Go for a walk, take some time. You need to process. Go."

Grabbing my bag, I darted out the door.

7

The door slammed behind me and I took a huge, gasping breath. Resting my hands on my thighs, anxiety grew hot and expanded through my chest, biting through my resolve.

It's so easy to lose control. I had only been here for a short time and I already lost what took years to obtain. Torn between my past, my draw to magic, this place, and terrifying fear, I focused on taking long deep breaths and counting through my exhales. The one thing Dr. Mack, the therapist my mother had forced me to see, had helped me with was managing my panic attacks.

I hadn't been completely honest with Rowan. Not even a little.

Control eased back into my body at a sluggish pace. The air, fresh and cool, filled my lungs as I stalked away from the house. Irritated I couldn't go far because I wouldn't know how to find my way back, I decided to stick to the river's edge, heading south down the path. *At least, I think it's south.* The remnants of the panic attack pounded in my ears as the soothing sound of the water lessened the pain.

I wish I had packed my anxiety meds.

Following a narrow path, I started up a small incline. Rocks steadily became boulders as I continued upward. Sticking my foot in a crevice, I pulled myself carefully to the top. Another lesson from therapy: physical motion helped to move emotional energy and shift the focus from panic. Peering down, I found myself at the top of a small waterfall, with only fifteen feet between me and the bottom. I wrapped my feet beneath me and observed the water rush to the pool below.

The water spray tickled across my arms in cool tingles. Heavy trees shaded most of the area except where tiny breaks of light fought through the leaves. Sunlight sparkled across the water, creating rainbows around the waterfall. The connection between me and the earth settled, and my control crept its way back to my body.

I focused on the rushing water and the sun on my skin to allow my heart rate to settle. It was probably the only technique from therapy that I actually enjoyed. For a short moment, I imagined I was in Minneapolis, sitting by Minnehaha Falls instead of in a world I didn't know.

Maybe the answer was not thinking at all. Reaching into my bag, I dug out my iPhone and my wireless buds, then jammed them into my ears. I scrolled down to my current favorite band and cranked the volume, returning my mind to the vision of Minnesota.

After listening to several of my favorite songs, I checked the battery. The power bar turned red, and I knew I wouldn't have music much longer. I thought about the charger wrapped in my bag and groaned. A lot of use that would be without an outlet to charge. *Yeah, pretty much screwed on that one.*

I picked up a tiny pebble. When I turned it over in my hand, I saw it was a shining shade of otherworldly purple. *For hell's sake! Is anything normal here?* Flipping the stone in my fingertips, I tossed it over the edge of the precipice, where it landed with a plunk in the water below.

With my earbuds crammed in my ears, I didn't hear anyone approach, but I suddenly sensed a presence behind me.

When I glanced over my shoulder in apprehension, I found a man watching me curiously. He appeared to be my age, wearing dark pants and a loose buttercream shirt like Rowan's. Hair the color of warm caramels flowed longer around his face, and of course, hard to miss were the common Hallervania crystallized blue eyes. His gaze gradually met mine as we accessed each other.

"Hello." His voice was softer than I expected.

"Hey," I said, tugging out my earbuds.

"May I ask what that is?" Curiosity rattled his voice as he pointed to my iPhone.

"Oh, my phone? Music." I shook my phone back and forth, and it dawned on me that my cell phone would be considered quite strange here.

He stepped up to the boulders around me, his face inquisitive, reaching his hand out in a tentative gesture.

"That is quite extraordinary." His voice was full of awe as he peered down at the small device.

"Wanna listen?" I offered an earbud.

He took it gently from my hand, examining the bud before he put it close to his ear. His eyes popped open in surprise as the music streamed into his ears.

"What is that?"

I couldn't help but smile. "X-Ambassadors. 'Unsteady.' Do you like it?" Discussing something as simple as music felt normal. The song finished, and he handed back the earbud.

"Thank you for sharing. That was pleasant." The stranger sat cross-legged next to me. I edged to the right a little to create space for him. Something about his presence made me feel at ease.

Should I be concerned? Usually, after a panic attack, I was on edge and frazzled. But the stranger brought a sense of calm.

"Well, I guess you should feel privileged because it just died." My iPhone powered itself off.

"What do you mean?" Worry and confusion settled across his face. I supposed saying "it died" would mean something else here.

"The battery is dead. You guys don't have electricity, I can't exactly plug it in to charge."

His eyebrows furrowed together in a perplexed way and I knew he didn't understand what I meant. "Why don't you just use magic?" he suggested, as if this would be the obvious solution to my problem.

"To charge my battery?" My eyebrows scrunched.

"Yes. Sure. Magic is energy, and that is what your electricity is, is it not?" Again, plainly obvious.

Yeah, why didn't I think of that? I must have been looking at him like an idiot because he smiled at me.

"May I?"

Handing him my phone with hesitation, I finally shrugged. Holding it in his right hand, he hovered his left over the front. When he spoke in a quiet whisper, my phone started to glow in blue light. Internally praying the damn thing wouldn't explode into a thousand pieces, I squinted my eyes and turned my head in mild fear.

"There. That should do it."

This time, I stared at the stranger in awe and amazement. I guess we could both show each other new things. My phone powered on and the battery icon showed a full green bar.

"That's amazing. Thank you." I beamed. "You make it seem easy and I know it's not."

"When it is all you know, it is simple." He shrugged as the corners of his mouth turned up. "Don't worry, Aislynn. It will soon be easy enough." He handed me my phone, and as the tips of his fingers touched mine a shock ran through me.

"How do you know who I am?" I shook my finger to dissipate the tingle.

"Everyone knows who you are. We have been waiting a long time for you," he said with ease as he jumped down to the grass below.

"Yeah, that part worries me. I have no clue what I am doing." I turned to look down over my shoulder at him, hoping my sarcasm hid my frustration.

"You will find your way."

I rolled my eyes, growling. "You sound like Rowan. Talking in riddles and mysterious reasoning."

The stranger laughed in response. "Well, I should go . . ." He seemed hesitant to turn and leave, though.

"Hey, wait," I began, "you never told me your name."

He jumped halfway up the boulder, taking my hand and bowing his head slightly. "I am Tristan MaCallohan of Gladdenbury, Hallervania."

His name sounded proper and regal. I smiled nervously as my cheeks turned hot. He gave me one last smile and a small wave as he turned away.

I shook my head as Tristan walked away. *Maybe things would be okay.* Then something shifted. A snap in the air bristled like a jolt of electricity. Fire exploded in star bursts of pain, burning in my shoulder like a punch to my chest.

8

I cried out in agony as I fell back toward the waterfall's edge. Tristan snapped his gaze back toward me, then crawled up the rocks.

"Oh, Goddess!" he exclaimed, looking around wildly and thrusting his hands out in front of him. Although in a fuzzy pain haze, I saw a stream of light erupt from his palms, surrounding us in a bright circle. I decided I must be delirious.

"Aislynn, you will be okay," Tristan told me.

My eyes darted back and forth as I clutched my chest. Then multiple voices sounded at once.

"Tristan!"

"Please! Let us in!"

"Tristan, please, it is okay. Please release your magical protections. We need to help her."

Ailianna and Aila's voices surrounded us from outside Tristan's protective circle. The edges of my vision were blackening as I faded in delirium. My sisters' voices were full of anger and worry, but more worrisome was how I could feel their emotions from them.

The blistering in my chest and shoulder rushed through my body, and the pure anguish rapidly took over my thoughts.

"Sorry!" Tristan insisted. "Sorry! I didn't know how quick you would be here." He must have done something because Ailianna and Aila rushed to my side.

"What in Hell's fury happened?" Dread oozed through Aila's voice. "Oh . . ." A low groan settled in her throat as she peered down at me. "Ailianna . . ." From my perspective on the ground, terror slid down her face in my awkward upside-down view. *Shit. That can't be good.*

"Shhh, Aila. She is going to be fine." Ailianna's stern eyes quieted Aila. The two of them muttered back and forth, and it helped to focus on them rather than the fire searing through me.

"Shit! It freaking hurts!" I screamed as another wave built, rising to a crescendo, and I writhed in anguish.

"Aislynn! Look at me!" Ailianna's turquoise eyes pierced mine. "Shhh . . ." She pushed my hair, sticky with sweat, off of my forehead. "It will be okay."

A calmness flooded into me, and though I was still aware of the pain, her soothing felt like a shot of morphine; I didn't seem to care as much now.

"Tristan, I need to know what happened so I can help her," Ailianna implored, and turned to look at him.

"I don't know. We were talking, and as soon as I turned to go, I heard her cry out and fall backward. I did not realize she was not protected." Guilt echoed in his voice.

"It looks like Daragon's work."

"Why was she out here by herself? You just let her go?" Aila stomped above me, and I didn't have the strength to explain that her blame was directed at the wrong person.

"She needed a moment," Ailianna explained. "Time to process everything she is going through."

"Unprotected? Goddess help us!"

"Stop bickering! Please! Just help her." Tristan's helplessness flitted through his words.

Aila muttered under her breath, while pain pounded in synchronization with Tristan's pacing. I thought, *Yes! Please help me.* The burning was becoming hotter until their voices were muted and the fire saturated my awareness. I glanced down to my shoulder, certain there would be a white-hot fire poker sticking out, but instead I saw burnt and blackened flesh. Unconsciousness almost won.

"Follow us, Tristan."

Blinking, I saw Ailianna with her arms out over me and Aila. I knew what came next: I no longer could hear the rushing of the waterfall, but instead the crackling of fire and the wood floor beneath me. At the shift of sounds, my stomach turned, knowing we had teleported. I heard Ailianna rustling in the kitchen, distracting me as Aila took my hand, stroking my hair.

"Let your magic fill you, Aislynn," she said, her voice soft. "It will help."

"But I don't know how . . ." My eyes flitted back and forth, tears rounding the edges of my vision. Panic filled the remaining holes around my vicious pain.

"Yes. Yes, you do. It is within you always, and all around you. Let it fill you." Aila's emerald crystallized eyes swam with tears. I saw her fear settle, subdued by a sweet calm. Warmth radiated up the hand she held, and a steady brightness consumed me. My breath softened as agony resumed in the background.

Ailianna leaned over me, packing a thick grainy paste on my chest and shoulder. A flowery aroma filled my nose. Lavender registered in my brain and soothed my skin almost instantly.

My breath evened with the strange awareness of the happenings around me until I heard Rowan's voice, rampant with worry as he conferred with Tristan.

When did he get here? The thoughts distracted me from the seething fire inside.

"Are you ready yet, Ailianna?" Aila's words were short as tension built.

"Yes." Ailianna set down the bowl of paste and took my other hand and then Aila's. As the three of our hands connected for the first time, the energy shifted, vibrating around us.

"We call upon the Goddess of Light, the Elementals and the magic of this Realm, and all others." Ailianna's voice was clear and vibrant.

"Air, come to us. We call you here and ask your aide."

"Fire, come to us. May you burn brightly to warm and heal."

"Water, come to us. Protect and shield by washing away the evil done here."

"Earth, come to us. Center and ground so that we may nurture and repair."

"I call upon the elements of Earth, Air, Fire, and Water. Come forth and bring your powers with guidance." Their voices sang together, and the magic of their home made my skin tingle.

From the corner of my eye, white light encircled us,

followed by bands of color: yellow, red, blue, and green, following with each of the elements swirling around the circle. My head resting to the side, I saw Rowan and Tristan standing past the circle of light that enveloped us.

Tristan's face was plastered with awe; he seemed to be moved by the magic being performed.

Isn't this normal?

My gaze jolted to Rowan, who stood with his arms crossed, watching with satisfaction. He expected nothing less. In my strange delusion of exceeding pain, pride was visible in his eyes.

"May the light warm itself over the darkness that has taken place on this day. May it be washed away and healed." The light around us began spinning into a vortex above me before it poured into my body.

The light filled me, magic pulling me into surrender. The pain all but disappeared, chased from my body by Light, which eased its presence into every aspect of my being. I realized the ache in my chest and shoulder was only the entrance of the damage; Dark magic had spread through my body like a disease, destroying me cell by cell.

Piercing white light occupied my vision and the room faded to whiteness. Floating bliss became omnipresent. Vague awareness clicked. *I must be unconscious because I'm not in the kitchen anymore. At least . . . I can't see the room. How strange.* Was it possible to be aware of being unconscious? Milky white fog surrounded me, then a voice reached my ears.

Oh shit. I knew that voice.

"Grandma?" I called out, unable to separate joy and fear. There was joy upon hearing my grandmother's voice, and fear because she had been pretty dead for about eleven years.

"Yes, darling."

I searched through the mist of white for her.

"I am only here to help you get where you need to go." Her voice was peaceful and serene.

Uh, thanks, Grandma. That only sounds slightly foreboding. Alarm trickled into my thoughts. Was I dying? I thought about how my pain had been obliviated. *Oh shit . . . is* this *the white light people talk about?*

And then, I heard a different voice:

"Do not fret, my dear Aislynn. You have not died. You are simply in the in-between." Her voice overflowed with power.

A beautiful woman appeared before me, sitting on a giant velvet pillow the color of merlot. The pillow floated in a mist of nothingness. Folds of amethyst, violet, and orchid velvet layered around her.

"We have thrust so much upon you so quickly. You have a strong soul, my dear Aislynn. I am here, supporting you through this journey." Dark chocolate hair curled in curtains around an ageless, ethereal face.

"And who are you?"

Her arctic frost-colored pair of eyes glittered and shimmered as she considered me.

"I am a Goddess of the Elements."

I had read enough books and watched enough television series to know Gods and Goddesses rarely were trustworthy; they tended to have their own agenda.

"But what am I supposed to do?" I cringed at the whine in my voice in comparison to her rich velvet.

"You must remember to always let magic fill you. Trust in everything that is shown to you and those who have been put in your path. Once you do, your path will be revealed. You are powerful beyond what Darkness can possibly imagine."

A part of me reveled in the magnitude of the Goddess in front of me, while another part rationalized and questioned the mystical bullshit of her wording.

"I surround you with Light and love, my dear child. You are never alone."

The Goddess of Elements faded away. Gradually, my sisters and the room reappeared before me. I fought back, trying to return to her, trying to fill the space with images from my mind. I wanted to cry out, to scream, and do anything to go back.

"Aislynn?"

My thoughts were cut off by Ailianna's voice. The images of the Goddess broke apart in my mind and my eyes fluttered open. Everything in the room took its place again, and I began to think I imagined it all. Maybe I died. As each moment passed, the memories felt more dreamlike and gave new meaning to "seeing the light." The thought brought a giggle bursting from my mouth. I was unaware the sound came from me until Ailianna sighed and Aila laughed.

"I think she is alright." The two of them peered down at me and I grinned. Glancing at my chest still covered in thick paste, I no longer felt burnt flesh beneath. I sat up on my elbows.

"Well, that was different."

"Shall we close the circle?" Ailianna gestured toward the power shimmering around us.

"You mean before she becomes more inebriated off power?" Aila scoffed, then pushed off her knees to stand.

She grabbed a thick cotton towel off the counter and handed it to me to wipe off most of the paste.

"Would you like to do your part, Aislynn?" Ailianna gave my hand a gentle squeeze, her skin warm in mine. My throat tightened as I instantly wanted to say no, but I paused my wiping, folding the towel on itself. Could I do this? The Goddess's words came back to me: *Trust. Believe in the flow of magic.* I could do that now because I wasn't alone, couldn't I?

My eyes darted as I thought about my part. *Water.* I needed to release the element from the circle. I wasn't completely sure how I knew this, but I tried not to think about it. Seconds passed since she asked, so I nodded, letting her pull me from the floor.

Aila stepped forward to take our hands. The magic reverberated within our circle and rippled throughout the room. Ailianna's face lit with power, and when she spoke her voice was clear.

"I release you, Air, and thank you for your gifts and presence here today. I bid you farewell." Ailianna's hair lifted as the air gently stirred away from her.

"I release you, Fire, and thank you for your gifts and presence here today. I bid you farewell." Aila's eyes closed with a small smile on her face, embraced by the magic. Heat brushed between us. My face flushed, knowing it was my turn. My voice betrayed me with a crack, and I tried again.

"I release you, Water," I said, my voice a whisper. "And thank you for your healing gifts and presence here today. I bid you farewell."

Magic flooded through me and an overwhelming sense of gratitude washed forward like waves. Cool droplets of water tickled my skin. For the first time in my life, I felt connected to magic rather than stampeded by it.

The three of us together released Earth, my voice stronger this time. "We release you, Earth, and thank you for your gifts and presence here today. We bid you farewell."

Ailianna began speaking, but I found myself interrupting her. Words tumbled out of my mouth before I could stop them. Ailianna gave me a curious glance, but I shook my head, changing my mind.

"Nothing," I said, cheeks flushing hot again. My fear stifled any chance of more magic. The thought of losing control was at the forefront of my thoughts. Ailianna stared a moment longer, then closed her eyes to continue.

"Thank you, Gods and Goddesses of the Elements, for your presence within this circle, giving us the power to heal our new sister." Her full smile reached her eyes as she squeezed my hand again. My belly tightened at the word *sister*, and I tried to smile. Instead, I was certain my face twisted into a demented version of a Stepford wife.

The magic faded, shifting into a neutral hum. Our hands dropped, and I attempted a better smile. They healed me with their gifts, the magic they had known all their lives, without hesitation. It left me humbled in a way that would upset them if they knew. Instead, I focused on appreciating them and my ability to use magic without losing control.

"That was quite incredible, Aislynn!" Tristan began, pulling me from my thoughts. "I am happy to know you are okay. The Goddess made you well. I must go now, please take care."

"Thank you, Tristan, for . . ."

But with a small bow of the head, he already disappeared. My mouth popped open in surprise; having people disappear in the middle of talking with them was a bit unnerving. I definitely needed to get used to that. Ailianna began putting away the things which were hastily used within the circle.

"Can someone fill me in?" Rowan pulled the corner of the bench, and it groaned in protest.

"I am not sure. I will need to look and see." Ailianna sat opposite him, with Aila and me following.

"I thought you saw the future?" I asked, pulling bits of lavender off my shirt. The edges of my V-neck were charred and frayed, a delicate reminder of how close the injury was to my heart.

"The past is just as important as the future. By looking back, you can better understand what is to come."

It made sense but seemed strange to me. I didn't understand what they needed to know; I was fine now. Ailianna's eyes changed, the whites, the iris, and the pupil a swirling deep turquoise. I stared in wonder.

"Oh!" She cried as her hand moved to her mouth.

"What?" Aila's hand reached for Ailianna's.

"He meant to kill her!" Disgust filled the room, and everyone else was shocked to hear this . . . except me. Ailianna's eyes swirled with color, still seeing.

"But . . . why didn't it work? He is just as perplexed. He knows you're fine now, but of course, he is not happy with such things. It should have worked. The magic should have killed her." The words rushed as she reiterated everything she saw behind the swirling turquoise.

"Then why did it not?" Rowan questioned.

"Thanks!" My eyebrows locked together, paired with a snide grin.

"Not like that. Here, when someone does magic with such intent, it does not fail. If he wanted to kill you, you should be dead."

"Well apparently, it didn't work." Their horror confused me. I thought it obvious Daragon wanted me dead.

"Therein lies the conundrum. What is different about this?" Rowan stood, pacing behind the table. Ailianna's eyes were still searching. Aila watched them both with disinterest, her chin resting on her hand as she stroked Jax with the other.

"Aislynn, murder and death are much simpler in your realm," Aila explained. "You can die much easier there, but here the rules are different. Magic protects us always. To kill someone, it is quite the accomplished magic. Like Rowan said, if Daragon intended to kill you, then you should be dead . . . hence the confusion."

Rowan stopped abruptly, turning toward me. "You had the box."

Everyone's eyes were suddenly on me. I forgot about the box.

"What box?" Aila's curiosity was offhanded as she continued to pet Jax. Ailianna stopped seeing and her eyes returned to normal.

"Box?"

"Yeah." I walked over to my bag, which thankfully had teleported with me. Sliding the zipper open, I pulled out the box and set it on the table.

"It keeps doing that," I mused, watching the box glimmer a steady white-blue light.

"Ah. Of course." Ailianna looked to the box with awe and understanding. I, of course, didn't understand anything.

"So how did the box save my life?" I asked, pulling on my necklace, swirling the pendant in my fingers.

"That would be the question." Rowan sunk back to the bench, his hands steepled at his mouth.

"Do you understand what this is?" Ailianna asked.

"Um. No. Because all I know is, I remembered, tried to open the box, and then he flew across the room to stop me." I jerked my hand at Rowan.

"Yes. Thank the Goddess, for that would have been . . ." Ailianna shuddered much like Rowan. "Aislynn, this box is integral to what will be."

"But what *is* it?" Frustrated and confused, we were back to mysteriousness.

"You are going to hate this, but I don't know. The Goddess will reveal its truth when the time is right."

"Uggghhh! Can this place give any straight answers?" Their conviction in their belief system was not enough for me. I let my head sink to the table. Ailianna picked up the box, placing it back in my hands.

"Here, Aislynn. Keep this with you always. As we know, it will keep you safe."

"At least we know why his magic didn't kill her," Aila said.

"Yeah, thank the Goddess for that," I grumbled from underneath my arms.

10

I didn't realize how much time passed as day shifted into night. The glowing balls of light floating throughout the rooms gradually brightened as the windows darkened. My attention turned to my body, and everything that happened in the last twenty-four hours caught up with me with wicked revenge. The high I received from the circle long faded away and left me in utter exhaustion.

Ailianna showed me upstairs to what she affectionately called "my room," and thankfully she also revealed a very "my world" bathroom. Internal gratitude flooded me, assuring me I was not backward in time, but across it, or something. I didn't fully understand. She left me to my own, knowing I was beyond worn out. Standing in front of the mirror, I glanced up and found I didn't recognize the person staring back at me.

Rapidly blinking, I pushed my body into the smooth granite counter to be closer to my reflection. Golden flecks of crystal shimmered through my eyes. They were crystallized, sparkling in ways I never imagined in my mundane chocolate brown.

It was one thing to see everyone else's eyes because I didn't know any different, but seeing this change in mine, the eyes I've known for twenty-seven years was *freaky*. Once I finished being mesmerized, I took note of how tired the rest of my face appeared and groaned. *Uggghhh.*

Peering into a deep, spacious bathtub, excitement ran through me until I noticed an absent faucet. *What the hell?* Annoyance grumbled in my throat. *Are they trying to torture me?*

Ailianna's voice filled my head. *"I forgot about that."* After a few moments, her face appeared in the crack of the door.

"Aislynn, your element is Water. Ask for it." She smiled and disappeared.

I turned toward the tub with my eyebrows raised. Just ask for it? Oh yeah. Real simple. I groaned again.

Alright, here goes . . .

"Come to me, water, to cleanse and purify . . . fill this tub for a relaxing time."

My words lacking confidence sounded ridiculous, but as fast as the thoughts came, they were replaced by amazement and pride. Water appeared as if from an imaginary faucet, slowly filling the tub. Realizing as I watched it fill, my experiences gave it restriction; the tub could have filled at once just the same.

However, this was pleasing, and reminded me of home and normalcy. I glanced through the bottles lining the edge of the tub, smelling as I lifted the corks. One was a lovely light purple, and the fragrance of lavender and vanilla filled my nose. I tipped the bottle and the silky liquid swirled into the water.

Unsure of how long I soaked, I begrudgingly removed myself from the cold water and realized I didn't bring in a change of clothes. After the attack and magical resurrection, the heap on the floor was not redeemable. I wrapped myself in a thick forest green towel, grabbed the clothes on the floor, and made an awkward shimmy run to my new bedroom.

Shutting the door behind me, I found a sanctuary of dark heavy furniture and a bed covered in layers of deep magenta blankets. Bowls of stones sat among candles and herbs, giving warmth and comfort to my exhaustion. Jax sat curled up in the middle of the bed in his usual place, and I wondered why I expected anything less.

"Because you are still adjusting. This is weird for you."

"Weird? Really? Jax, this is beyond weird. Weird doesn't begin to describe this." I spoke aloud because it felt awkward in my mind. In my world, we talked to our animals out loud, like normal people.

"It doesn't matter. I hear you either way."

"Ha. Ha. Have you always been this funny?" Wrapping the towel tighter around myself, I found my bags carefully lined against the wall. Kneeling, I began to search for something clean to wear.

"Yeah, aren't you bummed you've been missing out all this time?"

"I have a feeling you will be making up for that." I turned to look back at him after I pulled on my Imagine Dragons *Evolve* t-shirt and a pair of boxer shorts.

"Probably." Eyes closing, cat satisfaction melted across

his face. I shook my head, watching the cat drift to sleep oblivion.

A place I wanted to be.

I put the towel and my dirty clothes in a pile and wondered if they had washing machines. What if they didn't? My insides turned again, and I decided to not think about it. We left my apartment in such a rush, Rowan had shoved clothes in the bags haphazardly.

Unable to handle the chaos, I took out all the clothes, organizing and refolding everything into precise piles. Internally cursing myself for not taking control of the situation at the time, I pulled out a button-down dress shirt with raised eyebrows.

Business casual, the new dress apparel for all magical battles. A mini advertisement flashed through my mind and I laughed to myself.

Piling my stuff into categories of necessary and completely useless, I discovered half a bag of wearable clothes. *Men.* Freaking hell. It wasn't his fault, not really. After I finished, I crawled into bed, pausing as if to flip a light switch. I remembered the balls of light dimly glowing at the ceiling.

"I guess you can darken now," I said out loud again, certain I sounded absurd, but the lights twinkled into darkness. Slivers of light emanated from the long window in the corner from the pale glow of a full moon.

My body sunk into the blankets, my limbs heavy as my mind raced to process. *I'm in another Realm!* Insanity. Reaching over to the nightstand, I picked up the box, rolling it in my hands. I wanted to open the damn thing. Rowan had stopped me because I was in the Earth Realm. Well, I was here now, so it should be safe, right?

Flipping the little swivel latch, I tried lifting the top. Nothing. *Dammit.* Of course not. In frustration, I shoved the box back on the nightstand, rolled to my side, and watched the light pulse. Pulling the soft blankets over me, I shifted into sleep, a complete escape from destinies, magic, and Realms.

Leaves crunched under my feet as I walked through the woods. The air was warm on my skin as I let out my breath: I was home. Minnesota, home.

"Aislynn." A light whisper as the trees subtly shifted a ripple through the leaves.

"Aislynnnn." This time my name was drawn out in an eerie, disturbing sound from all around me.

"Aiiiiisssslllllyyynnnn . . ." Shivers ran up my spine and I searched in panic for the source.

As I turned back, a man appeared from nowhere. He leaned against a tree with one knee bent, head angled downward as he picked at his nails. His appearance was nonchalant, as if he had every right to be placed in the middle of my happy dream.

"Hello, Aislynn." His voice was smoky and matter of fact. He looked up through onyx hair, long and messy on top with shorter sides.

"Who are you?" My hands went to my hips in irritation. What was he doing in my dream? *Maybe I should be concerned I'm aware of my dreaming.*

"That healed rather nicely." His head gestured with smugness at my shoulder, indifferent to my irritation.

"Daragon," I spat. His eyes were as dark as his hair,

deep black, and crystallized in typical Hallervania fashion. They stared into mine.

"Mm-hmm." This too came with boredom and disinterest.

Anger filled me and I tried to remind myself I was in a dream, even though it seemed real. I attempted to find my magic, reaching around me frantically for any spark of energy and came up empty. Not a thing. Magic might be new, but I should be able to find power. Nothing. He observed my panic with satisfaction.

"You have to control your magic in our Realm before you can control it here," he said.

Frustrated, I gave up and instead crossed my arms in defense. "What do you want?"

"I wanted to see how you were fairing." From the angle of his face, gaunt cheeks with dark stubble and thick eyebrows drew me in.

"I'm fine." Something appealing and interesting about his presence begged me to step closer.

"You are extremely powerful, you know. Capable of so much . . ." He brushed his hands off and pushed himself off the tree.

"Uh-huh." My eyes narrowed.

"You could control and have whatever you wanted. Your sisters need you, but you do not need them." The corners of his lips raised in a small smile as he stepped closer.

"Screw you."

"Oh! I did not realize. You have such a deep connection with them. After all, they have done so much for you; growing up together, practicing magic together . . . oh, oh wait . . . that is not the case, is it? They abandoned you, leaving you in another Realm with nothing. Not even an awareness of who you are." He barely glanced up, picking lint off his clothing.

The words stung, piercing and cutting me with things I had not come to terms with yet. "Leave me alone." I stalked past him. He followed.

"What do you want?" I asked, sensing him behind me.

"I want to help you."

I halted abruptly, whirling around. "You tried to kill me. Remember?"

"Yes, *tried* being the operative word." He blinked deliberately.

"Oh, I am so sorry you didn't succeed." My sarcasm bit with a glare.

"And why is that, Aislynn?" An instantaneous smirk popped from both of us; neither could stop it. We had an understanding: we both knew *I knew* why his magic had failed. It wasn't confusing in the slightest.

"Why are you here?" I crossed my arms, looking around at the trees.

"You have a much bigger destiny, and you don't need your sisters."

Back to that? Seriously? I rolled my eyes. "Really? That is all you have? You. Tried. To. Kill. Me. You are going to need to try a lot harder."

His indifference pissed me off; I wasn't a toy. I turned, walking away from him. He reached out, long fingers grabbing my small wrist and whipping me around. His crystal black eyes penetrated mine.

"Don't worry, Aislynn. I will. Next time, you will not survive."

I jolted awake from the dream.

Sweat trickled down my back. I sat up, Daragon's voice pounding in my head. *"Next time, you will not survive."* I rubbed my wrist, surprised to find it hurt enough for there to be a mark. I crawled across the bed and stood at the window, turning my arm over to find a perfect handprint where Daragon's grabbed me.

"Bastard," I whispered aloud.

My curse was loud enough that Jax's shimmering sapphire eyes popped open. Sluggish, he stood, yawning while shivering his body into a full arch. Stretching and turning, he curled up into a small circle.

"What are you doing over there?" Lazily, his eyes fluttered back closed.

"Having a tea party." I glared at him, still holding my arm. Huffing out my breath, I realized I had no reason to be rude to him.

"Sorry, Jax. Only a stupid dream." Although, up until now, no other dream had ever left marks on my body. Crawling back into bed, I moved my pillow around in irritation, trying to get comfortable again. Jax walked across my body, standing on my chest.

"What kind of dream?" His crystallized cat eyes met mine.

"It was nothing. Go back to sleep." I rolled over, tugging the covers with me, letting Jax fall off my body.

"Dreams are not just dreams here. They have meaning. Sometimes they are not dreams at all."

I sat up on my elbows, turning back to him. "What do you mean, not dreams at all?"

"What was it about?"

"Daragon."

"It wasn't a dream."

"Then what was it?"

"Astral projection. I am sure you were dreaming, but Daragon astral projected himself into your dream. What did he say?"

I had a little knowledge of astral projection, but before being sucked into a magical realm, my belief in such abstract spiritual concepts was minimal. "He was disappointed he hadn't killed me."

"Oh, yes, I am sure he was. What else?"

I told him about the dream, and as Jax listened, he put his head on my arm over the mark. His purring vibrated against my arm, and the aching began to fade. I shouldn't have been surprised.

"How did you do that?"

"It is always within my capability to heal you."

"Oh." Looking at my arm, I noticed the mark was gone and, with it, my uneasiness. "Thank you, Jax."

"You will need to tell your sisters in the morning. You have much to accomplish tomorrow. You should sleep."

I fell back on my pillow while Jax laid against my body, his presence giving me comfort. I was pretty sure sleep had been what I was doing before being rudely interrupted. Thankfully, I fell into a dreamless sleep.

II

The next morning, the long grass and bright sky of the open field where we entered Hallervania surrounded me. Aila informed of its official name: Astra Meadows. Swayed by the beauty of this place, Aila kept reminding me to focus. Sharing my dream with Aila and Ailianna led to immediate lessons of my magical education.

A part of me was excited; perhaps by learning the basics I would control my magic rather than let it spurt from me in vicious explosions. *But how in the hell are they going to teach me to teleport?*

"You need to learn this, Aislynn." Aila's frustrated voice brought me back to the grass below my feet and the earth pulling me down.

"Why?"

"Because you're vulnerable, and this could be vital to your survival. If something like yesterday happens again, you will be able to leave quickly."

"You mean run away?" My eyes narrowed. Aila didn't

know me. There was no way in hell I was just going to make a hasty retreat just because I could teleport.

"No, it is not about running away. You were lucky yesterday. We cannot have something like that happen again." Her mouth was a thin, flat line.

"Now, concentrate. Teleportation is about focusing on where you want to go," she instructed, and stepped through the tall grass to my side. "Envision your destination with full clarity and make a conscious choice to move your energy. Remember everything around you is fluid, movable. It's simply a choice to mutually work together and create movement with the things around you." She pushed long strands of chocolate hair back off her face.

She made it sound easy and simple. Piece of cake. *Sure.* My eyes internally rolled.

"First thing you need to do is focus on where you want to go. For this first time, let's try the house. Close your eyes. Focus on being there; see the kitchen. Concentrate on that space. Visualize the room around you and allow yourself to feel the room. Be there more than here." Her voice was slow and methodical.

"Feel yourself standing in the kitchen, with the wooden floor beneath you. The heat of the fire is around you."

Aila's voice drifted further away. The room around me began to take shape, shimmering in and out of my view. Aila's voice was eventually in my head rather than next to me, and I was aware some of her magic pushing me, willing me away.

Opening my eyes, I found myself standing in the kitchen. In sheer joy of my success, I lost my concentration and the room shimmered away. I snapped back to the field.

My face teemed with excitement. *Wow*. A wave of dizziness, much like in my apartment washed over me, minus the need to vomit. Instead, my body tingled with an electrical charge. A current buzzed through me, leaving the hairs on my arms standing on end and chills flushing my entire body. I flashed a smile at Aila.

"Very nice! You are a quick learner." Her face lit up, and we tried again.

We practiced for several hours, me going to different rooms of the house, across the field, and to the stream. After a while, my muscles became thick mud and my brainhole seemed to melt with exhaustion. I managed to accomplish learning to teleport somewhere and stay for several minutes, but if anything broke my attention, I instantly snapped back to the field. Aila continued to encourage me, assuring me it took months for most to do what I managed in a few hours. I still felt slow and impossibly behind in my magical expertise.

We began our walk back to the house in silence. Head down, reflective of my new environment, I struggled with being in close quarters with my newly acquired sisters. Even the word sisters grated on me. I hadn't shared space with anyone for several years, let alone females.

After I turned eighteen, I moved from my parent's house to attend the University of Minnesota for graphic design. My parents helped with my tuition, along with the scholarship I received, but I needed to work and live on my own. I even worked two jobs at one point to support myself, which irritated my mother.

Then came my senior year and my relationship with Mitch. My mouth twitched at the mere thought of his name.

Biting the edge of my lip, I forced his name into my thoughts again, as a test.

Mitch.

Swallowing hard, I thought back to how easily he swayed me to move into his place when the lease on my apartment ended. It was closer, more convenient, and a barrage of endless other things made it a good choice. *The* right *choice*. He convinced me of a lot of things, including how worthless I was without him.

Involuntarily, I started chewing on the inside of my cheek, a habit I formed during the relationship. After I left or escaped, as I liked to think, I moved downtown. On the complete opposite side of Minneapolis, I tried to reject everything I had allowed to happen.

A part of me vowed to never live with humans again; after all, being alone meant no one could control me. Living with people, let alone women, was completely unknown to me and was like the Universe's idea of a cruel joke.

Lost in my thoughts, I startled when Jax began yelling in my mind. Up ahead his tail swished through the long grass.

"You must hurry!"

"What's wrong, Jax?" Aila asked.

"Ailianna has seen the White Witch."

Aila's eyes widened, and anger slid down her face. She grabbed my hand and in the turn of a second, we left the sun-warmed field, arriving in the kitchen.

"What is going on? Where did you see her?" Aila spouted at a distracted Ailianna standing at the sink. Depleted of all my energy, I grabbed a sweet roll and plopped down at the bench.

"It was a complex vision," Ailianna began with her back turned. "She was walking through The Orchard." Turning from the sink, a wide, elongated metal bowl filled her hands.

"The Orchard? How on earth would she be in The Orchard?" Aila questioned. I observed their conversation with half-attentive eyes, curiously pondering the strange bowl Ailianna set down. Intricate swirls infused into the silver metal ran around the circumference of the shallow oval shape. Jax jumped on the table, rubbing his body against me. I propped up my head with my hand, my elbow resting gently on the table. Jax wrapped his body in and out of the space between my arm and the side of my head.

"Um? Who is the White Witch? And what is so important about The Orchard?"

"Oh, Aislynn, I apologize. Sometimes it is easy to forget you have not been here all along." Ailianna's delicate words diffused my frustration at being uninformed.

Tricky little Seer.

"The White Witch is a mysterious part of our history in Hallervania," she continued as she waved her hand over the bowl, the color of metal transforming from a silver pewter to a deep obsidian black. "Most would say she supported Dark for many a thousand years, but others say she doesn't take a side from Light or Dark. We err on the side of caution, as we have seen her . . . play both sides."

"Thousands of years?" Surprise etched into my voice, between thousand-year-old witches and the vivid magic display before me.

"Yes, she is immortal. Fallen from the graces of the Gods and Goddesses. Her punishment is to roam this plane for all eternity." Ailianna sat opposite of me, her hands folded on the table as the bowl reverberated shimmers of magic around the rim.

"Um . . . remind me not to piss them off." That was a bit drastic, I thought, giving new meaning to eternal punishment.

"She betrayed her own. She still owns her free will to change her destiny, but she chooses not to." Aila's words were bitter; obviously she had her own opinions.

Enamored by the odd shimmers, I pointed to the bowl. "Uh . . . what is that?"

"It is the Mirror of Memnosyne." Ailianna's fingers danced over the center of the bowl and light cascaded down her hands, filling the basin. "The mirror has been an integral piece in Seer magic. We are blessed to have it in our family."

I blinked wildly at the brilliant display.

"So," Aila refocused Ailianna's attention, "the vision?"

"Like I said, it was complex. I am going to take some time to analyze what some of the other images mean," Ailianna replied. "She was in her white velvet hooded cloak, walking through The Orchard in the winter. I could tell she needed to be at her destination in time. I don't feel like it was The Orchard, though, even though that's where she was. She kept repeating the words, 'She better be there, please may she have made it in time.'"

"Who?" Aila asked.

"I have no idea. Completely unknown from me, almost like it had been blocked," Ailianna said, shaking her head.

"What do you think it means?" I wondered.

"I am not sure. I will scry more on the meaning, and look for other triggers," Ailianna said. Distracted, she rose and began collecting things from around the room like herbs and candles.

As Ailianna left the room, I came to realize how much work being a Seer was. It seemed like it should have been simple: you see everything you need to see, find the meaning, and do whatever you are supposed to do. This was the opposite; there was no clear meaning, no time frame, nothing. She was faced with a guessing game of putting together clues, ones that she didn't know where they belonged in the first place. As Ailianna moved around the house, I realized it was hard work, taxing and difficult.

"Aila, can you tell me the story of the White Witch?" I laid my head on the table, too tired to prop it up. Jax rubbed against me, curling into a ball.

"I am sure Ailianna would give you a less sinister version. But as it is, I will show you." Grabbing an orange, she sat at the table, thoughtful as she peeled.

Show me?

With delicate ease, Aila pulled the Mirror of Memnosyne toward her, carefully moving it across the worn grains of the table as the strange shimmers of magic bobbled with the movement.

"The White Witch, as we said, has been roaming this plane for thousands of years. Legend says her life started as simple as yours or mine, an average witch living in a town not far from here. She came from a long line of Fire magic, and power came easy for her, unlike some." Aila raised her hands above the bowl and spirals of red-orange flames danced in the smooth ebony stone.

"We are raised with a strict creed to abide by when it comes to magic. That is how and why our world works the way it does, far different from yours in comparison. Our people understand, knowing if there are any deviation from the path of Light, serious repercussions follow." The flames died down and flickered into glowing embers against the obsidian of the bowl. "Here, give me your hand." Aila held out her own.

Mesmerized, I laid my hand, palm up, on the table as Aila hovered her left hand over the bowl and her right over mine. She sunk our hands into the amber glow, and my vision went black.

"Our witch grew up and fell deeply in love with a man, a blacksmith," Aila's voice continued.

Images filled my mind, like a movie or a dream. Her words became alive before me.

"Most believed he was ill-matched for her magical abilities. But they were madly in love. And so, for him, she gave up her magic."

Submerged into the magical memory, I fell into the story of the White Witch, played out in resemblance to my favorite movie theater. Sights and sounds displayed themselves, filling every corner of my vision. All the while Aila's voice narrated smoothly in my head.

She was his world, and he was hers. The love between the two of them stopped everyone in a room. It was real, vivid, and everyone knew it. They celebrated their love, and it came time to marry, as things were done.

The day of the celebration of their new life together was filled with love, laughter, and music that warmed the soul. As the two of them celebrated that night, they were eager to make their union official, and they rode off on horseback to the home they would share together.

She held on tightly as she sat behind him, love filling

her heart as she knew they would be together forever. He urged the horse to gallop a little faster to be with his bride that much sooner. The path was dark before him, but it was one he had traveled many times and could have done it with his eyes closed.

The horses' ears pricked. Faint, the sound of horse's hooves thudded the earth ahead. He thought it odd but gave it no thought until the sound drew nearer, heavier with each step. The Sheriff's men. They had been expected to make their show at the wedding, but their lack of presence was forgotten in the lieu of celebration.

"Whoa!" the lead called to the horse. A group of five came to a quick stop, dismounting. One grabbing the reins of their horse. The White Witch twitched with awareness and fear of what they might require.

"And where are we off to this late in the evening?" the leader called out.

"My bride and I are heading to our home." The blacksmith's response was terse as he had heard stories of what these men were capable of. The horse, sensing his riders' fear, whinnied, stomping the ground below.

"Ah, the wedding, yes. I apologize for our late arrival. We do have well wishes from the King."

"Thank you kindly, sir. If we may pass now?" He gestured ahead.

"Ah, yes, there are certain requirements before we can give these good wishes."

The witch's fear was visible now as her grip tightened on her new husband's waist.

"That is quite the beautiful bride you have," one of the other riders jested.

"Yes, perhaps payment can be made in other ways." another snickered.

From atop the horse, the blacksmith looked down in disgust. He clicked his tongue to move the horse forward only to be stopped.

"There is no need. The money shall be paid. Just head south to the celebration. My family is waiting."

Instead of a reply, two of the men grabbed the witch, pulling her off the horse.

"So pretty you are. Maybe you can come with us for a while."

"No. There is no just reason for this. Unhand her." He reached to his side for his sword, and the man holding her pulled a short blade. Roughly holding her face, he pulled her head and pressed the tip of the blade into the delicate skin of her throat.

Her eyes filled with a fear he had never seen before, blood pumping ferociously through her veins. Sheer terror enveloped the muffled "Please, please . . . don't" as she tried to pull away from the man's grasp.

"Unhand her! We have done nothing. Please." His ground shattered around him as the love she held in her eyes blurred with tears. He pulled his weapon out as her tears streamed down.

"Unarm yourself. Now!" The lead man shouted at him. "We will take what is ours to have."

The witch cried out again as the blade pricked her, a small bead of red bubbling at her neck. Her eyes, so bright only hours before, filled with a passion surpassing anything he had ever known, now filled with panic. Another one of the men ripped at the beautiful gown her mother had sewn for her special day, leaving her feeling violated.

The blacksmith rushed forward but was stopped by a sword thrust at his chest.

"You shall not take another step."

Anger filled him. Even though he was outnumbered, it did not matter. He would do anything to save her from this fear. With a sword at his chest and another at his back, the men continued to taunt him with their sickening behavior. A show of power against both of them, their intent swam as an undercurrent. The witch cried out and a fire built inside of him. He struck out with his sword, slashing at the men around him.

The sharp clattering of steel upon steel as swords met echoed through the forest. The blacksmith's sword slid across the throat of one the men as he cried out in anger. Swirling around with incredible force, his blade striking across the armor of another. He raced toward his bride and the two holding her as they reached for their swords. Slashing at them, pure anger and hatred filled his being. One of the men pulled his bride toward him again, blade at her ribs.

The blacksmith's eyes followed her. In that quick instance of losing focus, the other man came at him and sank his blade deep into the blacksmith's side. The pain came but was quickly lost in his sense of failure.

The witch screamed.

Horror filled the air. Throughout watching her new husband, the thought of using magic to save them both never crossed her mind. She had abandoned her gift and was unable to summon her magic in her fear. His eyes met hers as he fell to the ground. They released her, and she collapsed at his side.

"No, no, no. This cannot be. My love . . ." Tears

poured from her eyes as she caressed his cheek. "They cannot take you from me."

His eyes, shimmering wet, locked on hers. "I will be with you always, my love." She watched his spirit drain from his eyes and he was gone. Her heart and their love shattered around them as he lay in her arms.

The images of the White Witch's story abruptly faded, and my vision returned. My eyes were damp with tears. The movie-like magic, with Aila's narration, had played out in such realistic display within my mind. Aila removed her hand from mine, and the orange glow of embers faded. The bowl returned to its original pewter color.

"No one knows how long she stayed with him, sitting in the cold dark road, holding his lifeless body," Aila added, her voice low. "We can't know how long her heart bled for him, but something inside of her broke and fury took control. The magic she had all but forgotten in her love came rolling back to her. Like waves, an ocean of a storm flooded from her." Aila's emerald green eyes sparked, and I could easily see her frustration with the witch's choices.

"We always have a choice in how we use our magic, Aislynn; it is a matter of free will, given to us by the Gods and Goddesses. Like I said previously, it was ingrained in the witch to use magic for Light, but fury took hold that night. She was broken beyond comprehension."

A part of me understood that lack of control. My own memories flooded to the surface and I shoved them back.

"It is said her magic swarmed around her as she hunted

each of the king's men. Using her magic, she cursed them into eternal darkness. She burned through the land, desperate to heal her pain, but found none, even in killing those who brought her harm and many more." Aila's anger danced through her words.

"Once your light shifts to Darkness, there is no returning. Finally, the Gods and Goddesses could take no more and they banished the witch's gifts just as they had given them. Her punishment was to roam this plane for eternity."

"You told it just as I would have," Ailianna spoke softly.

I looked away from Aila, still transfixed by her words. At some point during the magical replaying of memories, Ailianna must have returned and listened from the edge of the room.

"Maybe," Aila shrugged while pulling at the loose sea green shirt she wore.

"Dear sister, our history has as many dark, tainted parts as yours does. Aila's difference of opinion on our White Witch's reactions stems from her ... disappointment toward the witch." She sat beside me, stroking Jax with her fingers.

"I just don't see how she could abandon her magic in the first place. She was to blame for that, and then to get angry, letting her magic take over ..." Aila's frustration bit in her voice.

"It is unfair of us to judge her choices as they were hers to make." Ailianna glanced at Aila, unexpected sorrow suddenly settling in her gaze. For the briefest moment I could see something hidden behind her stunning Seer eyes, some bit of knowing that she wasn't sharing with us.

"You said in your vision she was in The Orchard," I

said shaking off the despair I could sense from Ailianna. "Why does that matter?"

"Well, when her magic was banished, The White Witch's presence in highly magical areas was thought unwise. The Orchard is such a place. It seems unlikely she would be there." Ailianna ran her finger down Jax's nose.

"Highly magical? What does that mean?" I asked.

"The Orchard is the entrance to the Amaranthine Portal, where she is forbidden," Aila answered while handing the Mirror of Memnosyne to her sister.

How many of these portals exist? I remembered the one I'd used to enter this Realm and now, from the way my sisters spoke, it sounded as though there were many more.

My attention refocused on the witch, my heart aching. "Is there anything she can do to . . . end her punishment?"

Ailianna smiled as she returned the bowl to the shelf. "Of course. Free will, remember? She must atone for her mistakes and reverse her magic by a deed of extreme Light to balance the scales."

I went to bed that night with my head filled of the White Witch and her story. The choices she made, and for some reason, the ones she *would* make, weighed heavily on my mind. I dreamt of The Orchard, a place I had never seen before, and a place I would never forget.

12

I didn't share my dreams the next morning, or during the weeks that followed. But every night she was there, in The Orchard. My magical lessons continued, and I became well versed in all things Hallervanian. Most days Rowan was missing from my training, attending council meetings and preforming other magical duties, whatever that meant. He informed me he was trying to locate Daragon and figure out who was working under him. I did miss him being close by, but I knew this was important.

The more we know about our enemy, the better. And since I didn't enjoy being attacked by Daragon, I supported his goals. By the time night rolled around, my exhaustion won, only to be bombarded with visions of the White Witch.

Some nights, she looked at me with sad, broken eyes. Because of her choices, she had thousands of years of punishment on this plane, without her love.

In the dreams she yearned for him, just to see him. The images had faded over time, leaving her with distorted memories. Some nights I awoke with such heaviness, filled with her sorrow for what she had done. Other nights I saw fire stream through villages and the anger which drove it.

I don't know why I held back from telling my sisters about the visions and dreams of the White Witch. Instead, I found myself questioning Ailianna or Aila about her, asking for details. They didn't notice and only assumed I was curious, as I was about most things in Hallervania.

Among the seemingly endless stream of everything I didn't know, Ailianna instructed me daily on herbs, plants, and flowers, and their magical properties and uses. One morning, weeks later, Aila deemed it time for me to learn the bow and arrow.

I rejected the idea, feeling I had gone back in time, but she insisted with a questionable wicked gleam in her eye. She dug through the large closet in her bedroom, determined to find the right bow. Eyebrows raised, I rocked back on my heels with my hands in the back pockets of my skinny jeans, trying to convince myself I could get out of this ridiculous idea.

The closet must have been expanded with magic, holding an arsenal of magical warfare. I spotted large crystals, wands of different lengths, jars of powders and salts. It was Aila's personal witch stash. She discarded several different bows from the rack they hung on, examining each one before making a final decision. A smirk crossed her face as she tossed me a bow.

"Here." I barely caught it with my hands. "I think you will appreciate this one. It is a beginner." Aila laughed.

I rolled my eyes; her jab only reminded me of my novice level. I followed her downstairs with bitterness snidely resting on my face. *I'll prove her wrong.*

Ailianna handed me a small bag filled with sweet rolls. "Be safe, sisters. And Aislynn, you'll do well to protect that hand."

I took the bag with an arched eyebrow, unsure of how to respond. Aila didn't give much time as she teleported us to the edge of a clearing not far from the house and immediately began her instruction. She informed me of the different parts, hand placement, and whatever else she could come up with.

"Alright, are you ready to try?" A wicked smile crossed her lips. I wasn't sure what to make of it, but I definitely wanted to try versus listening to her explain.

"Take your bow and hold here, like this." She placed the bow in my hands, and awkward and foreign in my grip, I struggled. "Now the arrow, here." She made the proper adjustments, stepping to my side.

"Okay, you will pull back here with your right hand." My arm shook as I pulled, taking more strength than I imagined. "Yes. More. Keep your eye on the target, there." She pointed. "Take a breath. Exhale and release."

I released, and pain shot through my arm. "Son of a—" Seething, I grabbed my hand. "What the . . . ?" The arrow forgotten in my slew of muttered obscenities, I jumped around the field clenching my hand in agony.

"Ailianna warned you," Aila giggled as she bent to pick up the bow. "Want to try again?" She held it out, daring me.

"Yes." I snatched it from her hand with a scowl. The second time was easier, probably because my hand was completely numb. Somehow, I hit the target. We took turns, my competitive streak pushing me to get closer to Aila's perfect shots.

"I am impressed, Aislynn. You keep surprising me."

Aila set herself up for the next shot. I tried to not be irritated as we walked to collect the arrows.

"Basic bow is great, and useful for many things, but when you add magic . . ." Aila's emerald eyes sparkled in the sun. "Well, that's a powerful weapon."

"Makes sense. So how do you do it?" We walked back to our starting place.

"Simple: essentially, you are spelling the arrow. Your limit is only the confines of your own creativity. So, an energy ball attached, a fireball . . . anything you can think of really."

Several ideas filtered into my mind and I filed them away for later.

We spent quite a bit of time practicing with magic until my hand could not take another shot. We laughed as my hand hung limply in front of me as Aila tried wrapping it. Even through the pain, I smiled, and for the first time I thought Aila might actually like me.

Aila whisked us back to the house, where Ailianna waited, preparing with a salve for my hand. A trickling of connection filtered into my soul and my discomfort began to wane. I accepted them as much as they did me, and in that moment, I decided that perhaps I could enjoy being a part of something bigger than myself.

13

I awoke the next morning with an aching inside of me, the White Witch taking center stage in my dreams all night. This particular "dream" felt different; an unseen anxiety filled her. She came close in a whispered voice and told me, "it is almost time."

I tried asking for an explanation, but she disappeared. Ailianna noticed my snippy agitation and knew something was off. No matter what lessons they planned, it all needed to wait.

So, I sat attempting meditation. Ailianna sent me to The Orchard, for some quiet time to myself. "Allow the magic of Hallervania to fill you and settle your mind," she said.

I groaned in frustration, pushing my bangs off my face. I didn't believe The Orchard was the best place for me, as it stemmed an aspect of my irritation. Perhaps Ailianna sent me here because she had "seen" it. I sighed. This was not working.

Leaning against a tree, I crossed my legs at the ankle

and mindlessly pulled at the threads stretching across the knee holes in my black skinny jeans. Refocusing I closed my eyes again. I tried to do the meditation thing and still my mind, but it was such bullshit. I tapped my head back against the bark. This was such an easy concept in theory. Shouldn't it be easy to just stop thinking? I called it maddening. My friend Amy had dragged me to a yoga class once. "Oh, it will be so good for you," she'd insisted. "You will love it!" I think I rolled my eyes then, too.

Meditation never worked for me. My brain simply wouldn't stop, as random errant thoughts suddenly decided *now* was the moment they needed to be heard. I started wondering how ridiculous I looked, sitting there with my eyes closed. Maybe I at least *looked* as if I was in deep meditation.

"Attempting peace, maybe."

My eyes popped open. The woman who stood before me didn't need to introduce herself, as I had seen her countless times already:

The White Witch.

She nodded. At last, she stood before me. Dream after dream, she came with messages I could never remember and never stayed clear, until last night. I knew they weren't dreams at all; visits, perhaps, was a better description. Her blood-red cloak hung to the ground, the hood draped around her shoulders.

"So, you have heard my story." Ice blue eyes I had accustomed myself to seeing so often stared into mine.

"A version of it." I pulled myself off the ground.

"Hmm . . ." Her thin lips smiled. "Indeed."

"There are many versions, I suppose, all bearing some aspects of the truth." Her voice was riddled with sadness.

"I won't deny, dear child, that the most terrible things left to the imagination in your version, as you put it, were true; I did these and worse. Much worse. After he died, my anger became alive inside of me. I embraced Dark. The anger rolled, becoming a monster which reached for the darkness and fed. I gave punishment with a vengeance, searing those who harmed me and anyone else I deemed unworthy. But we needn't talk about that; it is not why I am here."

I swallowed hard, fascinated and scared shitless. The witch was much taller than I realized, towering over my small frame. "So why are you here?"

"Because whilst many versions of my story exist, what happened and what I became, are countless. The story of why—the far more important story of why—has been neglected throughout time. Come, child, and walk with me. There is much to tell and show you." She pushed her white-blonde hair behind her ears as the heavy velvet trailed behind her. The thought of following a several-thousand-year-old witch didn't register; I didn't think but followed.

"You see, there is little to be found about what I will tell you next. The purpose to all of this." She waved her hand, encompassing the open expanse of The Orchard. "All of which has been kept secretly hidden from the many and held on to by the few. A few, who were avaricious, wanted and needed control. Power. Their endless greed brought us to this point. I do believe they relish the fact that my story took on a life of its own and directed the attention away from them. The question no one asks is who were those men that came? Why were they there?"

"I thought it was the King's men. They were asking for payment for something that was done . . . ?" I thought back to the images and gave her a glance. Narrowed ice blue eyes met mine before she nodded.

"Indeed, that is what has been told time after time. Something repeated is often believed as true. But payment? As you are fully aware, in Hallervania our world is not one of money. Now, at that time, we did have a King, as they called him, and with weddings came certain requirements. Not to the King, but to the Gods and Goddesses, as gratitude for the union."

Questions and thoughts tumbled together in my mind, about how quickly a story takes hold when repeated through time.

"Things had begun to shift from an incredibly good place of magic to a darker one, unbeknownst to our people. Small things, like the King's men, our 'sheriff,' were not following a path of Light, but a darker one, one not of their own.

"Rumors trickled throughout the nearby lands of things that had never happened before. The real reason behind their visit of the King's men was something I discovered much later and much, much too late. I have waited thousands of years for the truth to be seen, to be told, and . . . finally, it is time."

I listened with rapture, walking through the meadows at the White Witch's side. The world seemed to quiet, waiting for this moment.

"So, Aislynn," she began in the new silence, "I give you the truth, the secret, everything which was hidden so long ago. This is an important part of your destiny, as you will soon see."

Anticipation bled into me, a tingling current vibrated down my arms. *What in the hell?*

"You learned from your sisters that magic has many facets, all of which meet together to create this place. We can learn the vast properties and uses of herbs. We can practice spell work, the different kinds of energies, how to use emotion, and moving through time and space. And lastly, the elements: Earth, Air, Fire, and Water. You have found the one that speaks to you, which you have an affinity for, yes?" She gestured toward my arm.

Confused for the shortest moment I looked down.

"You've even painted it on your body." The witch raised her eyebrow.

My tattoo. I hadn't connected the dots. I thought of water, and the delicate watercolor wave tattooed on my wrist. Nodding, I tried to ignore the pulses zinging through my body.

"Believe me, dear child, you have not begun to reach the surface of your capabilities. Each element has its own unique properties and points of magic. What magical education has omitted for much of time is the origin of these elements. Long ago, four individuals embodied each element, two Gods and two Goddesses. They were, in essence, the element themselves, living in human forms. They created a line of magic for each element, which would be passed to their descendants, each future generation protecting the line of elemental magic."

"Waaiiiit a minute," I paused in the long grass, slowing the witch's history lesson. "Forever ago, at the start of magic land—" This gained pause from the witch as she pursed her lips. I continued, "There were four beings: one for each of the elements? A god of Air? Water?"

She nodded. "A Goddess of Air, to be precise. Aliro."

I blinked rapidly trying to process the new information.

Sweat began to bead at my forehead, the sun caressing in a relentless building of heat. I regretted my dark t-shirt and black skinny jeans. *Why is it so hot?*

"God of Earth, Goddess of Fire, and God of Water," she clarified.

"Okay . . ." I retreated to her previous onslaught, squinting against the sun. "Protecting how?"

"From misuses of the element, like an overseeing, if you will, making sure it was used in accordance with the rules and laws of magic. As time passed, one would be chosen to take the place as holder of the element. This was a birthright, and an extreme gift to be given. The downside of being given such a gift was a secret of sorts.

"Keeper of Elements are not known to everyone; we knew the existence of Keepers, but not their identity. This was kept secret for the protection of the Keepers, as they are sacred to magic. Their identities, if known, would be a danger to those using magic for Dark. As you can imagine, these Keepers were fiercely protected by the magical community and those overseers of magic. So, we come to me." Her eyes met mine, flickers of light dancing.

"By birthright, I am a descendant of Fire and was to be Keeper of the Element of Fire."

Shock registered, and I felt it spread through my body. In all my questioning, my lessons, and magical education so far, no one mentioned this, nor had I heard of the Keepers.

"How come . . . ?" I started uncertainly. I chewed on the side of my lip, thinking back to Aila's telling of the White Witch's story, the mirror memories, and specifically the *fire* magic she used to torment the land.

"Why has no one mentioned this?" she finished, and I nodded. "Because it was unknown, even to me. Let's go back to my story and those men. Again, we will ask the question why they were there. They knew much more than I did. I renounced my magic for my love, but if I was a Keeper, it did not matter. When called to my birthright, I would have no choice but to embrace my magic again."

I glanced out at our surroundings, an expanse of rolling green grass and endless trees. The beauty of their land hid the wicked secrets of their convoluted past. My heart ached for her; the poor witch had been doomed no matter her choices.

"Certain individuals knew I was next in line to become Keeper of Fire, and they did not want that to happen. Those men on that path were to keep me from my destiny. Now, whether they intended to kill me or not, I do not know, but their purpose was divinely met.

"With the death of my love, I did embrace my magic, but for Dark, and therefore would never receive my birthright. So, their goal was still accomplished. Again, remember I knew none of this then, but have gained this knowledge and much more with my many years of punishment."

"So why would they keep you from becoming Keeper?" The horror of her tale was terrible enough, but I realized this gave a more sinister twist.

"Therein lies the perfect question. If you control the Keepers, then you controlled the elements. Many years ago, a man named Viego, who came from a long line of powerful magic, wanted to use the Keepers to change magic forever. One shift would change all that is, and that was precisely what he wanted. A slow churning toward his eventual embracing of Dark. He scoured the land for any information on the Keepers, and using his powerful magic, he uncovered their identities one by one. He stole the elements."

Impossible, I thought. *Stealing the elements? I used elemental magic, didn't I?*

The White Witch seemed to hear my thoughts.

"The elements you use today, in this time, are not the same," she explained. "They're barely a glimmer of what they are in their true essence. And most who live in Hallervania are not even aware."

"How is that possible?" I peered up from the ground, glancing through my layers of chunky bangs. The red velvet of her cloak rustled next to me. *How is she not roasting in that thing?*

"Because most only want to live their lives as they know them. They don't wish to be bothered by the pesky past." She wrapped her hands behind her.

"So Viego?" I inquired. "What happened to him?"

"He succeeded in claiming all the elements. By doing so, he gained an insurmountable amount of power. Clever, he didn't use it unwisely, as history has no mention of him. What he did do was shift countless events, like keeping me from becoming a Keeper. He changed the course of magical history. The most astounding was that he kept the history of the Keepers silent, locked away in time." Anger and bitterness lathered through her words.

My mind ran with the new information, and I realized we had stopped walking. Raising my hand to my brow, I saw that The Orchard had cleared to an open field, empty but for one massive tree.

Immense, thick branches twisted out and upward from the trunk. The only thing missing from the tree was *life*. Bare of leaves, the weathered bark peeled up at the edges. Disintegrating before my eyes, my heart ached for the tree with no idea why. A sudden clenching in the pit of my stomach almost took my breath. A pain in my soul spread as I experienced a loss so deep, churning from the inside out.

Why do I want to burst into tears over a dead tree?

14

Welcome." The White Witch gestured toward the tree.
"Where are we?" I asked, glancing around the open field, trying to understand the cause of my heartache.

"We are at your destiny. This is the Tree of Elements."

My eyes darted from her to the tree. "Excuse me?"

What in the world is she talking about? I stared at the massive dead monstrosity before me that somehow tore a hole in my soul.

"This tree is the Tree of Elements, holding within the magic of all four elements. Look . . ." She moved behind me, hands delicately resting on my shoulders as she began pointing. "There, within the branches, you see Earth, Air, Fire, and just there, Water." With her direction, the vague outlines of where the elements would reside amid twisting branches took shape. They hung like empty vortexes waiting to be filled. "May I show you what it should be?"

I nodded, and the witch waved her hand over my eyes and the tree transformed. From the trunk upward, the bark darkened in a ripple as leaves unfolded in a rapid pace of accelerated magic. A shamrock green spinning light moved through the leaves, circling in a wheel of energy that embodied the Earth element. The center gleamed almost like a stone sitting within the smear of color.

Next, higher in the branches, Air, a yellow twirling moved in wind trails, settling toward the top of the branches. Then a spark of flames in shades of red twisted through the limbs, igniting Fire into the leaves. Finally, opposite of Earth, a roar of waves showered Water into the tree in tiny droplets of blue light.

Each of the elements was a bright swirling expanse of color, several feet wide. In the center of each became a solidified ball of faceted elemental light. Almost like a crystal.

Captivated by the unveiling before me, I stared in awe as the tree became alive with magic. The sheer force of the ripple almost knocked me off my feet as the magic breathed a moving vitality, stretching across the entire field. Everything appeared vibrant, aglow with dazzling lifeforce. The grass swayed in variant greens and colors seem to pop before my eyes.

Then, the image faded, and the bare desolate tree took form again. My chest tightened as a new degree of heartbreak gripped my body. This magic was concealed, kept from everyone for the benefit of the few. My eyes pinched with tears while sick dread filled my abdomen. I turned to the witch.

"In the world of magic exists a constant balance. Light and Dark," she began softly. "Even though Viego shifted many events to Dark, you cannot shift everything. Light will find a way to create a shift to restore the delicate balance."

"Okay . . ." My eyes shifted back to the desolate tree as I worked to absorb and understand everything.

"You, Aislynn, are that balance."

My gaze flew to her. An instant pressure crawled into me. The idea of being everyone's "chosen one" made me want to vomit. Swallowing hard, the fleeting thought of sitting at my desk downtown flashed through my head as I returned my gaze to the tree.

"This is why you are here," the White Witch shared. "You have been chosen by Light, and the Gods and Goddesses to restore balance and to reclaim the elements. More importantly, to reclaim the tree for Light." Her icy blue eyes met mine, convincing me of my destiny.

"I don't know how that's possible. I don't know what the hell I am doing!" I balked. I didn't want this. I didn't ask for this. I wasn't capable of saving magic, some girl from the Earth Realm who couldn't control her tiny spurts of magic. The witch's gaze was unwavering through my inner frustration.

"Remember there is always a divine plan. Whether for Light or Dark, fate is a twisting path which doesn't always make sense. But when you see the entire picture, everything comes together."

"You sound like Rowan." I averted my eyes, unwilling to roll them in front of her.

"Yes, he is a clever one," she agreed with a smirk.

"So, bring a dead tree back to life? Sounds totally reasonable." The sarcasm in my tone was not lost on the witch.

"In a world of magic? Of course." Her eyes glimmered. "It is nice to see some of your spunk, by the way. You are going to need it. The fates chose well with you." She smiled, and my mouth twitched at her enjoyment of my cynicism.

"So, is it a spell? Something with my sisters?" My face scrunched with desperation.

"If it were only that simple," she sighed, turning a ring of silver and garnet on her finger. "No. This is some of the most sacred, oldest magics of the world. The task the fates have given you will be difficult beyond your imagination." She paused and glanced back at me. "To bring the Tree of Elements back to life, as you put it, will require you to reclaim and control each element. By doing so, the tree recognizes the sacred use of elemental magic and ignites the life of the element in the tree."

"How do I reclaim the elements?"

"Each element has been hidden carefully through time. They are within areas, specific locations, objects . . . you must find them."

"An object? *Any* object?" My eyebrows shot upward with the daunting task.

"It will bear significance to the Element itself." She brushed a hand down the velvet of her cloak.

"That is vague and unhelpful."

She shrugged at my snarky tone.

"So," I began to clarify, "four objects or places or something. I have to find and control them, and this'll light up like a Christmas tree?" I pointed toward the heavy bare branches. Joking helped me ignore the oppressive aching in my heart every time my eyes landed on the tree.

The White Witch smirked. "Yes, essentially. To control the elements will require a magical event in which its use will be crucial."

"A magical event?" My voice notched higher. *Seriously? I do not need more magical events.*

"Yes, reclaiming an element and using its power will be

exponential, considering the power has been suppressed for centuries. It will be magnificent." The witch's eyes were wild with excitement. To me, it sounded dangerous and terrifying, nowhere near the realm of excitement.

"How will I know where to search?"

"You will know." Her eyes met mine again, searching.

Awesome, more vagueness.

"And finding them . . . ?" I kept probing, hoping for more information.

"Well, that should prove challenging."

"Perfect," I groaned with a sneer plastered across my face. "I feel like I am in a bad movie," I muttered under my breath.

The witch raised her brow.

"Never mind," I said, shaking my head, shoving my hands in my back pockets assessing the tree.

"Remember you were chosen for this. The Goddess challenged you for a reason. You are capable of amazing things, Aislynn. Believe by finding strength in yourself and everything you are."

And with that, she disappeared.

"Shit." She could have said goodbye. *"All the magic rests in your hands! You can do it!"* Freaking hell. Huffing out my breath, I gazed around the empty meadow and slumped my back against the tree. *Dammit.* I tilted my head back, closing my eyes.

Where did I even begin? This whole destiny crap was beyond me in so many ways. Stress piercing its way through my body, I longed for the monotony of deadlines and irritating coworkers. Saving the world, and magic, seemed impossible.

I peered up through the branches, listening to an eerie

rattling as they rubbed against one another in the breeze. My destiny weighing heavily on me as I sat, refusing to move. If I moved, then I would need to act.

"How in the world am I supposed to do this?" I said aloud to no one. Raking my hands through my hair I ran through the obvious things: finding the elements—which meant, if they were held by Dark for the past thousand years, I must somehow take them from Dark.

It did not go unnoticed that my witch friend left out that little tidbit. Magical event equals battle. I was pretty sure Dark wasn't just going to hand them over, saying, "Sure! You can play with them for a while!" FML. I knocked my head against the tree.

At least I had a few answers, a deeper line into my "destiny" which made me feel better in a strange way. I now had a goal to move toward: reclaim the elements. Check. Finally, I started my walk back to The Orchard.

After some time, a familiar black tail swished through the grass.

"There you are! I've been looking for you."

"Is something wrong?" For the quickest moment, I missed when my cat was just a cat and he annoyed me while reading.

"No. Ailianna was worried, so I told her I would come and check on you. Are you okay?"

My teeth grabbed my upper lip as I pondered the word *okay*. I let out my breath. "Yeah. Okay. Sure. Wanna hang out for a minute?"

He plopped down in the grass, licking his paw and swiping it over his face. I took that as a yes and sat in the thick blanket of green beside him.

"Do you know why I am here, Jax?" I tore a piece of grass, long and thin, between my fingers.

"Because Hallervania is your destiny. You have always been coming here."

"But why am I really here? What am I supposed to do?" Breaking the grass again, I peered at him.

"They say—"

"No, Jax," I insisted, and my lips pinched together. "Really. Not this mystical bullshit. What am I supposed to do?" My hands flipped outward, the blade of grass flying out of my grasp.

He stopped licking. *"Are you sure nothing is wrong?"*

My damn cat was sidestepping me, and I knew it.

"What do you know about the Elements?"

"There are four of them, I think?"

Sidestepping asshat *and* comical. What an awesome cat I had. But I did laugh out loud. "Yeah, there are four of them," I responded with an equal amount of sarcasm.

Questions began to rattle through my head, but I decided to keep them to myself. How was it possible that no one knew of the Keepers? My thoughts went to the wall of books back at the house. Perhaps I could find something which mentioned the Keepers in them, legend or otherwise. I wondered if I could find anything on Viego and his history.

"Is there something specific regarding the Elements?" Jax asked after my silence.

"It's alright, Jax. Forget it. Just something on my mind." I would do my own research first.

"As you wish."

"Go ahead and go home. Let them know I am fine. I think I am going to walk back."

Jax scoffed at my disregard to use my magical ability to travel, then stretched in an arch.

"You know, exercise is good for you!" I shouted after him. His laughter lingered after he vanished.

I stood, leaving behind a pile of torn grass. Following a path through a thick grove of trees, I headed west, trailing the dipping sun. I was confident I could find my way back to the house. *Maybe.* I thought about the new details I probably should have told Jax and eventually would need to tell someone.

Er, everyone. But not quite yet. I wanted to research and find answers to the nagging questions in my mind.

If the White Witch was a descendant of Fire and was meant to be a Keeper, what did that mean power-wise? She implied my affinity for Water could be more. By finding the elements and controlling them, did that make me Keeper? Keeper of all the elements?

One person holding all four seemed wrong. I could see why they separated them, with a Keeper for each. What happened when the elements were restored? There must be a book on the Tree of Elements . . .

Lost in my thoughts, I didn't hear my name being called.

"Aislynn? Aislynn! Hello?"

Tristan's voice shook me from my internal rampage of thoughts, and I glanced up to find him joining me on the path. *Where did he come from?*

"Oh, hey Tristan. How's it going?" I stopped, realizing I might be tromping through a trail in the middle of his yard. Did they have yards?

"I am well. And yourself?" He tilted his head, concern showing in his eyes. Giving him a half glance, I plucked a reed of grass and shrugged in the light of the setting sun. "I have not seen you around."

"I'm pretty occupied under the tutelage of my sisters, learning all things magic. Not much time for anything else." I blew out my breath and twisted the reed between my hands.

"Oh, but there is always time." He gave a glistening, knowing smile.

"Ha. I wish." I half smiled.

"There is when you can do this . . ." Tristan began to swirl his hand in small circles. A stream of pale white light circled, then his hand opened and went still. With the abrupt movement, everything around us halted, frozen in time. A bird in the sky paused midflight, the grass still in midbreeze. A motionlessness radiated around us, captivating my eyes.

"Tristan, that's amazing!" I turned back to him, dazzled by his magic. With a flip of his hand, everything was in motion once again.

"One of my gifts," he said with a proud smile.

"Can anyone do it?"

"I suppose some may learn if they are willing to master the magic." He pondered. "Our gifts vary for a reason; if everyone was capable of the same, we wouldn't need each other. There must be balance."

The White Witch's words rang in my head. That damn word again.

"My family line carries the gift of time throughout its history," Tristan explained. "Although no one in my immediate family has had the gift for many years."

"Interesting. Can you only stop time?" I asked.

"No, I can slow it and freeze. Speeding up time is tricky, as it can have adverse effects."

"Can you choose what to stop? Like me; I didn't freeze." His gift fascinated me. All my magical lessons were basic magic, learning from the beginning. I had been told of my gifts but had yet to practice them.

"Yes, I can decide. The more objects I freeze, the more magic it takes. I imagine there is a limit to the quantity." He alluded that he had not tested his gift's boundaries, but I had the feeling he was very aware of his capabilities regarding the reaches of his magic.

"Could you freeze something forever?" The question popped out of my mouth.

"No. Magic has a limit; time must always continue. Catch up, if you will. There are legends of such things, though," he said.

Again with the legends. More for me to add to my list.

"It's truly a spectacular gift, Tristan. Useful I am sure." I winked at him.

"It comes in handy, yes." He gave me another full smile. "What are you doing out this way anyway?"

"Sorting through things in my head. It's been quite the day." I tucked my hair behind my ears.

"I can't imagine what this is like for you, to come here. It must be strange." Tristan nodded, thoughtful with his words.

"Sometimes it's awesome," I admitted. "Being here is . . . the magic is indescribable. I just detest feeling like I am subpar at everything I do here." I tugged another reed of grass.

"I don't think that will last long. Trust me." He bumped my shoulder, and with it came the reminder of all I was *supposed* to do. "Your Realm must be fascinating."

I tried to stifle my laugh. "Something like that. Incomparable to here." I wrapped the grass around my finger.

"I think I would like to go there," he said.

"Well, Tristan, one thing I have learned is absolutely anything is possible." I arched my eyebrow and bumped his shoulder. "Do it again."

In response, he swirled his hands faster and faster before abruptly stopping, insta-freezing everything around us.

"It's sort of peaceful," I said, admiring the butterflies unmoving midflutter, and flowers pausing their waving movement. With a flip of his hand, all moved again.

"Amazing." My mouth turned upward in awe.

"I'm happy it brings a smile. Much better than a few moments ago." His cornflower blue eyes glittered, and I averted my gaze.

"I better get walking again. Otherwise they'll think I am lost."

"Of course. Would you mind if I walk with you for a bit?" He seemed hesitant to leave, and I wondered if it had anything to do with being attacked the last time I saw him.

"I would like that." Hopefully, I wouldn't get lost this way.

"So, tell me," Tristan began, "what were you trying to sort out?"

We started walking, and I appreciated that he didn't ask why I was walking instead of teleporting.

"Uggghhh . . . my destiny."

"I see." He folded his hands behind him as we followed a narrow trail. I found it pleasing that he didn't pry further.

"What made you show me your gift?" I asked after a moment.

"Well, I am not sure. I was practicing when you came along, but it seemed you needed a little magic." He gave me a wink. The irony made me laugh: magic was the source of my frustration but eased it as well.

"Have you always been able to do it?" I asked.

"Well, we generally have an age when we come into our magic or full powers, but they can also show up earlier. A lot of times it can happen in a highly emotional state, like when you are little, and things are out of your control" he said.

Memories of my childhood tickled at the edges of my mind. Yes, I knew exactly what he meant. "It seems you speak from experience."

"Yes. Yes, I do," he laughed. "When I was a child, I was a bit temperamental when I didn't get my way. The difficulty with my gift is that no one can catch on if they are frozen. It took a few times before someone 'caught' me using my magic, entering a room I had frozen. My mother worked with me when I was little, teaching me how to control and use magic and understand the rules. I don't suppose that was easy for her." A sweet smile crossed his lips with the memory. "I caught on rather quickly: you did *not* freeze Mom." He chuckled.

Jealousy nipped in sharp twangs; magic being allowed to flourish in contrast to my constant need to suppress something I didn't understand. His world, his upbringing was contrastingly different from mine. I shook off my frustrated jealousy and smiled, thinking of a towheaded four-year-old Tristan freezing his mother.

"Have you worked on your gifts?" He pulled back the branches of a bush for me to walk through.

"I don't feel like that's been on anyone's to-do list. Only the basics of magic, blah blah blah . . ." I rolled my eyes.

"That doesn't mean you can't practice on your own. Sometimes that is when we learn the most about our gifts."

I gave him a sideways glance and pushed my lips to the side. Why hadn't I thought of that? "How do you even start? Or know what to do?" My shirt snagged a hanging branch of another bush and I paused to pull it free.

"Well, start with something you do well, or something that's comfortable. Anything come to mind?" he asked as we stepped out of the trees and into an open field of long grass.

I gave this some thought. Water. *Not sure I want to play with the Elements after everything I've learned today.* My mind settled on my grandmother's stories and the prophecy of the three sisters.

"What about moving things?"

"Ah yes, the prophecy. Might as well give it a try." He walked ahead and turned toward me, long reed grass swaying at his knees.

"Um. Okay. What should I move?" A thrum of excitement trickled through me.

"How about this?" He formed a sapphire blue glowing ball of light in his hands. The orange and purple light of the day's end shimmered off its surface. Tossing the ball, it floated in the air between us. "Energy in its purest form is easiest to move."

"Okay. Should I use my hands, or . . . ?" Uncertainty

created an immediate anxiety as I overthought how to attempt the magic.

"Don't think about it," Tristan suggested, clearly seeing the struggle on my face. "Use whatever seems right to you."

Taking a breath, I focused on the electric blue orb and imagined it was an extension of my hands. With a small movement, I pushed my hands toward Tristan. The swirl of light moved toward him and he caught it.

"See?" He flashed another smile at me. "I told you it's easy!"

"I can't believe I did it." A grin lit up my face.

He threw the ball to me and this time I used my left hand, swiping it toward the right, pushing the energy ball away from us. When it moved several feet away, I gave a small cry of delight.

"Energy balls are easy. You will have to practice moving other things. Solid objects will be harder at first until you understand the energy and the amount of magic used to move the object." Tristan shrugged as if explaining simple math.

"How come this is easy with you?" I moved the ball back toward him. He held the twirling orb, letting it dance between his hands before closing them to extinguish the magic.

"Sometimes when we are with certain people, instead of being a lesson, it is fun. Magic is easy when it is fun." He stepped to me. "Come on, we better go."

"Thank you. Seriously, I've been so focused on the lessons, my sisters, and learning the way they show me, I haven't thought about having fun with it, particularly on my own." Using magic felt like plugging myself into a charger, magnifying everything. The restrictions I placed on myself were doing more harm than good.

"Remember, magic doesn't have to be one certain thing. It is whatever you want it to be."

We continued walking and I allowed my thoughts to roll around.

"Have you ever heard . . . ?" I started, wanting to ask about the Keepers. "Never mind."

Tristan gave me a questioning glance as we reached the top of the hill from the house, near where he had come to my rescue.

"I should go," I said. "Another time I will ask that question."

"Of course. Anytime. Thank you for the enchanting encounter."

We smiled at each other, and my cheeks flushed with heat. I smiled more in the past hour than I had in weeks. My mouth hurt.

"Thank you, Tristan. For everything."

He dipped his head, turning back the way we had come. "Enjoy your evening." He gave one last wave.

15

&mpty quiet greeted me when I walked into the house. After glancing around, I assumed my sisters must be off doing their evening rituals. I hadn't been invited to those, yet. For some reason, the exclusion made me feel a little hurt. *Witches sure stay busy. And they're used to doing things without me, anyway.*

Aged floorboards beneath me creaked in the silence as I walked toward the library of books on the east wall. The shelves reached the ceiling and even had a little ladder to move along the wall. The stash of books brought joy to my inner bookworm.

In my time here, I only had the chance to glance at the books, but nothing more. This time I was ready to search more thoroughly. Some of the books appeared newer, and some older, and most were material bound, but a few looked like family journals.

Upon closer inspection, I found some organization, arranged by spell books, potions, herbs, and plants. There was an endless amount of information. Ailianna's sense of tidiness and order were apparent in the shelves and the books which were used regularly.

Scanning through the titles, I dragged my finger down the books, searching for anything history related. Pausing, I found one with my grandmother's name on the binding. My brows furrowed as I pulled it from the shelf and slid my hand over the brown leather cover, brushing my finger across her name.

The first page was titled "The Elements." I instantly recognized my grandmother's handwriting and my heart ached. The handwritten pages were written like a journal but presented as a textbook. The corner of my mouth turned upward. My grandmother would have seen it as the most efficient way of presenting the material. I flipped the pages, and "The Council of Elements" caught my attention as I began to read.

> The Council of Elements was formed in the beginning to control the use and practice of the Elements. The Council was headed by the highest magical beings. There were nine in total: the Overseer, his council of four, and the four Keepers of Elements.
>
> In the beginning, much like a "secret society," their existence was unknown to the magical community until it was time for the Keepers to pass their Element to the next descendant. There is not much known knowledge on the original Council, the Keepers, or the identities of the members, as it was well hidden. Little research has been formally done, as most consider it only legend, and no one can confirm its existence. The Council that

exists in form today is a shell of what existed many years ago.

Four magical keeper lines exist, one for each element: Earth, Air, Fire, and Water. A fifth line, separate from the four, is the line of Affinity Keepers. These individuals were charged with re-assigning the Elemental Keepers if necessary. The ancestry of this line has been completely lost.

The current Council holds a larger range of members including overseers of magical laws and ordinances, protection of gift uses, and monitors of magic. The Council recruits from young ages those it deems worthy of service based on gifts, family magic lines, and other variables.

There have recently been questions regarding the current Council's direction, skewing the lines of Light and Dark.

My grandmother knew of the Keepers? Why hadn't my sisters told me? Did they know? And the Affinity Keepers? Now, the years my grandmother spent as a professor and her research on ancient documents made much more sense. I never gave much thought to her profession, as I thought she was a regular person from my Realm. I realized, however, that all the trips she constantly went on, being gone for weeks or months at a time, had most likely taken her here. Looking further, another chapter caught my eye: "The Prophecy."

Prophecies often hold mistruths in order to sway the outcome of the future. Seers and Visionaries often contradict one another. Subject to scientific possibilities of endless outcomes, this seems to be the trouble with following one prophecy over another.

Throughout my research, a similar thread of a prophecy has maintained. "One will reconstitute the balance of magic, bringing forth the light to the tree." This prophecy has been established across several realms, and even within the Earth Realm stories can be found.

I have searched the realms for any information in regard to the tree and what this would mean for magic in Hallervania. The prophecy is stated in different ways in each Realm, but still carries a similar thread. If elemental magic is not restored, then Hallervania and the other magical realms will wane and eventually cease to exist. But the location of the tree remains a mystery.

My grandmother never found the Tree of Elements? *How is that possible when it resides in the middle of Hallervania, not far from The Orchard and my sisters' house?* Unless . . . *it wasn't.* Thinking back to my walk with the White Witch, I couldn't recall the actual distance itself. The more I tried, the blurrier the memory became.

Shit. I remembered getting up and leaving The Orchard but had no recollection of anything around me until we reached the tree. I had been so enveloped in the White Witch's words and her story . . .

Dammit. Tricky freaking witch.

She obviously had taken me somewhere else. I imagined if I were to go back to The Orchard and retrace my steps to find the tree, it would not be there. Shutting the book with shaking fingers, I set it aside.

The magic Realms would cease to exist. With the sentence on vicious replay, I considered the ramifications if I didn't follow through with my destiny. Irritated with the White Witch, I searched the titles again, looking for anything about her, grabbing anything appearing useful. *The History of Hallervania* was added to my pile. *Legends of Our Land* and *The Meaning of Our Gifts* were added as well. But I found nothing specifically on the witch; she was just as evasive as ever.

Her true intentions started to weigh on me. It seemed she was a master of giving only what suited her. Aila's adverse opinion started to make more sense. I pushed the ladder to the next section of shelves and resumed my searching.

Some books I had to pull out to read the title. I was determined to find something. *Our Gods, Goddesses, and Guardians: The Purpose of Our Existence* captured my attention. There were just so many damn books. I tucked a few more I found relevant under my arm just as the door opened. Ailianna entered, carrying several baskets of fresh fruits and vegetables. I clattered down the ladder, the books falling to the floor in a heap.

Shit.

"Hello, Aislynn. You have returned. Are you feeling better?" Her voice was full of sincerity, watching me pick up the books.

"Hey. Yeah, much better." I pushed my hair out of my face with the back of my hand as I set the books on the ladder step. "Thought I would do some research and reading." I pointed to the shelves behind me, then rubbed my sweaty palms down my jeans nervously.

"Of course, they are yours just as well as mine." Her mouth was a thin smile.

"Would you like help?" I pointed to the baskets.

"That would be lovely, thank you."

I pushed the pile of books off to the side for later and helped Ailianna with the baskets.

"I am glad you are doing better," she said. "I know it must be frustrating at times."

We set everything on the table, and I gazed over all the beautiful food she had gathered.

"Yeah," I admitted. "I am so used to doing everything on my own that sometimes I think I don't know how to have sisters." I handed her a thin burlap bag of potatoes. "In fact, I have a question that has been bothering me." My words stumbled.

"Hmm?" Ailianna tucked the potatoes in a small basket on the counter.

"Well, it's the 'sisters' thing." I used air quotations. "Can you tell me about your parents? I just want to understand *how* we are related." I sat on the edge of the bench. The idea of either my mom or dad having other children in another realm was so laughable I nearly burst out with insane giggles. But I had to know: what did "sister" really mean here?

"Ah. Yes." She sat next to me, her eyes contemplative. "Our parents passed shortly after Aila was born, it was a long time ago. One day I will tell you the story, but it is not for this night. However, I shall sooth your worries. I understand in your Realm blood relation quantifies your idea of family. Here, our gifts, our threads of magic define our relations. We are bound by magic. And in our Realm, this sometimes supersedes blood." She ran her finger over the rind of an orange sitting on the table. "Do not worry so, Sister. In time all things will get easier."

I nodded and the tightness in my chest released, this unbearable weight of worry, that I had been kidnapped or been raised by strangers finally settled.

"And with the books you have pulled," Ailianna added, tipping her head toward my stack on the ladder step, "you may understand our urgency a little better now."

Glancing at the books across the room, I considered her words. *Magical Realms would cease to exist.*

"We need you, Aislynn." Her hand ran down my arm as she turned back to the basket.

The rest of the evening went with a blur. Aila returned soon after, and we ate and chatted. I realized both Aila and I were struggling. I didn't know how to have sisters any more than she knew how to have me as a sister. She let me see pieces of her personality more and more. A fire seemed to drive her, dwelling within her to fight for justice, fairness, and good.

Underneath Aila's rough exterior appeared to be a kindhearted person. Although I knew I couldn't tell her this, and *if* I did, she would probably find some way to show me how unkind she could be. That sounded a lot like my own behavior, and maybe that was our problem: in a lot of ways, we were too much alike.

After dinner, I grabbed the stack of books and headed upstairs. I felt awkward not sharing my encounter with the White Witch, but I wanted more information before telling anyone what she'd revealed to me. A part of me was aware they might be able to help, but an inner voice told me to wait. Laying the books on the bed, I pondered where to start when Jax darted into the room and jumped on the bed, walking across the books.

"What's this?"

"Light reading. Do you mind?" I pulled a book from underneath his paws. "I need to find some information."

"I see. Is this information in these books?" He sniffed the corners of one large tome and grated his cheek against it.

"Maybe. I am not sure . . ." I picked up *Legends of Our Land.*

"Perhaps I can help. What are you looking for?"

"I am looking for anything on the White Witch, or anything on the Elements." I perused through the pages.

"I see. You saw her today, didn't you?"

My gaze jumped to him, and I met mildly intrigued cat eyes. "How did you know?"

"Because I know things."

"Why didn't you say anything before?"

"Because you would come to it in your own time, which is the way you are. So, tell me: what did she have to say?" He laid down across several of the books, curling his paws underneath him. I groaned and fell backward on my pillow.

"She informed me of my *destiny.*"

"Oh! This sounds quite interesting. Interesting indeed."

I opened one eye to give Jax a dirty look.

"You realize my purpose here, now, is for you. To help you. That is why I was sent to you."

"I know, Jax. Well, sort of . . . I guess it's weird." I glanced toward him. "Talking to my cat about my problems. Up until this point in my life, I thought only crazy cat ladies did that, and now I am one."

"I don't think so." He sniffed the empty air. *"You don't smell like old stale mothballs."*

A bubble of laughter escaped my mouth. "Not yet, anyway," I said. Jax walked up my body, pushing his paws into my organs as he made my belly his new pillow. I resorted to rubbing his shiny black fur. "She told me about the Keepers of the Elements, the Tree of Elements, and the part I play with both. Do you know anything about them?"

"I do. A little." He slowly blinked as I stroked his head.

"You do? Why didn't you tell me?" Exasperated, my eyebrows furrowed to accompany my frown.

"Aislynn, unfortunately, I have limits. I couldn't tell you. Fate decided that was out of my hands and you would find out in your own time. Sometimes we are not ready to hear everything all at once, although that would suit you much better. If it comforts you, I know what you know. Right now, you are destined to reconstitute the elements and regain balance in the magical world."

"At least I don't need to explain it to you."

"There is that."

"So, I have to find the elements, save the tree, and let's save the world while we are at it."

"Why not? Might as well. It could use saving."

"Sometimes? You are so not helpful." I lifted Jax as I sat up, holding him in my hands above me. His paws dangled down as I stared at him. "You better not have anything else you are keeping from me."

His eyes told me it didn't matter if he did or not; he was unable to tell me regardless. Setting him down, I picked up one of the books.

"What do you think the White Witch gets out of this? If throughout Hallervania's history she's done nothing but roam the planes she was banished to, why is she stepping in now?"

"I imagine she was waiting for the right person. The magical

community holds strongly to prophecies, legends, Seers, and the like. But in all reality, she's been banished for thousands of years. I imagine she finally wants to move on."

"And to do so, she must perform a deed of extreme good. Telling me of my destiny isn't enough; she must do more. Hmm . . ." Jax allowed me to think. With the book in my hand, I turned to him. "Where do you think the Tree of Elements is? She took me there, but I realized afterward that it isn't in Hallervania."

"She took you to the Tree of Elements?" Jax stood, fascination sparkling in his eyes. *"You saw the tree?"*

"Yes? Is that weird?" I asked, perplexed.

"Weird, perhaps not, but definitely surprising. I wasn't aware she could travel to that plane. Interesting." His curious cat eyes stared beyond me, deep in thought.

"Well, we were there. I even stayed for a while after she left. Honestly, I wasn't aware we traveled. My grandmother's book made me realize—wait. My grandmother . . ." A thought occurred to me, and I searched through my pile until I found the book she wrote. "I think I should start here."

I awoke to Jax rubbing against my leg. Opening my eyes, I found myself on the floor propped against the window. When I attempted to move my body, I grimaced in pain. My neck announced its displeasure from sleeping at such an odd angle.

"What are you doing down there?"

"I must have fallen asleep reading." I picked up the book that had fallen out of my hands. Not quite morning yet, the sky was beginning to lighten at the edges. I ran my hands over my face. "I know what I need to do."

"Do you?"

"Of course. I am a genius, remember?" Jax rolled on his back, peered at me upside down, and meowed. "Okay, maybe not, but I do need to go home." His thin lithe twisted in cat precision to stare.

"Home?"

"Yup. We have to go back to Minneapolis."

My cat being speechless was a sight to behold. *Ha!*

"But . . . it's cold." Standing, his entire body shook as a shiver ran down his sleek black frame.

"Yeah, Fuzz Face. Don't you miss it?" This time we shared another shiver over our mutual disdain for the cold.

"There are a lot of considerations to be made. Your sisters are not going to like this. Obviously, you are after something. What are you looking for?"

"Something I found in my grandmothers' book last night. I think there is more. I don't think she dared leave the information in Hallervania. I know it's back in the Cities. I have no idea freaking where, but I will find it. This is the first step in finding these damn elements."

Sometime in the middle of night, purpose grabbed hold of me, and I felt inspired, determined, even. Facing my sisters would be tricky and I was unsure what to expect. I showered, changed, and gathered the crap I didn't need here, along with things I did. Taking a deep breath, I picked up my bag. "Well, here goes nothing. Wish me luck, cat."

Downstairs, I found Ailianna drinking tea. "Good morning."

"You are up early. Is everything okay?" She glanced up, her eyes drawn to my bag. Straddling the bench, I tucked the bag underneath, leaving her with a frown and confusion in her eyes. Probably not an easy accomplishment to surprise a Seer.

"Everything is fine. I just need to make a small trip."

"You need to go home." Her words were matter-of-fact.

Okay . . . not so easy after all.

"I do. I need to find something of my grandmother's. It's important."

"Are you sure it is there?" She cupped the mug with both hands, sipping.

"Yes. I'm sure. Nothing I need is here; she wouldn't take that risk."

"I see." She set her tea on the table. "There are some things we must put in place before you return. Rowan must travel with you. No question," she added before I could argue. I had expected more questions or complete disregard for my decision.

"Aislynn, if this is what you need to do, nothing I could do would stop you. Nor would it be fair of me to try," Ailianna explained, clearly sensing my surprise.

"Geez, you two! A little early for jabbering, isn't it?" Aila staggered into the kitchen with sleepy eyes. It wasn't fair; she wasn't completely awake yet.

"Aislynn is going to be traveling back to her Realm," Ailianna announced, setting down her mug on the table. "She needs to retrieve something."

Aila jolted awake. "Excuse me? By Goddess, she is not!" Anger flashed through her green eyes. *This* was the reaction I had expected. "She is nowhere near ready to be traveling between Realms. Send Rowan." She waved her hand as she plucked a mug from the shelf.

Complete disregard. *Yup,* exactly what I expected.

"Look, Aila . . . I am perfectly capable of going home. I can't just *send* Rowan." I used air quotations. "I wouldn't know what to tell him to look for. I need to go."

"Then you do not need it. This is ridiculous. Ailianna, you cannot be serious?" She crossed her arms, mug dangling from her grasp.

"Sister, you know as well as I that if Aislynn needs to go, then she must go." Ailianna's voice softened.

"You honestly think that is safe? That she is ready for this? She barely knows what she is doing!" Aila's arms flailed in frustration, and flyaway hairs escaped her braid, creating a crown of angry assertions.

"Thanks," I grumbled.

"Aila! She is capable, magically as well as the rest," Ailianna said.

At least one of them believed I wasn't a complete moron. Jax jumped on the table, interrupting the tirade.

"They need to know."

"Need to know what?" Aila seethed, making it clear that he'd spoken in all of our minds.

I sighed and met both of my sisters' eyes. "I met the White Witch yesterday."

"You what?" Aila responded first. Even Ailianna's head turned.

"She came to me, in The Orchard."

"Your vision," Aila said to Ailianna, panic reaching her eyes.

"No, it wasn't." I shook my head.

Ailianna looked between the two of us. "She is right; this is not my vision. That is something else. But what did she want?"

"She wanted to give me information." I filled them in about the Keepers of Elements, Viego, and the Tree of Elements. As I guessed, both were clueless and knew none of the information I'd just learned. Their faces were quite familiar as I informed them of my part in meeting my destiny, trying to process much like I did yesterday. I could practically see the questions running rampant through their heads.

"Jax, what do you know of this?" Ailianna asked. Apparently, she was familiar with the limitations of my cat. Lucky her.

"Everything is true. She needs to go."

Aila turned pale, the entire thing not sitting well with her.

"I will let Rowan know," Ailianna said with finality. Aila didn't argue. It was decided. I would travel back to Minneapolis. I would find what I needed and return. Hopefully, it would be as simple as that.

16

Simple. *Ha.* Not in a realm of magic. Rowan showed up and options were discussed regarding the trip back to Minneapolis. After a few moments of concerns and questions, he became action-oriented and started immediate preparations.

Ailianna required a "vision quest" to find the best time to travel through the Realms, and my dreams of a quick jump shattered into tiny bits. Apparently, there were spells to prepare, magical spaces to be created, and Ailianna wanted me to take several potions. *Just in case.*

In my mind, I'd hoped for a quick pop over to the other side so I could find what I needed and return, but that was just not going to happen. Unable to help with all the preparation steps, I retreated to my room to reorganize my backpack.

I checked to make sure I had both chargers for my cell and MacBook; God knew I didn't want to leave them here. The thought of using the internet made me want to pee myself. I was determined to find something, or at least I hoped. The mysterious box rested in the corner of the bag, and I wondered what part it played in my destiny. My grandma leaving it for me proved its importance. I pulled it out and tried lifting the top.

Nope. Still nothing.

The box sat on the palm of my hand, aglow with a blue-white light. I thought about my gift and Tristan. Concentrating on the box, I focused on it, levitating above my palm, staring intently.

And . . .

Nothing. I tried again, this time using my other hand. I waved it over the box, directing my energy as I did.

"Ah!" I exclaimed: it had wiggled, just slightly. I put the box back in my bag, tossing in a few of the books including the one from my grandmother. Then, begrudgingly, I shoved my coat in the bag.

"Aislynn," Ailianna called. *"Can you come down? Are you ready?"* Zipping my bag, I started to head downstairs, then turned and paused for one last glance. My hand was steady on the door jamb, smooth beneath my fingertips. I wondered if I would return.

"Are we doing this?" I bounded down the stairs.

"Yes, here are these. I have given you several different types of potions. I hope you don't need them, but I would rather you be prepared," Ailianna said. The small bag she handed me was much heavier than I anticipated. *Geez.* I also hoped I wouldn't need them at all.

"Try and remember everything we have shown you. Rowan, of course, will be there as well. You will be just fine." Their worry concerned me. What did they think would happen? The apocalypse? Too afraid to ask, I nodded.

"You will be leaving in a few hours. I found a time that will work where we can protect your travels best." Ailianna's face softened and she ran her hand down my arm with a gentle squeeze.

"Okay." My mouth formed a lopsided smile of gratitude.

"I found it! Sorry." Aila rushed into the room. I glanced back at Ailianna for answers, but her eyes were on Aila. "Here." Aila slid a necklace over my head. Its long chain ended at my heart.

I picked up the charm on the end, marveling at a stunning piece of fire agate that shimmered in my hand. "I charmed it, for protection, your travels, and anything that might happen," she rambled.

"Thank you. It's beautiful." I allowed the stone to settle at my heart, and her magic shrouded me like a warm blanket. Perhaps there was a softer side to Aila after all; her concern shimmered through the protection spell.

"Of course," she murmured, then turned away toward Ailianna, averting her eyes.

"You guys, everything is going to be fine. I promise! It's not a big deal. I will be back before you know it."

Their looks told me they didn't believe a word I said, and their worry rippled through the room. Jax picked that moment to stride in.

"When do we leave?" I was silently thankful for his entrance. I slung my backpack over my shoulder.

"Soon," Ailianna said, resuming her work.

When it came time to leave, we all gathered outside. They had a designated sacred circle for any intense magic, which I guessed included traveling. Aila came out of the house with a basket of items for the ritual.

"Okay. Rowan, Aislynn, Jax, please enter the circle." The earth was exposed, raw and open in the form of a perfect circle with four oak trees looming around the perimeter. My eyes were drawn upward to their branches that created a canopy perfectly meeting to form another circle to the blue sky above. I felt encased by the earth as it breathed life into the space.

"We are beginning preparations for traveling to the Earth Realm, Aislynn's home. For this journey, we ask that Aislynn, Rowan, and Jax are protected by the magic of Light, so destinies may be fulfilled." Ailianna walked the perimeter, placing twelve large quartz crystals in total. Aila followed with a line of sea salt. Ailianna stood at the north of the circle, her hands open to the sky.

"I use my gifts to surround this circle with love and light." Streams of magic shot from her palms, turquoise light enveloping us. Aila on the opposing side repeated Ailianna's words with emerald green light following her sister's trail. The magic was palpable not only two-dimensionally but above and below as a perfect sphere.

"We bless this space for traveling between the Realms and ask for protection and guidance by Light." Their voices sung together in harmony.

"Are you ready?" Rowan said, distracting me from watching my sisters.

"Yeah." I met his gaze.

Jax wrapped between my feet, curling his tail around my leg and sitting on my foot. Rowan opened his hand, exposing an amethyst crystal wand that emanated a mystical purple glow.

"Grab the other end and hang on. We will not travel to an in-between space but go straight to your Realm."

I nodded as the spell heightened, an electricity building thicker around us. Taking hold of the wand, I gave my sisters one last glance. They focused intensely on the magic they performed and eventually I turned my gaze back to Rowan.

The circle engulfed us in colorful light, an iridescent sheen. Before long, the wand became so bright, I could no longer see. Squinting, I tried to filter the intense brightness when light shot upward to the sky and I knew we were traveling.

A moment later my apartment appeared. I spun myself around, something tickling my subconscious. My eyes met Rowan's. He nodded, and I let go of the wand.

"Wait . . ." My eyes darted around the room. The hangers in the closet were swaying on the rod. "Rowan? When are we?" I had been in Hallervania for well over a month, almost two, but it felt like we never left.

"We are the exact moment we left."

"What? How?" My head snapped back in surprise.

"Well, magic and time exist together in a delicate framework maintained by the stability and foundation of our Realm. When in balance, spells can be created to move fluidly within the timeline. Therefore, we are now living the moment as we never left," he explained, setting the wand on the table.

Certain this didn't make sense, nor would our quantum physicists agree with him, I shook my head. "Wait. Wouldn't that mean Daragon is here looking for us?" I glanced toward the door.

"No. He left when we did and traveled back just as you and I did. Now he is not here and is not aware we have returned," Rowan said. My eyebrows scrunched as I tried to process.

"Time is a bit more . . . flexible than you previously believed."

My thoughts jumped to Tristan. *Isn't that the truth?*

"It was Ailianna's idea to choose this moment, and a brilliant move. Her skilled magic also has another part: the ability to return to Hallervania once we are ready." Rowan sat down on the couch, waiting for me to understand.

"So, we are exactly as we left? It's still snowing? No time has passed?" I moved my blinds and sure enough, snow plastered the window, still falling heavily. My brain tried to wrap around how this was possible.

Technically, had I time traveled? Teleportation was one thing, but time travel? Blinking rapidly, I closed the blinds. Inside my head existed a swirling mess of questions with zero answers. "Another time, you will explain this to me properly," I stated, glancing back at Rowan.

"I am sure." A half smile crossed his mouth. Jax jumped on the couch, pushing himself on Rowan's lap, forcing him to pet.

"Ah, it's good to be home."

"Um, Jax, I thought you didn't like it here." My eyebrows arched in question. His response involved curling up, head resting on his paws as his eyes settled closed. I shook my head. Freaking cat.

I was home as if I never left. It felt anticlimactic. When I left, the trip seemed unquestionably necessary, but now I wasn't sure where to start. I tossed the bag of potions on the chair and dug out my laptop. Pressing the power button, I inwardly cringed. There would probably be ten thousand updates or . . . would there? My brain hurt.

Meanwhile, I scrounged my fridge and the sparse contents made my stomach whimper, immediately missing Ailianna's food. *How the hell did I eat like this?* Regretfully, I closed the door and grabbed us glasses of water, digging out fruit snacks from my pantry. At my computer I opened Safari, searching *White Witch*. The results brought up Narnia, video games, and a movie. Backspacing, I tried *White Witch Hallervania*.

Your search did not match any documents.

Shit.

Well, it was worth a shot. I tried *elements*, and that was too broad. *Four elements tree of elements* brought up plenty. I surfed down the list: tree of life, tarot readers, four element spells, and charms. Clicking through several different pages, I read about the elements. Nothing answered my questions, so I tried *keeper of the elements*.

Ah, here we go. I scrolled through several different sites, gaining different cultural backgrounds and theories on the elements, reaching from the pagan world to the Bible and Christianity.

Changing my approach, I searched my grandmother's name. *Abigail Mitchell books* brought up several results. I scrolled through her tenure at the University of Minnesota, several books she had published, and different bios from various sites. These were all things I knew.

Clicking from site to site, I ended up on a blog of a student whose major was in quantum mechanics in relation to time travel. *Interesting.* I wondered how he would feel if I told him I had just traveled in time. *I could blow up the scientific community.*

#timetravel

Continuing through his page, I found he'd studied under my grandma and taken several of her classes. I perused a little longer and bookmarked the page, then found myself on a YouTube video of an MIT professor talking about the relationship between quantum mechanics and teleportation.

By then, Rowan and Jax had long since passed out, completely uninterested in my fascination. They didn't require an explanation of all this, as it simply always existed for them. I glanced over my screen, watching the slow rhythmic breathing of Rowan's chest. I hadn't seen him much lately, and I didn't realize how much I missed his presence. I felt less . . . magically inferior around him. He brought a sense of security and trust in my abilities.

I huffed out my breath. I was off track. My grandmother had left me something, somewhere. I couldn't think about Rowan and my emotions. My eyes squinting closed, I held the bridge of my nose. I knew I had to face the thing I had been subconsciously dreading.

My mother. I would have to . . . *visit* her. Obscene words crossed my mind. Not only would I have to visit, but also try and bring up the precarious subject of my grandmother. *At the same time.*

My mother and grandmother had a strained relationship. They had never seen eye to eye, on . . . well, anything. Ever. My mother was logical, a "follow the rules" kind of person, and my grandmother the absolute opposite. This could only go one way: horrendously.

Me being the spitting image of my grandmother didn't sit well with my mother, either. In fact, I was confident this drove her nearly crazy. My existence was a constant reminder of their tumultuous relationship. We tried to come together and tolerate one another, but it never ended well.

This was all much to my father's disappointment, who watched from afar, afraid to get involved. To try and confront her for information would be next to impossible. It had been eleven years since my grandmother passed, and I wondered if my mom would still have any of her things.

I ran my hands over my face, trying to ease the apprehension wafting through me as I thought about what needed to be done tomorrow. When I checked the clock, 10:43 p.m. stared back at me. Somehow, I thought it should be later and I wondered if jet lag from time travel was possible.

I closed my computer, set it on the coffee table, and exchanged it for my grandmother's book. My eyes became heavy reading and I drifted to sleep.

Sitting at work in front of my computer, I tucked my leg under me, shifting in my chair. Much to my displeasure, I felt uncomfortable and everything about my office appeared slightly . . . off, somehow. Unable to place the wrong feeling, I shrugged, continuing to work on an ad campaign for a beverage company.

But nothing seemed to work correctly. Each click of my mouse resulted in crazy colored shapes, in opposition to my client's request. Although unsatisfied with my work, I continued trying to fix the advertisement.

Leslie and Tina down the hall were snickering to each other, looking my way. *Laugh it up,* chicas*! My picture is going to win!* A strange awareness came over me that my thoughts were silly and ridiculous.

"Don't you miss this?" a voice said from behind me.

I spun my chair around. "Seriously? You?" Irritation

sat snidely on my face. What did this asshat get from harassing me while I was trying to sleep?

"Long time no see." A cigarette hung out of Daragon's mouth underneath a petulant grin.

"I almost forgot how irritating you are . . . almost," I spat, crossing my arms.

He responded with a wicked, knowing smile. "Yes, I know. I merely forgot I didn't kill you." He sat on the back of the credenza of my cubicle with his knee bent, foot resting on top.

"Yes, I could see how that might slip your mind. Sorry to be disappointing, still breathing and all."

He winked and jumped on top of the credenza. Panic sent my gaze frantically looking around, knowing his presence peering above everyone's cubicles might be noticeable. Flicking the cigarette to the floor, he took his right hand and created a sizzling red ball of fire, allowing it to bounce up and down in his hand.

"Don't! What are you doing?" I yelled, shooting out of my chair and checking who might be nearby. But no one noticed him; they all sat clacking away at their keyboards.

"I think we need to have a little fun Aislynn, don't you?" He threw the energy ball through the glass break room door, sending shattered glass everywhere. Instantly, screams filled the air as everyone ducked to the floor.

"No! Daragon! STOP!" Sick dread sang through me as I feared anyone getting hurt. Daragon attracted attention as he created more fireballs, throwing them at people in their cubicles. They tried to escape, but the doors were suddenly locked.

"Hello, darling," Daragon said to a whimpering Candice hiding under her desk. An energy ball slammed into her chest. Shock registered, then the light left her eyes. Inky black magic charred her body.

I watched, frozen in horror. "No more, Daragon! They're innocent and have nothing to do with this, or you! Enough!" I spun around, then shouted, "Everyone, go! Run to the conference room!" Terror ran down the hall as they escaped.

"Oh, come on, Aislynn. You're no fun at all." Daragon jumped with agile precision to the floor toward me. Taking short steps backward, I tried to see who was still trying to move to the conference room.

Leslie seemed to be caught in indecision, her movement catlike as she darted forward and back from her spot in the breakroom, too afraid to move. Watching in frustration, I willed her to run. Daragon caught her attention.

"Leslie, is it?"

Her eyes widened, bouncing between the two of us.

"Don't!" I insisted.

"Come on, darling. It's okay. I will not harm you." His dark eyes enchanted her to come forward.

"No, Leslie! Don't look at him. Don't say anything." I tried to throw my power at him, but he was barely pushing back. Breaking contact with Leslie, he looked to me. "Daragon, I said stop."

"And why in the world would I listen to you?" His voice was cool.

"Because you want me, not them." Finally, the fear he created crumbled around me. I found my balance, reaching for power, and created my own energy ball, bright white in contrast to his fiery dark magic. "Don't move."

I held my magic at eye level, and he paused, considering my threat. Tilting his head, he did the unthinkable and threw the fireball toward Leslie. I threw mine in return, which he put up his hand to repel. Glancing back to Leslie, the cupboard above her bore a burning hole. I found her dropped to the ground, covering her ears.

Gratitude washed over me as I turned back to Daragon. He raised both hands, and heat radiated from behind me. The walls set aflame. Fire crept across the floor and up the walls, eating everything it touched. I watched him concentrate on his spell as fire licked its way through the hall.

Throwing my hands out and extending my magic, I forced him off balance, temporarily distracting his spell. The fire slowed its wicked consumption. With one hand holding my magic at Daragon, I focused on my other hand, thinking of water. I demanded it flow through the hallway, extinguishing the searing flames. The movement was slow at first, as I was unable to put my complete attention with water while holding Daragon with my other hand. My magic was split—divided between the two needs.

Closer now to Leslie, I found her inside on the floor, coughing from the smoke. If I could get her next to me, she would be safe. Daragon sensed my thoughts and disrupted them as a fireball sailed past me straight into Leslie.

"*No!*" My scream racked through several octaves. My concentration was destroyed as I turned on Daragon in a rage. The slightest flicker of fear registered in his eyes as a subtle shift occurred.

"No more!" Furious anger tracked through my voice and my hands locked in front of me, acting of their own accord. I lost control, magic taking over like a death spiral. Somewhere in the back of my mind, I was aware of a line I was stumbling toward.

A massive sphere of shifting white light swirled between my hands. Daragon's gaze was on the orb, then it shifted to my eyes as he took the smallest step back. Stepping forward, I closed the small space between us and stared into the pools of black that were his eyes.

A deafening crashing sounded, like a wave, and snapped me from the dream. My eyes popped open, taking in my apartment. My chest heaved in terror. Magic still heightened around me and tingled my skin. Trying to soothe the adrenaline coursing through my body, I realized Daragon knew I returned.

I dug out the bag of potions from underneath me, clenching them to my chest. The tiny glass bottles clinked against one another. For the merest second, I expected Daragon to materialize before me. Evening my breaths, my heart slowed from the erratic pounding.

The end of the dream terrified me more than Daragon's presence: the magic I created was one I held with so little control. My thoughts jumped to the White Witch, and I imagined how easily she lost complete control, allowing magic to take over.

Shudders ran through me as I glanced to Rowan stretched out on the couch and Jax curled next to him, a small twitch of his ear and he tightened his position. Playing the dream out again in my head, I filed every detail. Daragon revealed he was watching and keeping track of me, and I swallowed hard. *What is his part in all of this?*

17

The next morning, my brain woke me at the ungodly hour of five, precariously mapping a conversation with my mother. After almost an hour with my spinning unhelpful thoughts, I procrasta-scrolled my social media until I decided to move from the couch and make coffee while Rowan showered. Savoring the delightful aroma of my brew, I spent several moments smelling the bag of beans like some drug fiend.

Ailianna's cooking aside, I missed my coffee immensely and considered bowing to my French press, begging forgiveness for abandoning its presence in my life. Jax jumped on a barstool, distracting my thoughts. I took a deep breath, then summed up the premise of my dream for him.

"What do you think it means?"

"I think it means he is a jackass." My cat, unimpressed, blinked slowly. I huffed out my breath.

"I think he wants me to know he is watching my every move. What Daragon wants has everything to do with the elements. Although, I don't understand how even he knows about them." I sipped my coffee, and a piece of my soul I didn't know was missing settled back into place.

"That would not surprise me in the least. He's only a tool."

My eyebrows arched in question, but the cat gave no answer. The heat of my mug warmed my hands and I secretly hoped it would warm the chill sitting deep in my belly. I didn't dare describe the extent of my use of magic in the dream, nor my lack of control. The thought freaked me out too much. I remembered the dream with such clarity, and the tiny moment when Daragon became frightened. A snippet of fear flashed in his eyes right before I woke.

"All done, Aislynn. The shower is yours." Rowan interrupted my thoughts. His black curls dripped at the back of his neck and I could smell my soap on him.

My lips twisted as I handed him his coffee, desperately trying to distract my nose. Without a word I went down the hall, taking my coffee with me.

Turning on the shower, my thoughts pondered Jax's comment about being a tool. What did that mean? Was there someone more sinister behind Daragon? I would need to ask Rowan, maybe he knew something from his Council meetings. My mind wandered to Naked Rowan standing here only a few minutes ago and I shoved my face under the cool spray.

Eventually, unable to find anything else to distract myself, I decided I was ready (physically, not emotionally) to visit my mother. The storm left the Twin Cities blanketed in over a foot of snow, and according to my traffic app the roads were purple angry lines of hell.

"Don't worry, we will just teleport," Rowan said, following my thoughts.

"We can't just teleport into my mom's living room!" The thought made me laugh. Saturday morning, she and Dad would be sitting at the breakfast table, iPads out as they read the news, coffee, orange juice, and a big breakfast laid out before them.

They would be discussing the latest politics or whatever current event took up prime media space. I envisioned us popping into the kitchen and plopping in a chair. Certain my mother would die, or at the very minimum, faint onto her travertine floor.

"Well," Rowan clarified, "I was thinking somewhere not visible and walking to the door."

"I like Aislynn's idea better." I burst out laughing at Jax. Rowan and I put on coats, and I pulled on a chunky pair of snow boots to keep my feet somewhat warm in the Minnesota frozen air.

"Let me tell you how disappointed I am that I am missing this." Jax jumped on the bed, stretched, then made a slow circle before curling into a ball, leaving me envious.

I completely understood his loathing of my mother. Last time she visited my apartment (which had happened less than a handful of times), she shooed Jax off his spot on the couch, informing us that animals did not belong on furniture. Jax and I shared a mutual look of disdain, and there may have been eye-rolling on my behalf. A giggle popped out of my mouth, wondering what he might have "said" to her that day.

"You don't want to know."

"Let's go," Rowan said, stopping our banter. He laid a

hand on my shoulder, transporting us to my parent's neighborhood. The sudden shift in temperature shocked my system. We arrived down the street from my parent's house, and a part of me was curious how Rowan knew where to go.

Fresh snow carpeted the neighborhood with an untouched delicacy, creating a pristine quiet. Something soon to be destroyed, I consciously released the breath I held and regretted my stupid plan. Rowan didn't understand how difficult it was for me to be here, not that I could explain it to him.

My parents lived in Eden Prairie, a suburb of the twin cities. It was a prosperous, wealthy area that was quintessential American living, and I never felt like I belonged. Everything was perfect, with robot children and well-kept houses. My mother embodied the typical Minnesota Nice, which meant she was passive-aggressive 99 percent of the time.

She held the typical "keeping up with the Jones'" mentality, which made me insane. Who cared what other people did? It drove my mom crazy that I shopped at thrift stores and lived minimally. In part because she thought I deserved better, but also because it might be an embarrassment to her.

The house sat back on the property, and I winced as we left deep footprints trailing to the door which would annoy my mother. They had built the house ten years prior, designed with impeccable taste by one of her snobby interior design friends. When the yard wasn't covered in frozen wet suck, flawless landscaping rolled over an assortment of shrubs, flowers, and trees that won them awards in the community.

Even the perfection in white promised an escape from reality. The only reality I wanted to escape was this one.

"It can't be that bad, Aislynn," Rowan commented as he observed my troubled energy with a sideward glance.

Finally, reaching the front steps, I rang the bell, knowing the door would be locked. My face puckered, and I folded my arms to withhold my shivers from the bitter cold.

After what felt like an eternity, the door opened, revealing my mother. She was dressed in dress slacks and her makeup was done, even though it was before nine in the morning, *on a Saturday*. Her mouth fell open in surprise when she saw me shivering in my coat.

"Aislynn! What on heaven's earth are you doing here?" She stood behind the door.

"Thanks, Mom. Good to see you too." I stomped my feet, shaking off excess snow.

"I'm sorry, I'm just surprised is all, and you have a friend." Curiosity peeked as she noticed Rowan, opening the door wider. "Come, come, don't let the heat out."

"Yeah, this is Rowan. Rowan, my mother." I stepped into the foyer and leaned against the wall to pull off my boots, sending bits of ice flying across the perfectly polished mahogany floor. *I'll need to get a towel.*

"It is a pleasure, Meredith," Rowan said, and took her hand with both of his, holding gently.

My head tilted as I struggled with my boots. *"Her first name?"* I projected at him. *"Really, Rowan?"*

My mom was surprised by his warm demeanor and couldn't help but smile while looking into those stunning (and what I knew to be the subdued version) of his blue crystallized eyes.

"Hey, Rowan," I half whispered, my eyes a steely glare. "No funny stuff!"

My mom didn't notice. His smile widened, and he gave me a wink. *"I am only making it easier, is all."*

I internally groaned.

"Well, it is lovely to meet you, Rowan," my mom said with a smile that reached her eyes, and I wondered what the hell he had done to her. "Please, come in and welcome to our home. John?" she called back toward the kitchen. "You will never guess who is here for a visit."

With Rowan next to her and me in tow, we went to the kitchen where my dad sat scrolling on his iPad. At last, he glanced up, and the pad was cast aside.

"Aislynn! What a surprise!" Joy filled his face as he came to embrace me.

"Hi, Dad." I returned the hug. My dad was always happy to see me, but because of the tension between my mother and me, it wasn't as much as he would like. Sometimes he met me downtown for lunch, so we could spend time together without the undue pressure.

"Good morning. And what do we owe this special visit?" He eyed me, aware something must be wrong. I noticed that he gazed unusually hard at my eyes. Perhaps the extra sparkle was somewhat noticeable.

"I missed you guys . . ." My inflection made it more of a question than a statement, trying to convince him and myself. He squinted, assessing me, and I averted my gaze.

"Well, it's good to see you." Dad hugged me again, kissing the top of my head. "Come sit down and have breakfast. God knows your mother made enough for ten."

My mom retrieved extra plates from the cupboard.

"John, this is Rowan, a friend of Aislynn's." I swear her eyebrows wiggled, which made me want to slowly die inside.

"Rowan, it is nice to meet you. Please join us." They shook hands, my dad eyeing us both again. Rowan happily sat, always willing to eat. After the sparse findings at my house, I was sure he was half-starved. I couldn't disagree as my own stomach rumbled.

I filled my cup with coffee and Rowan asked for tea. We ate in the comfort of small talk about the weather and the Minnesota Wild hockey team. My dad questioned Rowan ruthlessly on the team, who somehow "magically" answered everything right without a misstep. I rolled my eyes, certain Rowan's knowledge of the Wild's standings and team performance had been gained via telepathy.

When we finished, Rowan graciously thanked my mother for the meal, volunteering to help clean. All the while, I mentally worked up the courage to bring up my grandmother.

He insisted my mother not help, which was difficult as I noticed her twitch in her chair. Rowan picked up dishes and began washing them *by hand*. I stifled my laughter, knowing Rowan wasn't even aware of the dishwasher.

"How is work, Aislynn?" My mother poured herself another cup of coffee. I stuttered to answer, as I hadn't thought about work for almost two months. That Friday afternoon—er, yesterday—felt like forever ago.

"Uh, work's fine, Mom. Thanks," I answered with awkwardness, then Rowan's voice pummeled my mind:

"Get to it, already."

I sent daggers with my eyes. "So, Mom, I . . . was . . . ah . . . thinking about Grandma the other day."

My mom's face twisted, morphing into a hard, calloused stare. My dad shifted in his chair and a painful silence hung in the air.

"Oh?" She looked as though she wanted to crawl from the room.

"Yeah, I was missing her." Mom's face paled with the direction of the conversation, so I quickly added, "I am working on a project at work that is for the University."

The lie helped her regain some color; I knew that switching to my work always made her happy. "Oh? Well, that is nice. I didn't know the University used your firm."

I nodded, spinning my coffee spoon on the table. "Yeah, they do. Anyway, it made me think of her when she was a professor." My finger traced the edge of the spoon, sending it in slow spirals.

"Mm-hmm. That was a long time ago." She glanced up at Rowan. "Are you sure you don't need help, Rowan? You don't need to do that, really." Rowan disregarded her and insisted. My insides twisted at the excruciating pain of this conversation.

"So, I was wondering what you did with all of grandma's stuff. It was so long ago, and it didn't matter much then, but I think there are some things I would like. If you still have anything . . . or something." Fast, incomprehensible garbled words caused my mother's shoulders to lift and fall with an irritated, heavy breath.

"Well, most of it is in storage, but some of the boxes are downstairs in the closet. Those are more personal items. I don't know what you would possibly want with them," she said with disinterest, choking the paper napkin in her grip.

"Well, I'd like some of her books, maybe. I came across

some of her theories and . . . well, I was so young, they were a bit beyond me." I inwardly waited for the blow that was about to come. Glancing down, I realized I had stopped touching the spoon, yet it continued to spin. I clamped my hand down on it, looking up frantically.

"Oh, God. Not you, too. Please, please tell me you don't believe that nonsense." Aggravation sparked and thankfully, Mom was too caught up in her anger to catch my magic trick.

"Mom," I pleaded. "I am just curious, is all. It's kind of cool." I used my words to distract from the relief that washed over me that she didn't see.

"Your grandmother was a storyteller and lived in a fantasy world. She had unreasonable ideas based on no facts whatsoever."

I had hit the ultimate nerve. My dad's discomfort doubled, and my eyes closed in frustration. I didn't think now was the time to inform her my grandmother's theories were absolutely correct and the fantasy world was real.

"Most people believed your grandmother was a complete nut job," Mom continued. "Do you know what it feels like to have to explain that to people? To have that follow you around? The need to make a name for yourself and not have people believe the same of you?" Her voice raised with each question as her hand tightened around the napkin she crinkled.

"I know, Mom. I know." I turned to Rowan, glaring. *"I told you so!"*

"Meredith, sweetheart, she is just curious. It's her grandmother. She wants to look through her things; it's no big deal. No reason to upset yourself." My dad patted her hand. "Your mother told you that Aislynn would come to you one day and do this very thing."

My entire body lurched forward. "She did? When?" The sharpness of my voice further unnerved my mother and startled my dad.

"Oh, it wasn't long before she"—his eyes darted to my mother, who pursed her lips—"passed." My mother's face was stern, and I caught the stall and tilted my head in question.

"What did she say?"

"Oh, it was a long time ago; I don't remember much. She was here, her and your mother, well . . . you know." He glanced back and forth, stuck between the two of us.

"They were fighting," I interjected.

He nodded, barely. My mom shifted her gaze. "She was insistent with your mother, telling her that on the day you came asking for her things, if she wasn't around to give them herself, your mom must give you everything. She went on and on about how important it was. Seemed odd at the time, but hell, everything she did was strange."

I peered back at my mom.

"I said it was in the downstairs closet," she reiterated in a piercing, staccato manner. "Help yourself." She set the dead, crumpled napkin on the table with such force that the spoon in front me rattled as she walked out of the room. My head fell to the table, wrapped in my arms.

"I'm sorry, Dad. I really am. I just . . . I need . . ." My voice was muffled from under my arms.

"I know, Aislynn. It is just difficult for her. You know that." He tried his best to comfort me. "Come on, I will take you downstairs."

Rowan magically finished at that exact moment and followed. We made our way through the massive house to downstairs, which included an indoor gym, and a full game room with a bar leading to the outdoor patio.

My dad flipped light switches as we went down the hall, the temperature plummeting as he opened the door to the storage room. Bare concrete and exposed wood framing allowed a drab flat light through the window. My dad reached up and pulled the string, lighting the bulb above us.

"Well, it's all here somewhere . . . let's see . . ." He shifted boxes around. "Ah, here we go. Like your mother said, this is some of her more personal stuff. If what you need isn't here, let me know and we will go to the storage unit."

My heart lifted with my dad's kindness. He gave me a quick half hug and kissed my head again. "I will let you guys be. If you need anything, I'll be upstairs. And don't worry about your mother: she will get over it." He smiled.

"Well, that wasn't so bad," Rowan said. I groaned while he smiled. Obviously, he did not understand the complexity of a mother/daughter relationship, let alone mine. We began searching through the boxes. I pushed up the sleeves of my sweater as we began our search of the boxes. I moved several around, restacking while reading the writing on the sides.

"This looks like office things," Rowan commented, and pulled out a coffee mug with the University of Minnesota's insignia wrapped around the side. I peered in and pulled out her nameplate. *Prof. A. Mitchell, Ph.D.* My fingers ran over her name, and I wished she was here helping me instead of digging through her things.

"Did you catch how my dad stuttered? About her death?" I asked.

"I did."

Rowan's evasiveness didn't get by me, but I continued my search. I opened a box and found different awards she'd won and a couple copies of one of her more well-published books. In another, I found clothes, the ones she always kept in her office: a knit brown sweater, a tweed blazer, and a black trench coat.

"What?" Rowan questioned, looking up from his box.

"I just remembered how she kept these in her closet." I rubbed the soft knit in between my fingers. "I would always ask her why she had them, particularly in the middle of summer. She always told me, 'You never know where you might go.' Kind of funny now, huh?" The corner of my lip raised in a half smile.

Rowan nodded. My memories pleased him, and though it was subtle, I found it oddly comforting to be able to speak about her without the pressure of my mother eating at me.

Pushing the sweater back in the box, I folded the box closed. Moving it to the floor, I opened another, this one full of textbooks ranging from religious studies and occult practices to science, including quantum mechanics. A smaller book, the size of a paperback, had slid down the side.

Using my fingers to shove my hand down the box, I edged it upward. Leather-bound like the ones I had found in Hallervania, I turned it over in my hands and an envelope fell into my lap. My grandmother's handwriting scrawled across the front *For Aislynn*. With shaking fingers, I carefully pulled out the pages.

My Dearest Aislynn,

If you are reading this letter, then evidently, I've met my untimely demise. As you will soon see, I planned for all contingencies of this small problem of mine. You are searching for this letter within my things with nowhere else to go for answers. And to be reading this letter, you must have had to deal with your mother, and I can imagine that was . . . difficult for you. Please remember that has nothing to do with you and everything to do with your mother and me. And I sincerely apologize for its ugly nature.

Knowing you, my dear sweet grandchild, you have a thousand questions running through your mind with little answers and only more questions. I am hoping this will provide you with some solace as I spent my entire life searching for anything that will possibly come to your aide.

As you must know by now, I am fully aware of Hallervania's existence and your destiny which is so deeply entwined with it. As you may have guessed, I traveled to Hallervania many a time, along with some other places you may or may not have been to but will go with all eventualities. When I said I was "out of the country" and unreachable, I truly was! We can share a laugh about that now.

There is much to tell you and much to do. I studied and traveled through the realms to try and give you as much information as possible. I left you several books, documents, and other things which will come to your aide in different ways. I am hoping you found Rowan and he is helping you. Those who have been charged with assisting you fulfill your destiny are blessed souls; guiding and protecting you is part of their destiny.

For you to be here, you've learned of your true destiny to be the Keeper of Elements—to gain the magic from those who stole it and return it to the Tree of Elements. I know this must seem an impossible task for one person, but you are the exact right person for this challenge. The Gods and Goddesses chose wisely with you. I know in my heart you will do everything being asked of you and more. I only wish I could help you and guide you. Maybe by leaving this for you, in some way I am doing just that.

Now, here is the most frustrating part: I cannot give you everything you need. I have been barred from this. Believe me, I know your frustration. I've seen many a Seer, Visionaries, and Readers across the Realms but all shared a similar message. This is your journey. All the mistakes, twists and turns, and triumphs are yours to make. I can only guide.

There are several items I put together for you, I wish I could have labeled it with arrows and notations, but I could not. As you well know, others are looking for these items as well. So, everything has been done methodically and deliberately. I have faith in your clever abilities to find what you need.

So, this letter is the first of what will be a few more. I shall have the last word yet.

Remember, my dear Aislynn: you are exactly where you are meant to be, and a bigger picture will slowly come together on a fantastic magical path. Be who you are as your power comes from this very thing. I only wish I could see you in all your beauty of reclaiming magic for Light. An entire world of possibilities you never imagined is waiting for you.

With love and all the power of Light, may this find you well and safe as you travel your path. I am always with you.

With the brightest love,

Grandma

Tears streamed down my cheeks. Reading the letter and having her so "alive" through her words was a twist of a knife in my heart. I wished she could be here helping me, even though a part of me knew she had found a way to do precisely that. Rowan had stopped his search long before, knowing I had found what I needed. Handing him the letter and keeping the book aside, I closed the box.

"The rest of what we need is not here. It might be in the storage unit, but I am not entirely sure," I said as Rowan read through the letter.

"Your grandmother has a beautiful light." He folded the pages and handed them back. Nodding, I noticed the present tense he used. I stood, dusting off my pants and looking around at the stacks of boxes covered in dust and old peeling tape. This was what remained of the amazing human who was my grandmother. Sadness rushed through me as I pulled the string and vanquished the light.

18

My heart was heavy as I closed the door behind us. Thoughtful, I wandered to the patio doors, gazing at the drifts of snow. The already gray skies had darkened in the morning light as flurries fell from the sky. Leaning on the door jamb, I rested my head on the wood, my sadness palpable.

Of course, the letter gave me more questions to ponder. My grandmother knew she wasn't going to be able to help me. I imagined what it would be like, knowing death was imminent but still wanting, *needing*, to help someone.

Absently, I ran my finger across the bright orange color of the poppy tattoo on my left forearm. It was my first tattoo, for my grandmother, her favorite flower, forever a part of me.

Little pieces of my childhood spent with her came zinging back to me. Tracing the outline of the flower, I remembered the stories and fairy tales we would act out, finding hidden messages and pretending to save magic. She had prepared me for this all along and I didn't have a clue.

"If I know my grandma, this isn't going to be as simple as coming here and finding one thing." I held up the letter. Rowan stood opposite me with his shoulders resting against the wall. "She was a bit theatrical, and she put *years* of preparation into this, her greatest works." I glanced down, Rowan's feet almost touching mine. "I highly doubt our search will end at the storage unit, but there will be something there."

Rowan nodded, turning his attention outside, quiet. He seemed to have something to say, but chose not to share, and I decided not to press the issue. Unsure of how long we stood there, watching the snow gently fall to the quiet landscape, I decided it was time to move again. Without a word, I stepped toward him and pressed my lips against his stubbly cheek.

"Thank you. For letting me be me. For being patient."

Surprise sparked in the corners of his eyes before I turned and headed upstairs.

A swift, short knock on my dad's den was answered by a muffled "Yeah, come on in," making me smile. The room was incredibly *my dad*, and always made me feel comforted. It had become one of my favorite places over the years. I found him sitting behind the dark cherry desk that had been in his family for generations. He glanced up from his case files.

"Hey, Dad," I sighed and plopped into one of the old wingback chairs.

"Hi, sweetheart. Did you find what you were looking for?" He pulled down his reading glasses, closing the file.

"Well, you know Grandma. I found something, but not everything I need." I stared at the wall behind him filled with heavy caselaw books.

"Yes, indeed, that does sound like her." He watched Rowan wander the room, amused by the flat screen that hung on the wall turned to the Wild hockey game. "They are up, 4–2," he said to Rowan. "What can I do to help?"

"I am thinking the storage unit might be helpful."

He sat back in his swivel chair, nodding. "We can go this morning." His eyes veered toward the TV and the Wild offense making a play for the net.

"Dad, you don't have to go. Rowan and I can. I am sure digging through Grandma's stuff was not on your list of things to do today." I turned to watch the play. The puck rippled off the goalie's glove and the players followed swooping around the net.

"I welcome the distraction. Besides, then I can harass you." He winked. Twisting my lip in my teeth, I thought about him coming with. Perhaps the help would come in handy, although I couldn't tell him what we were looking for because I didn't know.

"And . . . I can show you the new car!" My dad's eyes lit up with a smile. "And test it out in the snow."

Soon enough, we weaved our way through the neighborhood in his new Audi Q5. Rowan nodded in fascination as my dad informed him of specs which he knew nothing about. I couldn't help but giggle. Maybe it didn't matter what realm you were from: guys just think cars are cool. My dad thoroughly enjoyed navigating the partially plowed roads as I clenched the "oh shit" handle with sheer terror. The drive was not far, but I hated being in the car on snow-covered roads.

The parking lot was desolate as we pulled in. The storage facility was one of those indoor climate-controlled buildings, with twenty-four-hour monitoring and security.

As we got out of the car, the four-story structure loomed down upon us, and I thought about the strangeness of humans.

We had an intense need to hold on to possessions, requiring them to be locked away in such a place. My dad entered the access code on the keypad and pulled open the door. A loud beep acknowledged our presence, and we walked to the elevator and went up to the third floor.

"The unit is down the hall to the left." He pointed down the long, carpeted corridor. Finally, we stopped at unit 3923. The number caught me off guard as September 23 was my birthday.

"Hey, when did you guys get this unit?"

My dad looked confused as he unlocked the door. "We didn't. Your grandmother did."

"But this didn't exist back then," I said, confused.

"Yeah, I know." Dad opened the door, flipping the switch and letting us enter first. As I expected, there were stacks of boxes, plastic totes, and a few pieces of furniture. "Well, where do you want to start?"

We began our search closest to the door, going through the plastic totes first. Mostly we found copies of her books and the research binders that went with them. Some we could easily close, others required more thorough scrutiny. Several we found filled with textbooks from her areas of study ranging from anthropology, theology, and religious ethics. It all seemed endless.

After a couple hours halfway through the boxes, my dad asked several times what we were looking for. I couldn't give him anything specific, but he would nod and told me what he discovered. As I restacked the boxes I went through, I moved to the next stack and a wave of heat rushed through me. I pushed up the sleeves of my sweater to my elbows.

I pulled down a small box first and found a tiny photo album I recognized as one she used to keep in her office. I flipped through the pictures of us: me at various ages, trips we had been on, and places we visited. The last one in the book was a closeup of me smiling at the camera.

I remembered this picture distinctly: when I was maybe ten or twelve years old, my grandma had taken me to one of her favorite places. We'd hiked all day to a secluded spot where we sat and had lunch, and I'd played in the shallow creek nearby. She'd insisted on taking my picture and something about that day stuck out in my mind, but I couldn't put my finger on it.

I closed the album and set it aside. Next, I found a wooden box about five by ten inches in size. It was ornately carved and eerily similar to the box I already had, but this one was much bigger. When I touched the wood surface, it immediately emanated a glowing light.

Quickly, I pulled my hand away, making sure my dad hadn't seen. A sigh of relief washed over me as I watched him dig in a tote nearby, not paying attention to me. When I turned back to the box, I let out a startled squeak: Jax sat on the box with wide blue cat eyes and meowed loudly.

"Was that you, Aislynn?" My dad looked over, then saw my cat. "Is that . . . Jax?" His head jutted forward in disbelief.

"We have a problem. Trouble is coming."

Before I had the chance to try and explain, Rowan let out a groan. A thundering crack followed. *Shit.* I knew that sound. An energy ball.

Haunted laughter came from the hall. "Hellooo . . . ?" called a voice that I didn't recognize, accompanied by the sound of a hand dragging down the wall.

Rowan held a finger to his lip from where he stood closest to the door. He quietly edged himself to the entrance.

"Come out and play with us," the voice droned.

My dad, not one to sit back, started to stand. I grabbed his hand, shaking my head. Something in my face must have convinced him of the severity of the situation because he stopped midstep, even though I knew it went against his very nature. We both looked back to Rowan, who now held a bright emerald energy ball swirling in his hands. My dad's eyes widened with disbelief as his mouth dropped open in shock.

"What the—" Another deafening crack issued, this one closer to the door. He cringed at the unearthly sound.

"Aislynn, you should go. Take your dad," Rowan whispered.

My insides turned. I couldn't leave Rowan, and the thought of teleporting my dad made me sick.

"Rowan! No. I can't!" My hands shot out in exclamation. Rowan shrugged, peeked around the door, and threw the energy ball. My dad watched in horror, followed by complete bewilderment.

"Hey, now! That's not nice." Another voice sounded from the hallway. Shit, there was more than one of them. This time, the energy ball came at an angle across the room in my general direction. On instinct alone, I put up my hands and pushed the energy away from us, sending the dark magic into the wall beside us.

"Nice," Jax said, sitting in front of my dad.

I turned to him with a glare. "I don't need a cheer-leader."

"What?" My dad looked around.

"Dad, grab that box." I gestured toward the box I had been digging in, handing him the album to put in as well. I stood, but my dad grabbed my hand, trying to pull me back. "It's okay. I promise.

"Hey!" I yelled across the room. "Don't you know destruction of private property is illegal?"

In my hand, I began a swirling of white light that I tossed out the door. I assumed it must be someone of Daragon's, and I chastised myself for not expecting something like this, especially after the dream last night.

"Dad, in the bag are bottles of potions. Get them. Jax will help." I pointed to the bag Jax had brought.

Dad pulled it toward him, but I could see he was perplexed about how the cat would help. "The cat?" he asked, and Jax meowuffed at him. "Potions?" The bottles rattled as he searched through the bag. He ducked as a red sphere of energy crashed behind him.

My dad shoved a potion into my hand, and I focused back on Rowan. "What's the plan here?" I demanded, getting worried.

He took the potion, gave it a quick glance, and handed it back to me. "That will work. When I say, you are going to throw it and we will repeatedly throw energy balls at them, as fast as you can, okay? Try and overwhelm them." His eyes fixated on mine.

Inhaling sharply, I swallowed, then nodded. On Rowan's count of three, we acted, and edged closer to the door with each throw.

"Grab another potion. If I know your sister, it should be the color of ice."

My heart scampering, my hand shot out to my dad. He complied, digging through the bag until he grasped one with silver, flowing liquid inside. Passing me another bottle, I felt his hand quaking in the exchange.

"We need to get out of here. Throw this and I will do what I can, but . . ."

"But what?" I shrilled. "What am I supposed to do?" My arms flailed in response. Besides energy balls, it's not like I had practiced much else.

"Be you. You can do this."

My legs wobbled beneath me. If I failed, we might die. *What the hell is he thinking?* Anger rippled through my face, and Rowan smirked.

"Throw the potion."

FML.

I rolled the bottle in my hand, shaking my arm out. Then I threw the bottle toward the two guys outside the door. I was unsure what to expect, and when I peered around the doorway, I saw that the potion had exploded at their feet. A cool, silky glow crept around their bodies in a steady swirl that left them motionless. Frozen. Like ice. Horrified, I stared as they struggled through the magic, trying anything to stall the spell as the cool light encased them.

Rowan went out the door, throwing magic in their direction, but I stuttered in my steps, too petrified to move.

"The potion won't last long. We need to hurry." Rowan encouraged us out the door. "Come on."

My dad acted fast. His face was ashen in response to the magic playing out before him.

"Come on!" Rowan shouted at me.

Being half dragged by Rowan's grip on my arm, I continued to look back at the men captured by the silk glow of the potion. Gathering in front of the elevator, Rowan pushed the down button in quick succession.

Glancing back again, I saw the spell begin to break; there were slight twitches of movement before they were freed completely. The taller of the two thrusted a mass of dark magic toward us. With my dad and Rowan behind me, I panicked; my first thought was to push the magic away, to keep the people I cared about safe.

Away meant back toward them. In an instant, his magic reversed direction. It slammed into the men in a roar of flames, killing them both. They evaporated in one swoop.

Gone, in microseconds.

A deafening silence shattered when the elevator dinged and the door slid open. Shaking uncontrollably in terror at what I had done, Rowan yanked my hand, pulling me into the elevator. My body was a limp noodle, and my dad reached out to steady my movement. I bit down on my trembling lip as I tried to comprehend what happened.

"I . . . I . . . what did I . . . ?" I stuttered. "I'm sorry, I . . ."

Rowan put his hand on my shoulder and a steady calm surrounded me. "Aislynn, you did exactly what needed to be done."

The sharp ding startled me again, and Rowan gently pushed me forward through the doors. *What did that mean? "What needed to be done"? Was I supposed to be a killer?*

"Everything is fine. Act normal." Rowan walked in smooth, fluid motions as if there hadn't been an insane magical battle three floors up.

"Um, Rowan," Dad started in a hushed tone, "I believe we have a small problem in regard to this facility having surveillance and security cameras."

"Yes, John, I took care of that. All that will be seen is we came in and are now walking out. The rest is gone."

My dad pursed his lips. My gaze shifted between the two of them in jerky movements, and I focused on putting one foot in front of the other.

A fierce cold wind blasted us in the face as we exited the building, numbing me further. Rowan opened and closed the door for me as I shifted myself into the car. Their doors closing caused me to jump as silence filled the car.

Images replayed in a constant cycle in my mind: I saw the magic slamming into them, and I shuddered as I was consumed by the thought of what would have happened if I didn't stop the black mass. No one spoke as we drove away.

❧ ⚬◈⚬ ☙

My dad pulled the car in the garage, and the door closed noisily behind us. His movements were jerky as he shut off the engine, trying to speak.

"Aislynn . . . I . . ." He searched for words.

Are there any?

"Thank you," he finished.

My mouth snapped closed. *Not what I expected.* "Dad, I . . . I . . . killed people!" I sputtered.

"No. You saved us." His lips turned up in the smallest smile. "Of course, you can't tell your mother."

Sound spurted from me, a half laugh, half groan.

"Look, I have no idea what just happened," Dad added

183

as he glanced in the rearview mirror. "I trust that you took care of things, to remove . . . any evidence?"

Rowan gave a small nod in response.

"Aislynn, I can't explain the things I saw. I am not sure I would want you to, but I know your grandmother well enough to know that she was involved in things . . ." He paused. "Things that were not anywhere near ordinary, which is what makes your mother crazy. I am quoting Abigail here: 'Just because we are not aware of something or don't understand it, doesn't mean it does not exist.' And . . . I have not been completely upfront with you."

A trace of guilt settled across his eyes as they met mine. I raised my eyebrows silently, waiting for him to continue. Really? More surprises today?

"In fact, I practically forgot until now," he continued. He put an elbow on the edge of the window, then rested his head on his hand. "Your grandmother came to me sometime after telling your mother you would come for her things. Actually, she made an appointment at my office, under a false name so I couldn't avoid her." His head rested back on the seat now, and his exhausted eyes shone as he smiled at me.

"It was quite funny, really. I thought I was meeting a new client and there she was, waiting in the conference room. I was very confused, and she said, 'John, sit down! Aislynn needs your help.' At first, I panicked, thinking something happened at school or you were hurt or sick.

"But she said you would need my help and it would be later, much later, years from then. I gave her one of those 'Abigail, don't start this nonsense' looks, but she cut me off, rather upset. 'John, this is important!' She even smacked her hand on the table. 'I know you aren't going to believe me now; in fact, you won't until it happens, but you must do as I say. Aislynn's life will depend on it.'" He rubbed his hands over his face.

"I have to say, I was pissed off by then, but I listened and agreed to do what she asked. She told me one day I would see impossible things, beyond this world. I thought she had gotten her hands on some tribal peyote or aya-huasca . . . until now. She said I would understand enough to do what I needed to do, and she was right: here we are. I am beginning to realize your grandmother was not the crazy person I thought, nor the one your mother makes her out to be. I just didn't know. It sounded so kooky at the time, but if I could apologize to her, I would." Sorrow resonated through his words and my heart softened.

"Dad, I am sure she knows." I placed my hand on his arm. "I can't say I was all that accepting when Rowan came tromping along." Amusement lit up my voice, but concern flashed over Dad's expression.

"I don't think I want to know." His eyes met Rowan's in the mirror again. "But I have something for you inside."

I sat for a moment as my dad got out of the car. The light dimmed in the garage, then I followed him inside. Back in his office, my dad proceeded to the wall beside his desk and stood in front of a charming landscape painting they had picked up from some art gallery downtown. I arched my eyebrow, waiting until he pulled the picture off the wall, revealing a safe. A burst of laughter shot from my mouth.

"Dad! Seriously? A safe in the wall?" Laughter came easily as an explosion of excess emotion rolled through me.

My dad shrugged with a lopsided smile. I realized he felt cool, which made it that much funnier. Opening the safe, he moved a few things before turning around, holding a box in his hands. It was slightly bigger than the one my grandma gave me all those years ago, covered in the same engravings.

"She gave me this, to give to you. I know what's in it, but she insisted it needed to remain in the box. I thought it was silly because it's only a key." He flipped the box in his hands.

"A key to what?" I asked. Rowan stepped closer to me.

"To a safe-deposit box, downtown. In both your names. No one else is on the account. I advised against this, but she generally didn't listen." He set the box in my hands, which started to glow a blue iridescent light.

"What the—"

I half smiled. "Yeah, don't worry, it does that."

"I am scared to even ask for a detailed version of what is occurring here. Apparently, someone just tried to kill us, which I find concerning as I have no idea how to help or keep you safe. When your grandmother came all those years ago, I had no idea you would be in danger." Defeat melted through him as he sunk into his chair.

My heart twisted. "I know, Dad," I insisted. "I promise, I am alright." My words, however, were unconvincing as his eyes met mine.

"I assume you can open it. I am ashamed to say I tried, with no avail." He flushed with embarrassment.

"I think that's the point."

"Yes, John, if magic sealed the box, then magic must be used to open it. No mechanical attempts would suffice," Rowan's sing-song voice cut in.

My dad grabbed a pad of paper with a sheepish grin and began writing. "Here is the address to the bank. I would assume she is still there, so when you arrive ask for Marcia.

It should all be simple. Oh, the box number is your birthday, of course." He handed me the paper.

"Thank you, Dad. Seriously." Wrapping myself behind the desk, I gave him a hug.

"Please be careful, Aislynn." He squeezed me, and tears stung my eyes.

"Do you need a ride? How did you get here, anyway?" He immediately put up his hand. "No, never mind. I am not sure I want to know."

Rowan smiled. "No, John, you probably do not."

"At this point, I'm not sure if I can help you with anything else, but if there is, Aislynn, please call." His mouth was a firm line, and I saw bravery settle back into his shoulders.

"I will, I promise. Love you." The words rushed out of my mouth. Normally I was not affectionate with my family, so the words sounded somewhat strange coming from my lips. I loved my dad, but my family didn't say 'I love you' regularly . . . or at all.

"Can we go out through the garage?" I asked.

"Sure, whatever you need."

I put the small box in the bag with the potions, and Rowan picked up the cardboard box from the storage facility. Leading the way back out through the garage, I wondered if my mom was still here.

"I figured we could leave from the garage because I refuse to go outside. It's freaking ass cold." I peered over my shoulder, and Jax jumped on the box he carried.

"Can I catch a ride?"

The cat was like a ninja! Where did he come from? The three of us stood in the garage and in a turn of a second, it disappeared. The surroundings of my apartment appeared.

19

"*Well, that was eventful. I am exhausted.*"

My face scrunched, and I glanced down at my cat, bemused. "Really, Jax?"

"*Quiet, human. Need sleep.*" He jumped on my bed with his tail straight in the air, padded across my pillow, then curled up to sleep. Without words, mouth gaping, I turned back to Rowan.

"Okay ... first things are the key and safe-deposit box." I glanced at my phone, checking the time. "The bank is closed, which means we can't do that until Monday morning. Super annoying. We could teleport in, but is that a good idea?"

"Aislynn? Can you stop for a moment?" Rowan asked as I dug through the bag.

"Huh?" I emptied the contents on to the table. "We should probably go through this stuff and figure out where else she may have hidden things."

"Hey." Rowan grabbed my hand, but my eyes darted away in avoidance. Gently, he pulled me to the end of the bed. I felt his intense blue eyes searching mine. "Are you okay?"

Swallowing hard, I kept my gaze deliberately away. I knew what he meant. Of course I did. But I was trying not to think about *that*, and here he was bringing it up. My hand retaliated against me, shaking in Rowan's grasp.

"That was powerful magic you accomplished," he pushed.

My mouth opened, but words did not follow.

"I cannot imagine how you must feel." He pulled my hands in closer.

My emotions, the ones I pushed deep down, started a steady creep to the surface, promising to swallow me whole. *This isn't me. I can't allow this.*

Chewing on my lip, I held my breath and pushed the emotions down. My stomach burned while my skin tingled, and I mentally stomped out the fire. Rowan was aware of everything, as I was too raw to block anything.

"I don't . . ." My lip trembled. "I can't go there."

Rowan sighed, releasing me from his steady gaze. "You are going to have to, eventually." Taking a breath, he let go of my hands. "And I will be here when you do." He stroked my back, soothing me with tidbits of his magic.

Torn between giving in and crying out my eyeballs, my emotions wavered. I just wasn't ready, and I found myself slightly offended by his insistence of forcing me to face everything. I searched the room trying to find a distraction. His magic persisted, comforting like a cool wave lapping at my soul, pulling away pieces of my anxiety. I sighed, relishing in the peace.

However, steadfast in my deserving of self-punishment, a part of me needed to feel the pain. I didn't appreciate my emotions being stripped from me, leaving behind a muted empty hole.

In response, my magic flared, driving his bits back. Stubbornness claimed victory and I reclaimed my unsettled emotions.

"So how do we unlock these boxes?" I stood resolutely and gathered all three, lining them up on the old, weathered coffee table. The one my grandmother gave me all those years ago, the one from the storage unit, and the one from my dad. Rowan gave me one last glance before his final resignation in allowing me to distract myself while simultaneously rejecting his magical valium.

"Well," Rowan began, and picked up the largest box. "There are several ways to perform lock spells, from simple to complex. Some merely are time-based: they open at a certain moment in time, or maybe only a certain person can unlock the spell. Others have keywords or spells attached. There are numerous possibilities." He inspected the box. "I would imagine your grandmother created a spell where only you can open them. She could have a whole set, and they could only open once they are in your possession."

"Perhaps something is in the books?" I reached for the little box. My grandmother had accumulated an excessive amount of information as a professor and throughout her travels. How would I ever home in on the specific things I needed?

I tugged out the book which held her letter, setting the box aside. It was a journal of sorts, and I browsed through the pages which were a scatter of thoughts, ideas, and even spells. Some of the writing I did not recognize.

"Hey, Rowan. What does this say?" I tapped the page. Taking the book, he flipped through several pages, then back, turning the book sideways to read words running up the length of the page. His eyebrows raised periodically as he read.

"And . . . ?" I prodded, but he ignored me for several moments.

"This is rather complex magic . . ."

He skimmed through a few more pages, then muttered, "Wow," followed by a few remarks of "That's interesting" and "Never thought of that."

My leg bounced and rattled the contents of the coffee table. Rowan finally noticed my impatience.

"I don't know who your grandmother worked with, but these are intricate spells, things I have never seen before." He turned the page again. At least he was talking to me now.

"Like what?" I inquired as patiently as I could.

"Well, in Hallervania our magic is ritualistic. As a people, we learn from our ancestors, each family having their own 'line' of magic. But we all follow the same thread when performing magic, like rituals, spells, etc." He rubbed his chin. "For example, everything you did with your sisters, we each carried our own individual flair. This book is beyond that; it takes magic at its core, taking the excess out. Almost like . . . *being* magic."

"Being magic? What do you mean?" I curled my leg underneath me on the couch.

"Well . . . how do I explain? Growing up in Hallervania, learning magic is something we use, a thread of energy we pick up and facilitate to create a potential. But we are not magical. We are using what is already available. This book is about creating magic from yourself, or from nothing."

My thoughts scrambled to a screeching halt. "But you must create from something or somewhere, right? You can't create something from nothing. Doesn't that defy the laws of physics? The universe?" I thought back to a class I had taken and the laws of energy. "Energy cannot be created or destroyed, only manipulated." I wondered if I could apply the physics laws of my Realm to a magical one.

"Exactly," Rowan confirmed. "The complexity of this book is beyond my comprehension." He sat back on the couch, tapping the book on his knee.

My grandmother was a highly intelligent woman who spent an absorbent amount of time in the academic world, obtaining two Ph.D.'s, writing several books, and sitting on multiple committees. She had a voracious need to consume information. If subjected to a world of magic, I could only imagine how intensely she would research every aspect.

"Give me an example of something in there," I asked.

"Well, this isn't a huge example of what we are talking about, but . . . think of the work and ritual in leaving our realm to come to yours. The spells in here are as simple as we teleport. Essentially, it is the same thing, but our people are ingrained with respecting the ceremonial aspect of magic. It seems so perfunctory."

"Okay, so this is about taking the fluff out." I chewed on my fingernail.

Rowan sat thoughtfully, handing back the book. "What else was in the box?" He dragged it closer to inspect.

"Well, a photo album from when I was little and some other books." I peered over the top of the book. He fished around, pulling out a notebook that he inspected right away. After that, both of us were quiet, absorbed in our own thoughts.

"What's this?"

Sometime later, Rowan held up a small white envelope he found stuck between the notebook's pages. Reaching across the couch, I took it from him, inspecting the blank front. It was the size of a small thank you card. I opened the flap to find exactly that: in shimmering silver, the words *With Gratitude* were embossed on the front. Flipping the card open, I read aloud.

Abigail,

I cannot simply describe the gratitude I have for the things you've given me. Knowledge, as we know, is a magnificent gift. I will do the things you have asked of me, not in return for this gift, but because it is my responsibility to do so in this life. The darkest hours are just before dawn and I know you fear the things you learned, but I have hope that nothing is set in stone and we are here to challenge any path set before us, therefore changing it. There are endless oppor-tunities therefore infinite possibilities. You possibly already set in motion the changes necessary to alter the outcome. Do not forget this. When Aislynn comes, as we both know she will, I will give her what she needs. Thank you for opening my eyes to a whole new world.

Always—Winston

"Who the hell is Winston?" I flipped the card over to the back and then the front again. I hadn't been too involved in my grandmother's personal life, as I was fairly young, but I never met anyone she was involved with, nor heard of this person.

"You don't recognize the name?" Rowan questioned.

"No. I don't." I slapped the card against my palm. Winston . . . Winston. Something was buried in the edge of my thoughts. Had I seen the name? Closing my eyes, I thought through everything I had read and seen recently.

"Wait!" Jumping up, I searched the stack of books I had chosen to bring back from Hallervania. I grabbed the one I wanted. "I think . . ." I searched through the pages quickly. I remembered it was on the left side of a page, something small, barely noticeable. I flipped again. "Yes!"

I peeled myself off the floor, handing the book to Rowan. "I knew I saw something." I pointed to the scribble of words.

"This is hardly legible. What does that say?" Rowan squinted his eyes.

The words scrawled in the corner of the page didn't seem to relate to anything else, and suddenly the intricacy of my grandmother's plans was overwhelming. This book had been hidden in Hallervania; the off chance that I brought it here had to be a miracle.

Or magic.

The note from Winston was in a book from a storage unit in Eden Prairie. Two separate objects as far apart as physically possible, seemingly unconnected, both tied together to make this clue. I pulled my MacBook into my lap, waking it from its slumber. A part of me was astounded by the extent she used to keep things hidden.

What drove her need for this? Fear?

The scrawling on the page that seemed insignificant read *U–Winston*. I remembered seeing the words one night in Hallervania. At the time, it made me curious but didn't mean anything. However, with the note from Winston, it became obvious.

Clicking on the Safari icon, I opened the University of Minnesota website. My grandmother taught at the U of M at the end of her career and always referred to it as "the U." The connection was only simple in context. In the Administration tab, I searched for the name Winston.

"U–Winston? What does that mean?" Rowan asked, eyebrows raised.

"This." I turned my MacBook around. The results had yielded an Edwards III, Winston, edwardsIII@umn.edu, Dept./College Astrophysics.

"How did you know that's what this meant?"

"I remembered seeing it. In the book by itself, it meant nothing, but with the card, it's simple." I curled my legs underneath me, bouncing on my toes.

"So what do you want to do?"

Glancing to the corner of my screen I considered the time. The midafternoon hour gave me little hope. "Well, let's go to the U and see if he is there. Anything is possible."

20

I shrugged into my coat again, adding a thick black scarf and beanie, and stuffed the card into my pocket. Tendrils of my bangs hung over my eyes and I shoved them under the beanie. I gave Rowan a general idea of where we were going: Winston's office in Tate Hall. Fairly familiar with the campus and the Tate building, the Lab of Physics was located on the East Bank. Rowan settled his hand on my shoulder and my apartment disappeared.

Shadowed by the side of the building, secluded from prying eyes, the campus seemed quiet in the dusky after-noon light. Secluded meant we stood in about eighteen inches of drifted snow. Looking down at my buried boots, I sneered at Rowan.

"Sorry," Rowan said with a sly grin. My nose scrunched as I shook my boots off one at a time.

We stomped our way to the sidewalk running the length of Tate Hall. The front entrance had been recently remodeled, giving it a more modern flare, but I preferred the massive old columns that had stood sentinel to the essence and history of the building. Rowan pulled open the door for me and I checked the directory, looking for an office number.

"This way." I pointed as we headed upstairs to the third floor. Following the signs, we weaved our way to office 313. The frosted glass on the door was etched with the name *Professor W. Edwards III.* Glancing at Rowan, I took a breath and knocked. I was certain there would be no reply. I began to turn to leave; the chances of him being in his office were slim.

"Come in!" a clipped British accent muffled from inside the office called out. Lifting my eyebrow in surprise I pushed open the door.

A rather tall, slim man sat behind an impossibly unkempt desk. The office was stacked full of books, file boxes, and layers of whiteboards littered with math problems of some kind. It all left the room feeling cramped and teeming with unfilled potential.

Several large framed degrees hung on the wall behind the whiteboards, barely visible. A small lamp glowing an amber hue sat on the desk, lending light to the papers he read.

"Hello." He met my eyes with a narrowed expression as he set the papers on the desk.

"Hi, um . . . are you Winston?" I asked with hesitation, chewing on my lip. Not how I would usually address a professor in normal circumstances; clearly my nerves were eating away at my manners. My grandma would have smacked me on the side of my head.

"Yes. *Professor* Winston Edwards the Third. How may I help you?" His precise British accent corrected my use of his first name. Offering his hand, I found it warm and soft in contrast to the cold of mine.

"I am hoping you can help me."

He gestured for us to sit. I reached in my pocket, offering him the card. His hand wavered for the quickest moment as he recognized the familiar white cardstock and his lips turned up slightly.

"So, today is the day." Peering down at the card for a moment, his eyes pinched at the corners, as if truly seeing us rather than glancing at some random students bursting into his office.

I nodded with a small smile. "I'm Aislynn."

"Aislynn, it is a true honor and pleasure, let me assure you. And you must be Rowan." His smoky gray-blue eyes brightened. Rowan nodded as he sat back in the chair.

"I have been waiting for this day." The professor held up the card in gesture. "Your grandmother came to me so many years ago. I really do miss her." A sad smile crossed his mouth.

"How did you meet her? Was it here at the University?" I questioned, my curiosity peaked.

"Actually, no. We met many years ago in the late eighties or early nineties. She came to a lecture of mine at Cambridge. I just finished my doctoral work at Oxford, and she sought me out distinctly because of my area of expertise."

"Physics?" I asked, perplexed. What did physics have to do with this?

"Physics, Astrophysics, and Quantum Mechanics, particularly my thesis work. Nuclear Transmutation." He leaned forward, elbows resting on the desk with his hands in a steeple under his chin. I raised my eyebrow, pulling off my beanie and shoving it in my coat pocket.

"Abigail was a unique woman. I finished my lecture, began to gather my things, and she came on stage, telling me how much she enjoyed the lecture. She asked if I had time for some questions. Your grandmother was stunning in her day, and I made sure I had the time." He winked at me and I couldn't help but giggle.

"I was a bit pompous at that particular time of my life, having just finished my second Ph.D., but I was not quite prepared for the things she brought to my attention." Something about the way he spoke made me instantly like him.

"She, gregarious in her approach with me, wanted to know if I believed in time travel or if teleportation was possible. I must say, I was quite surprised and a bit irritated. I tossed it off as some American woman with a half-deluded fantasy, unaware of actual mathematical science, the workings of the universe, and the laws that govern it. But your grandmother . . . deluded she was not. She had done some very interesting research on the subject and presented it all rather humbly. She enamored me, fiercely intelligent and entwined in her work. We began working together more closely, delving into areas I hadn't previously considered." He smiled at the memory of her, removing his glasses and folding them on the desk.

"A part of me was aware she was not telling me everything, and there were aspects I was certainly missing. Because she fascinated me. Perhaps a smidge twitterpated, I didn't press too much. But I knew we were not researching these possibilities because she was merely interested in the idea. I hoped eventually she would tell me, and one day she did." He held up the card.

"This card is a symbol of the workings of the universe, almost too impossible to comprehend. When I wrote this all those years ago, it was part of a test, you see. The letter was in part a note of sincerest gratitude to your grand-mother, but it also held another purpose, which brings us to this moment." He toggled the card in the air, and I imagined how his students must love his flair for the dramatics. "This card traveled through time to bring you to this moment, a catalyst for future events." He handed the card back to me. In my hands, I acknowledged the complexity of what he said. *Without this card, would I be here? Possibly?*

"You see, there are endless possibilities, always. But to receive an outcome you desire, you must play an active role in producing the outcome."

I didn't want to admit to myself that this delved into a world which was a complete enigma to me. It was like trying to wrap my head around the intricacy of the space-time continuum. When I thought of time and all the choices I made daily, I acknowledged that each resulted in different consequences. If I examined the variables of if I had done this instead of that, where would I be, the outcomes were endless.

We were all inevitably tied to those that were in our lives by the choices we made, and sometimes, like in the case of Winston, the choices others made, even though we had never met. The Butterfly Effect at its finest.

This brought on another question: were we destined on our paths all along? Were there no such variables? My mind reeled. I hated philosophy.

"Ah, but I am getting off track," Winston said, and he winked again. "You just have no idea what an enjoyable journey this has been for me. Your grandmother and I worked for a number of years before she finally disclosed everything. She had been traveling between Realms for some time, without my knowledge, devilish fox. But when she had been followed back, we came across a little problem. Obviously, she had no choice in telling me everything and rather hastily.

"Of course, I was bewildered and astonished she had not only teleported, moving from one location to another, but also traveled to another dimension. Science's most enthralling theories! It took time for me to believe this new reality and I tried to analyze it from a scientific point of view, as is my nature. But your grandmother would have none of that. She said to me, 'Winston, it just is. There is no explaining magic. That is *why* it is called magic.' Who could argue with her?"

Only an astrophysicist, I presumed. "She was followed?"

"Yes. Imagine my surprise when she came rushing into my lab, followed by two rather unsightly chaps who were none too pleased that she escaped their magical attempts of torture."

I sat up in my chair, eyes wide. "Wait, what? How involved was she?"

Until this point, I had been dismissive of realizing what part my grandmother played thus far. She traveled to Hallervania, was aware of the prophecy, and was trying to help me fulfill my destiny . . . but was that it?

"How involved, love?" the professor smirked. "My

dear, she uncovered the Tree of Elements, the lost magic of the Elements, and your part in the rebalancing."

My heart jumped when Winston mentioned the Tree of Elements. "She *uncovered* it?"

"Of course. Don't you have the amulet?" Bewilderment filled Winston's face.

"Amulet?" I repeated in confusion. Rowan looked back and forth between the two of us.

"But . . . how is this possible? Abigail said you would," Winston stammered out the words in frustration.

"What amulet?" I insisted.

"The Elemental Amulet, of course." He started moving around his office in search of something among the mess. "I suppose, perhaps, I should have started with this." He dug through his filing cabinet.

"Here we are." He set another wood box on the desk.

This one was larger than the rest, a stunning walnut carved intricately with spirals bounding out from the center design to the corners and down the sides. Inlaid into the design were bright colorful crystals representing the elements. From the center a swirl of limbs and branches edged out from the main stem of a tree. I was unsure why I didn't recognize it before, but being larger in size, made it easier to see.

The boxes represented the Tree of Elements.

Winston held his hand over the center of the box, igniting a steady blue light. He watched the light brighten and dim before he flipped the lid open. I glanced at Rowan, catching his eye.

"Ta-da!" Winston laughed. "I am afraid that is about as magical as I get. I wish Abigail had taught me more, but she said I lacked any real talent." Another full belly laugh filled the room, and I couldn't help my smile. I imagined the two of them; what a pair they would have been.

"Ah, here we are!" the professor moved several things around and handed me an envelope. Instantly, I recognized my grandmother's handwriting across the front.

My Darling Aislynn,

Bravo! I do hope you aren't tiring of these letters. However, you must have put together a clue or two, to find my dear Winston. Isn't he just delightful? Keep him focused; he gets off track easily. I have to say this has been rather fun to put together, like a good, thrilling book.

Back to the important things. I do hope you are well. I know you've experienced difficult things and you are doing your best to not deal with them, but please allow those around you to help. I am asking the impossible, I know.

You can trust Winston unconditionally. He will give you the things I left for you. He helped me many times and always kept my secret safe. I do adore that man.

As Winston may have told you, I discovered the prophecy many years ago. I found the Elemental Amulet and began a quest to find its purpose, our purpose. Of course, I did not expect what I found, as is the case most of the time.

The Amulet is the beginning, Aislynn, and it's already in your possession. I gave it to you all those years ago to keep you both protected. It's been hidden in magic, although at this point, I imagine the strongest aspects have worn off considerably, which is why there are others after you. It became magically available to be "seen" once again.

The Elemental Amulet is the most important aspect of the Prophesy, holding each of the elements safe as you collect them. It was magically created to hold the power of each element as a failsafe in case of a magical cataclysmic event. Each of the elements would be held in a singular place together in safeguard.

If you are not wearing the Amulet, please put it on immediately, designating you as the new Keeper of Elements. The ancient magic used to create the Amulet will protect you in ways you may have experienced by now, but please *do not think it will protect you indefinitely. There is no magic available to do this, not completely.*

Find the other things I have left for you and continue your journey.

As always, with all my love,

Grandma

These letters were becoming intense. I wiped my eye as I handed it to Rowan.

"I do have the amulet. I just wasn't aware." I cleared my throat to speak. Winston nodded in response.

"How did she come in possession of the Amulet?" Rowan asked.

"Well now, that is a thrilling story!" His eyes sparkled. I guessed Winston's true passion was in telling stories. "Your grandmother was quite the adventurer. As you know, she studied many areas and attended many educational lectures across the world. On one of these trips, she was studying in the area of ancient civilizations and documents, on a tour of sorts, I believe. Multiple lectures as well as touring the local areas, historical buildings, areas, and so on.

"They were in Newgrange, just outside of Dublin, at an ancient temple constructed long before Stonehenge and the Egyptian Pyramids, which fascinated Abigail. After touring the temple, everyone broke for lunch, and your grandmother was working on one of her books, collecting research, et cetera. She found a spot away from everyone to work, take notes, and eat.

"Distinctly clear in her description—although she didn't know at the time—but magic began to build around her, and the energy shifted. She stopped reading and glanced around, trying to understand the thrumming in the air, which no one else seemed to notice. Then, as quickly as it started, it ceased.

"Abigail looked around, searching but found nothing she could discern as the source. Giving up, she resorted back to her reading when she saw something in front of her, glistening in the dirt. As she brushed away the dirt, she found a rather large crystal. Curious, she kept at it until eventually, she uncovered a box, much like this one, but smaller. She continuously checked to make sure no one was watching her. Thankfully, she had gone far enough away from everyone on the tour.

"After digging out the entire box, she opened the lid. She said it glowed and inside was the amulet. Like a dream, she held it out in the sunlight, besotted with the piece. The tour group gathered to leave, and she hastily put the necklace back in the box and in her bag. Later, she told me how upset she was with herself treating an artifact in such a way. She couldn't explain why she did what she did, almost like she was drawn to do it.

"Of course, upon returning from the tour, she began searching for information on the necklace, trying to find the origins, beginning with Ireland. Let's face it: what she did was unquestionably illegal, so she had to be discreet. However, no one could help her, even through all her connections.

"The necklace became an obsession. But how do you find information on something which is not of this world? Almost impossible, until destiny cut in. About a year later, she was visiting a little college in Pennsylvania or maybe Virginia . . . anyway, she showed the necklace to a friend of hers, an archaeologist. Though fascinated by the necklace, she could provide no new information for Abigail. In turn, the friend asked another colleague of hers to take a look, who was instantly captivated and inspected it with enthusiasm. She insisted on knowing where it was found, when, and how.

"Your grandmother was thrilled she finally found someone who was interested. They met later for dinner to discuss the amulet further. The woman couldn't believe an artifact actually existed; you see, she'd been studying for years the history of a lost land. That was how she referred to it: a lost land. She had generational stories, written accounts of events, but nothing as concrete as evidence. It all appeared as only a story, a fable or legend, much like Atlantis. This was a side project to her doctoral work, finding these small pieces of an unknown history. She may have been as obsessed as our Abigail." Winston gave a small chortle. Rowan reached forward in his seat, resting his elbows on his knees.

"When your grandmother studied her work, she concluded there must be more. This couldn't be a series of made up fables; the necklace proved this place existed. I think, in all reality, her belief that it was more kept her searching. With the new information, she dug deeper and we both know once your grandmother has her teeth in something . . ." He smiled, gazing to a faraway place that held the memory of her. An intimate fondness emanated from him.

Several thoughts came together at once for me: Winston revealed a side of my grandmother I didn't know, a tenacious woman who became determined to uncover a secret realm, intertwining my destiny while doing so. I had in my possession an elemental amulet with the capacity of holding ancient elemental magic. The happenstance way in which the amulet appeared seemed strange, and it occurred to me that it was hardly chance at all.

"The ever-questing astrophysicist and cosmologist in me has always pondered: because she found the amulet and began her journey of knowledge, did she unknowingly draw you into a destiny that would have been obtained by someone else? Or was this your destiny all along, and the amulet was just the catalyst setting your destiny in motion?" His thought trailed, and I could see after all these years this still troubled him.

"Really, Winston," I began, deciding it was now appropriate to use his first name. "I don't think it matters, because I'm here and the elements are now my destiny."

After I said the words, I realized I'd just voiced my own form of acceptance. Rowan tilted his head in my direction. Winston eyed me with a quiet acquiescence.

"You know, my dear child, perhaps you are the perfect person for this impossible quest. More so than I ever believed until this moment."

"You are absolutely right, Winston." Rowan let his hand settle on my shoulder. He'd been quiet until this point, allowing his conviction in me and my destiny to permeate. Winston's face held a certain reluctance. Like with my father, he had given me small pieces to my puzzle but, they could do no more. Neither of them was accustomed to feeling helpless.

"Well, I hope I helped you in giving information you needed at this point," Winston said. "I am sure there will be moments when my assistance might be needed again, and for those, I shall be waiting to help in any way I can. Let me give you my cell. I recognize you have other ways of reaching me, so do not be shy about 'popping in' at any moment." He scribbled his number, handing me the paper.

"Aislynn," he added, "I am certain you are more capable than anyone to follow your grandmother's trail down the rabbit hole."

My lips turned upward as we stood. "Thank you. For everything." I looked around the small office.

"You can leave from here if you would like." Winston's eyes sparkled. "It delights me to see scientific impossibilities." A small wink from Winston and we disappeared.

21

Half a second later, my apartment once again appeared and I sloughed off my coat. Jax peeked at our existence through glazed sleepy eyes and tucked his head tighter against himself.

Taking a breath, I sat cross-legged in front of the coffee table, pulling the smallest box toward me. This one held the amulet, the other held the safe deposit key, and the bigger one . . . well, who knew?

I gave Rowan half a glance and chewed on my bottom lip, realizing once I opened the box, I was sealing my fate and accepting my "destiny." I would be Keeper of Elements, Reclaimer of the elements from Dark, and overall Saver of the universe.

Okay, so the last bit might be pushing it.

Sarcasm aside, I recognized when I claimed the amulet as mine, I could not fail. Of course, I could fail, but I refused. I would reset the balance of magic with a fierceness of—

"Would you just open the damn box?"

"Jax! I was having a moment!" I snapped. Rowan stifled a roar of laughter.

"No. You were dragging your feet."

He padded toward me, jumping on the table and sitting among the boxes. I arched a brow at him. Perhaps his comical wit was the distraction I needed to set aside the enormity of what I was doing. Or maybe he was just an asshole.

I picked up the carved box, turning it in my hand. This entire time, a powerful magical artifact had been in a little girl's possession. An incandescent blue light pulsed brightly, and I was aware of the amulet inside. A throbbing of power tingled up my arm.

The trail of magic trickled into me, connecting and intertwining with my own power. How could I deny what I felt? Hovering my hand above the box, I closed my eyes. With a click, the box opened, along with my eyes. Right away, the amulet within reminded me of the Tree of Elements.

Twisted silver created the base and prongs to hold each of the elements. A perfect faceted amethyst sat in the middle with a chain of infinity twists wrapped over one another. I pulled the chain delicately, holding up the amulet as the power pulsated through me.

I caught Rowan and Jax's eyes as I settled it over my head, the amulet resting at my solar plexus. A deep violet light radiated from the silver looping through each of the infinity chains, expanding into me.

A distinctly different magic coursed through my being as the amulet accepted me as the new Keeper. Now, I became aware of each of the elements and their existence out there, somewhere, as if they called to me.

"Huh, I thought there would be music. Perhaps a booming voice that said: 'You are now Keeper of Elements!' I am somewhat disappointed." Jax jumped off the coffee table, landing with a "Hmph" as he sauntered away. *"I guess that only happens in the movies."*

My eyes closed slowly. "That cat . . ."

"He is something else." Rowan looked after him with a smirk. "Well, how do you feel?"

I was aware of him reading me, trying to sense me and the magic, but a hesitation in his face made me curious. "Good. I feel great; awesome, really. I can sense the elements out there."

"Do you know where they are?" An expectant hope drizzled through his voice.

"No. Just that they are there, waiting. I think . . ." I focused, and although it was indistinguishable, I had the idea that one was in this Realm while the others were elsewhere. *Strange.*

"You think what?" Rowan tried when I faded off.

"I'm not sure," I replied. The feeling fizzled. It was like trying to remember a dream in the morning. "I will need to focus on them." A charged excitement overtook me, and I thought about teleporting to the bank. *Screw waiting!*

But dealing with alarms, cameras? Not completely sure what Rowan had done at the storage unit, I wasn't sure I wanted to risk that again. It was probably better to go legitimately, which meant we had a day and a half to kill before Monday morning.

Plus, I had another box. With my newfound power, I hovered my hand over the largest box. Nothing happened. My lips pursed, and discontentment settled over me.

"I am not sure what type of spell your grandmother

used on those boxes, but I am guessing you are not meant to open that one yet."

"Maybe so." I huffed, resting against the couch. "I feel like we should be doing something, but I have no idea what, or where."

"Well, we have the amulet and we know you are supposed to find and control the elements. It's a start," Rowan said, leaning back in the chair.

"I am holding hope in the safe-deposit box. A map would be nice. Earth is here! But I know my grandmother well enough; she wouldn't dare. Everything has been outlandish thus far, and I'm impressed we have figured out this much."

"Do you think after the bank we should return to Hallervania?" Rowan asked.

"I can't imagine why not. Not much else to do here, except being maimed by Daragon . . . although that seems to happen anywhere. I wonder what his place is in this?"

"Besides chaos, destruction, and malicious intent?" Rowan spat.

"No, he has a bigger role in this. In fact, I think he knew I was destined to reclaim the elements before I did. I think his attacks were preemptive."

"Preemptive? Daragon? Hardly. Ailianna would have seen it." Rowan dismissed my thoughts.

The more I thought about my dreams and Daragon's smug, nonchalant attitude, I was certain he knew more than we believed. "I also think he recognized that he couldn't stop this, but he wanted to scare me. Perhaps he thought he could kill me or change some aspect of the future. Deep down he knew he couldn't, so he created chaos, distraction, anything to slow me. Which may mean he has the element's locations or is after them."

The White Witch's words "magical event" crossed my mind. I knew I needed to find more information about Daragon.

"What about your Council meetings? Did they uncover anything?"

Rowan leaned forward in the chair, resting his elbows on his knees. "Nothing specific. Their Seer, as well as Aili-anna, can only see that he is after you." He seemed to be considering my train of thought. "If they know about the elements, that is news to me." Agitation filtered into his words, as he considered his position in the Council and the knowledge they shared with him.

We searched through my grandma's books again, look-ing for anything on him or the elements. After a while, my stomach protested the lack of lunch and I realized it was almost dark again.

"Hey, Rowan? Does Thai food sound good for din-ner?"

"Thai?"

"Oh yeah, never mind. You'll like it. I promise." I made a quick call to my favorite Thai place and informed Rowan the food would arrive in forty minutes. He seemed a little perplexed by the entire process but shrugged. Ailianna was much better at this hosting business.

Jax convinced Rowan to watch a movie, mentioning something about fully immersing him into our culture. When I sat down next to them, I realized that Jax picked *Harry Potter*. I held back my laughter, but I relished the mo-ment to zone out for a while. The food arrived, and Rowan and I greedily ate our dinner while sitting in front of the TV.

Harry Potter and the Sorcerer's Stone neared its end, and Rowan was completely entranced. I was not about to inform him there were seven more movies, although Jax probably had already done so. My thoughts were interrupted by the doorbell ringing.

"Who the . . . ?" Face scrunched with confusion, I dragged myself off the couch to the door. I peeked through the peephole.

Shit! My friend Amy stood on the other side, scrolling through her phone. Pinching the bridge of my nose, I contemplated not opening the door, then gave in.

"So, you aren't dead!" Amy proclaimed, beginning to shed her coat and scarf revealing a Twins sweatshirt and jeans. She pushed her way inside.

"No, I'm not. Am I supposed to be?" I asked, shutting the door behind her.

"Well, yeah! Because you didn't answer my texts. Or phone calls. Since last night! So I kind of figured you got knifed by Leslie or chopped up by one of those serial killers that lurk about." Amy may or may not be slightly dramatic.

I forgot about my phone and her texts in the diner. *Shit.* Thankfully, I only had missed twenty-four hours and not two months. Not that I had service in Hallervania; that would be a new kind of "roaming."

"What have you been doing anyway?" Oh!" Her own question was cut off when she noticed Rowan sitting on my couch, Jax perched on his lap. "Oh indeed! Hellooo!" She drew out the "o" sound, making it flirty.

Inwardly I groaned. I shouldn't have let her in. "Rowan, Amy. Amy, Rowan." I waved my hand at them, then drew Amy toward the kitchen and away from Rowan.

"Well, no wonder she hasn't answered her phone."

I couldn't see her face, but I was certain she wiggled her eyebrows.

"Pleasure to meet you, Amy." Rowan delighted her with his sing-song voice.

"Oh, where are you from?" She cocked her head toward me and mouthed, *Oh my God!*

"From very far away!" I groaned. This wouldn't end, not with Amy.

"Ooh, foreign hotties. Yum." She raised her eyebrow, setting her purse on the counter. "I brought back your book. I figured if I found you dead, I would keep it, but I guess I'm outta luck." She slid the latest best seller across the counter.

"Thanks."

"Sure. So, what's with Mr. Hottie McStuffin's over there?" She pulled out the stool and rested her chin in her hand, ten thousand questions swimming in her green eyes.

"It's not what you think." I handed her a glass of water.

"He is on your couch, petting your cat. Like, it totally *is* what I think. Wait . . . your cat is allowing himself to be touched?"

"Yeah, well, I don't like to be touched by the crazy folk."

My lips instantly pulled in to hold back my burst of laughter. "Uh, yeah, they . . . like each other." I took a sip of water to hide my smile.

"That doesn't say much about Hottie. That cat is an asshole."

"Right back at you, Squirrel."

Behind Amy, Rowan grinned like a fool. I continued to hide my inner knowledge of the other half of the conversation. "Well, he's . . ."

"Hey, what is that?" she interrupted again when I faded off. Amy reached out to grab the amulet. A sudden surge of magic shot through me, and Amy gave a small cry of pain as the amulet zapped her. She pulled away, shaking her fingertips.

"Um . . ." I didn't know what to say. *Oh, that's just an ancient elemental amulet which I will use to save magic for Light, and save the universe, too. Why?*

Before I could gather any coherent explanation, Amy plowed on.

"It looks familiar . . ." She leaned in closer but refused to touch it. I wondered if the choice was conscious.

"It does?" I asked. "I highly doubt that."

"No, it does!" Amy insisted. "I swear I've seen the design somewhere."

"You have?" I glanced past her at Rowan, raising my eyebrow. Jax sat up on his lap.

"Yeah, I just . . . I am not sure where. So familiar, though." She was hyper-focused on the necklace, as if she couldn't look away. "Maybe from work? I will think of it."

As a fellow graphic designer at another local firm, both Amy and I came across a lot of design concepts. It was entirely possible she saw something similar, but still, this was strange.

I grabbed her arm. "If you do, will you please tell me?" I pleaded.

"Sure . . . if you answer your phone," she snarked in response. "I guess I better go. You enjoy Mr. Hottie." She wiggled her eyebrows again. My eyes shot upward toward the ceiling as I shook my head. "Oh, and I'm glad you aren't dead. Nice to meet you, Rowan!" she added in her sweetest tone.

We half hugged, and she waved and sauntered out the door before Rowan had the chance to respond.

"She is exhausting." I plopped down on the couch just as Dumbledore awarded points to the houses in the great hall.

"Are you ready for the Chamber of Secrets?*"*

I laughed at my cat, but my inner Harry Potter geek was content as I curled up on the couch to enjoy the movie. Then I remembered my phone.

I dug it out of my bag, and sure enough, there were three missed calls from Amy with two voicemails and at least twenty-six texts from her. *She is absolutely insufferable.* Mostly she did that to annoy the crap out of me. She found it funny. My smile faded, however, when I also saw a missed call from my mother, and a voicemail. *Shit.* I clicked to listen.

"Hi, Aislynn. I wanted to apologize for this morning. I hope you understand. When it comes to your grandmother, well, I just . . . I am sorry. I hope you had a good day. See you soon."

My thumb hesitated over the delete button. I knew it was left purely on behalf of my father and his insistence. I deleted the message and wrote out a quick text to her as Harry was pulled into the flying car.

Hey, mom. No worries. I am sorry I upset you. XOXO

I grabbed the microfiber fleece blanket off the back of the couch and wrapped myself into the world of Hogwarts. Eventually, I fell sound asleep.

Two paws kneaded into my arm, one subtle push after another, again and again. His precisely sharpened claws pierced my skin with each push, and I forced my eyes open.

"Seriously?" I groaned. "You can talk to me, but you have to be all catlike and knead me?"

"I must knead." Jax continued his pushing with dirty cat eyes.

"Uggghhh!" I threw the blanket over my head, curling up against his incessant claws.

"Your phone has been lighting up like a Christmas tree for the last hour. I think it's crazy girl."

"I don't care!" I snapped, my voice muffled from under the blanket. I wanted to go back to my happy sleep place, the best sleep I had in months. The best part? There were no dreams involving Daragon. Embarrassment crept over me, realizing I had slept on the couch all night. Jax ignored me, resuming his kneading.

"Fine!" I threw the blanket off my head. My phone lit up again with another text and I grabbed it. Sure enough, it was Amy. I scrolled back to the beginning of her ramblings.

OMG! I remember.

I knew I had seen it before.

The necklace, I mean. The one you were wearing?

I had the CRAZIEST dream the other night.

It was SO bizarre. I was in this other place, like another planet or something, I don't know. But I could do magic! So freaking cool. All Darth Vader like—throwing energy balls at douchebags that wanted to kill me. ANYWAY.

All of a sudden you show up and start saying we have to get out of here. Dude, you were sort of crazy. But you had the necklace on! Except it was different. Somehow. I don't remember.

I remember. It had colors. That's why I didn't remember. There was blue, red, and yellow glowing within it. I remember thinking I wanted to design something similar for a client. Anyway. Crazy. So yeah.

I told you I had seen it.

Call me.

Jax leaned over my shoulder with catlike disgust. *"Darth Vader uses a lightsaber. He doesn't throw energy balls. Idiot."*

"Be nice, Jax," I said, laughing. This was interesting. Why would Amy of all people be dreaming about me and my current predicament? Although it shouldn't have, a fleeting feeling of hope settled through me. She *saw* the elements within the necklace.

"Interesting, indeed. Who knew that one had an ounce of magic in her?"

"You think she has gifts?" I said, looking at Jax and smoothing out my blanket.

"Well, everyone has magic within them. But it's more about the availability to reach the magic. It all depends on how far down the family line the magic lies, how strong it is, how suppressed it is . . . there are many variables.

"For most people, it is so far away, buried and inconceivable, that it doesn't exist. Which is why in your Realm magic remains hidden. But when you look, it's there, hidden in the shadows."

Hidden in the shadows? What did that mean? If magic powers, elemental magic, and talking cats for crying out loud, all existed, what else was there? My mind leapt through possibilities which I immediately shut down. I didn't want to know. And yet, I had the feeling I would find out regardless.

We spent most of Sunday being lazy. Another front moved through during the night, leaving another couple inches of snow to the already thick blanket. Apparently, Jax and Rowan made it to the beginnings of *Goblet of Fire* before Rowan surrendered to heavy eyelids. They renewed their enthusiasm and continued the Harry Potter marathon.

After showering, I bounced between half watching the movies and sketching a pencil portrait of Rowan's profile. I dragged my pencil in sharp points, adding the stubble on his jaw line. Drawing always soothed my anxiety and helped me feel in control.

Our plan was to head to the bank first thing in the morning, retrieve the contents of the safety deposit box, and return to Hallervania. Rowan was concerned that the longer we stayed here, the more we left ourselves open to another attack from Daragon.

After a while, I switched to charcoals, working on an image of Jax curled in Rowan's lap. I tossed the drawing pad down on the table and switched to my grandmother's books, trying to find more answers.

I was excited when I found a little information on Daragon in the books I had brought. His family was listed in a short section of Dark Practitioners my grandmother compiled. His family line had a deep fracture because of those who embraced the Dark side of magic—*talk about family drama problems*. The choice to use Dark included a skewed version of the rules.

For Rowan and the people of Hallervania, using magic

for Light was to harm none. Dark, well . . . they didn't care so much about a small, pesky thing. Those who practiced Dark seemed to take a slow spiral to the sinister side of magic. *How Dark did Daragon take his magic? And who might he be working with or for?*

When they were deep into the *Half-Blood Prince* learning of Horcruxes, I read my grandmother's book. My mind drifted to the elements. I wondered about the complexity of hiding an element and what that entailed. What in the world were they thinking? How did sending a twenty-seven-year-old who knew nothing of magic on a quest to do the greatest magic in thousands of years make sense?

Great freaking idea. I tossed the book in my hand on the coffee table in frustration. My mind ran incoherent with a million different ideas, but I chose to dismiss them and fade into Harry Potter Land, drifting away . . .

I found myself standing in the deep snow outside the physics building at the University of Minnesota. The sky was dusky from the sun sitting low on the horizon, casting gray shadowed light across the snow. Looking around, I found Daragon standing about fifty feet away, dressed in his usual black with the addition of a long black trench coat.

"What are you doing here?" Daragon asked, startled by my presence.

"I might ask you the same." I trudged through the snow toward him, chunks sticking to my skinny jeans.

"Perhaps. I need to ask a certain professor a question."

"Perhaps you should stay away from him." My voice held a biting edge. Closer to him now, I saw slight hesitation sitting in his eyes. Then it hit me: for the first time, I had just astral traveled to him in current time, rather than him to me in dreamland.

"Well, aren't we full of ourselves?" he smirked at me. "Find a boost of confidence, did we?"

"Missing some friends of yours?" I asked as his eyes sparked with anger.

"Yes, that was mildly annoying." Hesitation distracted him, and I moved closer. A quiet "ah" sound escaped as he caught a glance of the amulet.

"You are mildly annoying," I said. The campus was deserted due to the cold and the hour, so I created a white-hot energy ball in my hand. I kept it at my side in case anyone came near. I watched Daragon as he decided on a plan. His eyes darted to the few lit windows of the physics building, then back to me.

"Don't even think about it!" I spat.

"You have no idea what you are doing. I am and will always be five steps ahead of you." He retreated to his usual smug attitude and took a casual step toward me. "You will never succeed in getting all the elements."

I, however, could take his taunting; I'd successfully drawn his attention away from Winston. Now he was focused on me, a panther stalking his prey.

"I guess we will have to wait and see, won't we?" My expression shifted angrily, and tiny shards of fire sparked through me and into my hand. The magic transformed with my emotions, the white ball now bleeding with vibrant reds. "Or maybe we should see right now."

I pushed my magic at him. My energy ball hurled forward, but he blocked with his own black ball. The magic collided with a sound reminiscent of thunder and a shock-wave rocked back toward us.

The wave pulsed through me and threw Daragon to the ground. My mouth rolled into a smirk as I took a few steps to him. Empowered by magic, I finally felt like I had the upper hand. Resting on elbows sunk in the deep snow, he furrowed his eyebrows and his lip curled in disgust. I gathered another ball of energy.

"Don't move. I *will* reclaim the elements for Light and no one is going to stop me . . . especially not you." My voice resonated through the cold air, riding the wave of confidence that the magic bolstered within me.

Daragon's eyes darkened before he vanished. I extinguished the magic in my fingertips. Blowing out my breath, I glanced down at my hands, now completely normal in the wind's chill. Just moments ago, I'd felt like I could take on anything . . . but now, a bit of fear crept into my stomach. How much control did I really have? I looked toward the physics building. Thinking of Winston, I blinked then stood in his office.

The room was empty.

"Dammit," I said to myself, rolling my lip in my teeth. I was aware this was an astral projection, but I was unsure of the limits of my capabilities.

I thought about my phone. I reached in my pocket and to my surprise I could feel my phone in my fingers. I punched in Winston's personal cell.

"Hello?" Winston's voice called, and my heart calmed.

"Are you safe?"

"Aislynn. Why yes, just enjoying some tea. Is something wrong?" Concern rolled through his voice.

"I think it's okay, I wanted to make sure. Talk soon." I hung up and felt myself being pulled.

"Aislynn, wake up."

Suddenly I was aware of Jax's heavy body on my chest. I blinked and met sapphire cat eyes boring into mine.

"Where were you?"

Sitting up, I noticed my phone rested on the table in front of me. Scooping it up, I checked my recent calls. Sure enough, an outbound call was made at 4:37 to Winston. My eyes widened, and I thought my head might explode.

"Best to try not to make sense of it," Rowan suggested, interrupting my thoughts.

"I was dreaming, but it was too real to be a dream." I explained to Rowan and Jax what happened.

"Your power is expanding with the amulet and will continue to do so."

"Things are becoming more dangerous by the minute here. I am not sure how much longer we can stay without some sort of event. Daragon will only become more restless." Rowan shifted into warrior mode and his need to take action settled around him.

"I know." I dragged my hands through my hair, thinking about the expansion of power and the dangers that followed.

22

Fidgeting, I pulled out my phone yet again. 7:43 a.m. We were waiting impatiently outside the doors of US Bank in the Crystal Court. The bank should have opened at 7:30, but for whatever reason, the bank was still dark. All the potential problems with our plan raced through my mind: *What if Marcia isn't here this morning? What if Daragon shows up?* I physically shook off the thoughts, refusing to think about the what-ifs.

Monday morning delighted us with an air temperature of a balmy eight degrees and a windchill of negative twelve. The skyway was littered with people bundled in coats, scarves, and hats. Indoor snowmen waddling around obscured Rowan's endless search of Daragon or his people. I rolled the small box from my father in my hand, keeping it under sealed magical protection. I resumed my pacing of the doors.

After an eternity, lights began to flicker on throughout the bank and a tall, thin blonde woman unlocked the door with an apologetic half smile on her face.

I stalked to the reception desk with Rowan in tow, where Blondie now resided in her ergonomic chair, booting up her computer.

"Hi, I'm wondering if Marcia is in today?" I asked before she could speak.

"Good morning," she said cheerily. "Sorry about the time! I was stuck on 394 because of that accident. The roads are awful." Blondie, or rather, Christina, I realized after peering at her name tag, glanced up at us through thick fake lashes. "Marcia? Do you have an appointment with her?"

"No. We don't." I tapped my fingers across the top of her desk.

"I don't think she will be in until nine, but I can double-check her schedule." She flashed another apologetic smile at us, the essence of Minnesota Nice. I tried to exude the same politeness, but I was certain I lacked that gene in my DNA.

"Please, I appreciate it."

A ticking sense of anxiety built within my body, with an awareness of Daragon pacing at the edges, waiting for this moment. My fingers continued their dance across the desk. Blondie, aka Christina, peered at them with a sideways glance as she clicked her mouse at her computer screen.

She frowned. "Yeah, I am so sorry, she isn't here until nine. But with the roads . . . gah, it might even be later."

I despise Minnesota winters.

"Is there anything I can help you with?" Another warm smile filled her face. It occurred to me then that potentially I didn't need Marcia specifically; you can visit your safe-deposit box anytime, right?

"Well, I need to get into my safe-deposit box."

"Oh! Well, I can certainly help you with that!" Christina was eager to be able to help me after all, probably because she was late in the first place. "Do you have your key?"

"Yes." I squeezed the box within my coat.

"I will just need to see your ID and pull up your account." She started to clatter at her keyboard. Finally, she stood smiling.

"Right this way."

We followed her toward the back of the bank to a hallway and down an elevator. Rowan was on high alert with watchful eyes and my heart thumped in my chest. The amulet pulsed against my belly, leaving my skin tingling. The elevator dinged and opened, and we were met by a security guard outside the vault doors.

Christina nodded to him. "Hi, Mac." The tall man, dressed in a bank security uniform, nodded as she entered a code on the keypad.

"Good morning, Christina. Glad you made it in okay. The roads were a mess," he said to her while eyeing me and Rowan.

"Uggghhh, it was terrible! And you know my car is awful. I slid all over the place," she said.

I slammed my teeth together. *Not a word, Aislynn. Not a word.* The door beeped and clicked.

"Alright," Christina said. "Just get your key and we will unlock your box. We have a private room through this door to use. Just let us know when you are finished."

In the pocket of my coat, I felt magic thrum over the box, releasing the key. I hoped to hide all traces of magic, my heart pounding the entire time.

"Calm down, Aislynn," Rowan insisted in my head.

The amulet's magic radiated through me as Christina

held out her hand for the key. As I handed it over, my thoughts ran wild, including the scene from the movie *Seven*: *"What's in the box?"* Could there be an element? That would explain the magic pounding in my ears. Anticipation built, spreading up my throat. I could barely breathe.

"Nine-twenty-three. Right this way."

Surrounded by rows of boxes, I tried to focus. Christina inserted her master key, then mine, turning both. Her manicured nails slid the box from the wall. "Just here." She led us into a small private room, setting the box on the table. "I'll be here when you are ready." She closed the door behind her with a smile.

Somehow, Christina had missed the ethereal blue light beaming from the box. The entire room shivered with magic. My heart racing, I shot a glance toward Rowan and slowly pushed back the lid.

Of all the things I expected to find, these were not on the list: some cash, a passport, and legal documents. Nothing else.

What the hell? Frantically, I pushed everything aside, then set everything on the table. The two bundles of fifty thousand dollars in cash sent my eyebrows creeping up my forehead in surprise. I flipped open the passport and saw my grandmother's photo, but the name listed was Sara Thompson. Handing it to Rowan in confusion, I lifted the box, checking the bottom. Metal.

There must be something else! The box protested, shimmering brightly.

"Could there be an illusion? Or magic hiding something?" I asked.

"Of course. With your grandmother, I would not expect anything less." He picked up the box, examining it from all angles. I kept reaching out for the box, both of us wanting to examine it simultaneously, somewhat impatient.

Rowan finally set it down. "I think this will only open for you, much like the others."

He turned the box toward me, the metal scraping against the table in a squeal of sound. Blinking rapidly, I held my hands over the top, trying to concentrate on the magic permeating the room. I wished I knew what I was doing.

Come on, Grandma. A little help here. With my eyes closed, I focused, thinking about the box opening for me. Magic was palpable around us, continually heightening the more I concentrated. The box began to shudder. Metal trembling against metal made me open my eyes. The box shook violently, and with a loud crack duplicated itself before us. Two boxes sat side by side.

"What the . . . ? Okay, not what I expected."

"She duplicated the box, hiding it within itself. Quite genius, really." Rowan was smug as I reached out to touch the second box.

Glimmering in a blue hue, I slid the lid back and found several things inside: a thick notebook, an ornate box, crystals, a leather-bound journal with the Tree of Elements embossed on the front, and miscellaneous papers stacked and sticking out of the notebook. Once I emptied the box, it disappeared.

"Well, that's convenient." *Thank God I didn't need to explain two boxes.*

I picked up the journal with the tree on the front, thick and heavy in my fingertips. Ripples of magic pulsated. It felt old, but not as if it would fall apart, or that it was delicate.

Instead, it emanated its age like an ancient item from Rome with the distinct awareness of history.

Caressing my hand over the cover, Rowan held out his hand for the book. When I held it out to him, his hand fell through the book as if it didn't exist. He reached out again, swiping through thin air, yet I could firmly feel the book in my hand.

"Maybe it's only for the Keepers?" I mused and turned the book over in my hand.

"I imagine there is a depth of magic protecting that book that predates anything I am aware of." He crossed his arms, rocking back on his heels.

"How did my grandmother come into possession of it?"

A rhetorical question, yet Rowan shrugged. "I do think we need to move along. Let's gather this into your bag and we will examine everything back at your apartment." He glanced around at an invisible source of agitation.

At this point, I trusted his instincts and we quickly shoved everything in my bag. With the lid back on the box, we opened the door. Rowan called to Mac in the hallway who proceeded to call Christina. We wrapped things up, returned the box, and left the bank.

Relief washed over me when we returned to my apartment. I slung the bag into the chair, retrieving all the items from the safe-deposit box. As I carefully set everything on the coffee table, the crystals captured my attention. Curious, I examined the four crystals which were at least eight inches tall and several inches in diameter. I was by no means a crystal expert, but clear quartz was easy enough to identify. Each was a stunning piece with rainbows glittering throughout.

Thinking about everything I had learned from my sisters, I arranged them into a circle formation on the table. Rowan watched, half-propped on the armrest of the chair. The air shifted as I placed the last tower into place and the amulet shivered against my skin.

Rowan crossed his arms across his chest as the crystals emitted a bright white light, each individually, then they connected together, shining into the center. The light became brighter until the room was saturated with white light. A loud pop sounded through the air, and I shielded my eyes, squinting from the brightness. The room returned to normal, and my eyes adjusted.

Then I saw her.

A tall, confident woman stood in the middle of my apartment. I looked at her, then Rowan, and back again. Rowan stiffened with wide eyes.

"Hello, Aislynn, Keeper of Elements." Her voice, like music, reached the corners of the room. "And Rowan, Protector of Light."

Rowan bowed his head diligently as she spoke his name. My eyes darted back and forth between the two of them, still unsure. I was captivated by her stunning emerald green gown and long chestnut hair that flowed around her. She finally turned to me.

Eyes of crystallized milk chocolate met mine, blazing into me with a depth of understanding. A flood of emotion was interrupted by Jax, who darted across the room, swirled against the woman's legs, and leaped into her arms. She graciously and greedily held him.

My cat is snuggling. I wasn't sure which was more bizarre, the cat or the strange, beautiful woman.

"Jaxon, our gentle guardian." She cooed and murmured against his fur, and purring filled the air. I glanced back to Rowan, eyebrows raised.

"I am Evalina, Guardian of Aurora Falls." She continued to nuzzle Jax against her face before letting him leap back to the ground. "The Aurora Towers," she gestured toward the four crystals on the table, cascading with ribbons of colorful light, "are a very special gift from your grandmother."

She glanced around. I inwardly cringed, wondering if I should be embarrassed by my shabby little apartment, particularly from the eyes of a mystical Guardian.

"This book"—the Tree of Elements book flew across the room, gently landing in her hands—"is only for you. As you have already seen, it can only be touched by you and is protected by the strongest elemental magic. You will find the guidance helpful."

A calmness eased through my soul as she handed me the book.

"The Aurora Tower crystals were gridded and created to bring you those who can help in a time of need. May you use them wisely." An underlying cautionary tone entered her voice as she motioned to the coffee table. "Aislynn, the magic you are connected with is an ancient magic that runs the depth of our existence."

I gulped as her crystallized eyes bore into mine.

"Please remember just as there is Light, there is Dark. The depth of Darkness is unfathomable, and Daragon is only the tip of the darkness that lies ahead of you." Her mouth set in a firm line.

My nose scrunched as the phrase "only the tip of the darkness." What did that mean? *Shit. Shit. Shit.*

"My dear sweet child, you have before you a daunting task, but one you are more than capable of. You were born for this, created for this purpose." Her eyes narrowed and anger flooded me. I was tired of being told how capable and born for this I was. Blah blah blah.

"The magic and power that runs through your veins is incomprehensible to you." Evalina took a few steps toward me, holding my chin in her delicate yet powerful hand. Her spellbinding eyes scoured through my soul, and my anger soothed to a dull roar. "But you shall soon see. May you always be blessed by the Light." Soft lips met my forehead.

"Rowan, Jaxon, may your travels be protected by Light." She met my cat's gaze in a curious manner before nodding, and then she vanished.

"She is my favorite."

My brain took a moment to process as my forehead tingled. Amy would have said my third eye opened, and I would've laughed in her face. And rolled my eyes for good measure. All *three* of them.

"Seriously? A Guardian of Light magically appears in my living room and that is all you can say? *Jaxon?*" I quipped as Rowan smirked. I realized with each passing moment that I knew absolutely nothing about my cat. He sauntered off, tail up.

✎

I plopped on the couch, staring at the crystal grid that still zinged with power, only barely visible. Not daring to touch it, I picked up the notebook instead. Stacked papers and notes were stuck haphazardly throughout, shoved with no rhyme or reason. My slight OCD drove me to remove all the papers and organize them one by one.

Some of the pages were folded, others wrinkled, and eventually I came across a hand-drawn map. Turning the page in my hand, I tried to read the small notes. The map appeared to be of Hallervania. I recognized my sister's house, The Orchard, and the stream. Another page was a drawn picture with a description of the layers of dimensions.

Layers of dimensions? What does that mean?

Notes scrawling up the side of the paper read, *Levels of dimensions—T of E hidden in layers of dim. 5 layers deep.*

Of course my grandmother would find the purpose of my journey and decipher the physics of the possibilities/existence of the magical dimensions. This led me to believe she was aware that the Tree of Elements was not located in Hallervania but buried within the dimensions of magic. Grimacing, my brain hurt trying to wrap my head around the idea. A small note in the margin exclaimed, *5=!!!*

Another page had each of the elements listed with possible locations and last known whereabouts. Sheets and sheets of handwritten notes had been written over what seemed several years of time. It was impossible to know what was what, so I flattened and organized the pages as I went. Flipping another page, I found something on the towers.

Elemental Crystal Towers—Clear Quartz (4)

Uses—Circle work, bring forth those who can assist at that moment

Represent 4 corners/elements.

Created for Aislynn to help reclaim the elements. Riona.

Useful. *Thanks, Grandma.* I began to realize how much stuff I accumulated over my time here. *How in the world can I lug all this crap around?* I would soon need a Harry Potter trunk or maybe Hermione's bottomless bag. I pushed the papers back in the notebook.

A small notepad had been shoved in the back of everything else, reminding me of something a detective used in movies. Flipping the book open, I folded back to a page in the middle of the notebook and found scribbles and random words. I spotted Riona's name again. *Who the hell is Riona?* And the next several pages had numbers on them.

48.41.

95.55.

11

Gritting my teeth, I threw the notepad across the coffee table and huffed out my breath. Seriously, I was over this mystical riddle bullshit.

Rowan arched an eyebrow at me. "Are you ready to go back?"

Huffing out my breath, I nodded. *More than freaking ready.*

After shoving all the stuff we'd found into the bags, I really wondered about the Hermione spell. Rowan held out the amethyst wand, and we stepped together face to face. Jax jumped on my feet. Activating the return spell Ailianna had created, we each grabbed an end and traveled back to Hallervania.

23

A subtle glow illuminated the space around us, announcing our return to the magical Realm. As my eyes adjusted to the early afternoon light, I noticed we stood in the Astra Meadows, where I'd practiced my teleporting skills (or lack thereof) not long ago.

Jax darted off through the grass and I took a deep breath, letting the clear, crisp air of Hallervania wash over me.

"You've returned," Aila called, instantly spoiling the wave of peace I had felt upon returning. She nodded in Rowan's direction, arms folded as she leaned against a nearby tree. "Did you find what you were looking for?"

"We did," I answered for him.

"Word traveled that you killed some of Daragon's men," she said cautiously, apprehension hanging in her voice as she shifted her weight.

"It sort of just happened . . ." Guilt washed over me. Emotions pushed to the edge tried to resurface, and I swallowed hard, burying them deep.

"What are you wearing?" Aila motioned her head at the amulet. Glancing down, I noticed the necklace emanated a bright indigo light.

"Aila, I told you she had no choice. Let her be."

Ailianna's voice rattled through our heads as she strode through the grass, the tension building around us.

"Aislynn, we are glad you returned safely." Ailianna let her hands slide down my arms, holding my elbows as she gently hugged me. "As Aila said, we heard about Daragon's men. I tried to keep a close watch on you both, but through the Realms, it becomes a bit difficult." Her eyes dropped to the amulet. "You have much to tell us. Come, let us talk."

Her peaceful tone easily diffused the discord and we followed her back through the fields to the house. Aila trailed last with reluctance.

Rowan and I recanted our trip as we walked, from the dreams, to Winston, to discovering the amulet and retrieving the safe-deposit box. Ailianna reached out to touch the amulet (much like Amy had done) and I was aware it zinged her as well. However, Ailianna's magic protected her from a full force shock.

"Yeah, it doesn't like being touched." I held the base of the amulet, twisting it in my hand.

Ailianna smiled. "No, I imagine not. With the ancient magic that protects it, the elements, and you, well, I imagine it is a tad . . . testy."

"Do you know someone named Riona?" I asked suddenly. We hadn't reached the house yet, but I couldn't hold back my questions. "A witch, perhaps? The name was mentioned several times in the notes from my grandmother, so I thought she might be a starting point in finding more information."

Ailianna's gaze shifted, meeting her sister's eyes for the briefest moment before pursing her lips. "Yes, I do. Although, I am not sure she will be much help. She has been in hiding for many years. She does not practice the same . . . sort . . . of magic we do." Ailianna spoke carefully as she pushed open the door to the house.

I looked at her expectantly as her gaze fell to her hands. "Dark magic?" My words were sharp as I flew through the possibilities, wondering what sources my grandmother trusted.

"No, not Dark magic per se. In fact, she chooses no side, Light or Dark."

"Okay . . ." I followed Ailianna into the kitchen, sitting at the table.

Aila chose that moment to slide out the bench to sit across from me. I gave her a quick glance and found her mouth set in a firm line. *Seriously? What is her problem?*

"As you understand, those who practice for the Light follow strict guidelines and a creed which keeps us in balance; in check with magic, if you will," Aila explained. I thought back to my conversation with Rowan regarding my grandmother's notes and "being magic."

"Riona chooses neither side. She embraces all sides of magic, which has caused her trouble in the past. Several years ago, she met with the Council to explain her way of doing magic. She followed ancient threads, and said we were being far too restrictive with our magic. She foresaw a heightened, more present magic. The Council, appalled, felt it opened magic for misuse and ultimately rejected her ideas. After that, she became a bit of a recluse and sheltered herself from most people." Aila leaned her body forward on the table.

Listening to my sisters, I started to chew on the tip of my thumb. This was exactly the reason my grandmother had sought out Riona and why I would do the same. Guilt trampled over me as I always seemed in conflict with my sisters and their version of magic. They wanted and believed everything needed to follow the strict guidelines set before them. That was rarely how life worked, as the world was not black and white, but a thousand shades of gray and everything in between.

"Aislynn, I do not think you should seek her out," Ailianna pleaded as she trailed my thoughts. "Her magic is dangerous. And I couldn't begin to tell you where to look for her."

I gave Ailianna a small nod while glancing at Rowan, whose thoughts mirrored mine.

"Where do you plan on starting your search for the elements?" Aila inquired.

"Honestly? I have no idea. They could be anywhere."

I had hoped Riona could be a starting point, but that didn't appear to be possible. I could sense Aila internally rolling her eyes, and I gritted my teeth against further propelling the tension. Jax chose to saunter into the room, jump on the table, and lay in front of me. He distracted my thoughts by forcing me to pet him.

"We need to find Riona. I have a few ideas. Come with me."

Rowan appeared to be privy to Jax's thoughts, but my sisters were not. *Interesting.* An odd tension settled across the room as Aila's eyes bored into mine.

"I am going to take my things upstairs." I pulled my bag up from under the table, averting my eyes. Something had shifted since I was last here. For some reason, I had now become the outsider, the misfit.

What happened while we were gone?

Rowan and I met Jax outside. Sneaking out of the house like I was fifteen and breaking the rules felt silly, but I didn't want to hurt them. And if they weren't willing to help in the way I needed, we had to keep moving.

"We need to go to town. Come."

My cat, demanding as ever, disappeared. Rowan grabbed my wrist and we followed. At least teleporting didn't make me want to vomit anymore. There was that.

C ﹒ﾗﾔﾋ ﾗ

Town was an odd word to describe what reminded me of the farmer's market on Lyndale Avenue in Minneapolis. My sisters had brought me here on several occasions over the last couple months, and I always felt as if I was in a strange parallel universe. The layout was extensive, and most of the buildings were permanent, much like our outdoor shopping malls. This, however, was more intimate and quainter. And magicky.

Along with flowers, vegetables, fruits, jams, and the like, there were also magical goods. A quirky shop called Devi's Apothecary, its name written in funky script, made me look twice at a sign in the window that advertised: "Supply your own pine needles for trade on sleeping potions." We followed Jax, weaving through people who shopped.

"Hey, what's with Aila? She was awfully bitchy." I narrowly missed running into someone who stopped to peruse a small table with jewelry.

"Protection for your children!" the vendor called, enticing over new customers.

"I am not sure. She was very abrasive, which isn't unlike her, but . . . something has changed," Rowan said with thought. "I understand why your grandmother sought out Riona, though. Her magic is in line with Elemental magic."

"I thought the same." We passed Thyme for Tea, and an earthy aroma escaped the open door, begging me to stop. "Funny how your history of magic is so convoluted that no one knows the truth, only their perceived belief of the truth. If Riona's magic follows elemental magic and if this magic has been hidden for thousands of years, then wouldn't she be showing the Council true magic? Instead of something that's been toned down and restricted so far beyond belief that it's easy to . . ." I paused.

The purpose suddenly occurred to me: control.

My thoughts flitted back to the first day I arrived in Hallervania and had compared their way of living versus ours. I'd realized there wasn't much difference at all. There was always a governing power to hold control over its people; they just thought they were free. I wondered about Riona and her purpose in this.

"This is why we must find her. Come on, you slow bipedal creatures."

Eyebrows furrowed, I turned my hands up in question, glaring at Rowan. *What in the actual hell?* Rowan shrugged as Jax shot into a shop. I hesitated in the doorway reading the sign: *Matoya's.* It seemed innocent enough, but as I stepped over the threshold, tingles raced over my skin.

The name didn't give way to the things I saw inside. The main counter was surrounded by shelves upon shelves of jars. Some of the containers held items suspended in liquid. *Ew.* Other jars offered powders, dried herbs, and more strange floating items. My eyebrows raised. *Gross.* Jax jumped on the counter and mewled louder than seemed possible.

"Yeah, yeah, Jaxon. I am coming!" a muffled call came from behind the counter in the back of the shop. "You know, I do not have to be at your beck and call. I am the human here!" Dripping with sarcasm, the voice came closer.

Ha. That was a language I took up regularly with my cat. Jax plopped his butt on the counter, twitching his tail wildly as he mewled again. The sound was deafening in the small space.

"Alright, alright! Sheesh. Not like I am trying to run a shop today or anything . . ." The grumbling belonged to a cheerful face and a man full of smiles. He appeared carrying a little brown mouse by its tail. A *dead* mouse. I became more disturbed by every second that passed.

"Do you want your present or not?" He dangled the dead creature back and forth.

"Why yes, yes, I do. Took you long enough. Hand it over, funny man."

He tossed it at Jax, who deftly caught it in his mouth, hopped off, and meandered out of the shop. Rowan smirked as my eyes filled with disgust.

"Matthew!" Rowan called as he reached across the counter to give a half hug, male-bonding ritual. Matthew's shaggy brown hair almost covered his eyes as he glanced in my direction. He appeared maybe a year or two older than me, and he turned his attention back to Rowan.

"Rowan! Good to see you. Glad you returned safely." Matthew's jovial presence warmed the shop.

Slivers of anxiety trailed over me. *How does everyone know about our travel plans?*

"Yes, we came back early today. Jax brought us here, assuming you might be able to help." Rowan turned to me and I gave a half-wave salute trying to brush off the remaining worry trailing through my mind.

"Matthew, this is Aislynn." Of course Matthew knew *of* me, even though we had never met. Although supposedly, he knew my cat.

"Aislynn . . ." His tone softened, eyes curious. His gaze made me uncomfortable and I began to take an extreme interest in his jars. "Are you in need of something for potions? Spells?" he questioned with curiosity, attentive to my every move.

"So, you have Eyes of Newts, frog legs, and stuff?" I tapped one of the jars, glancing back at him.

"Eyes of Newts? I am not sure I know what that is . . ." He looked to Rowan, then around his shop, wondering if he had something comparable.

I tried not to laugh. "Apparently, they are all the rage in our fantasy books," I said, picking up a jar.

Matthew's face pinched more bewildered than before. "I did recently acquire some essence of Dragon's Blood." Excitedly, he continued mumbling something about a rare black Truvian Dragon.

Dragons? *Gulp.* I preferred the Eye of Newt. Thankfully, Rowan saved us.

"We are looking for someone." Rowan's voice lowered. "A witch."

Matthew rested his elbows on the counter and leaned in. "I see. And is this someone I know?"

"Well, Jax seems to think so."

"Perhaps this witch is of the variety that keeps to herself and has struggled with the Council?" Matthew rubbed his hand across the worn wood of the counter.

"Perhaps."

"I may know who you speak of and may know how to reach out to this witch," Matthew's said in all but a whisper. "She is waiting for you." His eyes pierced mine, a crystallized hazel where the entire universe dwelled. Profoundly struck by their uniqueness, I had to close my eyes and shake my head to break the trance.

Matthew held out his hand and snapped his fingers. A piece of paper appeared and flitted through the air toward me. I stood dumbfounded as the paper dangled in front of me. Matthew nodded, encouraging me to take it. All the magic up until now had been ritual-like, a process, but this was raw. Simple. Finally, I reached up grabbing the paper.

Do not read this aloud. You are being watched. We will meet under the cover of darkness. The edges of the Truvian Mountains.

The moment I finished reading the piece of paper, it burned at the edges and disappeared.

"So, that's two ounces of powdered frankincense. We are out of the frog legs you spoke of, but I do have plenty of lizard legs. I imagine that shall work fine for you. And to top it off, one Seer stone straight from the Spirit Sea. Does that complete your order?" Everything about Matthew shifted to a fake cheerfulness. I raised an eyebrow as he packaged my order.

"Yes, that shall do it, Matthew," Rowan cut in, taking the bag from him. "Thank you again for your time."

"Of course," he nodded with wary eyes.

I had entered The Twilight Zone. The music played in my head as Rowan grabbed my arm, turned me around, and pushed me out the door. My head turned over my shoulder, looking at Matthew as he waved.

"What the . . . ?"

"Shhh. We are being followed. Smile."

"How about the Wild, huh? Such a great team. I think they might make the playoffs." The pitch of my voice was awkward and loud.

Rowan's face screwed up as he pushed past people. I guess in Hallervania they didn't talk about their local sports teams when the subject needed to be quickly changed. *Weird.*

"You are so very odd sometimes," Rowan commented with a sideways glance as we walked.

"I'm odd? Really? You *really* want to go there?" I demanded, trying to keep up with his fast-paced walk.

Rowan reached back to grab my hand, and we disappeared from town.

24

Y ou really should give a girl a little warning, ya know?"
We reappeared in an open field. It may have been near
the Astra Meadows, but I wasn't sure. The sun was beginning to lower in the sky behind the distant mountains.

"What did the note say?" Rowan ignored me, currently
engaged in warrior mode.

"It said we're being watched, to meet under the cover
of darkness at the edges of the Truvian Mountains. All very
mysterious and clandestine." I waved my hands around for
extra measure.

"Interesting . . ." Rowan searched the field meticulously. Apparently, we were back to the part in the show
where I am clueless.

"Are those the infamous Truvian Mountains?" I jerked
my thumb to the mountain line.

"No, those are the Crescent Mountains. The Truvians
are much farther away." He didn't notice my blank, impatient stare. "Oh, and you need to hide that." He pointed to
the amulet shining at my chest. "It is a beacon of magic."

I tucked it down my shirt. I presumed he meant more than this, but for now, it would have to do. I sort of felt like Ironman with the steady indigo shimmering through my shirt. *Sweet.*

Jax appeared in front of me. *"Um, Ironman? I do not think so."* He shook his head with disgust.

Rude.

"You must go to the house and get your things before they get there."

"Before who gets where?" I asked.

"The Council," Rowan answered for Jax. "This is worse than I thought."

"Yup."

"Wait? What?" Dammit, I was tired of being ten steps behind.

"GO!"

Not completely sure if it was how he said it or what he said, but without a second thought I focused on my bedroom and with a blink, I appeared in it.

A combination of my sisters' and male voices sounded from downstairs. I grabbed my bags and the jacket I had left on the bed. With another blink, I appeared before Rowan.

"Holy shit! I did it!" Astonished at my own self. I had teleported many times, but I always second guessed myself, moving through an entire process, thinking about what I needed to do. That was instantaneous.

It was magic.

"Uh, yeah, you are a magical being. When will you understand this?" Jax sat staring at me as if I was a complete idiot.

"Shut it! Not another word, fur-face!" I wanted to gloat, and I should be able to, dammit.

"That was quite impressive, Aislynn," Rowan commented, "whether Jax says so or not."

"Thank you, Rowan." I gave my cat a dirty look.

"The clearing at Morning Pass will work for now. But you will have to walk quite a distance. There is no other way."

"How do you know so much?" I snarked.

"It doesn't matter. Go now!"

Rowan, listening to my asshat cat, grabbed my hand and we twisted off, reappearing among a gathering of trees.

"This will be unpleasant," Rowan said. Without giving me a chance to respond, we zipped again. This time, he took us to the top of a mountain. The wind cut sharply across the precipice we stood on, and dizziness washed over me.

"Row . . . an—" My call cut off as we traveled again.

I think I need to puke. Now we reappeared on the edge of a river. I wrenched my hand out of his as I turned to the edge of the bank, throwing up what little I had in my stomach. Breathing unevenly, I stayed there for a moment with my head hanging, trying to absolve the nausea. As I pulled my head up and wiped at my mouth, Rowan grabbed my hand again.

"Ah hell . . ."

My words cut off as we arrived nestled in Morning Pass, a canyon of thick pines. Saliva pooled in my mouth as I tried to force down the need to vomit. The dizziness was overwhelming. I wanted to yell at Rowan, but even that seemed impossible. He pushed me at the shoulders and gently moved me to the ground, his face near mine.

"I am sorry, Aislynn. I needed to confuse our magic, otherwise they would have followed. Are you okay?" His crystal blue eyes looked deep into mine, searching.

"I'll be okay. But I left my intestines by the river." Closing my eyes, I half smiled and took my time to stand. "Do you want to explain what the hell that was about?"

"The Council. They have decided to intercede on your behalf. I don't know why. I don't know what happened while we were gone, but this isn't good." Rowan kept a watchful gaze on the trees surrounding us.

Gazing around the small open clearing, I stopped mid-motion: about ten feet behind Rowan stood a wolf. A huge wolf. His silver fur flowed as he stalked closer to us, hazel blue eyes watching mine with intensity.

Shock and fear took away my voice, so I smacked my hand against Rowan to try and point behind him. He didn't pay attention. I turned his body toward the wolf, who took another step forward.

Using Rowan as a shield, I peered around his arm. The wolf drew his nose toward the sky and howled, and the sound resonated through the darkening forest.

Jax appeared in front of us, facing the wolf. He mewled, the sound deep and throaty. Carefully, I edged my way toward him, scooping him into my arms.

"He will eat you," I whispered in Jax's ear.

Jax's ear pivoted as he stared at the wolf. Laughter filled my head, and Jax jumped out of my arms. I tried to hang on as his silky fur slid through my hands, claws piercing my skin as he went.

"Jax! No!" I called out in distress. Jax, whom I had no control over, sauntered over to the wolf, tail up, friendly as ever. My hand clenched Rowan's arm in fear.

The wolf sat on his haunches, watching Jax, ears pricked and head cocking to one side then the other. Jax rubbed his body against the wolf's legs, and my fingers dug deeper into Rowan's arm.

The wolf, massive next to Jax's small body, nudged the cat with his snout, pushing him away. Jax continued his rubbing, flipping his tail in the wolf's face. *This will not end well.* We stood motionless, not wanting to spark any sort of cross-species animal violence.

"So, are you going to tell them, or am I?"

A new voice rang in my head. A voice I thought I recognized.

"I think the cat's out of the bag." Jax rolled on the ground, rubbing himself into the dirt, ferocious laughter rocking his body.

"That was a good one!" The wolf shook his head, snorting.

"What is going on?" I debated, inching closer to the wolf. Rowan tried to hold me back. The wolf spoke again, seriousness filling his voice.

"Put on the cloaks and follow me."

He gestured to material hung over a tree branch. Certain they had not existed moments ago, Rowan cautiously retrieved two black cloaks. When he held them out, magic shimmered in black-gray waves.

"They are spell cast to shroud you and your magic into darkness. You cannot be tracked."

Rowan handed me mine and swirled his over his shoulders, pulling the cloak over his head. I followed, and magic settled over us. Everything stilled and quieted as silver and black ribbons cascaded outward from the cloaks.

"That's better. Now come. She is waiting."

I recognized the voice: Matthew! Several things flew through my mind at once: *Matthew is a wolf. Wait . . . Matthew is a wolf?* My thoughts flitted back to the shop and a giggle burst from my lips.

"You just figured it out, didn't you?" The wolf, Matthew, turned his head back with a lopsided grin, tongue lolling out the side of his mouth.

Rowan paused. "Wait? Why didn't I recognize you?"

"Sorry, my friend. I had to mask my energy signature to be certain I wasn't followed." Matthew turned back toward the trail. I could feel Rowan's concern ribboning out behind me. He didn't like missing small details, and I knew the Council thing weighed on his mind. We followed Matthew's sleek wolf body trotting at an easy pace down a narrow path worn through the thick forest.

"Can someone tell me why the Council is suddenly interested in what we are doing?" I questioned Matthew in front, then glanced back to Rowan behind me.

"When you returned with the amulet, they realized you were not some dumb girl who they could control anymore."

"Excuse me?" I growled. *Freaking rude.*

"Well, they were sort of banking on the fact you wouldn't succeed. They never thought you were powerful enough to gain the knowledge to accomplish the magic you are destined to do. Which is why they put you with your 'sisters' in the first place. Do you actually feel like you have been learning magic?" He scoffed in my direction as he trotted the path, watching his step.

"Put me with my sisters? What does that mean?" I clenched my fists beneath the cloak. His tone regarding my sisters triggered a slew of emotions. A part of me continually refused to define their relationship in connection with me. Instead, I forced myself into acceptance of something I didn't understand.

"It means you have been fooled since the beginning. You were misled on purpose, by the Council. They wanted to control everything, including your time with your sisters. Not that it matters; it would never work. You and your destiny cannot be controlled. She will explain it to you."

"Are you telling me that the meetings with the Council were a ruse?" Rowan fumed. I glared over my shoulder at him.

"A distraction, yes. They were not pleased when you went back to her Realm, as it shifted things out of their control."

"I am not someone's puppet." Rowan's anger shimmered off him in tendrils of smoky gray. The cloak encompassed a larger mass as the emotion shifted around him.

We trailed through the forest in silence, everyone stewing in their own thoughts. I wanted to know what freaking meetings he was referring to. In the time I'd spent training with my sisters, he'd been meeting with the Council discussing me and my destiny? I thought he had been focused on Daragon.

My footsteps became quicker the more I thought about how little control I had over this situation. I picked up a narrow stick, breaking off small pieces and tossing them to the ground, grinding my teeth in silence.

The trees began to thin and larger chunks of the night sky became more visible. I wanted to be humbled by the incomprehensible number of visible stars, something I could never see under the orange glow of Minneapolis, but instead apprehension trickled over me in slow waves.

25

As we broke through the edge of the forest, an enormous mountain line shadowed the night sky surrounding us. I didn't need to be told these were the Truvian Mountains. They beamed with magic, demanding my full attention and beckoning me to their power. Matthew bounded through the inky grass to a cloaked woman who instantly lowered her head, petting and cooing him.

Eventually, she gazed up as we neared her. Her hair shimmered gray-white, wild and free at her shoulders, and cradled her glowing eyes. Fine lines warmed the corners of her face, giving away her age.

A thick black cloak was clasped at the top of her sternum with a silver brooch. Immediately, I recognized the Tree of Elements. Glowing crystals were embedded into twisted metal swirling with magic, much like the tree the White Witch had shown me.

"Welcome, Aislynn, to the Ancient Black Truvian Mountains, where elemental magic scores the earth from long ago." Her voice was throaty and strong while her thin lips curved at the edges and her hands met in front of her. Matthew sat happily at her side, his hip falling into her leg. "I am Riona, Witch of the Ancient Keepers.

"The journey to this point has been long and tedious. I know you have many questions and I believe I've answers to most." Her words were thoughtful as she watched me. "If you will trust me a bit more, I will take you to my home and share the truth with you." A delicate eyebrow raised, waiting for my response.

For the first time, someone was willing to give me answers. The apprehension I carried dropped away and without hesitation, I nodded. Her hands flew up forcefully, palms open wide as silver magic flowed from them, surrounding us in glimmering tendrils. Moving her hands together, we all traveled. I felt a serene floating sensation as we were caressed by magic that willed our movement until we reached our destination.

We reappeared in a small cottage, where the tiny living room was lit with a warm glow from the fire in the corner. Cozy chairs draped in thick fuzzy blankets were inviting and comforting. The heaviness in my chest released and I felt encased by Riona's magic, this woman I just met, safe and at ease. The amulet, usually a constant zinging at my chest, became still and quiet.

"Welcome to my home, Aislynn, Rowan, Jaxon." She gestured with her hand for us to sit.

The room beamed with magic, pulsing in the walls, as if waiting for this moment. Glancing around, I finally sat on the edge of a chair, not willing to surrender to the comfort I felt. Rowan relaxed a bit more and Jax jumped on my chair, curling next to me and resting his paw on my leg. The fire cracked, filling the air with the sweet smell of nutmeg.

"Thank you for trusting in me. Now I shall trust you to bring forth the truth and return elemental magic back to this Realm." Riona settled back into the chair across from me.

"Okay, but honestly, I have no idea what I am doing," I insisted, spurting out my mental gremlins.

"I know, dear sweet child. You have been deceived and led astray, but it was the only way. I tried many things, believe me." Her mouth was firm, full of apology.

"Many years ago, when the prophecy began to unfold, I went to the Council to convince them to find you, to nurture and train your magic. I knew it was vital to help you reclaim elemental magic for our Realm, but they would not hear of it. In fact, afterward, I was carefully watched and routinely chastised for my magic and my part in the prophecy. After being shunned by our community and the Council I turned away, left my family, and began my search for you." After steadying her voice, Riona continued:

"The prophecy with your 'sisters' was created to form a distraction from your true destiny. They were used, coerced, and deceived into helping you. Those girls were only given tidbits to satisfy their continuous questions in regard to your destiny, and were instructed to only give you basic, elementary magic lessons. The Council wanted you to be naive. Everything you have accomplished thus far proves they are complete imbeciles and shouldn't oversee anything!"

Anguish filled me. My "sisters" had only been doing what they believed was their destiny.

Riona scoffed, her emotions getting the best of her. "But that is neither here nor there. The magic you are capable of is beyond what you know, and I will teach you to control it." Leaning forward, she graciously offered me the one thing I desired most.

"Did you know my grandmother?" I questioned.

"I sent her the amulet," she said matter-of-factly. Disrupting our conversation, a little bird flew in the window, landing on Riona's hand, chattering and chirping incessantly.

"Ah, thank you, my sweet friend," she said to the bird as it flitted away. "My friend tells me the Council lost your trail and is searching the Crescent Mountains for you and Rowan."

A satisfied smile crossed her lips and the news brought Rowan some relief as he settled even further into his chair. In contrast, I inched myself further to the edge.

"How did you send my grandmother the amulet? Why? How did you even have it?" My rapid succession of questions made her grin.

"Ah, yes, a good place to start. Abigail was already being directed by the Divine Source to receive knowledge of your destiny in obscure ways. For example: the deluded prophecy. But it wasn't enough, and as the Witch of the Ancient Keepers, it is my duty to . . . help things along. The magic protecting the amulet, which was waiting for the Keeper to be born, had waned significantly. To put it under new protection, I sent it to Abigail. Together we were able to lengthen the magic, protecting you and the amulet. The Council heard murmurs along the way and tried to restrict things when they could, but we diligently worked through our precise plan."

"So, my sisters?" I asked next. "Why did I end up with them?"

"That was a necessary evil," Riona replied. "Your

grandmother and I could find no way around it. If we didn't allow that to happen, the Council would have realized we were deceiving them as they were trying to deceive you. We needed them to believe they had you under their control and watchful eye."

I let my body fall back into the chair as I digested this new information. These two sides were pitted against each other trying to outwit one another.

"Why doesn't the Council want me to reclaim the elements? Won't I be doing good? Saving magic for our Realm?" My hands went up in the air.

"When you restore elemental magic, it will change magic at its basic core level," Riona explained. "As the White Witch informed you, the magic used now is a fraction of what is actually available. This frightens them. How will they control this type of magic? And the people? An extremely old and outdated way of thinking." Riona rolled her eyes. "Their Council is infiltrated by the very Dark they oppose." A smirk crossed her mouth.

"Wait, are you saying there are people who practice Dark on the Council?" Rowan charged forward in his chair.

From an outside perspective, this didn't surprise me; it was much like my politics at home.

"Of course there are!" She let her head fall back with the absurdity. I leaned forward again, running my hands through my hair and down my face.

"When you returned with the amulet, the Council needed to take new measures. Jaxon could only reach out to me once this occurred. The Council is full of a bunch of nitwits who can't see past their own toes! And they oversee magic for our Realm?" She rumbled to herself.

I smiled. I could only imagine my grandmother and

Riona working together, forming a plan to outsmart a bunch of "nitwits." My grandmother had used the term often in referring to the department heads at the university.

"Okay, I just find it hard to believe the Council doesn't want me to fulfill my destiny because it will change magic. That doesn't make sense; everyone always wants more power."

"Ah, Aislynn. You are as clever and smart as your grandmother said. Precisely the right question to ask. Why has this remained hidden?" She tapped her fingertips against her mouth.

Her eyes darted to the fire, and she jutted her hand forward, palm open. A ball of fire released itself from the logs and shot into her palm, swirling just above her skin. It wasn't an energy ball, but actual flames hovering for her.

I stared, entranced by the movement. Quickly flashing open her other palm, a sphere of water appeared, liquid and tranquil. As Riona brought her hands together in front of her, Rowan and I sat forward in our seats, watching with intensity.

"Fire and water. They oppose one another but are well-matched when forced to contradict one another. You remember your dream?"

I blinked rapidly. *How did she know?* My thoughts flashed to the dream in my office with Daragon. His fire met my water, the will of each feeding the two forces. Chewing on my lip, I secretly hoped she didn't know the entire dream.

"Now, imagine a much larger scale . . ." She pushed the two together, a wall of water and fire almost touching. They were ready to vanquish each other, fighting with a fury to connect and disintegrate.

"Now add in air." Blowing her breath toward her hands, the air grew fierce as it separated the two further from one another.

"And last, earth." The floor beneath our feet trembled.

Riona allowed the magic to ride a wave of energy, then turned her hands and extinguished the magic. Everything dissipated, moving to stillness again. Her eyes sparkled as she looked at us.

"This example is minuscule in comparison to the potential available. Nothing. A parlor trick, insignificant to the actuality of elemental magic, of what *you* are capable of, my dear child." She held my gaze. "Do they want that power? Are they holding the keys? Absolutely. But they cannot fathom allowing one person to control it. Because you will not hold it for them; you will not let it fall into the wrong hands because that is who *you* are. What place will they hold then?"

She sat back in her chair, hands sliding down the armrests. Matthew's head rested there, and she softly massaged the back of his ears. I pushed my bangs across my face, trying to distract myself from everything I had just seen.

"You have much to work through, Aislynn. You've been caught up in this whole charade from the beginning with false beliefs and misdirection, continuously leading you here."

She allowed me time to process. My thoughts took me back to when Rowan followed me.

"When Rowan first told me the prophecy of the three sisters, it was similar to the stories my grandmother told me when I was little. But there is also the prophecy of the Tree and me reclaiming the elements for Light. So are there two prophecies?" I asked, trying to keep the information straight.

"Again, misdirection to get you to follow. The Council wanted you to believe you were part of three, to suppress your gifts. Ailianna and Aila are talented, gifted beings. They have a divine purpose in helping you return elemental magic, but that prophecy is nothing but a tale the Council weaved to twist their own desires."

Rowan's head jarred forward in disgust. "This entire time, the Council lied to me? They've just been getting me to do their bidding, leading me around on a leash?" His voice became louder with every question.

Jax lifted his head from the tucked position. *"And this surprises you?"*

"Why didn't you tell me?" Rowan demanded, glaring at the cat. Jax curled his head back into his body with a small squeak and closed his eyes.

"The Council considered using you to regain the magic for them," Riona said, "but they were warned by their own Seers it would never work. Your will is too strong; you would see through their falsities and go about things your own way." She arched an eyebrow in my direction. I smirked; she described me perfectly.

My thoughts circled back to my sisters. "Ailianna and Aila? Are they my sisters? Ailianna mentioned something about magic family lines and not blood . . . and . . ." The term had little meaning now, and my head wanted to explode.

"They are connected to you through magic, so in the context of the heritage surrounding magic, they are your sisters. But they used the prophecy to suppress your true purpose." She stroked Matthew's head, drawing her finger down his snout.

"Sisters in regard to magic, but that's it." I sighed and rested my head back on the chair. She gave me a soft smile, nodding gently. Relief washed through me. Final confirmation solidified in my heart. Some part of me had still been wrapped in this idea that I was stolen at birth, living a hidden life from my true destiny. Even though they weren't my sisters, I developed a closeness with them, and I cared for them. Again, the anguish returned when I thought of how they had been used just as much as me.

Riona could tell my energy was beginning to wane. "Alright, that is enough truths for one evening. Through that door . . ." She pointed across the room to a door that hadn't existed a moment ago. My eyes tried to process this new extension of magic. "You will find bedrooms and a bathroom complete with all your needs. Be assured this space and those rooms are secured by the strongest protection magic. You are safe here." She stood and Matthew shook his body, sending fluffs of hair across the dark floorboards.

"Rest well, for tomorrow we will see what you are made of." Riona flicked her hand toward the sky and the fire dimmed to coals and the candles blinked out. There was a confidence to her magic that rivaled anything I had seen. Ailianna was graceful with her magic, Aila was a forced tempered will, and even Daragon used his to create fear and hostility. Rowan's magic was practiced and used with a profound respect for its guidelines. Something about Riona's was different; it held a rawness channeled into pure confidence.

Rowan and I diverged to our own separate rooms with quick good nights. I laid down on the small bed, Jax curled next to my body. A quiet stillness rolled through me, something I hadn't experienced since before I was ignorant of magic. Threads and tendrils of protective magic blanketed the room and peace washed over me.

Deep sleep stole away my consciousness, and it was probably the best sleep I had in my life. I didn't doubt I needed it.

26

Awareness slowly crept in, and I felt a furry head pushing itself into my open palm, forcing me to touch him. The hand connected to the still-sleeping body was not active enough for the furry being, and he began to push his head into my face.

Caressing his fur against my skin, his whiskers tickled my cheeks and nose. I groaned, rubbing my face with force and rolled with a grunt. Paws moved to stand on my shoulder, then he leaned in with a short sniff and continued his incessant face rubbing.

"Need love. Now."

"Nooo . . ." I pulled the sheet over my face. Was this necessary?

"It is my loving time. Pet me, human."

"You are doing this just to be an asshole," I snapped and flipped the sheet off my face.

"Perhaps. Now, pet me."

Rolling to my back, which to Jax meant crawling across my body and plopping on my chest, I brought my hand on top of the blanket to massage his fuzzy head.

"Two hands. I request two hands. Simultaneously."

"Good God! Could you be more demanding?" Despite my sleepiness, I obliged, using both hands to fully massage his ears, scratch his head, and rub under his chin. He particularly liked when I used my thumb and rubbed the bridge of his nose.

"I could . . . that . . . feels . . . amazing. I wish you understood." His eyes practically disappeared to the back of his little cat head.

"You are making this awkward." I raised my eyebrows.

"Shhh . . . keep petting."

The purring increased, and I closed my eyes, trying not to feel used. This went on for several minutes until he suddenly stood on my belly, dug paws into my organs, and glared with disgusted cat eyes.

"What?"

"Too much. One pet too much." Disdain filled his cat face.

"I have no words." My steely glare meeting his. "Next time, I won't pet you." My eyes narrowed.

"Riiight. Whatever you say." He hopped off the bed, black silky tail straight in the air. Turning, his sapphire eyes pierced mine. *"Riona is ready for you."*

I plopped my head back on the pillow and stretched my arms over my head, confident I was not ready for what this day would bring.

Until that point, I believed I had a fair grasp of magic. Or at least I thought I did. Riona, however, was patient with me. That was probably a good thing as I didn't have much patience for myself. She chose to start with water because of my affinity for the element. We stood at the edge of a small lake nestled deep within the Truvian Mountains.

"Aislynn, the elements are yours to control," she explained kindly. "More than how I manipulate them with simple magic. You were born to control them. Do you understand?"

I gave a tiny nod, clenching my teeth as I held a beach-ball-sized sphere of water in the air ten feet above me.

"Your imagination is the only limit of how you can use the elements," she offered.

I concentrated, knowing my imagination sucked. Clapping my hands, the sphere of water shot upwards like a volcano and came back down upon us in droplets on a misty rainy day. I heaved out the breath I held.

"Very good." Riona let a small smile break across her mouth. "Now think bigger," she challenged.

I brushed my hands across the holes in my black skinny jeans, preparing to try again. Rolling my shoulders, I took another breath. Maybe I should rethink yoga classes and the damn pranayama shit Amy always wanted me to go to; my arms trembled with exhaustion.

"It is only exhausting because you are forcing the magic. You need to let it be a part of you, an extension of you." Riona's hands rested on the top of a staff or walking stick, I didn't really know what the damn thing was. She lifted the curved, polished wood several inches, then forcefully tapped the ground, sending rolling movement through the earth. A rumble tickled my feet, sending tingles up my body. "You are the maestro of the symphony, Aislynn. Lead the magic; do not force it."

Damn her and her shitty analogies, I grumbled inwardly. She was like a freaking wall of motivational posters staring at me until I dug deep inside to pull out all the little pieces of my soul and offer them out to the world. *Bigger. She wants bigger.*

I pushed my lips out and turned to the lake. Shaking my hands, I gave Riona one last glance. *Bigger, she says. Symphony, she says.*

Closing my eyes, I thought of the air pushing against the water with such force that the edges of the lake would start to push backward, creating a wave. The wind gusted from behind me, propelling me forward and I dug my feet into the earth to hold myself steady.

In a dance movement with my hands, I swirled the air and thought of it freezing, colder and colder until the water started to freeze under the pressure. I thought of the water behind the wall, and with a gesture of my hand, I brought it over the top of us, freezing everything as it moved to encase us in a dome of ice.

"Brilliant!" Riona exclaimed, her eyes glittered, gratified by my efforts.

I took a moment to observe the beautiful clear ice above us, admiring how the sunbeams sent a mirage of geometric shapes across the earth at our feet. A faint smile hit my mouth and I noticed I wasn't out of breath, or tired. An odd sensation rippled through me: connection. There was a tether binding me to magic, alive and sparking an unfathomable bond.

For a second, I pondered how to close the magic. Peering up to the ceiling of ice, I imagined snowflakes falling gently on my skin. The ice transformed into snow, covering the ground with a light dusting. I grinned. The water melted, bubbled, and trailed back to the lake as the air warmed and the sun reached us again.

"This is how you have a relationship with the elements. You must feel them within you and orchestrate their movements. Excellent work, Aislynn." The light breeze lifted the loose chiffon material hanging at her arms, and she gestured for more.

I looked to the lake, and the water that lapped at the shore. I perceived the tether within me, like a heartbeat of its own, and began to understand what Riona meant. The elements would become a part of my being, an extension of myself. Finally, perhaps this was real magic. Balance trickled through me, loosening the fear and need for control. I focused on the center of the lake and thought of my favorite animal. For the briefest moment, I wondered if they knew of tigers in Hallervania. Closing my eyes, I connected to the water and the image of a tiger.

Gracefully, he took shape. The water rippled into the form of a tiger and he slowly began to stalk toward us, as if the lake was a smooth surface for him to walk on. The water was fluid as he moved; through his stripes, I could see how the water twisted and shimmered. Golden eyes scrutinized us intensely as he prowled closer to the edge of the lake.

Riona's interest peeked from behind me as I brought the tiger to the wet sand. He gave me a second glance, his form becoming more solid and lifelike.

He moved across the land, his heavy water paws stalking closer to her. I turned, watching as I controlled the magic. She stood motionless as the giant cat crept carefully, padding one paw at a time, watching her with primal intent.

Suddenly, Matthew appeared in wolf form at Riona's side. His lips raised, growling at the massive water beast. Matthew's hazel eyes glanced in my direction, confusion melting through them before his focus darted back to the tiger.

His hackles raised as he dropped his head, snarling, prepared to attack. I smirked, bringing the tiger's focus to Matthew. The tiger leaped at Matthew with massive paws expanded wide. His sharp claws extended out, grasping to meet the wolf's body. Matthew jumped as they flew at each other.

The tiger became a shower of water upon impact, drenching Matthew. He shook his wolf head in disorientation. His body rippled from head to tail into a full shake, cascading the water from his fur. A sharp whine escaped him.

Riona roared with laughter as she bent to nuzzle Matthew's face. "Oh, my sweet friend, it is hard not to laugh." Wrinkles lined the corner of her eyes. Matthew sneezed in her face as he turned sharply toward me.

"Th-that . . . what was that?"

I tried to hold back my laughter. "A tiger. A water tiger. I'm practicing my magic." I winked at him, still snickering.

"Quite impressive, as well. You had Matthew convinced." She smiled. Matthew walked over to me, giving his body another shake and, this time, getting me wet.

"I suppose I deserve that!" I laughed, giving Matthew's head a pat.

"Well, that is enough fun for one afternoon. Why don't we find something to eat? Hmm?" Riona turned on the spot and disappeared. Matthew followed.

I, however, stayed behind for a moment. Watching the sunlight shimmer across the surface of the water, I breathed deeply to observe the magic thrumming underneath my feet. The towering mountains encircled me with confirmation of my destiny.

Maybe I *could* do this. The amulet pulsed at my solar plexus, connecting with the elements. Like a GPS, they pinged back to me. Somewhere, out there, they were willing me to find them. I took one last glance at the lake and then disappeared.

27

Back in Riona's little cottage, we sat around the table happily shoving our faces. Okay, I was shoving my face as my stomach protested its starvation. Using elemental magic burned through energy like using your allotted data stash for the entire month in a matter of two hours.

I filled my mouth with another half a roll. This gave high metabolism a whole new name. Riona pushed the plate of bread toward me with a sly grin.

"You did well today. We shall practice using each of the elements in the same way. There is much to show you in limited time," she said.

My head bobbed as I tried to swallow, my mouth still full of food.

"I need to attend to some things this evening, so do as you please. But please be aware of your surroundings and use the cloaks if you decide to leave." She motioned toward Matthew, who had been asleep on the floor. He jumped up in a floof of fur and they both disappeared.

Groaning, I laid down on the bench, my food baby

extending from my stomach. "I think my eyeballs were bigger than my stomach," I said to Rowan on the bench next to me, who had long ago stopped eating. Apparently, he enjoyed watching me gorge myself and only laughed.

"Riona told me of your water tiger. Pretty clever." Rowan rested his head in his palm.

"Thanks," I grinned. "I don't think Matthew thought it so clever."

"Perhaps not, but it's fun to ruffle his feathers."

"What is his deal, anyway? He is so loyal to Riona, and what's with the wolf thing?" I asked, looking up from my horizontal position.

"He is a shapeshifter. Riona saved his life, and he indebted himself to her." He spun his glass on the table, giving me a sideways glance. "I think he likes the wolf form, which is why he chooses it most often."

"Shapeshifter?" I perched myself on my elbows. "He can be any animal?"

"Mm-hmm. A more uncommon gift now, but certain family lines still carry it." Rowan focused back on his glass.

The idea was appealing, transforming into any animal and the thread of gifts throughout family lines. "How did she save his life?" My stomach's discomfort forced me to lie back on the bench.

"Matthew and his family were being sought by the Council for their gifts. This was when Riona still worked with them. When she learned what the Council wanted, she opposed them immediately. She recognized it was wrong and adamantly defended his family; no one should be used for their gifts. Unfortunately, they already sent out trackers to collect them, and if they resisted, they had justification to use force. Riona found out and got there in time to save

Matthew. She tried to save his little sister, but she didn't survive her injuries." His eyes drifted to the glass in his hand, shoulders drooping as he filled with sorrow.

The shift in his attitude sent me upright, putting us almost face to face. I laid my hand on his arm, aware of the sudden closeness between us on the bench. He continued staring at nothing as his chin dipped downward and remorse seemed to overwhelm him.

"Rowan?" I asked, guessing there was something more that was troubling him.

"I was one of the trackers." The confession came softly, tearing apart his resolve.

My grip on his arm tightened. "Does he know?" Even though I asked, I was already aware of the answer: if Matthew had known, he would have ripped out Rowan's throat.

"No, he doesn't," Rowan confirmed, his head hung in regret. "I didn't harm any of his family. I was a new tracker and it was one of my first assignments. In fact, I was still in training. When you are obtained by the Council, they have a very . . . precise way of training." He chose his words carefully. "You are given limited views of a situation, and you do as you are told."

I frowned. The more I heard about the Council, the less I liked them. "I think I understand your response last night a little better now." I thought back at how surprised and angry he had become when Riona discussed the Council. I imagined there were layers of convoluted history in his time with the Council that I couldn't possibly comprehend.

"But Riona must know . . . that you were there that night."

"She does. But she also understands me and who I

became after that event. She knows . . ." He paused again, and the internal struggle visible on his face made my heart clench. "She knows I would never allow that to happen again. And as for Matthew, I think she believes he doesn't need to know as it would only hurt him." His eyes settled back to me.

"I think so, too. Your secret is safe with me." I squeezed his arm again with a half smile. Rowan moved his arm and wrapped it around my shoulders, pulling me in. He rested his chin on my head.

"Thank you. I appreciate that."

I permitted myself to relax into him as his two-day scruff tickled my scalp.

We had spent so much time together, yet I hardly knew anything about his past. Constantly on the move since I met him, we didn't have time for much else. He was always in warrior/work mode, and rarely relaxed.

I thought about how many times he had saved me in one way or another. This was the Rowan I had come to appreciate: an inherently good soul. What happened in the past shouldn't carry over to the now and I knew Riona felt the same. Sitting up, I released myself from our half hug.

"So when you first came to me, you were working for the Council?" I tried to pull together a timeline in my mind.

"Not working *for* them necessarily, but I was asked to retrieve you. With knowledge of the prophecy and you, I didn't want you falling into the wrong hands. Another tracker would not have been kind nor patient with you. After working with Ailianna and her visions, I knew you would not tolerate harshness. That would only make you balk more." He rubbed his chin against the back of his hand.

He was right. If someone else would have come and been forceful, I would have never gone with them. It occurred to me they could have "forced" me, and the thought gave me chills.

"It isn't worth thinking about. Remember, the divine plan. I am meant to be here with you and be a part of your journey. Even your grandmother understood that." With a smirk he nudged me with his elbow, and I returned the nudge for him jumping on my thought train like he had the day we met.

"You know, you freaked me out! I thought I needed to admit you to the psych ward!" Laughter burst from me when I thought about a psychiatrist making sense of the "I am from another Realm" business.

"Well, you aren't the easiest to convince." He smiled, and something in his eyes made me divert mine.

"I know, but seriously, you caught me on like the worst day, in the middle of a deadline. I was a disaster." I thought back to that Friday, and how snippy and rude I was with him. Shame rattled into the crevices of my thoughts.

"We should probably get this cleaned up," I said, distracting myself with the mess scattered across the table. The fork in my hand clattered across the table sending bits of food flying. He kept his gaze on me for a moment longer, then relented to helping me clean.

Afterward, we hung around in the living room. Rowan laid across the couch reading one of my grandmother's books and I decided it would be fun to create fire. It wasn't fun. Failing miserably, I could only create small sparks of light within the logs.

"You are trying too hard again." Rowan peered at me

over the edge of the book. I glared playfully, sensing the smirk hidden behind the book.

The thought of his mouth, that sexy smile of his, broke my concentration with the element. Needing a break, I stood, my legs stiff from sitting awkwardly on the hard floor. Stretching, I noticed how dark it had become, and opened the door to admire the night sky, overcome by the elaborate show of stars.

The moon beginning to crest over the top of the mountains illuminated the forest below. A serene peace emanated in the quiet darkness in contrast to the constant movement and noise I was accustomed to under the city lights of Minneapolis. I took the moment to enjoy the silence and the crisp smell of the night air.

Rowan propped himself in the jamb opposite of me. His legs, longer than mine, reached across the doorway. We had stood much like this at my mother's house, which seemed forever ago, but in reality, it had only been days. But I wasn't exactly sure. This time orientation business was a lost cause.

"Do you miss home?" Rowan asked, looking down at his feet.

I paused, contemplating the question. *Do I miss home? Did I miss the monotony of my dull life? Getting angry with coworkers for their ineptitude and laziness? Avoiding anything which made me feel real or a part of something?* No. I didn't. For the first time in my life, this spark of purpose and innate response to be a part of a collective, something I never chose to be a part of before, called to me. I smirked.

"No, Rowan. I don't miss home at all." My smirk met

with his own. We reached a place of comfortability with one another. I had allowed him into my inner circle without even realizing it. I would definitely need to overanalyze how *that* happened, but I pushed the thought away.

"Do you? Not miss home, but your life? Or is this normal?" I peered up through my lashes.

"This is *not* normal." A small snort escaped him. "I am not usually on the run from the Council, jumping Realms or trying to convince a gifted being of her magical destiny." He grinned as he pushed his hands through his thick dark hair.

"Weird! You would have thought this sort of stuff happens all the time." My laughter intertwined with his, followed by playful eye rolls.

"I know, right?" he joked.

For the first time, I saw Rowan, the real Rowan. He was relaxed and at ease, finally ditching warrior mode. Not teaching or protecting; just human . . . or magical being . . . or—

My thoughts were halted by the back of his hand gently caressing my cheek. Every muscle froze, locking into place. His eyes met mine, watching or feeling me, my energy, or something.

Shit.

Bars clamped down over me, and my habitual walls of protection securely locked into place. *What was I thinking?* If I let him in, he would only get hurt, as everyone did.

"What happened to you, Aislynn?" Rowan's hand fell away as genuine concern settled into his eyes. My own fear blocked any responses deep in my throat.

"I . . ." *What happened? Why would anyone want to open that door of shit?* "I . . ." The words wouldn't follow. How could

I put my screwed-up life into a few sentences? It was best not to share those secrets—not this century, anyway.

He sighed, and with both hands held my face. "It's okay," he whispered and laid his lips on my forehead.

The tingle of his magic prickled my skin. Rowan had become the only person, besides my cat, whom I absolutely trusted and relied upon through all this.

But I knew I had to hold back from him, just like I held back from everyone in my life. It was for the best. It kept me safe. And more importantly, them.

28

For several days, I practiced elemental magic, gorged myself with food, and succumbed to the sheer exhaustion that followed. We settled into a routine, and I flourished, finally feeling like I was accomplishing real magic. And I was pretty damn good at it.

Behold, my magical destiny! When I practiced fire magic, I almost burned an entire side of the mountain. Thankfully, Riona's quick response with water magic extinguished the damage.

Lying on the couch thoroughly sapped from the day, my head rested in Rowan's lap. The movement had been unintentional; it sort of sloughed its way there as exhaustion took over. Each day through our time together and the magic, we became a team, relying on one another. Riona went somewhere with Matthew again that night. We weren't sure where they went, but I was too tired to care.

"Why do you push everyone away?"

My eyes popped open when I heard Rowan's unexpected question.

"I believe that is a question for a psychotherapist involving a lot of sessions on a couch," I deflected.

"Mm . . ." He waited out my deflection.

"I don't know. Because it makes things easier?" I offered.

"Easier? Life needs to be easier?" he asked.

"Well, it would be nice!"

"Isn't our purpose to be challenged, pushed? To create a better version of ourselves?"

Sitting up, I ran my fingers through my hair, thinking my short style would need a trim soon. I gave him a sideways glance, wondering why he needed to be so damn mystical. *What does he want from me?*

"Maybe I don't want anything but authentic Aislynn," he said. My eyebrows furrowed as he hopped on my thought train.

"Hey, sometimes it's the only way to know what you're thinking."

"Intrusive, though, don't you think?" I arched my brow, pulling my legs into a crossed position.

"Perhaps. Alright. How about you ask me something. Be intrusive, if you will."

It was an interesting offering, and I pushed my lips out as I thought. Rowan was allowing me to pry. This might get interesting.

"Okay," I began, and turned my body toward him. "What prompted you to leave the Council? Or at least question their integrity?"

Rowan blinked, rapidly, surprised. He debated for a few moments before answering. "A lot of things happened," he replied, and blew out a breath. "Even leading up to finding you, I technically still worked for them . . . well, until we ran." His eyes shifted to a faraway place.

I rested my elbow on the back of the couch, propping my head in my hand, intent on his words.

"One of the biggest moments when I grasped that things had shifted was an assignment with another Council tracker, Eirnin. We were sent after Liam Bracken, whose family is well-known for their scrying gifts. We arrived at the location, and he was there, but with his daughter. Zarah was six? Maybe seven?

"It was a complete shock to me, although looking back, I believe Eirnin knew. I quickly realized we weren't there for Liam, but his daughter . . . something else I didn't know. Liam was out of his mind, of course; there was no way we could take his child.

"I tried to convince them both to come with us, to meet with the Council, trying to be peaceful. Eirnin was rough, harsh, and that only created more tension. His behavior was heinous, something I had never seen from a Council member. Completely desperate by then, Liam threatened us, to expose the Council, and everything spiraled out of control."

Rowan's voice got heavy. Quiet, my eyes urged him to continue.

"Eirnin threw an energy ball at Liam, killing him instantly, in front of his daughter. Zarah screamed, a scream I will never forget. I ran to her, horrified, her earth-shattering screams filling my head. Somehow, Eirnin beat me to her. I still don't understand how, but he did. He scooped her up and took her."

"What?" Disgust filled my face. "How could someone do that?"

Rowan only shook his head in response. "I returned to the Council, told them what transpired, and questioned Eirnin's actions, but it was swept away. Eirnin's behavior was excused. 'We will not tolerate such action against the Council of Magic' were the words they used. I tried to explain that there was absolutely no reason for Liam to be killed, as it went against our own code of conduct, but . . ."

"It was all dismissed," I finished for him. Rowan nodded. "What happened to her? The girl? Zarah?"

"I don't know. I searched for her for years. I tried to get any information on her, where she went . . . nothing. I am sure I know why they wanted her." He rubbed his face with his hands in despair.

"Power, I am sure," I said. His head fell in agreement. "What about Eirnin? Did you ever see him again?" The idea of working with someone like him made me ill.

"No. Believe me, he wouldn't be here if I did. They hid him from me, too, sending him on assignments more suited to his abilities, I presume." His mouth became a grim line.

"You mean killing?" I scoffed.

"He wasn't always that way," Rowan defended him. I pursed my lips. "You aren't born Dark, Aislynn. You become Dark. A slow spiral of choices takes you to places you never believed you would go."

"Sounds like he enjoys it, though," I snipped, unable to help myself.

"In his twisted sense of reality, he probably believes he is doing right." He rested his head against his fist, soft dark curls splayed between his fingers.

"He was your friend." My voice softened, realizing the depth of his pain more than what occurred to Zarah and her father. This was also the betrayal of his friend. Rowan cast his eyes downward, remorse filling them.

"I should have realized. I should have known what was happening." For the first time, weakness surrounded him with spurts of guilt and shame. I reached out, putting my hand on his arm in comfort. It surprised me a bit when he placed his hand on top of mine, then wove our fingers together.

"I am so sorry, Rowan."

He nodded silently, squeezing my hand more tightly than I anticipated. We sat like that for a while, lost in our own thoughts.

A few weeks later, Riona sat us down at the table which had become my favorite place in her house. Well, except for maybe my bed. All my grandmother's documents and note-books were a messy array strewn throughout the kitchen.

"The time has come to tell you that you've trained well enough, for now," Riona announced. "We must move forward."

Well enough? I thought to myself. *What the hell does that mean?*

"Okay?" I arched my brow inquisitively.

She sat silent for several moments. "Your search for four elements is actually three."

"Excuse me?" I sputtered. *She has an element?* Rowan jerked his head toward Riona, and satisfaction filled me. At least this was news to him, too.

"At a certain point, your grandmother and I located the water element and retrieved it from its hidden location. Of course, we only hid it again, for the obvious reason. Neither of us had the capability to control it adequately; however, we could not pass up the opportunity to secure one element for you."

"I . . . what? Okay . . ." I digested this new information at a slow rate. "Okay, so where is it?"

Riona's face suggested I wouldn't like the next words out of her mouth. "That is the problem. I don't know." Her eyes lowered.

My shoulders sunk, and I let my head drop to the table with a groan.

"Don't be sullen! We have a map to find it." Her words were sharp, and I peeked up from behind my arms.

"Map?" I whimpered.

"Well, not an actual map," she said, laughing.

Laughing. *Agggbhh!* I couldn't freaking handle this anymore. Every time she spoke, she dangled hope before me, only to rip it away again.

"Your grandmother, her books, and things . . ." Riona waved her hands emphatically across the table. "She left you all the clues you need to find the element."

"Wait. So, you don't know where it is? You found the element and decided to what? Wait till I was around to find it for real?" Confusion melted my brain and my temper flailed. "You just *re-hid* it?"

"She was responsible for protecting it." Riona's voice was soft, disregarding my temper.

"She hid Water but didn't tell you where?" My words were desperate.

"Of course she didn't," Riona argued. "We needed to keep the element safe. If we both knew the location, then one of us could be used against the other, and we refused to allow that. We explored every contingency, creating our plan with supreme care. I understand you are frustrated and tired, Aislynn, but everything is here. We only need to put this together."

I looked at her across the books and papers scattered across the table. "I am so tired of the puzzles, games, and hidden messages!" I motioned at the table in frustration. My anger weighed on me, suffocating me with the eventuality of my *destiny* and the maze I was trapped in.

I had practiced magic for weeks and as proficient as I had become, the impending magical events were a constant pressure digging at my consciousness. Pushing my chair back, I walked out of the room, stalking out the door. I knew better than anyone that unless we wanted to be searching charred crisps of paper, I needed a break. My magic tingled, fraying at the edges.

I felt Rowan and Riona watching me go, Riona in interest and Rowan's worry palpable. That worry only pissed me off further. I plopped myself into the grass and I could hear Rowan's soft footsteps behind me. I ground my teeth in irritation. He knelt behind me, hands on my shoulders as he gently massaged.

"Riona can be exasperating, which is why she was at odds with the Council so much of the time," he said. "She doesn't give. Ever. Which is exactly why she *is* the Witch of the Ancient Keepers; her family line of magic doesn't allow for anything else. She is deeply rooted in her destiny."

He kneaded through the trigger points in my shoulder blade, soothing my anger and flushing the frustration. I huffed out my breath. I knew this. I did. I realized she and my grandmother didn't leave room for leeway; every step was planned methodically to help me. I tried to convince myself I wasn't being ungrateful.

Shit.

"Don't worry, she understands. She understands you better than you may know yourself at this point, which is why she knows precisely how hard to push." He used his thumbs to smooth away the knots in the base of my skull.

I chewed on my cheek. *Dammit.* I hated admitting I was being an asshole. "I'm sorry."

Rowan brought his head near mine, looking sideways at me. "Aislynn, don't apologize. I wouldn't be surprised if she is testing you."

"What do you mean?" With my face near his, my anger diluted. I pulled my lip under my teeth.

"She wanted to see if you would control your magic. Would you hold it in, or would it come spurting out of you, unbridled and uncontrolled?" He squatted, balancing on his toes.

It made sense. My thoughts trickled to my past. She knew. *Dammit.* I should have realized; Riona had worked so closely with my grandmother, of course she did. I tapped my teeth against each other. *She can't know everything, can she?* I tucked my worries away for later.

"Give yourself some credit, Aislynn," Rowan tried to soothe, still believing I was upset with Riona. I had turned to more ferocious concerns.

"Thanks, Rowan." I forced my smile, head turning toward him. I gazed into those warm, bright eyes. Discarding my frustrated thoughts, I recognized perhaps part of his destiny was to keep me on track. How many times had he soothed, calmed, and eased me into taking the next step?

Or pushed when necessary? *If he knew the truth of my past, he wouldn't be so generous or kind.* I released my breath as the depressive thoughts charged through my subconscious again. Tidbits of his soothing magic streamed around me, and I savored the moment even in my emotional turmoil.

After a while, we headed back inside the house. Shoving my inner demons aside to engage with later, I settled on the fact that my grandmother had not left me stranded without answers. I missed something. We sat around the table, charging through my grandmother's things. A new resolve drove me back to the problem at hand.

If she *had* hidden Water, then we needed to find it first, because Daragon wouldn't be far behind us. Something in the back of my mind bothered me, all the way back from the beginning, when I remembered the box my grandmother gave me. As Rowan informed me about the prophecy, which mirrored the childhood stories my grandmother told me, that had created a tickle. When we found the album from the boxes in the storage unit, something nagged at me. I tried to pull the threads together, but nothing fit.

My bag made a chirping sound. It had been tossed into the corner after we started our search of all the documents, papers, and books. I immediately recognized the sound, but—

How is that possible?

My phone. How the hell could my phone receive a text message in another Realm? With pursed lips and hesitant movements, I retrieved my phone, sliding my thumb across the screen.

Amy. How the . . . ?

Hey. Wicked dreams last night. Where the F are you? I stopped by your office and they said you were out. Um, my bad juju senses are hitting the roof today. Just wanted to check in.

I read the text again, my mind reeling. Why and how did I receive her message? More importantly, time is passing, which meant we were up shit creek. Another beep.

My dreams. Wicked. Didn't your grandmother pass when you were little? Or younger? She was in my dream, not sure what THAT means.

Chewing on the side of my lip, I wondered why Amy would dream about my grandmother. I had long given up on coincidences and believed this must be all connected. The missing link stared at me, but I still couldn't put the puzzle together. *Dammit.* What was I missing?

"It's Amy," I told Rowan, who was standing behind me as I stared at my screen. "She dreamt about my grandmother."

"That's interesting. What do you think it means?" he pushed.

"I am not sure, but I am concerned." I paced the room, muttering my thoughts out loud. The amulet in my Realm, the stories, the storage unit, the books . . . everything always led to my Realm.

Would she have hidden Water in our Realm? It would've been dangerous. Exceptionally dangerous and ill-advised by most, I was sure, which is precisely why she would have done it. I pondered if Daragon recognized Water was hidden in my Realm but didn't know where. That may explain why he followed me like a damn puppy.

It had to be there. Finally, like little pins slowly falling into a lock, I understood exactly what she did. On one hand, it was a genius plan, on the other absurdly obvious. My hand shot to my mouth as it hit me. I couldn't say where my grandmother hid it. If I uttered the location, Rowan, Riona, and Matthew would all be at risk. My grandmother's choices all became clear, and a fierce new determination swelled in me. How did I not see it before?

"I know where Water is," I whispered.

Rowan reacted first, turning toward me. "What? Where?"

"I can't tell you. It's too dangerous. I won't risk it." I frowned, eyes pinching. It was my turn to be protective.

"But we need to know so we can make a plan," Rowan insisted and shook his head. His eyebrows locked together as he looked at me. His magic probed at me, but I pushed back, not allowing him anything. My hand pulled at my lip and a plan began to formulate in my mind. The how's weren't quite there, but I knew what I had to do.

"Riona," I began, looking to where she still sat at the table, "you are going to have to show me how to pull the element from its hiding place."

"It is an ancient magic, one you have already done once on a smaller scale. However, this will be far more diffi-cult . . . almost impossible."

"When? She couldn't have." Rowan's tone was adamant as he turned on Riona.

"But she has." Riona looked to me.

"The boxes," I began, understanding what she meant. "The safe-deposit boxes. Remember how she hid one inside the other?" Riona nodded, and Rowan's eyes filled with understanding.

"There are several dimensions, layers of magic," Riona explained. "Your grandmother managed to layer the magic and hide the element within the layers, hiding in plain sight. It was her idea, a risky magic as it's temperamental, but she insisted." Pride was visible within her face, and I imagined them working together. It tugged on my heartstrings.

"The magic to separate the dimensions is dangerous and complicated. It's nothing like what was used on the boxes, which was simple and was used as a clue to guide you. This will not be easy." She settled back into her chair.

"Like any of this has been easy?" The word *easy* didn't seem to be written in my destiny.

My mind drifted back to Amy. I pulled my phone out of my back pocket to reply to her. I usually scoffed at Amy and her "spidey senses." She refused to call them that, but I insisted, just to make her crazy because she *hated* spiders. Loathed. Sometimes I sent her spider videos just to torture her, and in return she sent me on awful dates.

As crazy as she made me, I loved her, and worry trampled over me. The dreams appeared to be her magic coming out in her subconscious mind, before with the amulet and now with my grandma. I started my reply.

Hey. I'm okay, just taking care of some things. Yes, she passed when I was 16. What was the dream about?

I hit send, doubting it would go through.
Failed to send.
Dammit.

Riona interrupted my thoughts. "I will need to prepare myself to show you how to invoke and separate the dimensions. It will be the most difficult magic you have done yet, so be ready." Her eyes were steady and serious.

My throat hot and dry, I nodded.

29

The cottage was quiet in the early morning. While Matthew was out hunting and Rowan was still sleeping, Riona and I enjoyed tea at the table.

"Aislynn, for this spell and the magic you need to perform to retrieve Water, you need to understand a few things." The morning light filtered through the dusty rose color of her curtains, illuminating the steam rising from our cups. "You are now aware that the rules of the universe are far more intricate than you previously realized. As hypothesized by some in your Realm, there are layers to our world: layers of dimensions, Realms, and even parallels. In your Realm, the dimensions are weaved within the Realm, hidden and unseen by most." She splayed her hands open.

"But some people can see them?" I asked.

"Of course. Think of your mediums, angel workers, witches, and those who believe in gnomes, fairies, werewolves, vampires, and the like. It exists, just unseen to most." She took a sip of her tea.

"And of course, the ones who can travel among the dimensions and are *of* those dimensions keep these secrets for a reason," Riona continued." Do you honestly think vampires want humans to be aware of their existence? Of course not! Wiccans and Pagans play with magic, but amid teenagers finding themselves, there are witches with actual powers. But why would they out themselves to society? It didn't end well for them last time." Her words were harsh, and I had to agree; our history had been cruel.

My thoughts stuck on the word vampires. I didn't want to think about the fact that vampires existed somewhere in our Realm. I focused my attention back on Riona.

"So, on one dimension or more, all these magical beings exist," she clarified, and I nodded my understanding. "Now, the dimensions are stacked within each other. The walkers of the dimensions, those with magical gifts, have the freedom to travel as needed across the Realms. You will soon discover, as your grandmother did, that all the fluff that went into preparing to travel Realms was completely unnecessary. Nevertheless, the history of witches and Hallervania's magic is one of ritual and ceremonial protocol that runs in their blood."

"I can travel by myself between the Realms?" This information would've been useful weeks ago; I could've traveled to check on Amy. Worry creeping back to me, I rubbed my sweaty palms down my jeans.

"Yes, of course. It might be difficult at first, but with practice it becomes easy. We are off track. For most, your grandmother included, this kind of magic is difficult. For you, as Keeper of Elements, I suspect you will have a learning curve." A small smile formed on her lips.

She held up her hands, right hand stacked on top of the other. Her right fingertips rested on top of her left wrist, and her left fingertips touched the bottom of her right wrist.

"Imagine this is one dimension stacked within your realm. To retrieve the element, you will need to separate and pull apart the dimension." She slid her hands away from each other, creating an opening between her fingertips. "You will do this, times five."

Shit. I tried not to groan out loud.

"So, not only will you create an opening in your Realm, but you will also hold five dimensions aside in order to pull the element through." Her words were stated simply.

My eyes raised to the ceiling and I held my head at the temples. I contemplated the physical and mental strength it took to hold a water tiger or a band of fire. Now I would need to hold five dimensions of magic? *Freaking great.* Internally I whimpered, heat seething in my abdomen.

"Keep in mind that most are only aware of maybe the first two dimensions," Riona continued. "Very few are aware of the third, past that the fourth or fifth. It takes an extreme magical being to even be aware of them, let alone access them."

How in the hell can I do this?

"Wait, then how did my grandmother do it? Let alone hide the element?" I inquired. As proficient as she became, she wasn't an important magical being like Riona described, so how did she accomplish this magic?

Riona's face dropped. "Aislynn, this is something I questioned for years. I do not know how she hid the element. From what we learned together and the things I knew, I have no idea how she accomplished the feat of hiding the element deep within the dimensions of magic."

Concern drifted into her eyes. "I secretly hoped I would find answers when you came through. However, she is as elusive as ever. I don't think your grandmother fully trusted me, at least not with your magical destiny." Her eyes saddened, and I could tell these worries had troubled her for some time.

"You think someone helped her?" I searched her face for answers.

"I do," she said in whispered tones. "I understand why she kept it from me; it was part of our plan. But, seeking outside help and from someone unknown to me, I just . . . I have not been able to reach any answers."

"Someone helped her, then, or assisted in some way," I thought out loud. "There's no way she could accomplish this by herself, right?"

"Absolutely." Riona let out a huff of air and her mouth settled into a line.

So who had helped her? I was certain Riona had searched the magical Realms for anyone who might have assisted my grandmother. That left my Realm. Was it possible a simple "human" helped her? Winston? No. There is no way. I tucked it into my thoughts for later.

"There's one more thing you will not like." Riona hesitated.

"I like any of this?" My mocking tone only led to her shrugging.

"I can give you the magic, I can teach you the words, and I can tell you what to do, but we cannot practice the magic."

Silence prickled the air.

"I'm sorry, what did you just say?" I rattled through her sentence again. "What do you mean I can't practice?"

"There isn't a way, Aislynn; this is a one-shot deal. If we practice separating the dimensions, holding back magical layers, people will notice. We can't chance that."

My eyes went wide, staring at the witch. *Of course we can't practice.* Snarky sarcastic comments filled my mind, but I clamped my mouth shut. I needed a plan. A damn good plan. Ideas started to string together, as well as the people I needed to make this happen. The chance of success was probably next to zero, but that hadn't stopped me yet.

Morning light cascaded across the walnut wood floor, dust motes suspended, awaiting disturbance. I peeked out of the bedroom door before closing it carefully, trying to avoid the inevitable creaks. After a few days of plotting, I decided to covertly follow through with my plan without telling anyone, including my tattletale cat.

My eyes scrunched tightly, certain I would end up in Transylvania or somewhere worse. *Focus, Aislynn.* Relaxing, I thought of Amy's apartment in Coon Rapids, a suburb of north Minneapolis. She lived on the second floor of a three-level complex. We often joked that she was stuck between two levels of Hell. Literal, actual Hell. Not the nicest part of Coon Rapids, she had gotten stuck in a lease with an ex-boyfriend and had been trapped for precisely another four months, eleven days, fourteen hours, and twenty-one minutes. We'd kept track.

We decided the neighbors above her were an actual herd of elephants owned by demonic overlords, and the lady next door was her own brand of crazy. She would pound on Amy's door to inform her she needed to blast her stereo at 110 decibels and sing karaoke, *really* loudly, because the people in the walls enjoyed it. This usually occurred at two in the morning.

Sometimes she would invite Amy to sing with her. Why did this happen? Why did she need to do this? Not a freaking clue. This was the madness of Amy's life. I told her we could create a reality television show entirely based on her neighbors.

Focus. I envisioned everything: her kitchen, dining room, the small bathroom down the hall, and the lotus flower painting that hung above her bed. I imagined the sliding glass door with a view of her patio. I could smell her diffuser with her favorite blend of orange spice oils wafting through the living room. The light piano music she played met my ears, and I slid over through the dimensions.

And just like that, I stood in her living room. *Wow.* Easy-peasy. *Freaking cool.* Maybe I could get good at this destiny business. Of course, my pride in myself was quickly interrupted by foul language and screaming.

"OH MY GOD!" Amy shouted with a squeal. I had disrupted her, curled up in her chair reading a book. "Where . . . WHERE did you come from? What . . . what the . . . ? What? How? What?"

The probability of me getting in a word edgewise to explain myself was limited. Instead, I plopped on the couch and waited for her to finish her tirade.

"Hi."

"HI? That's all you say! HI?" At this point she stood above me, dramatically waving her arms to fully encompass her emotions. I suppose I didn't blame her. "Don't you dare come in here and say hi! Where the hell have you been? I've looked for you for *three* days! Three! *And* your mother told me you were there last Saturday with the hot guy! At her actual house. You took him to your mom's house? I about spit my coffee in her stoic face! What in the hell is going on?"

Well, at least she was over me magically appearing in her living room. I raised my eyebrow at her while scooching back on the couch as she got closer with her . . . enthusiasm.

"Are you done yet? Do you want me to answer those questions? Or no?" My mouth twitched.

Amy went quiet, breathing heavily. *This is good.* Then, she crossed her arms. *Shit.* I was in trouble. She tapped her foot. She expected and wanted answers. Now.

"I've been in another Realm learning magic because I need to save the elements and the magical realms for Light. My cat talks, the asshat you always believed he was; Rowan, a.k.a. 'hot guy,' is pretty awesomesauce; and do *not waggle* your eyebrows at me." My cheeks flushed with heat. "There is this douche, Daragon, who is a royal pain in my ass and wants me dead, and probably other guys, and this shitty Council of Magic. My grandmother was involved, which is why you had dreams about her, oh, and I am pretty sure you have magical gifts, too." I spewed everything like a fast-paced train wreck.

Amy's eyebrow marched upward.

Grabbing the amulet at my chest, I held it up. "This? It's the ancient Amulet of the Elements, and I am Keeper of said Elements. I must rescue each of them: Earth, Air, Fire, and Water. I must find them from unknown, hidden places and return them back to a magical tree. I have magical powers, and I've been destined to control magic that has been hidden for centuries. I need you to help me reclaim the first one. I'm 99 percent sure I know its location. You'll never guess where."

I waited. Her eyes narrowed, staring intently at me. Finally, she sat down, recollecting her Kindle that had been tossed to the floor in her overly emotional state.

"Well, that would explain why your eyes look like a twinkle shit show."

That's my Amy! My insides turned gooey, and I wanted to hug her.

"Your cat totally hates me, doesn't he?" She looked at me pointedly.

I bit my lip. "Uh, yeah. But if it makes you feel any better, he kinda hates everyone."

"I knew it!" she almost yelled.

I cocked my head, surprised she hadn't asked the obvious questions. Perhaps that wasn't that surprising.

"First one is Water, right? Blue?" Her eyes narrowed again, waiting for a reaction.

How the hell does she know that?

"Uh, yeah," I replied. "How did you know?"

"Well, I don't tell you *every* dream I have, especially since you don't answer my damn texts!" *Point taken.* "And what magical powers do I have, per se?"

"Uh, obviously, powers of premonition!" I rolled my eyes. "I am sure other stuff, but I don't know. I barely know what I am doing!"

"So, where were you exactly?" she asked, rubbing her hand across the Kindle.

"A magical Realm called Hallervania."

Her sharp "Ha!" laugh cut through the room. "Is that by Transylvania?" I shook my head in laughter. "So, you were actually unable to answer my texts."

I nodded.

"I guess I can forgive you, then." She seemed satisfied. "So, where is it? Water, I mean."

I tried to keep up as she changed directions yet again.

"Well, technically it's hidden in five layers of magic that I am supposed to magically hold back whilst I retrieve the element. But to answer your question: the lake property."

"I *freaking* knew it!" Amy exclaimed. "I *told* you that place has weirdo energy! I knew it! It always felt creepy, like the edge of something was going to curl up and swallow you."

Of course the fact that I had to hold back five layers of magic wasn't what caught her attention but the lake property. I inwardly rolled my eyes. *Oh, Amy.*

The lake property had been in my family for years, near the Lake of the Woods on the northern border of the state. My grandmother often spent her summer weeks at the cabin, and I would go with her. The clues were there all along: the numbers in the notepad (longitude/latitude), and that photo album in the box included only pictures from our summers at the cabin.

Minnesota owns the label of Ten Thousand Lakes, and though there were more than that, I guessed ten thousand was a nice even number. Water was hidden in a state of lakes? Absurd and obvious.

And I believed Daragon realized the element was hidden in my Realm, in my own state, but he didn't know where. Water was a needle in the proverbial haystack, or one fish in ten thousand lakes.

Amy and I had stayed at the lake house the last three summers. My mother had been happy to let us use the cabin as she despised the lake, camping, and giant, bird-sized mosquitoes. Over the years, we had big parties, hangouts, and lazy weekends; however, Amy was always torn. The cabin was amazing for the epic parties of twenty-something-year-olds, but it always gave her the heebie-jeebies. I thought her description apt; I imagine Water did want to swallow her up.

"So . . . you have a plan." Amy encouraged me to continue.

"A half-assed one, yeah," I admitted, then explained it.

"Yeah, that's a shitty plan," she agreed. "But I have some ideas that might work." She tapped her fingers to her lips. "Oh! And this Daragon dude?" she added, suddenly animated again. "With dark, dark eyes, almost black? Black hair? Smug and sort of jack-monkey-like?"

"Yup, that's him!" I thought it was an adequate description. "How did you know?"

"That jackass has been bugging me for weeks! He's a sneaky little shit." The validation made her happy.

"Yes, he is. Bugging you how, though?" I worried what hell he provided to Amy.

"Well, first he started showing up in my dreams. He baited me with the 'you're worthless' card hard, toying with my head. In general, making me feel shitty about myself. Then he moved to showing up at work and on the bus, kind of like pausing time?"

She threw her hands up. "Like, I was in my head imagining all of it, but I knew it was real. He would show me things like my mom being better off without me . . . really screwed up stuff. I mostly told him to go away. A few times he scared the shit out of me, though." She internally trembled, and I could tell she gave a very mild version of her experiences.

My jaw tightened. *That little . . .*

All this time, Daragon had been relatively quiet on my end because of my magical protection from Riona, but he'd been torturing my friend. I vowed to make sure he paid for his douchery. If he was willing to attack from multiple angles, perhaps he was uneasy about his current position. The thought gave me some satisfaction.

"So. You believe me?"

Amy scoffed, offended. "Of *course* I do. Why wouldn't I?"

A spurt of laughter burst out of me. "Why, indeed?"

"Look, Aislynn: I see you. Past all the crap you use pretending to fool people. You have this brightness about you; this light that's fierce and spunky, and I've seen you do things I can't explain."

My head moved back. *What has she seen? Have I done things? What things?*

"I don't think you are aware of most of it. So you coming here and telling me you are an almighty magical being is *not* a surprise." She arched her brow. "At all."

"I am *not* almighty." I shook my head with disgust, but Amy shrugged.

"Wanna go to Hallervania?" I asked with a grin.

"Let me get my things!" She jumped up, sauntering toward her bedroom. I sat back on the couch with a smirk.

"Sooo, is it cold there? Do I need a coat?" she called from down the hall.

"If I told you it's warm and perfect, will you kiss my feet?" I hollered back.

She appeared in the hall with her mouth hanging open. "Wait . . . are you saying?" She brought her hands together. "Are you saying there is . . . no evil white suck?" She collapsed to her knees and threw her arms into the air. "Praise sweet baby Jesus!" she exclaimed with sheer joy, which sent me into a fit of giggles on the couch. She hated snow almost as much as I did.

Eventually, Amy came down the hall with packed bags. Bags. As in plural. I raised my eyebrows at her.

"What? I dress by mood." She heaved her bags on her shoulder. *Giant eye roll.*

"So how does this work?"

"Well, it might make you throw up." I didn't give her a chance to respond and grabbed her hand. I focused on Riona's cottage, the warmth and the safe harbor it had become, and just like that, I slid back into the magical Realm.

30

Amy's face drained of blood. I was familiar with the feeling, and although nice to be on the other side, I tried to comfort her.

"I think . . . I think I need to sit down." She sunk to the bench behind her.

"Yeah. I'll give you Rowan's advice: breathe," I said. Amy glared within her grimace and I sat down next to her, letting my hand trace small circles on her back.

"Welcome to Hallervania," said a whisper coming from the corner. Riona. She stepped from the shadows, appearing more "witch" than I'd seen since the first night. A royal blue velvet cloak shrouded her with the Tree of Elements broach holding at the center of her chest.

"I am Riona. You are a part of Aislynn's destiny to reclaim the Elements for Light and will be an intricate aspect of helping her succeed. You will be pushed in ways you cannot fathom. Every limit you know will be tested." A smokiness sauntered through her words.

"Riona, don't scare her. She just got here," I argued.

Amy's mouth was semi-open, glancing from me to Riona. That might be the first time I had ever seen Amy speechless.

"She should be terrified. She is playing with the balance of magic for our world. This is the accumulation of thousands of years of waiting to reestablish balance and the existence of magic for all kind."

A silence filled the room as the enormity of her words took over. Chills crawled up my legs and arms. Gulping, I realized how gentle Riona had been with me.

"Because it was the only way." Jax strode into the room. *"You are a sneaky little Keeper."* His blue eyes filled with judgy cat displeasure. I supposed he was angry with me for ditching out without telling him. *"It's you,"* he hissed as he sat in front of Amy.

"Your cat talks." Her words were disjointed with shock.

"I told you."

"But he really, actually talks!" she insisted and pointed, her eyes wide. My head bobbed in unison with her hand.

"So, I have to put up with you."

"He *is* an asshole," she said. As if I would've lied to her.

"Whatever, Squirrel."

Disdain riddled Amy's face, like I could somehow control the fuzzy creature's mouth. I shook my head.

"Don't bother. You will lose," I offered. Jax threw his body against my legs, swirling and shedding black fur onto my pants.

"We do not have time for such trivial behavior. Yes, the cat speaks," Riona snipped. "Amy, do you accept these challenges, your destiny, and helping Aislynn reclaim magic?"

Riona's eyes were intent on Amy. Tendrils of colorful light poured in from the edges of the room, a steady pulse as a thread of Riona's magic weaved around us.

"Here we go!" Jax watched with excitement.

Amy's eyes darted around the room, sensing the unfamiliar magic around her. A throbbing hum filled my ears when Amy glanced my direction. I shrugged, putting my hands up. This was new to me, too.

"Yes," she replied, her voice unsure. Then she stood, the gravity of Riona's request melting over her as she spoke clearly. "Yes, I will. I will help Aislynn do whatever is necessary to fulfill her destiny."

I was dumbfounded by her surge of passion for me, magic, and taking a leap of faith into the unknown. Without hesitation, Amy believed in something she only just learned.

My throat tightened. Amy trusted effortlessly with an internal compass she never defied. I wished for half the balls she had and tried to focus as the magic began to take shape. Intertwining threads encompassed us in a circle, reminding me of a Celtic weave of light.

"Then I, Riona, Witch of the Ancient Keepers, cast you, Amy, into this circle of protection. I bind you to Aislynn and her destiny of Light, to reclaim the elements and the magic across the Realms." Her words sung through the cottage. The magic, growing stronger and brighter, moved in a steady thrum of motion.

My own stream of magic burst across my chest. Much like how I was aware of the elements, I could feel Amy; there was a light inside of me, an awareness of her being connected to me. Everything settled, the thrum in my ears becoming an indistinct buzz.

"Aislynn, as you begin this quest, those who vow to help you will be bound to you through magic and through the interconnectedness of creation. You will be aware of them, their feelings, and their essence, always," Riona said, explaining the tingling of light I felt.

Well, isn't that nice? I thought to myself while sensing Amy's bewilderment.

"You will need to find your time manipulator soon."

I hoped Tristan would be as willing as Amy.

⚜

I thought it best to beg Tristan for his help by myself, mostly so no one would have to see how pathetic I could be if I needed to resort to begging. But alas, I had an audience. Amy pleaded to come, curiosity getting the best of her, even after being nauseated by teleporting. And with much opposition, a very irritated Rowan came as my protector. *Jumping Realms without telling anyone didn't go over well.*

Almighty being of magical kick-ass, holder of the elements, keeper of light, I reached for ridiculous titles . . . okay, I totally needed a protector. The three of us whisked ourselves to Tristan's home. There had been a lengthy argument about the safety of the trip, the Council still after us, blah blah blah, but I continued to be adamant with my decisions. After all, I was captain of this screwed up shit show.

Tristan's house was surrounded in an uneasy quiet, alerting us to the emptiness. Not only was the house empty, it appeared disheveled. *Dammit.* I wondered who had come first: The Council? Daragon? I shuddered.

"We need to go," I said. Without another word, we whipped back to Riona's.

"Well, that was uneventful," Amy said, pulling the bench out from under the table.

"Do you think it was the Council?" I asked Rowan.

"I am not sure. I will check on a few things. Will you *please* stay here this time?" He didn't give me a chance to respond as he disappeared before our eyes. *Yeah, he's definitely still angry with me.*

"That isn't going to get old, is it?" Amy questioned, tucking pieces of her purple chunks of hair behind her ears and I half smiled. Pacing the kitchen, I tried to settle my uneasiness.

"Nope. It does get irritating, though, after the awe wears off." I settled next to her on the bench, leaning back on the table.

How would I find Tristan? I needed him, or my plan would never work. I pushed my palms across my jeans, standing again.

"Uh, Aislynn . . ." Distress flooded Amy's voice. I turned to see her eyes wide in fear and followed her gaze.

A mass of silver fur appeared in the doorway, ears cocked as he sniffed the air. Amy stood quickly, trying to put distance between her and what I knew to be Matthew. The bench groaned as it pushed into the table, causing Amy to stumble to her feet. Beaming, I walked to him and ruffled his ears, massaging the soft fur at the back of his head.

"Hey, friend," I said to him. I admit, it was weird when he was in wolf form wanting attention like an animal when I knew he had a human form. Jax was different; he was always a cat, but like most things here, I tried not to think about it.

"Aislynn!" Amy's distress wandered into uncertainty.

"This is Matthew." I squatted down, and he licked my face. *Ew, Matthew!* "Matthew, this is Amy." I peered over my shoulder, nodding in her direction. "She is one of my favorite humans."

"I am not sure . . . I . . ."

Poor Amy. I stood, glancing back at Matthew.

"Maybe, Matthew, you should . . ." I wiggled my hands. "Maybe it would be easier."

Matthew nosed around my legs, eyeballing Amy carefully as a small whine puffed his cheeks. His beautiful wolf shape shimmered, magic shivering around him as he took human form, dressed in clothes. I wondered how that worked and vowed to ask him sometime.

"Uh . . ." Amy fell back to the bench again. "What the . . . ? What?"

Guilt washed over me. I wasn't being fair. "Matthew is a shapeshifter. He prefers wolf form, but I figure you might appreciate the human, for conversation purposes." I offered a smile.

"Hello, Amy, human from Aislynn's Realm." His voice was soft as he cocked his head. "Welcome to Hallervania." Matthew's shaggy hair fell over his hazel eyes.

"Um. Thank you." Amy's cheeks reddened, and courtesy of the new bond I shared with her, something else tickled through my senses. My eyes shot to her, then to Matthew and back again.

As they stared at each other, I stood in a place I liked to call "awkward town." I tried to make myself invisible as they assessed each other, but I was also curious about the emotions pinging away inside me. Amy admired Matthew's stocky human form, and Matthew . . .

Uh . . . no. Just no. I rubbed my lips against each other, closing my eyes, trying to block everything I felt. I busied myself with the towel on the counter, trying to count away the awkwardness.

Matthew broke the gaze first as he came back to planet kitchen land, and I further stamped the emotions emanating from both of them. Some things I did not need to know.

"Aislynn," Matthew began, still distracted. "I came because of Tristan." His eyes *finally* turned my direction.

"Do you know where he is?" I asked. "We went to his house, and it looked ransacked."

"The Council made an attempt to disrupt your plan." Fury rocked his hazel eyes. Amy caught the tone and arched a brow in my direction. I would need to explain later.

"How did they know he's part of my plan?" My hands tightened into fists.

"Their Seers, I am sure. But it doesn't matter; Tristan was able to stop them and help his family escape. Thankfully, they are safe." Matthew's jaw tightened and his anger fused through his words. "He will be here shortly, but he's taking extra precautions."

I nodded. Nothing up until this point had been easy and my nerves edged into raw land. The need to retrieve the element was a constant pounding in my mind. Matthew decided he could stay awhile, so he and Amy began to find something assimilating lunch.

Trying to distance myself from their flirty eyes, long gazes, and Amy's cute giggles, I stalked the room like an outraged panther, but it didn't seem to help. Amy pulled me to the side of the kitchen, tipping her head toward Matthew.

"So . . . why is it that everyone is so dang good-looking here?" Amy whispered as I tried not to notice her ogling Matthew's backside. She focused back on me, realizing I was distracted. "Relax, Aislynn. Tristan is coming. Everything will be fine."

Grating my teeth, I didn't answer and resumed my pacing. Tension throbbed in my shoulders, zinging pulses up the muscles of my neck, the intense feeling of being perpetually behind consumed me.

The room suddenly slowed. Amy paused midstride, and Matthew's turn slowed as he smiled in Amy's direction. All movements were like heavy sand until they came to a complete standstill.

Tristan.

He appeared before me.

"Hello, Aislynn. I apologize for the freeze of your friends; however, I refuse to take chances." He gestured toward Amy and Matthew.

"It's fine. Are you okay? Your family? I am sorry for all this." My face twisted with guilt. I couldn't stand the idea of other people's lives being thrown into chaos because of me and my destiny. *And my shitty planning.*

"Everyone is fine. Don't worry so. This is my destiny. As a family of time magic, we have always been entwined in influential magical events; it is our destiny much as this is yours. And though my family has not seen a talented time manipulator for several hundred years, we are prepared for the roles we play in the history and existence of magic." He searched my eyes. "Aislynn, I have always been a part of this. My purpose as a time manipulator is to help you restore the elements. I have always known this."

"But you didn't tell me." I gnawed on my lip.

"I couldn't. You know the rules," he said. My eyes rolled on reflex. *Of course not!* "Tell me your plan to reclaim Water."

I told him my ideas and shitty plan. I hoped he didn't take offense to my expectations of his magic, and double crossed my fingers *and* toes that he wouldn't laugh in my face. Fortunately, only contemplation and gentle nods in agreement flashed across his face.

"This might work," he contemplated. "I am more than capable of the tasks you need."

A part of me was profoundly grateful while the other was worried, praying he wasn't being cocky about his abilities.

"Don't worry; I am far more proficient in my magic than anyone realizes." He winked, following my thoughts. Smiling, I allowed myself to relax a little as I rubbed my fingertips into my neck muscles.

Riona chose to appear then, head tipped with eyes questioning the two frozen people in the room. "Tristan, would you mind?" She gestured toward Amy and Matthew, still in midmotion. Tristan turned his hand with half a glance, and Amy and Matthew continued their movements, stuttering before seeing the two extra people.

"Thank you," Riona said with kindness. Amy tried to speak, but her words were stuck as her mouth bobbed open and closed. Speechless again. A new record. Matthew eyed Tristan apprehensively, and I sensed an internal debate weighing on Matthew as to whether he should shift back into wolf form, unappreciative of being caught off guard.

"We have our time manipulator." Riona's eyes glittered. "Tristan, you are well-aware of your destiny to help Aislynn reclaim the Elements. I now bind you to her and cast you into the protection of Light to retrieve the elements to return to the Tree and restore the balance of magic."

Whips of light in shades of iridescent blues weaved around me and Tristan, linking us and our magic together. He accepted the flood of power and the magic shimmered through him. There was something perceivably different this time as he *allowed* the threads to move within and interlace with his own.

The protective magic receded, and the kitchen became alive with normalcy, filling with laughter and excitement. Leaning on the back of the couch, I watched everyone interact, settling on Riona's satisfied smile.

And so, there they were: my little group of misfits, joined to help me accomplish ancient magic which hadn't been seen for centuries. Their lives were held in my hands, wrapped tightly amidst my own destiny.

31

We went over the spell repeatedly until it became ingrained into my being. Bu without physical practice, it felt flat and lacking, leaving me worried. Wondering if I would actually be able to perform the magic, I tried to hold on to hope, knowing that destiny was supposedly on my side.

I ran through the steps again in my head. We had a well thought out plan. I could do this. The ancient words repeated until they became natural and fluid in my voice.

"What happens if I can't control it?" I asked, drawing my head away from the paper in front of me to Riona across the table. "Or if I lose control?"

Riona was thoughtful before answering. She tapped her fingers across the table. "Do you remember when your sisters told you the tale of the White Witch?"

"Sisters? They aren't my sisters," I snapped, still a bit hurt. "But yes, I remember."

"Aila hardly touched on the rage that poured through the witch and the people she desiccated with Fire magic."

My dreams lingered at the edge of my thoughts.

"If you let the elements take over, if you give them the tiniest amount of power, they will be a wildfire in your soul. You will be a vessel to hold and carry the magic. Aislynn, it will burn you alive as it consumes your essence."

My swallow was audible as my eyes enlarged, and I folded the paper underneath my fingertips. "Well, that sounds rather unpleasant."

"You must hold control at all times. You are the Keeper. You hold the power to reign the magic." Crystal flecks in her eyes shimmered at me, reflecting my past and all the times I had lost control. "If you do not, the Elements will be lost forever, and Water will be released upon *all* the realms."

Rolling my lips against each other, my eyes twitched with emotion. Once again, I was being forced to hold control over myself, something I had done since childhood. I pushed the memories down, as far away as possible. If Riona saw those moments, she might lose faith in me and my abilities.

"Will my plan work?" I questioned, distracting myself by willing my thoughts in a different direction. Taking a sip of my tea, I grimaced at the cold, bitter flavor in my mouth.

"I think it will. Rowan is still not pleased with your choices, but he recognizes your power to decide. He does not believe Tristan is ready to hold such an immense level of magic, nor does he think you should bring a mortal human into the mix."

Riona snapped her fingers and my tea mug warmed underneath my grasp. The instant radiating warmth pulsed, and the magic traced up my arms, surprising me with reassurance, calming my heart.

"Amy might be the most prepared. She expects me to succeed. I've got to say she really has processed this whole existence of magic quite well." With the tea steaming now, I sipped again.

Riona shifted her weight, pulling on the long sweater she wore.

"Tristan can hold the magic," I assured her. Honestly, I wasn't sure if he could, but I had to *believe* he could. He might be my only chance.

The day rolled into night as I continued practicing on my own. Scattered clouds hung across the sky, leaving the full moon shadowed in heaviness. It reminded me of the passage of time here in this realm. Even in my moments of frustration, something here always comforted me.

That evening Amy insisted I fill her in completely. Apparently, she was annoyed with only having pieces of information. She pestered me with nonstop questions regarding the White Witch, the prophecy, and my *sisters*. Amy tended to bring questions to the surface that I hadn't considered.

A little after ten, Amy ended her barrage of questions. With her brain melting in an overload of new information, she decided to follow Riona to bed and everything became still and quiet.

I wandered behind the cottage to one of my favorite spots: a massive cluster of granite boulders. Leaning against the hard stone, I closed my eyes, thinking about my life before magic. My general sense of floating through life had lacked any purpose. My mouth twitched. How things had changed.

For the second time today, my sisters entered my mind. Riona generally dismissed their role in my destiny; and although the title of sisters bothered me, I missed their presence: Ailianna's soothing attitude and Aila's opposing, feisty one. A part of me wanted them here actively participating with me, but it seemed impossible. I couldn't reconcile two conflicting parties never willing to work together on different sides of the magical spectrum.

"It's beautiful."

I knew it was Rowan before he spoke. Sneaking a glance from the corner of my eye, I saw him ease his way to the ground with me. The line of his jaw shimmered in the low light, contrasted against the scruff on his face. "It's almost time."

The apprehension and aversion to my plan he held were hidden within the lines of his forehead. I couldn't help smiling; it was kind of adorable.

"It's going to work," I said, patting his leg. This was a switch in roles, me convincing him. I tried not to laugh.

"Aislynn, if anyone is capable of this magical feat, it's you." The lilt in his voice gave me confidence as his blue, crystallized eyes peered into mine. Although he didn't approve of my plan, a deep trust settled into his gaze. Warmth washed over me as his faith sank deep.

Trust, with his life, and his world of magic, were all held in my hands. He had been here every step, protecting and guiding me through all my snarky comments, frustrations, and freak-outs. His head tipped near mine, and our foreheads met in the shadowed moonbeams.

In that quiet moment in the starlight, the realization of all the things I didn't believe were possible began to build around me. Magic thrummed between us. His chin tilted down, bringing his lips close to mine . . . a perfect moment.

It was shattered with the sound of an energy ball

cracking through the air. Rowan's eyes instantly shifted from enchanting to icy vigilance.

Seriously?

We both stood, potential kiss forgotten. Without any awareness of our movement, our sights set on the cottage. Its windows were suddenly filled with flashes of magic, and my mind whirled as I thought of everyone inside. Red shards of Dark magic flew across the windows, causing dread to swim over me.

"Rowan, we have to help!" I darted toward the cottage, but Rowan grabbed my wrist, stopping my dash.

"Aislynn, this way," he insisted, and looped me behind him with a finger at his lips.

Of course, I had intended on blasting into the cottage full of magical rage. However, Rowan forced me to pause and create a plan, quiet and contemplative as ever. My heart twisted with feelings for him. Begrudgingly, I sat on my heels beneath the window with his hand clasped on my arm, holding me in place.

So much for the trust. Teeth grinding against one another, my magic—snippets of furious reds—spurted from my fingertips.

"No, Aislynn. Control it. We don't know who it is!" Rowan warned.

Does it matter? Frustration struggled around me, and ribbons of colorful magic continued to swarm. Rowan glared in my direction, and I flipped my hands up in question as fountains of light extended from my fingers.

Voices suddenly thundered through the window.

"Riona! You meddling little witch! Do you not realize you have failed?" a male voice blared. I didn't recognize him, but from the way the color drained from Rowan's face, I could see that he did.

"Eirnin, you fight for the wrong side," Riona replied. The casted magic slammed back and forth. The walls of the small cottage trembled with the force of bright explosions. When our eyes met, I now found myself clenching Rowan's arm to keep him in place.

"You want to release an ancient, uncontrollable magic! This cannot be allowed!" Eirnin shouted, followed by a snap of magic.

Rowan wiggled underneath my grasp, and I watched the anger seep into his eyes. Deep rumbling growls resonated through the cottage from Matthew in wolf form.

"All lies which have filled your little mind," Riona sneered back as more bands of light flashed.

"Give her to us and let this be done!" Eirnin demanded. The swirls of their magic were reflected on the slabs of granite behind us. Vibrant streaks of colorful light emphasized the tirade within the cottage.

"I would never. Her destiny will not be interfered with by the likes of you!" A thunderous blast cracked through the air. Rowan counted his fingers down: *Three. Two.*

One.

His grip tightened, and we appeared at Riona's side. Behind her Matthew and Tristan were prepared for a fight. Farther back in the hallway a sleepy-eyed Amy peered around the corner, fear rippling in waves around her.

So, this was Eirnin.

"Oh, the little girl decided to make an appearance," he snipped, and my eyes narrowed, focusing on his gaunt face.

Little? Didn't he know it was rude to make fun of

someone's height? His mouth smirked as he threw a green shard of magic across the room.

My hands flew up simultaneously and with them came a crashing flood of water that ran from the floor to the ceiling, creating a wall between us and them.

Through the ripples of water, I saw that Eirnin did not come alone: there were three other Council members at his sides. A satisfied Cheshire cat grin slid across Riona's face when she looked at me: her prodigy of magic finally stood before her.

"You know not of the magic you wield. Nor the potential." Riona's sharp words cut through the water, and I knew the men on the other side could hear her.

In response, they continually threw sinister black energy balls at the barrier of water, but I sighed a breath of relief knowing that Amy, Tristan, Matthew, and even Jax were fine. Through all the magic cascading around the little cottage, those I cared for were safe. Stewing anger radiated from Rowan, however, and my concern shifted gears.

Holding the water barrier with ease, I pushed cold air past us and into the wall, sending shards of ice across the room. Just as the shards pierced the edges of all four of my enemies, I stopped the magic. Ice swords held each of them in place, with one about to drill the center of Eirnin's eye. He could barely blink for fear of the ice penetrating him.

"This *little* girl . . ." I threw his words back at him as I stepped closer, putting myself between them and my misfit family. I hoped Rowan would stay put and trust me. "Is going to fulfill her destiny and restore magic as it should be. Not you or any of your *little* Council members will stop me."

Courtesy of the bond I shared, varying emotions

slammed through me: Rowan's anger coiled within him, Riona's elation, and Amy's pure shock and awe to the magic streaming around the room.

"Eirnin, is it?" I asked, grabbing one of the ice shards hanging in the air. Alarm raced into his eyes, and I could tell that the Council hadn't really prepared him for coming here tonight. They sent him on their missions with disillusionment scattered through the purpose. Awareness trickled across his face, and I watched the realization dawn on him: this was a suicide mission, a test of *my* power, and nothing more.

"It's all coming together now, huh? Your Council misled you." My voice was as icy as the shard I held.

He swallowed hard, his Adam's apple a slow bob in his throat as I stepped closer.

Power, an electric current eating through my nerves, presented my choices. My gaze settled on each of them as uneasiness twitched through their bodies. For the first time, they were apprehensive; without the upper hand, fear trickled through them budding in the darkest places.

From the corner of my eye, I saw the one furthest from me react. He wanted to fight, to break free of the magic that locked him in place. Matthew took several steps forward in response, snarling and snapping his teeth with sharp barks of vehement fury. His rage toward this one individual rocketed through me, and Rowan's voice filled my mind. *"Lorcan."* This must be the one who filled the Council's wishes so long ago against Matthew and his family.

The wolf's wrath poured out of him. Consumed by his revenge, he stalked closer. I couldn't trust his reaction; the anger was too alive within him. Summoning Air, I pushed a fierce wind toward him, propelling him back a step. His snout shook against the harsh gust of air, and he snarled at me in disagreement.

"None of you understand me at all. Did you honestly think I would go with you? That I would bend so easily? You underestimate me." I was unsure if I had filtered some of Matthew's rage or if it was the magic coursing in my veins, but in that moment, something shifted inside me.

Lorcan wiggled, trying for an escape. I saw his mind wading through alternative plans as his eyes darted back and forth. With a turn of my hand, the ice shard flew, pushing him back into the wall.

"Most importantly? You underestimate the elements only I can control." Another flip of my hand and the ice shards collapsed to the floor, sending a roar of flames upward. Reds and oranges danced at their feet.

The other two men gave up, begging me to stop. I wondered if they were trainees, much like Rowan had been, and I knew they wouldn't harm me or my friends. I released the magical prison holding them, the flames dying just enough to give them a clear path to the door.

"Go, and do not return. If you try to cause harm to me or anyone I care about again, you will wish I had killed you, here and now." The unrelenting staccato snap to my voice was unrecognizable even to me. Riona's opposition to my decision rolled over me. The connection I shared with my group was both annoying and convenient.

I knew that Lorcan and Eirnin would not give in without a fight. Matthew resumed his aggressive growling at Lorcan, who was held at bay by my magical flames. These two would never surrender to each other. They were both ensnared by the past and the rage between them.

"Aislynn, perhaps they have learned enough this evening. They are insignificant to you and your destiny." Riona's voice cut through my internal debates.

Meeting Lorcan's stare, I disagreed. No, he wasn't insignificant at all; something hidden in those dark eyes told me he was not finished with me or Riona. Considering a moment longer, I swung my hands together, then blasted them apart. As the fire magic dissipated, Lorcan and Eirnin disappeared.

32

"Oh." Rowan's voice hitched. "Aislynn, did you . . . ?"

I turned, staring into his wide eyes, full of shock. "Kill them?" I finished, eyebrow arched. "No. However, they have quite the swim ahead of them. I put them at the bottom of the lake. I hope they can hold their breath."

Open mouths audibly snapped closed without response. Amy caught my attention, watching me with an apprehensive stare. *Did I frighten her?* I dropped to my knees in front of Matthew.

"I am sorry," I said. "Another time, I will let you rip off his face and shred his limbs, okay?"

As I ruffled his soft fur, his eyes filled with regret and hidden beneath perhaps there was a bit of relief. The wolf nuzzled my face and licked my mouth. *Gross.* Not the kiss I had hoped for, but better than nothing, I supposed. The magic relinquished its hold on me, and I glanced up to Rowan. A mixture of relief and pride washed over his face as a smile found both our lips.

Matthew excessively nuzzled me, and excitement saturated the room. He wiggled underneath my arm, tail wagging profusely like a feather duster. With a bout of laughter, he knocked me off my knees.

"We should celebrate!" Riona tossed magical sparks throughout the room, and clapping and hooting filled the small cottage. I scrutinized the situation with hesitation, unprepared to celebrate quite yet. The pressure from the Council was only the beginning of more to come.

Retrieving Water became even more imperative in my mind; if the Council was willing to make moves against us, Daragon wouldn't be far behind. His attack wouldn't be reckless or ill-formed. It would be calculated like a grandmaster chess player.

Everyone else rode Riona's excitement, pouring drinks and recounting their favorite moments of me threatening the Council members. Separating myself from the group, I stood in front of the window, moonlight once again shining upon me. The impending magic stifled inside me was ready to detonate at a moment's notice. I watched the puffy clouds roll across the moon. Rowan circled the room, finding his way to me and eyeing my apprehensive attitude.

"Not going to join in the festivities?" He folded his arms, leaning into the windowsill and giving me a sideways glance.

Lips rolling against each other, I glanced behind Rowan toward everyone in the kitchen. "Seems a tad early for that," I said. I wanted to tell him about what I had seen in Lorcan's eyes and the fact that it scared the shit out of me. I had focused my attention narrowly on Daragon without realizing that Dark would attack from several directions.

"Mm-hmm," he responded, tight-lipped. "Riona is

pleased with you, satisfied that she finally has the upper hand. It's good to be happy about such things; however . . ." His thought trailed off.

"Don't count your chickens before they hatch? Something like that old adage?" I asked.

Rowan's face scrunched as he pondered the odd sayings of my realm before finally giving in to a small nod. "Indeed, something like that." He rubbed the back of his hand against his chin, quiet for a moment. "You handled Eirnin interestingly, considering what I told you."

"I wanted to destroy him. For what he did. To Zarah, to you," I admitted. "But I couldn't."

"Thank you for that."

"I don't think he was prepared for me." I pushed off the window, balancing my weight on my heels.

"No, I don't think he was." His mouth pulled to the side in agreement. "You are worried about them, Lorcan and Eirnin."

"And about ten thousand other things," I confessed.

The clouds swarmed over the moon, covering it in a haze, leaving an ominous feeling behind. What had the Council hoped to gain from coming here? A test of my power, my capabilities, but what else? Riona implied the Council was infiltrated by Dark, which meant they knew what we were doing.

Eirnin was high on my suspicious list for obvious reasons, leaving Lorcan not far behind. The mood inside the cottage was still carefree even through my cynicism. My friends needed this, the excitement giving strength and pride to build comradery between everyone. Eventually the laughter died out and everyone scattered to their beds.

Unable to sleep, I curled up in the oversized chair in

front of the fire, watching the flames dance. The room was quiet except for the occasional pop within the wood as it exposed itself to the element. Flipping open the Tree of Elements book, I searched for Water. Each element was separated by an embossed image, and I traced my fingers over the swirling blue emblem.

In the silence, the amulet pulsed at my chest, magic rising from the floor and creeping up the walls. I placed my palm over the element, focusing on Water. Cerulean blue swam in my vision, and my family's lake property took shape in my mind.

The element was nestled within the lake and the magical layers which held it pulsed beneath the water. It called to me, weaving me into its fluid grace. The movement rushed over me as the element nudged, pleading for freedom.

Opening my eyes, I returned my gaze to the spirited play of the flames. Dazed by their hypnotic and alluring dance, I suddenly found myself deep in the woods, standing in a circle of exposed dirt. The trees surrounded me in a thick darkness as the moonlight cast shadows on the forest floor. I spun around, looking for the person behind the magic.

"I apologize. I cannot go to Riona's, but I can bring you here." The White Witch floated from the inky black tree line. The moment she reached the clearing, fire shot up from the perimeter. "I do promise to keep you safe and protected."

I crossed my arms, trying to hide my surprise. Ice blonde hair layered around her face in stark contrast to the blood red cloak shrouding her head. The fire illuminated her skin, creating a beautiful dangerous glow.

"Not so long ago you sat in The Orchard, unsure of yourself and your path." Her eyes tracked mine in contemplation. "I know you have set your intentions on Water being the first element . . ." Sliding her hands from the cloak, she brought them to a temple in front of her. My eyebrows crept upward with suspicion. "But I must interfere. There are things you are unaware of that must be tended to first."

"Like . . . ?" I asked, a slight edge in my voice.

"Air magic."

"Air? But I don't know anything about Air yet." My words sounded whinier than I intended.

"Think of it this way: much like a magician of show, they make you look here, while over there they are doing something else."

"What do you mean?" I asked. But I knew. Everything became clear: she was referring to the Council and Dark and whoever else was behind this disaster.

"Yes. Exactly." She confirmed my thoughts. "The Council specifically has been quite satisfied with your obsession on Water. They came here tonight hoping to push you into retrieving that element first, because meanwhile they have been cleansing the lands of Air magic." Her mouth was a grim frown.

My thoughts immediately jumped to Lorcan.

"Yes, he is a nasty excuse of a being, isn't he?" Her head tilted and the hatred danced in her eyes, mimicking the flames behind her. "They have diligently sought out all those connected to Air magic."

My mouth twitched with anger as I thought of the senseless devastation and loss.

"Aislynn, you cannot protect everyone. But you need

to move quickly." She halted my empathy before it took hold.

"Okay," I relented. "But I don't even know where to begin." My Water plan was now shot to hell, and the fierce determination I had crumbled. Fear tromped over me.

"I do." A knowing smile lifted her lips.

Of course she does. I had a feeling I wouldn't like where this was going.

"I know of someone who can help you." Her eyes were alive and dancing. "Although, you are not going to like it." Her laughter carried through the pines.

Shit.

I pushed my fingers to my eyes, grimacing. "Why? Who?"

"Her name is Ravenna," she said.

I waited for more. The more was coming; I could feel it.

"She is a Vampire Queen."

"Oh, no! No. No. No. *No* vampires. No. Uh-uh. No. Nooo!" My slew of noes was met with her impatient stare. She waited for my tirade to finish. "No! Vampires? Are you freaking kidding me? Absolutely not! No blood sucking kind, no sparkly kind, no. None. Zilch. No."

She continued her steely gaze.

Shit. Dammit! Vampires? Seriously? I read enough and knew enough that anything involving vampires never ended anywhere good, even in fiction land. And I particularly enjoyed keeping my blood *in* my body.

Dammit.

Vampires.

This was going to happen. Freaking vampires! My eyes fluttered closed and I heaved out a slow breath.

"Fine." I caved. Freaking fine-diddly-fine. Her mouth broke into a full smile, which made me frown.

"I knew you would understand." Contentment nestled around her.

"Understand? Oh, no. I don't understand. And I don't like it either," I snipped. White Witch or not, I needed to stand my ground somehow. She only laughed. *Again.*

"Oh, Aislynn, how I do adore you," her laughter filled the moonlit clearing.

I rolled my eyes. I didn't want to be *adored.* "Ravenna? Where am I going to find her?" I questioned.

"I will tell her you are coming." Her icy blue eyes glittered, and the magic ended. I returned to the living room and let my head fall back on the chair. My groan shattered the serene quiet.

Vampires. I had to go find vampires. Rowan would be pissed.

The morning sun began to crest over the tips of the mountains, casting light onto the shadows of the earth. Leaning against my favorite boulders, I realized the earth was forming a perfect divot for my butt.

I hadn't slept much, the thought of meeting vampires and the ever-pressing magic of the elements kept me from anything near the realm of sleepy land. Soft footsteps gave way to Rowan's approach.

"Good morning!" His voice became a song when I saw the two tea mugs in his hands. "Here." He handed me the steaming mug. My yearning for coffee was indescribable, but I had acquired a new affinity for tea and honey, particularly strong black tea.

"It's a bit chilly this morning." He took note of my hoodie. Shrugging his shoulders against the chill, he sat next to me, legs extended and crossed over each other.

"Mm-hmm," I murmured, taking a tentative sip and wincing as it scorched my mouth. For some strange reason, Rowan liked his tea scalding hot. I gently blew across the top of the cup.

"Did you sleep well? I know magical battles can be a bit unnerving," he asked.

I almost laughed; I had actually forgotten about that part of my night. My thoughts were consumed by blood sucking vampire queens.

"Ah, no . . . I had a visitor."

Rowan eyed me carefully, full of alertness.

"The White Witch," I explained, glancing at him over my cup of steaming tea.

"And what might she have wanted?" he asked, settling back against the boulder.

"Oh, this little tidbit of information that we need to find Air because the Council is destroying its existence."

My words were blasé as his eyes darted to mine. I nodded, taking another tentative sip. *Hot!* Rowan did make excellent tea, and he had no issues taking big gulps. *What a weirdo.*

"Okay . . . so?" he inquired. "We need to go after Air? After we get Water?"

"Oh, no, my friend. She thinks we need to find Air *first*." I sipped cautiously again. I wondered if I was rubbing off on him when Rowan performed an excellent eye roll.

"That's what I said." I inferred my agreement with another blow across my mug. "But wait. I have one better . . ." Here was where Rowan would freak out and head to crazy town. "She has someone for us to meet."

An eyebrow cocked in my direction, but I pretended not to notice and instead took another slow sip. "Ravenna."

He practically spewed his tea over the front of himself. *Yup. Crazy town.* I assumed he knew exactly who she was.

"Absolutely NOT!" he exclaimed, almost jumping to his feet. "No. Vampires? Absolutely no!"

I waited. Much like the White Witch had with me. I sipped. This was rather amusing; no wonder she had been entertained.

"Aislynn, no. Vampires are dangerous. I don't care what kind of books about vampires they have in your Realm, but *no*. Vampires are the categorical bottom of the magical bucket."

Did he just say, 'magical bucket'? I about died. Lips curling at the edge of my mug, I gave him a sideways glance. *Wait . . . he read* Twilight*?* I could hardly contain my laughter.

"Aislynn, I am serious!" He became more animated with each passing second.

"Rowan," I began with a sharp laugh. "I know, believe me. I reacted . . . um, much the same. Vampires are not my thing. I told her no. Precisely 847 times."

This satisfied him, and he settled himself while taking a sip of tea. He thought I was on the same page as him, and well, I was . . . kind of.

"But we have to."

He glared at me and began mumbling in his own language.

"Whoa! Hold up there, mister. Is that swearing? You can't go off in another language I can't understand. That isn't fair." I nudged him with my arm.

He blew out his breath, glaring from the corner of his eyes. "We can't take anyone," he said, taking the final gulp of his tea.

"You mean my yummy human friend who would probably be a five-star three-course meal? Yeah, she isn't going!" This gave Rowan little satisfaction.

Of course, there was a giant ruckus among those in the cottage over the two of us going to meet vampires. Eventually, Rowan did his fair share of convincing Riona. I promised my firstborn child to Amy in lieu of a detailed report on how vampires function in Hallervania and other Realms, with specific ratings on how hot they were. Being here was beginning to affect her brain.

This was happening. Vampires. Freaking vampires.

33

Apparently, vampires didn't hide their existence in Hallervania, but everyone kept themselves a safe distance away out of principle. Magical bucket, after all. We teleported to Ravenna's doorstep and knocked. In regard to the full report for Amy's needs, this would be disappointing.

"Remember they can hear us, even now," Rowan said. Nodding, I thought of the creatures on the other side of the door listening to my heart pounding in my chest as blood flowed in and out of its chambers. *Great.*

Rowan knocked.

The vampire's house was out of place from every other house I had seen in Hallervania. It had a modern appeal with a feel of an updated Italian villa. I glanced around the large archway we stood under that was decorated with pots of flowers, reminding me of a gardening magazine cover photo. The oversized door was a deep, rich wood that looked hundreds of years old. It groaned with restraint as a petite redhead pulled it open.

"Welcome. She has been expecting you." The redhead's voice was smooth like caramel.

"Of course she has," Rowan said tightly. We stepped through the doorway and magic shimmered around me.

"Magical protections. Interesting," Rowan commented in my head.

The petite girl led us down a hallway through two magnificent arched doorways, and our steps echoed against the walls. She opened another massive door covered in intricate carvings of angels and demons that twisted throughout the ebony wood grain. As Rowan and I marveled at the elaborate high ceilings and artsy furniture, her approach was almost unseen.

As she made her way toward us, my mouth gaped open. *Ravenna.* Scrambling to close my mouth, her hypnotic movement melted me into the floor. Skintight black leather wrapped around her long legs, and her lacy bodice top barely contained her chest. Her movements mimicked a panther.

"Aislynn. Well, aren't you just absolutely stunning?" Her voice seductive and sultry sang across the room.

Her dark raven hair hung straight, cropped just above her shoulders, and wisped as she stalked closer to us in the highest heels I had ever seen anyone (not on a pole) wear. I guessed the thousands of years to practice walking in them served her well. She towered over my small frame, her mocha skin glowing in the light that broke through the windows.

"Our mutual friend does not lie, now does she?" A satisfactory grin slid across her face. She turned toward Rowan, and he shivered with apprehension. "You are just as beautiful as she."

She dragged a fingernail, formed into a pointy stiletto, down his cheek and jawline, causing Rowan to clench his teeth. Bracelets of silvers and golds with writing and designs weaved into their metal rattled at her wrists.

Her attention turned back to me, crimson lips twitching and causing my heart to scramble against my chest. I tried to remind myself that I could control the elements, that I was a powerful, magical being, but Ravenna's inky void eyes peered down into mine. I knew then that I could never create magic in time to respond if she decided to rip off my head.

"Aislynn, your fear is so palpable. You fear me so?" Her delicate words met my ears. I swore that I could feel her smelling me. *Awkward.* I inhaled sharply as she began circling me like a decadent dessert.

"Well, you guys don't have the best reputation, it seems, in any Realm." I jutted my jaw at her.

Her sly smile widened again. "Perhaps not, but we are not evil." She drew out the end of the word. "In fact, we participate in neither light nor dark magic."

I had heard that line before. *Vampires are ruthless, deceptive, and conniving.* I had to remember that. Running the thought through my head again, I kept a watchful eye on her. A sweet fragrance met my nose, making me weak.

"Vampires are ancient, immortal beings," Ravenna continued when I did not speak. "We do not trouble ourselves with the constant bickering of the childlike existence of magical beings. We've watched this for centuries, as two sides battle for power. It is amusing, but nothing more."

The alluring fragrance whirled around me, and I swallowed, trying to block the draw radiating through me.

"Then why are you helping me?" I asked, realizing that talking helped.

Contemplating my question, her heels struck the floor with resounding clicks as she circled us again. "A favor for a friend." She flipped her hand to the air. "However . . ." She smiled, those dark, seductive eyes turning back to mine and causing my head to tilt. There was something more hiding within her quick dismissal. "Helping you has its own intriguing benefits." She covered herself well with the corner of her lips turning up and her tempting voice. I knew why humans stumbled over their feet for her; for them, vampires captivated by their presence. I, on the other hand, enjoyed the blood pounding through my veins.

"The White Witch implied you know something of the Air element," Rowan spoke up, clearly eager to break Ravenna's spell and keep the meeting in motion. She glanced over her shoulder, and the look she sent him would have put our A-list actors to shame.

"That title is so silly. Do you not know how much she detests it?" She blew out a small breath, pursing her lips. "No matter." She turned her back to us, walking away.

Click, click, click snapped her heels as they met the marble. Standing in complete stillness, Rowan and I glanced at one another from the corners of our eyes. When Ravenna was about ten feet away, she turned back.

"Well, are you coming or not?" she asked in a seductive purr.

I hoped this would be the first *and* last time I followed a vampire queen into her lair. But, with the way my life had been going as of late, I figured I was hoping unrealistically.

She led us, surprisingly, to an outdoor space, and my eyes widened. I had expected dark caves, people in cages, and blood everywhere. Okay, so maybe I overindulged in my imagination. But an outdoor pergola wrapped with tender vines, rare flowers, and overstuffed chairs begging me to stay in them for hours accompanied by a gorgeous view of mountains and distant waterfalls was *not* what I expected. I decided in that moment, the writers in my Realm had gotten all this vampire business wrong. *I must add this to my Amy report.*

"Our ways may come more surprising than you expect." Slyly smiling at me, I realized I need to control my thoughts better. She settled herself into one of the chairs, lounging her body in a sexy and suggestive way that made me reconsider my plopping hastily into the chair across from her.

"As I have said, we usually partake in neither Light nor Dark. Nevertheless, I have watched as magical beings have ruthlessly destroyed for years and for senseless reasons, which will not be tolerated by me any longer." A callous edge to her words sent me leaning back in my chair. "There are many who have been watching you, waiting for your arrival. They have anticipated whether you could fulfill the prophecy. Most had little hope for you."

Gee, thanks.

"I am partial to the magic of Air, as it keeps us hidden in the shadows. Particularly those who find their homes in other Realms. Vampires have their own hierarchy, and I have many who rely on me to keep their lives as they are accustomed." She drew her hands across the smooth leather of her pants.

Probably a good idea to keep the vampires in all the Realms happy. That was an idea I would advocate for.

My thoughts were interrupted by the redhead reappearing with a platter of fruit, cheeses, juice, water, and what looked to be champagne. She set the tray on the table between us.

"Thank you, my sweet." Ravenna ran her finger down the girl's arm, and I observed the exchange with intrigue. The girl almost purred with delight, her eagerness to please the vampire palpable.

That's not creepy, at all.

"I wasn't sure what you might like, so a little of everything should please." Ravenna waved her hand at the tray of mounded fruit. Breaking off a small bunch of grapes, I wondered curiously at my need to please her as well. Rowan hadn't moved, the man of stone. *Bastard.*

Ravenna smiled with pleasure at me, and my insides turned in a mixture of delight and anxiousness. "Well, on to the things I know." She leaned back in the chair. "There are several members of the Council who diligently worked to eradicate those who have hidden Air magic. Looking for the Keepers of Air to . . ." She stopped as my eyes widened. "Of course I am aware of the Keepers. Aislynn. I have been a vampire for over two thousand years. I have more knowledge than anyone who has helped you thus far."

I tried to relax my expression. "Do you . . . ?"

"No, I don't know where it is. Respectfully, it's been kept hidden. It is up to you to locate it." She answered my question before I could finish. "In the Council's attempts to find the element, obliteration of those who practice Air magic is taking place. Air Faeries are almost extinct." The loathing returned to her voice. "Lorcan," she spat his name.

I nodded. "Yeah, I met him. I know someone who would like to rip him apart from the inside with his teeth." I said.

She cocked her head with a devious smile, revealing, for the first time, vicious fangs. "Me first." Her eyes pierced mine. "He will see my wrath." Her promise was made with scalpel sharp fangs glistening in the light. At times, Matthew could be scary, snapping snarling wolf teeth full of pent up rage, but Ravenna with her calm, steely promise sent chills directly to my bones.

"Vampires used elemental magic long before it was destroyed. What we use now is mere ashes of a diminishing remainder. You must restore the elements, or magic will continue to dissipate and vanish completely."

I shifted my weight in the chair. *This is new.* So far, no one had painted a picture quite so extreme. However, Ravenna may have been the first "person" who witnessed its demise. Chewing on my lip, I debated whether this was an advantage or not.

"So Lorcan and his cohorts of evil have been destroying anyone and anything to find the location of the element?" I asked.

The vampire queen paused, searching my eyes. I felt as though she was deciding what to tell me. "Yes, except they already know where it is. 'Where' isn't the problem." She chewed the tip of her nail, enticing me into her mental mind games.

"But if they know where . . . ?" My confusion settled across my face. "I mean I don't want them to obtain it, but . . ."

"The problem is the *who*." She angled her body forward with seductive eyes that melted my concerns. I found myself drawing nearer to her. Her voice was alluring with a sensual smokiness, and suddenly I was thankful for the table between us. "There is only one, perhaps besides you, who can get to the location. They want this person, but their attempts are lacking." She sat back, again a mischievous grin planted on her mouth.

"Because that *who* is under my guard."

I sensed Rowan's response building before he exploded. "Then *you* are responsible for these deaths. If you are protecting this person and the Council is killing air magic beings, you are responsible!" His anger propelled him out of the chair as he threw his words at her. Ravenna merely arched an eyebrow in annoyance.

"But, Rowan," I began, "was she supposed to just surrender this person? Give them access to the element? She couldn't." My voice, full of indignation, only aggravated him further. Clearly, defending the vampire made it worse. Pleasure rippled through me as I became aware of Ravenna's contentment with me.

"Aislynn is exactly right. Would you rather I gave the Council the element?" Her words traced my frustration with a steel point.

"How many lost their lives over this?" Rowan asked, his sorrow for the unnecessary loss bleeding through his question.

"They would die again if it meant they protected the element. Do not doubt this." Ravenna's vicious words chilled the air. "I've witnessed more devastation and loss over countless years than your measly little life could endure. What I am protecting supersedes anything else." She stood, matching Rowan's posture, and tension built between them. Clambering out of my deep seat, I threw my hands out. I pushed air between them, forcefully sliding them apart.

"Hey!" I shouted. "We are on the same side here."

Ravenna's eyes darted to mine. I didn't think she was accustomed to being pushed around by the elements. Holding the elements, I recognized her innate reaction to snap was being held back. Another moment passed, and her posture relaxed, her temper tamed.

"Unquestionably." The silkiness of her tone was restored as she brought her hands together. Rowan observed the exchange with frustration, ready to intervene.

"So, who are you protecting?" I asked, redirecting the conversation. Steely eyes deciding once again, she pouted her lips.

"Follow me," Ravenna said finally.

Ravenna led us past her magnificent open kitchen, through to what I assumed was a fancy butler's pantry. I tried not to ogle the gorgeous granite and exquisite design. She paused in front of a somewhat out-of-place glossy white metal door, pressing her thumb on a small square.

Magical keypads? Unsure where we were going, I found myself blindly following down a set of stairs. The walls slowly gave way to rocks, taking us deeper into the earth. *Down, down we go, like the rabbit hole.*

Rowan was hesitant as ever, and a constant rigid awareness caused the hairs on my arms to stand on end. Ravenna was casual as she led us down the path, radiating confidence that was only attainable after being alive for twenty-eight hundred and some odd years.

Sound prickled my senses: I heard the low hum of music, harps and strings blossoming in the air and tingling my ears. Soft and distant at first, it became more distinct the farther we walked.

"Ah . . . so it is finally time. You have come."

My head turned sharply toward Rowan as the new voice entered my mind. His blank stare informed he had obviously heard nothing.

"Do not fret, little child. He cannot hear me. I have been waiting for you. Waiting, waiting." His voice became a song with the music. How peculiar.

Ravenna glanced over her shoulder with a wicked smile. "Oh, how he loves to play."

Rowan gave me a questioning glance, and I shrugged in response.

"Oh . . . she's here, she's here. The breath of Air to save us all!" A singsong string of poetry became more excited with each word. The Vampire Queen halted before a door carved into the rock.

"This room . . ." She paused, seeming to search for the right words. "Is not going to be . . . well, you shall see." She winked and pushed the heavy door inward.

Light filled the dark hallway, enveloping us in brightness. Shielding my eyes, I squinted against the vibrant white and followed the vampire into the room. Instantly, I lost my balance.

The room did not have a floor. My feet planted themselves on a solid surface, but as my eyes adjusted to the light, I saw only the sky filling the space beneath me. An endless blue surrounded us. In the distance, clouds floated in an expanse of an immeasurable vastness, and we floated . . . or stood. I wasn't sure which.

"What in the—" Rowan tried to find his own balance. If the magical being was shocked, what was I supposed to be?

Taking a few hesitant steps forward, an eerie fear filled me as though I would fall through a precipice of sky which had no bottom. But each step was met with a sturdy place to stand within the air.

"Where are you, you tricksy little creature?" Ravenna called out to the empty space.

The reply, this time audible to all ears, resonated across the air. "Seen and unseen, my being and this scheme, we shall all float!"

My eyebrows raised with a twisted fear. Stephen King's clown filtered into my thoughts, and I shivered on the inside. *Way to be creepy.*

His laughter filled the room. "Your thoughts float on the air, just as you do!" His fairly hideous laughter disturbed me. In a cave with a vampire, floating on air in a room defying logic, I figured being creeped out was only icing on the cake. This would receive an entire section in the Amy report.

"He's somewhat theatrical." Ravenna rolled her eyes in a dramatic fashion. "Come on, Aeolus, enough."

His voice, airy and now a bit lackluster, albeit still loud, sang through the air again. "Fine, fine, we've work to do." I followed Ravenna's gaze to the endless blue above us. "As vast as this room is, it is still just a room, and alone I am."

From a place of no distinction, he flitted down. Rowan crossed his arms with his eyebrows shooting upward, and my mouth popped open in a perfect round circle.

The voice which reached across the immense space, loud within the singsong sound, came from a creature no bigger than eight inches tall. I promptly closed my very open mouth. Aeolus hung in the air at eye level, reminding me of a fairy but without wings, his yellow skin in contrast to the blue sky around him.

Designs embedded within his skin reminded me of tattoos, swirls and patterns that were illuminated from within. Large eyes bulged from a tiny head and a tuft of white hair spiked upward from between huge batty ears.

"Better to hear you with, my dear." He giggled ferociously at his own joke, and my eyebrows crawled up my forehead, too shocked to respond. "You should mind your thoughts; they float in the air for the plucking of any." He shook his tiny finger at me as he flitted closer.

Ravenna stood with one hand lazily holding her hip. She flipped her other in the direction of us. "Aeolus, at last, I present to you Aislynn, Keeper of Elements."

Darting closer in quick movements, he examined my face. Then, like lightning, his hand shot out and grabbed my nose.

"Hey!" I cried, rubbing my nose in return.

"I thought she would be taller." Mystified, he glared at Ravenna with disgust. Rowan rocked back on his heels, trying to hide a smile.

"I wouldn't be talking about height if I were you," I snipped. This *thing* was worse than my cat. "Aeolus, after the Greek God of Wind?"

His face took instant offense. "No. He is named *after me*." The little fluff of hair wiggled in outrage.

Ravenna cut in. "Aislynn, this is Aeolus, King of the Air Faeries."

I eyed the nose grabbing little king. "Nice to meet you." He shrugged off my niceties and I raised my eyebrow at Ravenna.

"Well, I never said he was pleasant." Indeed, she had not.

"What is this room?" Rowan questioned the king. I could tell he was trying to understand our odd orientation of standing in midair.

"I have been stuck in this miserable place far far too long!" the King whined.

"This *room* was magically created to *his* standards and needs," Ravenna hissed in his direction. "It is highly protected so the Council, Lorcan, and the rest cannot find him. As I said, he is the only one with the location of the Air Element."

"And bugger off, if you think I should tell any of you." He folded his little arms across his chest, batty ears wiggling in defiance.

"Aeolus, you must tell Aislynn as she is the Keeper," she chided.

"Yes, well, we shall see if she is worthy of holding the brilliance of Air, now won't we?" Testy eyes met mine. "How many elements have you reclaimed, Little One?"

I raised my eyebrow again. "I was about to retrieve Water, but I'm here instead."

This time, my voice held snideness, and his face twisted in repugnance. "You send me a Keeper with no elements in hand? This is not the way!"

"Aeolus, things change. No one way is written in stone, you know this. Do you want to save Air magic or not?" The seductive vampire reduced to irritation in response to the petulant king.

He heaved a breath in response. "Fine, fine. Her magic shall be seen. Show me. Show me what you know of Air and the depths of its magic."

Shit.

I didn't think this was the moment to inform him of

my novice abilities. My thoughts stuttered as I remembered he could hear them.

"Don't discount what you are capable of, Aislynn." Rowan's thoughts filtered through my mind. Perhaps another approach would work better.

"Aeolus," I began, "I have worked hard to obtain the knowledge I have in very little time. However, I believe my understanding of Air would be far superior with your assistance and insightful tutelage." I forced my voice to sound meek.

Switching gears gained me odd glances. Rowan covered his mouth to hide the smile bursting on his lips, and Ravenna eyed me, acknowledging my cunning.

"Well, yes, yes. Of course I could help you." He rubbed his chin as he gave the offer thought. "I have much knowledge in the craft. Yes, I may have the ability to do such a thing."

"Great! I would appreciate the help of such an esteemed being with considerable talent." I laid it on thick, and thankfully the little king ate up what I fed, just as I expected. "Well, tomorrow, then. I am sure you need your rest and, of course, the time to come up with how best to help me."

"Oh, yes! Tomorrow I shall be ready. You better come prepared to learn." Excitement filled him as his little body trembled.

"We shall leave you, Aeolus. We will return tomorrow," Ravenna said, turning to the door hanging in the air. He already zipped off joyfully, muttering to himself.

My breath huffing out of me, I stepped on the cool, sturdy stone surface, making my equilibrium dance. Ravenna closed the door behind us.

"Quite the clever one, my sweet," Ravenna cooed with her sultry voice.

"Pshh." I ignored her provocative stare. "I deal with egotistical chauvinistic asshats like him all the time. You pet and feed them the garbage they expect, and they eat out of your hand like a baby." I shrugged.

Rowan's eye twitched, seeing a different side of me.

The vampire's sensual laughter bounced across the cold rock. "You would make a stunning vampire."

"Uh . . . I'm good. Thanks."

"We shall see." She smiled, jutting her chin forward. "Aeolus is a temperamental little creature, who on most occurrences I want to throttle and throw across the Realms. But he is the King of Air Faeries and the only one who knows the location of the element, which is why I keep him protected and meet all of his demands."

"How long has he been here?" Rowan asked.

Ravenna took a breath. "Two hundred fifty-three years too many."

"You might be a saint in my book," I replied. My insides shivered at the thought of having to deal with him on a daily basis for even one human lifetime.

"A saint I am certainly not. I enjoy eating people far too much." A seductive grin enveloped her lips as she ran her tongue across her teeth.

Ew. Okay, maybe not a saint.

"You could have informed us we would need to coerce the element from him," Rowan said.

"My job isn't to reclaim the elements, it's hers." Ravenna's lips pursed.

Rolling my lips, my eyes angled upward. She had a

point. At least I didn't need to find the location. There was that.

We left Ravenna's quickly, deciding to spend the least amount of time possible in a vampire queen's house. Besides, I didn't want to stick around for dinner. Back in the warmth and blood safe zone of Riona's cottage, Amy began her barrage of questions.

"I am just against the entire thing. Why would anyone want to drink blood? It's not even sanitary." Amy shoved a huge portion of food into her mouth.

"I think sanitary is the least of their concerns." I tore apart my roll, internally thankful for normal human food.

"Right. But I wonder if some people taste better than others. What about health nuts? Vegans versus meat eaters? Who tastes better?" she pondered out loud, leaving me laughing.

"I don't *want* to know the answers to those. But after meeting her, I doubt she cares." I focused my magic and filled my water glass with a thought.

"You should ask." Amy offered out her glass for a refill.

"Yeah, I don't think so." I stared at her glass and water began to pour from thin air, filling it. Amy winked in gratitude.

"So, the little Faerie wants to test you? Interesting," Riona interrupted.

"I am not sure if it's a test or if he is just a fickle faerie," I said, grabbing another roll, purposely avoiding the meat on the table.

Jax's laughter emanated from the other room. *"Fickle Faeries are the worst kind."* Sauntering into the kitchen, he threw his body to the floor, twisting and rubbing against the wood. *"Although, if you think Air Faeries are bad, wait until you meet Fire Faeries."*

"Oh, help us all if I have to retrieve anything from any more faeries." I turned back to the table.

"I am curious what his plan is," Riona mused, disregarding our bantering.

"What do you mean?" Amy asked.

"Faeries are notorious for their deception and devious ways. Aeolus is no exception. He has ulterior motives. I am not convinced Ravenna is helping us, either." Her untrustworthiness bled through her words as she tapped her fingers on the table.

"Ravenna definitely has more than she is telling us. There was something in how she acted. I don't know, but I am sure she wants to use me to her advantage," I said, and Riona tipped her head at my assessment.

"You know, if I came along, I could be helpful in deciphering her motives," Amy piped in, taking her plate to the counter. Rowan and I both jumped and responded with harsh noes.

"Absolutely not! I am not allowing my friend to be eaten by vampires." I tried to soften my response. "That is a direct violation of my friend code. I watched her with humans. You would be following her around like a puppy."

"I believe I have more self-control than that," Amy said with coolness. I could tell my objections hurt her, but my only concern was with the blood flowing in her veins and making sure it stayed there.

34

The next morning Rowan and I stood in the kitchen, ready to leave for Ravenna's. Dread ate at me as I finished my tea, not particularly excited about spending the day with the Faerie King. But I didn't have much choice.

Instead, I would kiss his faerie ass if it led me to retrieving Air. Offering Amy a refill of tea, she shook her head, cool eyes barely giving me a glance. Grimacing, I assumed she was still angry with me for last night.

"You ready?" Rowan asked.

I nodded, thinking about Amy. I didn't want her to be upset with me, but I knew bringing her here was a bad idea. Rowan's hand settled on my shoulder, and simultaneously Amy shot across the room grabbing Rowan's hand. Timed with perfection, I realized she hadn't been angry, but plotting. We appeared at Ravenna's door and my stream of words began.

"Dammit! Amy!"

I softened my tone upon seeing her pale face, still not

350

accustomed to the teleporting business. Rowan said nothing, only staring with disappointment.

"Amy. She is a vampire. She eats people!" I tried to yell at her, but instead I pushed her head down and forced her to breathe.

The heavy door opened gracefully by Ravenna as if it weighed nothing. Blood red leather enveloped her long legs, paired with black lace stilettos and another skintight bodice top.

"Good morning. I generally don't eat people's friends. That would be considered rude." Her smile was a small pout as her smoky eyes glinted in the sun. "Welcome Amy, Rowan, Aislynn." She opened the door wide, motioning us through. Today her black hair was slicked back and held in a small knot at the base of her neck.

"I promise not to eat you, or even sample." She ran her sharp nail down Amy's arm, and I watched Amy shiver. Chewing my lip, I worried about my friend's safety and followed the vampire once again into the depths of her villa.

"I . . . thank you?" Amy said almost inaudibly. I watched apprehension and dread flood over her as she reconsidered her decisions.

A little late for that now.

"Amy, I so look forward to spending time with you today," the vampire purred, and my eyes shot to hers, my teeth on edge. "I enjoy those who live in the Earth Realm. I don't get to go as often as I like." Ravenna ignored my agitation and focused on Amy.

This is not going to go well.

"Do not fret, my sweet Aislynn. I rarely break my promises." Her wicked smile and bright white teeth did not comfort me.

"I will hold you to them," I promised.

She gave a gentle nod in understanding and we began our descent down the substratum maze of the lower portion of her home. This time I paid close attention to the doors and hallways we passed while Amy began her crusade.

"So, how long have you been a vampire?"

Ravenna's sultry laughter saturated the narrow hallway. "Oh, my dear child, you are never supposed to ask a woman's age! But to meet your curious appetite . . ." She let the word hang for a moment. "I have been a vampire for 2,893 years. Coming up on a big birthday soon." She winked at Amy, whose mouth fell open. "I know, right? All those vampire novels with characters a measly couple hundred years on them." She laughed. Amy's mouth was beginning to resemble a fish.

"Now mind you, there are plenty of freshlings around, but vampires are held to strict standards when it comes to creating new vampires. They are chosen with care and specific reasons. Any vampire who breaks the covenant of rules is immediately ended."

"No vampire armies, huh?" Amy concluded.

"Absolutely not. Besides there is no need for such things, and obviously, we need humans to feed on."

"Of course." Amy swallowed, and I heard her trying to contain the horror in her voice.

"Now it has been many years since visiting your Realm. There was a delightful little place called . . . New Orleans? Is it still there?"

"Yes, it is."

"I adored that little town, so much allure and life. Oh! They had these delightful treats . . . what were they called?"

Ravenna's eyes danced in the dim light. "Little bits of dough created in a way . . ."

"Beignets?" Amy offered.

"Yes! That's them." She looped her arm within Amy's.

"So, you can eat real food?" Amy asked. I knew the question came automatic, a small problem of hers.

"Well, of course. I rather prefer blood, but things like a perfectly cooked beignet are a delightful treat from another world." The vampire animated her words by using her hands to kiss the tips of her fingers.

Rowan glanced over at me as we trailed them walking ahead of us. *"What in the world?"*

"Don't ask me! I'm just letting Amy do her thing." I began to wonder why the vampire willingly offered up so much information.

"How long ago were you in Louisiana?"

"Let's see . . . oh, I believe it was 1919, if I am not mistaken."

"O-oh," Amy stuttered. I thought she expected maybe twenty years, not registering that to a vampire, "not long ago" would be more in the vicinity of a hundred years. "Things have changed a bit since then. Do you come to our Realm often?" At this point, I was certain Amy was asking for her own safety.

"Unfortunately, not as often as I would like. Not all vampires can travel the Realms, but for us few that can, it is difficult. Portal choices and such. When we go, there is usually a purpose for the trip."

I could hear Amy's thoughts, *Portals?* She recovered quickly with another question. "Why did you go this particular time?"

"Well, that was an unfortunate situation." Her voice

softened. "There is a family of vampires who reside in New Orleans, a very close-knit group. They maintain a healthy relationship with the magical beings in the area . . . overseers, if you will."

Amy's gulp was audible at the mention of "magical beings" residing in New Orleans, and it made my mouth twitch. Amy had no idea what she walked into by hitching a ride.

"They had a bit of a problem which needed to be resolved, and I was there to make sure things were handled properly." The vampire tilted her head at the memory.

"Mm-hmm, and what sort of problem would warrant such a thing?" Amy's voice caught within the question. I should give Amy credit; she was relentless through her natural reaction to escape the depths of this hell.

"Aren't you curious?" Ravenna's thirsty eyes flashed to Amy, clearly deciding what to tell her. "Sometimes order needs to be reestablished and it must come from a place of power. I am that power." Her smoky, dark eyes shimmered.

"I see." A sharp inhale led me to believe Amy held a pang of regret.

"You have no idea, sweet child. There are few moments of being a vampire which are unpleasant. In twenty-eight hundred years, though, that moment is not something I look fondly upon." Slight contrition filled her voice, but within seconds it shifted. "Ah, here we are. Aislynn, are you ready for the madness that shall follow?" She glanced at me over her shoulder.

I waved my hand in response.

I walked past Amy, giving her shoulder a gentle squeeze as I entered the strange room. Amy's slew of muttered profanities began, and I realized there should have been more warning. Behind me, she gripped onto Rowan's arm, clinging in fear of the unseen ground below.

"I don't like this," An emphatic whimper escaped her. Grimacing, I remembered her intense fear of heights, and guilt washed over me.

"Now where is he . . . ?" Ravenna looked around the expanse of blue.

Abruptly, Aeolus appeared hanging upside down at eye level. His fuzzy white tuft was in a point, reminding me of a troll doll. His large eyes peered into mine.

"You are late!" The little king's insufferable voice droned. I crossed my arms in defiance.

"You have brought me a present!" Excitement ran through him. "Someone for me? Can I keep her?" Aeolus zipped through the air. He loomed in front of Amy's face, zooming in a mere two inches from her. He reached his yellow hands out and grabbed her cheeks, pinching in what I knew to be a not so delicate manner.

"What? No! You cannot keep her. This is Amy, whom I am certain is regretting her decisions as each moment passes. Amy, this is Aeolus, King of the Air Faeries." I gestured in his direction. Amy rubbed her face, disdain pushing into her scowl.

"Well, I am not interested if I cannot keep her." Aeolus thrust his nose high into the air and whooshed back to me.

"What a—" Amy started, but Rowan's sharp look kept her mumbling the rest under her breath.

"I am here to earn your trust as Keeper, Aeolus," I said, distracting the king.

"Yes, yes." He twirled through the air, peering at me sideways. "Tell me what you know of Air."

"Obviously, moving wind, using the air to move things, you know . . ."

"And flying, you mastered this, yes?" he asked mid–barrel roll.

"Flying? Excuse me? No. I don't want to fly," I stuttered, blinking rapidly.

"But you are flying right now."

"No. I am standing, in a very weird room."

"No, this room is Air. There is no bottom; you automatically created something to stand on because you insist upon it. You restrict yourself because you choose." He resumed his rolling through the air. "Do I have wings?"

"Clearly you do not." I crossed my arms.

"Because I do not need them," he clarified.

Clenching my teeth together, I avoided snapping at him. His insistence upon communicating with me as if I was an inane child began to grate my nerves. From behind me, Amy squeaked.

"Um, you guys . . . ?" Her feet began to lift upward, no longer standing. Rowan grabbed her ankle, trying to hold her in place.

"Ahhh, see! That one understands!" Aeolus said with cheer.

"I have a name!" Amy spat as she inched higher.

"You need to understand that Air gives you freedom to move lightly anywhere you deem. The Air carries, so you may listen and hear things spoken from afar. Moving wind . . . that is nothing!"

Rowan pulled Amy back to her feet, struggling with the magic. She latched on to Rowan's arm like a vice grip.

"It's about being free, Aislynn," Amy spoke quietly. "You constantly restrict yourself."

I blew air past my lips in frustration. She was probably right; that didn't mean I wanted to hear it, though. Let go. Let go of the control I held? Shitty things happened when I did. Since childhood, I held on to that one paradigm. Because of that belief, I always tried to stay focused and in control. That was what kept everyone safe.

Shit. Let go. My eyes drifted closed, connecting to my magic and the room. I freed myself from the tethers holding me.

"Think about the Throat Chakra meditation I gave you. Take a step and lift off the ground." Amy broke my concentration and my eyes popped open. I didn't think now was the time to tell her I had never listened to the meditation. *God, I am an awful friend.* Aeolus's glaring eyes filled with ridicule and annoyance.

Refocusing, I closed my eyes. *I can do this. No one will get hurt; it's only practice.* I tried to convince myself. I took a step, letting go. I didn't want to float around aimlessly, so instead I shot off upward and out, past Aeolus. His excitement tickled my ears, but I was too distracted by the liberation flooding through me.

Air prickled over my skin and the magic rippled as I moved. Traversing across the endless "room," connecting with the element, I realized I had traveled quite a ways, yet I could still hear everyone below me.

So, this is what he meant. I tuned in, focusing on the sound, reaching with the magic to the tone of their words. *Sweet.* I pushed their words and voices away, finding pleasure in the silent air rushing across my ears. It reminded me of a flying dream, doing somersaults and dancing on the heavens with complete freedom. A lightness filled my chest as I embraced the magic. I never wanted to return.

Awareness of Rowan straining to contact me trickled in my mind, an indistinct sound, calling me. They wanted me to return, Amy's anxiety shooting like darts, but freedom drove me further. Out. Up. Away. The idea of drifting forever was appealing, and time began to disappear.

Why does time need to exist? I could just float in an eternity of freedom.

"Aislynn!" Rowan's voice became louder, more significant, pushing into my mind. *"You must control the magic! You are letting it control you."*

Control me? No, I was enjoying it. Ripples of wonder and pure happiness fluttered within me. Why hadn't I wanted to fly? I couldn't remember. The amazement was so distinct in my mind that I didn't want to let it go; instead, I streamed my body further into the expanse of alluring blue.

"AISLYNN!"

An annoying call came from a remote indiscernible place. *Fine.* I concentrated on their voices and knew their precise location. In no hurry, I pushed my body down to them. With an arabesque followed by a roll through the air, my toes landed on an invisible ground. It sent joy screaming in my heart. Below me, they stood searching, and begrudgingly, I let myself move toward them. One foot landed, then the other as giddiness fluttered over me.

"Ah, you see?" Aeolus grinned, and my eyes glittered in exhilaration. Compassion toward Aeolus gnawed at me; now I understood him, or at least his behavior. The freedom of the element couldn't be denied.

"The liberty Air gives you frees the soul from the restrictions the Realms place upon you."

My head bobbed along to his wise words.

"There is nothing wrong with keeping your feet on the ground." Amy snapped her hand on her hip.

"Ah, yes, well . . ."

"Your feet don't know what they are missing." I winked at Amy, finishing Aeolus' sentence for him. A thread vibrated through me, invigorating my soul. "Let's do more!" Excitement raged through me.

Rowan clamped his hands down on my shoulders. *"Let's hold on a moment,"* he insisted and held me in place. Antsy streams of energy ran up and down my legs, trying to lift and push me upward again. He found my eyes, held my gaze, and pulled me to the present. My knees were twitching, bouncing.

I don't want to stay. Or stop. Ever.

He held me steady, watching my eyes dart around. Slowly his magic saturated me, washing away the pull of elemental magic. As it dampened to a dull roar, my head began to clear. Out of the corner of my eye, Aeolus crossed his arms in front of his tiny chest.

"I . . ." *What the hell just happened?*

"It's okay, Aislynn. This is why you are here, to learn to control the magic." Rowan's voice softened.

Riona's warning filtered into my mind, making me realize this would be much harder than I thought. The elemental magic seized responsibility without me realizing it. It easily held the control, and I focused, shaking off the last tendrils of magic thrumming around me.

"It will become easier. You will become more aware of the magic." Rowan released my shoulders, dragging his hands down my arms and soothing the bits of anxious energy.

"You mean when it takes over," I snarked, biting my lip. He nodded with a half smile and Aeolus groaned in frustration.

I felt the little king's annoyance build and briefly thought about blasting him across the room, but I didn't want to be rude. It also occurred to me Aeolus liked the feeling the magic left. I could understand the slightly crazed, uncontrolled aspect now. His body fed on that unbridled lack of control, and perhaps, it contributed to his kooky behavior.

"Wait a minute," Amy interjected. "This flying business . . . ?" Aeolus, interested again, rolled through the air. He raised an eyebrow in question. "Are we going to be able to fly outside this room?"

Aeolus frowned like a sulky three-year-old, leaving Ravenna to answer for him.

"No. This room holds unusual magic, allowing Aeolus the freedom he required. In fact, flying magic is a coveted gift and attainable by few because of the dangers involved."

"Thank God, Aislynn. I can't handle this shit." Amy's posture slumped in relief.

Aeolus's shrill voice cut through the air. "Mastering flight in this room is imperative to retrieving Air."

Of course it is. My stomach twisted as I rubbed my temples.

"What do you mean?" Rowan asked.

"Flying is about trusting oneself and the element."

"And?" Amy inquired.

Aeolus, stubborn as ever, tumbled though the sky toward her again, peering at her upside down.

"You shall see."

I gave Amy massive props, because I was certain she wanted to take her fist and punch him in the throat. Instead, her jaw muscles twitched rapidly as she clenched her teeth.

"Let us do more." Aeolus spun off, flying out of sight. Giving one last glance to Rowan, I huffed out my breath and followed. Rowan called out after me, *"Be careful."* His voice was wistful and unconvinced.

The flying business came easier than I expected, but I was certain I was enjoying it far more than I should. Aeolus zipped in front of me, darting one way then another, making it difficult to keep up. In the distance, he spiraled downward, twisting through the air at a speed that made me nauseous. *How will I ever catch him?*

Squinting, I descended as fast as I dared. The wind whipped painfully across my face and the "fun" began to wear off. Where was he going? A rocky cliff appeared below me, coming up faster than I could register. *Shit!* I was going to smash into the rocks.

Slowing myself as much as possible, my body slammed heavily into the rock. Pitching forward, I threw out my hands to catch myself. Pulling myself to my feet, I stared at the little king, contempt distorting my face. My mouth was a flat line as I rubbed my hands together to release the pebbles and dirt embedded into my palms.

"Really?" This time I wanted to boot him across the sky.

The tiny king shrugged, taking little steps forward to peer down off the edge of the cliff, a jut of rock hanging out over an endless amount of sky. I followed awkwardly, leaning to glance over the side. My stomach twinged, clenching as a wave of fear passed over me.

In my mind, I knew I could fly, but peering over the

ledge brought out the natural human fear of falling. My eyes tracked the rocky wall below for an immeasurable distance, clouds crossing the air below to an unseen bottom. Instinct screamed at me to step back to safer ground.

"The element of Air is hidden where no one will go," Aeolus told me. "Fear limits one's potential." Again, with the riddles. Edging closer, he stood at the tip of the drop off. "The Air Faeries are taught from a young age that fear is only an illusion to hold you back from your greatest achievements. You must realize this. You cannot fear your power or restrain it by holding back. You will never reclaim the elements if you do." His voice was pensive as he peered down.

"When I lose control, people get hurt." I didn't like how whiny my voice sounded.

He turned, peering at me with his oversized eyes. "Only because you allow fear to rule." My response was a grumble in my throat. "It is true. The very thing you fear, you create. Humans struggle with this."

I arched an eyebrow. "And magical creatures don't?"

He wrapped his hands behind his tiny body, looking out over the edge again. After a moment, he met my eyes. "When you release the fear, your soul is free. Only then can you fly."

He let his body fall headfirst off the edge of the cliff. My eyes sparked and irrationally I called out his name in gut-wrenching fear. I found myself at the edge, peering down and watching his little body tumble and roll through the empty air.

Panic filled my chest, a tightening in anticipation of what was to come spreading like a fire through me. Biting my bottom lip, dread blossomed and expanded, making it hard to breathe. I swallowed through the tension as it tried to consume me. I wanted to push it down, push it away, put it *anywhere,* as long as I didn't have to *feel* it.

An animalistic response, it was instinctive in its brutality. But I stayed bound to the rocky edge. I stood and allowed myself to feel the fear, letting it pummel my body as thousands of what-ifs burned through my thoughts. The anxiety was a fireball in my belly, insisting I couldn't do this, telling me to turn, to run, to do anything but what I must.

How much time do I have? The seconds burned through me. My muscles jolted, ready to move, then the fear locked me in place. Goosebumps were zinging across my flesh and fanned out across my body. *Release the fear.* The words slammed into my thoughts. I took two steps, then three, and catapulted myself off the edge.

35

A litany of swear words thrust themselves out of my mouth as I fell. There was a moment of stillness when my body dropped, without control, and I flailed in the air. *Focus, Aislynn.* I reached out for the elemental magic. It thrummed all around me, calling me to use it. I oriented myself upright in the emptiness and then dived downward, headfirst, searching for Aeolus.

Increasing my speed, I propelled faster. *There,* just visible, was a tiny speck ahead of me, tumbling and turning at odd angles. My throat was tight, burning inside of me, and trickles of fear tried to find their way to govern once again. Mists of gray clouds rolled over my skin as I rocketed through them. I kept my eye on the little king, still falling ahead of me. Ignoring the prickles, finally I gained on him.

Then I spotted something beyond him, coming closer to us. *What is that?* It was dark in color, but I was unable to determine or comprehend what it was.

Is that water? An ocean? Fear slammed into me again. Thoughts of falling into an open ocean at this speed made me certain we wouldn't survive. It was impossible. Open ocean water terrified me.

Tears filled my eyes as the air scathed across me. I was almost upon Aeolus, and I tried slowing so I wouldn't slam into his tiny body. I reached my hands out to grab him, fingers just caressing his yellow skin, clawing and stretching to grasp on. Eyes closed, his body cascaded down in perfect serenity.

Seconds dragged into an eternity, and we fell much too fast as water approached at lightning speed. I had him, pulling him into my body and rotating my back to the water. I cradled him in my chest, my only thought to protect him.

We slammed into the water. The roar of the waves crashed on the surface as my body plummeted downward. Descending at uncontrollable speeds, my mouth open and closed, gasping for air that didn't exist. Fear took hold, possessing my mind, my thoughts, and my body. Water streamed over my eyes, and I forced them closed. *Magic.* Lines pulsing through me would protect me, wouldn't they?

Fear. *Magic.* Magic. *Fear. Fearmagic.* Knitting together, they became one, and I tried to separate them. Driving the fear aside, I drew on the magic. The tingle and rush of elemental magic thrummed, and I let it expand. Eating at the fear, the magic consumed. I held tightly to Aeolus as we descended, pushing through the water to impossible depths.

It's only an illusion. He had said it earlier himself. The room was only an illusion. Fear was an illusion. I took a breath. Air. Air was life. Breathing in deeply, I consumed beautiful streams of air and everything slowed.

Our descent softened, cocooned within a cushion of white. A fluffy cloud of cotton surrounded us, and we stopped, me on my back with Aeolus held gently in my arms in white froth. Relaxing my body, a shaky exhale escaped my mouth.

"You have traveled through fear. Now you can embrace your magic." Aeolus climbed off me and stood at my head, looking down. He reached his tiny hand out for mine. "Come." His immense eyes were expectant.

The idea of formulating thoughts, let alone moving, was impossible. Shifting my leaden muscles, I tried to prop myself up on my elbows. *He wants me to move.* Words were still unable to sort themselves into cohesive sounds to produce sentences as heaviness saturated my body.

Hands resting on his waist, he stared at me in annoyance. "Come, come," he said flippantly.

Groans murmured in my throat, the only thing I was capable of at this point. I asked my body to cooperate and it edged more upright in an impossibly slow manner. Taking in our surroundings, hanging in the empty sky, my brain melted in confusion. *Maybe we're Care Bears,* I thought. Perhaps a rainbow slide would be next. At least I could force thoughts now, and I clambered up to my feet.

"There, you see? Not so bad," Aeolus said, and my eyebrows narrowed. "Air Faeries have hidden the element for centuries. We've always moved it through time, and when it eventually came to me, I chose my only option. See, it is our very belief as Faeries that we must move through what is impossible." He turned to me. "You have within you the strength and determination to save our kind, save our element, and return magic to Light. But *you* must believe it." He rose upward, hanging eye level with me.

"Those moments you referred to," he added, his eyes glinting, "the ones where people get hurt? These things only happened because of fear." The crystal specks in his eyes seemed to reflect to me the images of that day. Seconds slowed, and time became stagnant. "So!" The trance broke. "You can stay in the illusion of fear or not. The choice is yours."

As I released the breath I was unaware of holding, he zipped out in front of me. "If you are my Keeper, and that is a *big* if!" I wanted to roll my eyes at him. We were back to this, then. "Then you shall see . . ."

The sky changed before me. Mountain tops careened by, trees layered within the dips, and valleys revealed small lakes nestled between them. The view was peaceful and stunning until thrashes of magic shot back and forth. Sparks of light were blown through trees, and fire erupted.

Further travel showed the back side of the mountain burned, the earth beneath scarred with smears of black. Traces of magic were left everywhere. Another flurry of movement led my vision to the Tree of Elements, or what was left of it. The trunk fissured open exposing blackened, seared bark. Evil oozed in onyx tendrils, seeping into the earth and destroying the tree from the roots upward.

"This is what is to be, if Dark takes the elements. Dark uses fear to control and manipulate," Aeolus explained. "You must be willing to push through the murky madness, blindly forging ahead even though you do not know how. You must persist."

The images shifted again, elemental magic igniting through the Tree of Elements once more. A flood of light reached across the Realms. The bright, golden light of Air swirled in gold ribbons before me, transformed into a floating orb.

It encompassed my field of vision. The tree was

restored, magic fluid and available once again. Then the amulet filled my eyes, with the elements held secure and safe.

My eyes swam with the orb of yellow, then I felt a sudden sharp poke, followed by searing pain in my forehead. I was falling again. Amy would have said it was my third eye, but I didn't care. All I knew was the searing pain bursting in stars throughout my head.

I landed with a thunk on what seemed like ground, and the pain stopped as quickly as it had begun. I tentatively opened my eyes, blinking in rapid succession.

Rowan, Amy, and Ravenna stood above me, staring down in bewilderment.

"Where the hell did you come from?" Amy offered her hand, and I took it, bringing myself upright.

That little bastard king dismissed me and sent me packing.

"Where is Aeolus?" Ravenna asked.

A thousand thoughts careened through my mind as I searched for him. "I guess I am done with my lesson."

"Let's get out of here, please," Amy whimpered. I nodded, beyond finished with this damn room.

Ravenna closed the door behind us with an audible click. A loud gurgling filled the air as my stomach protested the lack of food. My brain felt foggy with exhaustion. In some ways, the day had been more draining than my time with Riona learning the elements.

As we entered the damp hallway, magic crackled the air, sailing past me and smashing into the door. Adrenaline kicked into gear, pounding through my veins. I grabbed Amy and shoved her behind me just as Rowan threw energy balls across the dark hallway toward the unseen enemy.

"Stop! Now!" Ravenna's voice rang out against the

stone. Rage shimmered from the vampire, rippling in acidic tendrils. The magic consuming the space dropped.

"Show yourself, now!" Her voice bellowed in the empty air.

No one appeared.

"Now!" she repeated. An icy edge in her words scared me, and we were on her side.

"Come now . . . don't you want to play?" said a voice I knew.

Daragon.

Anger sputtered through my adrenaline. I had been waiting to cross paths with him again after what he made Amy endure.

"How did you get past the magical protections?" Ravenna snipped, moving her body slightly in front of us.

"It wasn't hard. You should find a new witch, by the way," he said in his offhanded way. Shifting into the light of the hall, he glanced up from his heavy eyebrows. The tendrils of fury from Ravenna became more palpable with every second, swirling around the vampire. "What are you doing here?" she demanded.

"I am here for the Faerie King." Daragon picked lint off his clothing, obviously unconcerned about being outnumbered. "And I rather enjoy irritating her." His finger pointed toward me.

Rowan shot his hand out, stopping me from my forward motion. My anger was taking control, which seemed more dangerous than the elements.

"He is under my guard, as you know." Ravenna paused, eyeing Daragon. "You made a mistake coming to my home."

In a movement so fast, my eyes barely registered it,

three men came to stand behind Daragon. They were unmistakably vampires . . . scary as hell vampires. Dressed in dark clothing that made them scarcely visible in the rocky, shadowed hall, only their eyes gleaming in the darkness.

They had a new twist to the crystallized Hallervanian eyes: sparkling, but with an underlying edge of *rip your heart out and drink your blood* look. Amy sunk deeper behind me, and I had a feeling she was beginning to prefer the room with no floor. A part of me wanted to slink back with her, but I stood terrifyingly still, holding my ground.

Ravenna matched the movements of her cohorts. She stood feet from Daragon, yet still placed directly in front of us in a form of protection.

"You are surrounded." Cold penetrating pinpointed her words.

Daragon shrugged, casually drawing his gaze back to me. "You really have gone to a new low, Aislynn. Hanging out with vampires? Even I am not that bad."

Ravenna didn't take kindly to being ignored, and in swift movement was at Daragon's side. Her hands exposed his throat as she peeled her lips back and unveiled her fangs. Their tips glinted in the dim light.

I was unsure what was more disturbing: the quickness of what happened, her teeth, or the fact that Daragon appeared unfazed. Something bothered me about his behavior.

"Wait!" I pushed forward, calling to Ravenna. Amy clenched my wrist trying to hold me back. Daragon arched a brow at me, still disregarding the vampire at his jugular.

"Why are you here, alone and obviously outnumbered?"

Daragon always made intelligent moves with fore-thought and precise planning. Why was he here, and what did he hope to gain besides dying? It didn't make sense.

A sly grin took over his mouth. "You're catching on."

Ravenna straightened, curiosity piquing as Daragon stared, waiting. Then it all unraveled in my mind. *SHIT. Shit. Shit.*

"Keep him here," I pleaded to the vampire. Grabbing Rowan and Amy's hands, I teleported back to Riona's, fearing we were too late.

The kitchen looked as if its contents had exploded against themselves, and beneath the debris I saw a lifeless furry form. Screaming, Amy fell to the floor next to Matthew. Rage rippled from my skin as I checked the rest of the cottage. Riona was missing. And where was Jax? I assumed he artfully escaped any danger. Returning to the kitchen, Rowan knelt before Matthew. A stream of magic cascaded from his hands, flowing into the body beneath. My head tilted, and I caught his eye.

"He will be okay, but he is badly injured."

Matthew's tongue timidly licked Amy's gentle hand that was stroking his fur. "Who did this?" Amy's voice was empty as tears swelled in her eyes.

"Lorcan." I spat. I swirled on my words and disap-peared. My rage carried me back in front of Daragon. Ravenna's eyebrows shot upward at my quick return.

"Where is he?" My staccato words reverberated in the small space. Ravenna loosened her grasp in the slightest amount. Daragon's eyes fluttered, intrigue burning inside them.

"Whoever do you mean?"

Fury flew through me, and my tolerance of his never-ending coy behavior snapped. My nerves burned. Throwing my hands outward I allowed magic to sail out of my fingertips, sending him against the jagged rocks and holding him in place. Ravenna held up a hand to stop the minions behind her.

"Where is Lorcan?" I yelled.

"Long gone by now, I presume."

My thoughts raced to Matthew in a heap on the floor. I pushed the magic into Daragon again and like a fierce wind it forced him deeper into the rocks, causing him to wince in pain.

"Just give me the king." Cringing against the magic, his lips pursed as Ravenna flew up next to him, her face inches from his.

"Not on your life," she said, dragging a sharp nail down the delicate skin of his neck, chin jutting out in defiance. His eyes tried to watch both of us.

"You honestly believed we would hand him over because you attacked my friends?" I spat, and Ravenna's head snapped my direction.

"Well, I kind of hoped." His Adam's apple bobbed as Ravenna dug her nail into the soft part of his throat. A red bubble instantly blossomed, causing her nostrils to flare.

"Where is Lorcan?" I demanded again.

"I would be more concerned about where the witches are." His eye caught Ravenna's, and he had the audacity to smirk. Distracted, my magic faltered in the slightest bit; I assumed Riona had escaped. But now I second guessed my assumption, and that was all he needed. Using the small hesitation, his hand shot out, blowing back Ravenna. He disappeared.

"Dammit!" I gritted my teeth against my anger.

"Go check on your friends. I will have him tracked," Ravenna said. Stray hairs had escaped her sleek ponytail, and she pushed them back as she rubbed her jaw. She gave a short nod to her vampire minions and in invisible movement they disappeared.

I nodded and vanished, leaving the vampire in the darkness.

36

The kitchen held an eerie quiet, disrupted only with sounds of wood scraping across the floor as Rowan tried to establish order in the disheveled chaos. I shoved my hands in my back pockets, hesitant to help. The muscles in his neck twitched in staccato movements as he avoided eye contact. Remnants of the kitchen crunched under my feet as I reached down to help him put the bench upright.

"Daragon escaped."

Rowan muttered an inaudible response as he lifted the top of the table against the wall. Behind him I could see Amy in the other room with Matthew's head in her lap.

"How is he?" I asked.

Rowan glanced up, past me, toward Matthew. His lips thinned, and his eyes sparked with anger as they met mine.

"What?" I growled while holding a bag open for trash. "Are you mad at me?" I demanded. The silent treatment rekindled the anger in my veins. "Are you serious right now?"

Amy's head snapped toward us at the increase in volume. Rowan kept his eyes averted from mine as he pushed a broken chair out of the way.

"Why in the world are you angry at me?" I hissed, barely managing to lower my voice. Blood pulsed beneath my skin.

His head jerked up. "Why? Because people are getting hurt!"

"Hurt by me, right? Is that what you want to say?" My voice hitched higher, and I wanted to scream. "I told you! I told you I couldn't do this! But you insisted. You and everyone else said I could do this!" The muscles in my jaw writhed behind my clenched teeth. "And now you want to be mad at me? You have got to be kidding me!" Rage pounded.

Without warning the few glass bowls left sitting on what remained of shelves popped loudly, shattering across the room. Rowan ducked as the glass scattered in tiny pieces.

"Aislynn! You need to control your damn magic!" Rowan turned on me, throwing down pieces of broken chair.

I flinched in response to the intense volume that made Rowan's voice almost unrecognizable. In all the time we spent together his voice never raised. Not once. My muscles trembled, and I gathered my anger to throw another response at him. Then Amy flew into the room.

"You guys! Knock it off!" Her face was filled with disgust. "What is the matter with you?" She looked between us expectantly. "Matthew is in there, half-alive, we have no idea where Riona is, and you two are fighting like damn teenagers."

My eyes darted to the ground, and Rowan returned to his silent cleaning. *Un-freaking-believable.* The anger alive and fluid in my body propelled me outside, letting the door slam behind me. I headed down the small path leading me along the thick line of pine trees.

I can't do this. I'll never be able to control the elements. This was a dangerous game, and lives were at stake. *Innocent lives.* Guilt washed through me as I forced my hands through my hair. I wondered if Riona was alive. Outrage with the current situation and how badly I'd screwed up launched me farther from the cottage, shooting loose gravel and dirt from beneath my feet in my quick pace.

In front of me, a chipmunk crossed the path, pausing midway in fear. He chirped noisily at me with wide eyes before scampering into the thick underbrush. I could still hear him chattering as he went. *I'm pissed, too, buddy.*

"Aislynn!" Amy's voice called from behind me. "Wait up!"

I tried to slow my angry stalking to a normal pace, allowing Amy to fall in step beside me.

"I am sure Rowan is just frustrated with what happened," she tried. I said nothing in response. "Matthew's ribs were broken. Rowan said he healed them, which is completely nuts, of course. This shit is all nuts."

I kept my head down, watching and stepping over the rocks embedded in the path. Amy would keep talking, and I'd let her.

"I think Matthew will be okay, but I can tell it is tender for him to breathe." She stumbled on a rock I had stepped over, taking a few odd steps to right herself again. "Do you have to walk so damn fast?" Her breath quickened.

"Sorry." I slowed a little. "I can't do this."

"You have to. All other applicants are underqualified. You're it, cupcake." She nudged me with her elbow.

Giving her a sideways glance, I came to a stop. Realizing my fury had led me quite a distance from the cottage, I gazed across the open grassy field before me. The walk had helped. I checked in with my emotions as my heartrate steadied, and my anger had simmered into dull, pissed off land. That was better than the DEFCON 1 level it had previously resided. Amy watched me carefully.

"A lot different than home, huh?" Amy held her hand above her eyes, shielding the sun. The last of its light cut across the valley as it began to dip behind the mountains. The long grass moved with the wind, twisting the wildflowers in a spirited dance. I took it all in and tried to let it soothe me. Instead the wind made me antsy.

I considered sharing with Amy what I had gone through, and what I'd realized about myself in the room with Aeolus, and the words hung on the tip of my tongue. But I also knew that my anger was precipitated by those events, my sheer exhaustion, and my lack of food. Rowan's attitude had been the last straw. The images of Air were so clear in my mind, I knew I should tell her.

My confessions were disrupted, however, by a man appearing across the field. He was tall and lithe, and his raven hair hung in strings around his face.

"Who the hell are you?" I tossed across the field.

His demeanor was apprehensive as he looked toward us. "Markus. Ravenna sent me." He brushed his hand across his dark clothing.

Eyeing him, I walked his way. Upon closer inspection, it became clear he was a vampire. *Great.*

"Hey, don't vampires burn in the sun?" Amy yelled, staying rooted in place.

Markus rolled his eyes. "Is that what they tell you in your Realm?" His voice took on a caressing tone as he peered at Amy. "Does it make you feel safer?" He stepped closer, his eyes never leaving Amy's. She began walking toward him. "Believing we are vulnerable." His words were silky now, alluring and captivating. His tongue rolled over his full lips as he stepped into her space, running his finger down her arm, gentle and slow. Amy was utterly taken, and I observed her entire being move to him, falling into his beautifully laid trap.

"Ahem." I cocked my head at him. "Do you mind not seducing my friend into your Vamp brain melt?"

Markus' eyes closed slowly, probably in annoyance of me, but he released his gaze on Amy. She almost whimpered next to me.

"What do you want?" I crossed my arms.

"We have a problem."

My eyebrows raised, waiting for more.

"Aeolus. He is missing."

"Fu—" My teeth clamped down on my lower lip. At first, I thought I heard him wrong. Aeolus couldn't be missing; he was in a magically locked room. Everything had quickly rolled into a giant shit storm.

Markus's hand shot up to stop the questions forming on my lips. "I don't know. I am just the messenger." Then he disappeared.

A loud sigh took place of my questions, and a slew of violent language flooded my thoughts. I pushed my lips out, turning to Amy.

"We are fucked," she stated simply.

Glancing to the empty field and back to her, I shook my head. "Yup, we certainly are. Right in the ass." I put my hand on her shoulder and took us back to the cottage.

Rowan, who was sweeping up glass, only gave us half a glance. No way was I going to speak to him. Amy gaped at the two of us, rolling her eyes. She appeared to be pleading with whoever was in charge of this shit show.

"Look, you guys can't do this!" she exclaimed.

The fiery absolution in my eyes called bullshit. "Rowan, we are all going back to Ravenna's," I said shortly.

His head snapped up midsweep. "You might be. I am going to find Lorcan," he said.

"Aeolus is missing. Which means we must find him, now," Amy said, meeting our eyes again.

I continued to stand with my arms folded across my chest in defiance, casting my eyes away from Amy's glare. Minutes passed in deafening silence.

"Fine." Amy sighed, her words final absolution. "Come on, Aislynn. Let's get Matthew. We can't leave him here." My gaze followed her to the other room. I stood still a moment longer, waiting for Rowan to respond. But it was pointless. I turned and walked out of the room.

❦

"Rowan wouldn't come with you?" Ravenna asked as soon as we appeared on her covered patio. She lounged gracefully in one of her comfortable chairs, playing with the necklace sitting at the hollow of her throat, rolling the chain between her fingers.

Amy beat my arm repetitively in awe upon seeing the view. I didn't blame her; it was impressive. The mountains in the distance were cloaked in a foggy haze of clouds that somehow perfectly mirrored our current predicament.

"No," Amy answered, still staring at the vista before her. "I think he needed some time."

I huffed out my irritation as a response and let my hand fall to Matthew's soft fur, who was lying on the chair next to me. He whimpered under my touch.

"Well, no matter," Ravenna said, shaking back a section of her hair. "We need to find Aeolus, and we need to do it now."

"How do you think they even got to him? Wasn't that next to impossible?" I asked.

Ravenna's expression was contemplative for the quickest moment, her black eyes deciding what to say. "I am unsure." Her response was quick. "However, this doesn't change our situation."

I noticed her discreetly giving Amy a glance while irritation prickled my skin. "I am assuming they took—"

Ravenna's words were cut off by a sharp crack of thunder and lightning shattering brilliant white light across the sky.

Amy squealed, and my body involuntarily jumped in my chair. Ravenna cared not to notice as rain began to pelt down around the covered patio. Pushing myself to my feet, I went to the edge of the patio, sticking my hand out into the biting rain.

Something was wrong. It hadn't rained the entire time I had been here. *Why now?*

"It's only a bit of rain," Ravenna spoke from behind me.

I turned sharply at the closeness of her voice, crossing my arms in annoyance. The rain blew into the covered area, a cool mist spraying across my face. There was absolutely nothing about this situation I liked.

"Aeolus is in danger. We must leave for the Air Mountains immediately," Ravenna insisted.

"Why do you think he is there?" I peered over my shoulder.

"Because that is where the element is hidden . . . well, sort of." She leaned against the post, bending her knee resting a stiletto against the wood.

My teeth snapped together, frustration rising again. "I thought you didn't know where the element was located."

I turned on her now. The images Aeolus shared with me were in the forefront of my mind.

"I don't," she clarified, completely unconcerned with the irritation in my voice.

"What aren't you telling us?" I demanded.

Another loud crack of booming thunder issued forth, followed by splintering light that sent shudders across my skin. The energy in the air pressed down on me. Matthew's whimpers filled the air, and Amy's eyes radiated concern.

Something is very wrong. I stepped closer.

"Tell me."

Raising her eyebrows, Ravenna turned and walked back to her chair, sitting slowly, crossing one leg over the other. Her mouth pursed, and I could feel her deciding. Deciding what to tell us. Crossing my arms, I glared and waited.

"He could only leave the room if he chose to leave of his own accord." Her gaze drifted to the side.

My eyes flickered as I took in her words. "So, no one *took* him?" I asked with exasperation.

Meeting my eye, Ravenna shook her head, then glanced down.

"Why would you lie?" Amy and I said at the same time, both our voices rising.

The vampire's eyes snapped to mine. Black and piercing anger sliced through her words. "I am a Vampire Queen. You will not question me or my motives."

Her staccato and icy words were accompanied by a rush of harder rain pelting down on the patio covering. Amy's open mouth slammed shut, and terror slapped across her face. Jaw twitching, I swallowed the fear shooting through me. Riona's words ran through my mind, and I wondered what Ravenna's motives were indeed. Then I decided I didn't want to know.

Jax appeared on the ground in between us.

"We need to go."

He faced the vampire queen, his little black nose sniffing at the air whiskers twitching. Violently hissing, a growling meow escaped his small body. In return, she raised her lip, showing her own teeth. My eyes narrowed, watching the exchange.

"Jaxon. I should have known," Ravenna spat.

I tilted my chin upward. *The vampire knows my cat?* He stalked in front of her, grumbling incoherent cat sounds.

"It figures you would have a paw in this," she sneered. Jax said nothing as his tail furiously snapped the empty air. They continued their stare-down until Ravenna finally looked at me.

"I guess I am not the only one lying." In a movement faster than my eyes could handle, she was gone.

"I said, let's go."

Arriving back at the empty cottage, a thousand questions burned in my mind. My lips pushed forward, and I held a finger up. I tried to choose the best one, started to speak, stopped, and then started again.

"Was that vampire scared of you?"

Jax meowuffed, jumped on the chair, circled once, and in lazy contemplation laid down with his back toward us.

"Oh, uh-uh, fur-face." I picked him up and held him eye to eye, his long body stretched downward. His blue eyes, full of displeasure, were cast down away from me.

"Perhaps. But it is neither here nor there."

Freaking riddles.

"What about that lying business?" I asked next, staring hard at him. His eyes slowly blinked in annoyance. Convinced I would receive no answer, I furrowed my eyebrows and set him down.

"The king left of his own accord. He knows what is best."

"How is it you suddenly know so much?" Amy asked.

"Oh, that dick has known *a lot* from day one. He fed me some crap about how he can only tell me what I need to know," I answered for him.

In response, Jax lifted his back leg at an impossible angle that would make dancers jealous and started licking himself. Amy muttered under her breath.

I wondered where Rowan went and inwardly chastised myself for caring. *But I do care. A lot.*

Fear pounced through my heart at the thought of him in danger, especially because I didn't know where he was or if I could help. Another shatter of lightning blasted across the sky, sending a blue crackle of light throughout the cottage.

"What about Riona?" I asked the cat, hoping my question would interrupt the intense licking of his ass.

"Riona can look out for herself."

I closed my eyes in frustration. He resumed his licking. Leaving him, I went into the kitchen, noticing Rowan had finished cleaning before leaving. I sat down on the bench, putting my head in my hands, trying to process. Amy sat down next to me.

"I think Ravenna wants the elements for herself," she said.

"Probably," I acknowledged. "But why would she even bother with me, then?"

"Because you could lead her straight to them." That was obvious, of course. "Where did Aeolus go?"

"Who the hell knows?" I sighed. "That little bastard could be anywhere."

"So, why would he leave?" The question was rhetorical, but Amy and I had a process: we would take apart problems and talk through them until we had a solution.

"Okay, well . . .danger?" she thought aloud. "He's in danger and knew he had to leave? Perhaps he had learned Ravenna would double cross him?" From her unsure tone, I could tell Amy wasn't convinced by her own words.

"Maybe he has to move the element?" I provided.

"Oh, like he recognized it was in danger?" She put her thumb in her mouth, biting on the tip. I nodded to her thoughts. "Or one of his people sent him a message?"

Possibly.

"And why the rain?" I asked, still bothered by the unconventional weather.

"What do you mean?"

"Well, the entire time it's been perfect. He leaves the room and there is a massive storm? Sort of elemental, don't you think?"

"Okay. Storms. Water, wind, air . . . makes sense. The element is exposed?" she concluded.

My eyes widened. Amy was a genius. *Why didn't I think of that?*

"It's exposed! It isn't in hiding, hence the storm. Amy!" Excitement rattled through my words. "So, he has it out in the open, which means we need to figure out where the hell he is."

"Ravenna mentioned the Air Mountains," she offered, but I shook my head. I began to pace the kitchen floor.

"No, he wouldn't go there." Another boom of thunder rumbled overhead, and the little cottage shook. "In the room, he showed me all these things . . ." There was too much to tell her, and we didn't have time for the details. "There was a flash of mountains, with magic ripping through them. He said I had to release my fears."

"Duh." Amy glanced up from the bench.

"Seriously?"

"I *am* serious. You are a basket of fear. It is all you know. Fear and how to traverse around it while being blanketed in more fear," Amy snarked.

I bit my lip. She was right, of course, but I didn't have to like it, nor admit it, for that matter. But what did that mean for me and the element?

"What is your biggest fear?" Amy asked. She peeked at me, offering more clarification. "In finding Air."

I gave her a dirty look for all the things she didn't say, but I knew what she was thinking. "Screwing up. Not being able to control it. Hurting people. Not being enough." The words spewed out of me like vomit.

Amy's eyebrows rose in response. "I have things to say, but we will save those for later." She eyed me. We had been over this many times before: my insecurities, my worthiness, my blah blah blah. Mitch had carefully and methodically destroyed all those things.

"What would make you face those fears?" she asked quietly, filling the silence.

I blew out my breath, finally stopping my pacing. "Going by myself to find him," I replied. "To help him? Get Air with him? Without a damn clue as to what I am doing." I sulked back down to the bench.

"Yup. Which means you have to leave us here, unprotected," Amy finished for me. Huffing, I ground my teeth together. That was the part I really didn't like.

"But—" I started.

"Nope. Don't want to hear it." The rain pelted the roof and ferocious wind howled in agreement. Amy glanced upward toward the sky. "That's your cue."

Damn it all.

37

I was going to get myself killed. Standing at the top of the peak, wind cut across the jagged surface, whipping me off balance. I dug my feet into the rock, holding myself steady. Amy had pulled a cloak off the back of the door before I left, and the material tugged at my body, billowing out behind me.

My thoughts fleetingly went to her and Matthew, unprotected and alone, and I shuddered. I teleported again and again across the peaks of mountains until something looked familiar. I had to find anything similar to what Aeolus had shown me. The peak to the right called to me as the wind nudged forcefully, reminding me of everything it held for me.

Here goes nothing. I didn't think; I acted. Taking several steps, I flung myself off the edge. For the shortest second, fear crawled under my skin, reminding me of its presence. Instead, I allowed the magic to take over, roaring through the fear and . . . I flew.

Well, I fell in style, perhaps. The air rushed over me,

little pins prickling my skin as I plummeted down. Scanning the ground below me, I searched the treetops for any sign of him. It was an impossible task to find a foot-tall being in the endless tops of pine trees, but I remained determined.

He has to be down there!

With a soft push downward, I landed in an open clearing between towering pines, my feet skittering across the ground as I tried to keep my balance. A noise captured my attention and I glanced upward to find Aeolus sitting on a thick branch, his tiny legs dangling underneath him.

"I knew you would find me."

Shielding my eyes with my hand, I craned my neck to see him.

"You left the room?"

"It was time."

Pondering this, my neck began to ache. I decided to improvise, teleporting myself on the branch next to him. Examining the narrow wood, I silently hoped it would hold my weight.

"You know my people have been responsible for keeping the element hidden for centuries?" he began. I shook my head in response. His mouth settled into a grim line.

"Yes, my ancestors have taken turns hiding the element, but it was always traceable, always found after a few short years. Darkness held control for some time, and then we would hide it again."

"Sounds exhausting."

"Indeed. But it is our purpose as Air Faeries; we took responsibility long ago."

I nodded. A strong breeze blew across the pine and I put a hand on the trunk for safety, which was silly when I thought about it. Aeolus seemed completely content.

"When it came to be my turn to hide the element, there was much discussion as to where it should be placed."

"Did you have any idea that in your lifetime a Keeper would exist?" I asked as the limb bounced in the wind.

"It was seen, yes." His lips twitched. "I did not approve of the places which were suggested. Believe it or not, I was a bit stubborn in my time." He made the statement with a straight face, and I tried to hold back the laugh. "I did not want to repeat the past, determined to find a place no one would ever find."

"I believe you accomplished that, considering." I still did not understand why he chose to leave the security of Ravenna's magical room.

"Things are not what they seem."

"No kidding. That seems to be the theme of Hallervania." He was right, though; every time I thought one thing, the rug had been ripped out from beneath me to find another version of the truth.

"He will be here shortly." Aeolus leaned forward in a way that caused my heart to skip.

I became alert. "Who?"

"Lorcan," he clarified, his voice pensive and soft. "Rowan, too, I am sure."

"What? How?"

"Because it is to be."

Again with the damn riddles. I gritted my teeth, searching for my patience. "So, what?" I questioned. "We are just waiting here for them?" *Is that why he's here?*

"Well, it seemed convenient."

I might have to throttle him after all. "We need to get back to safety," I insisted.

"Oh, that time has ended. I was only waiting for you."

He peered at me with his big, woeful eyes. "You see, it is time for you to take Air."

I almost fell off the branch. He couldn't be serious. I hadn't prepared. I wasn't ready. Even though Amy alluded to this very reality, I secretly hoped she was wrong. I thought about grabbing him and teleporting back to Ravenna's.

"Please do not. It wouldn't work anyway. And you *are* ready," he said. I swore under my breath, and my heartbeat increased rapidly by the second.

"I don't think so." My words were weak, and he disregarded them. Sitting quiet for some time, his little legs swung underneath him at ease in the old pine.

"Why do you think no one has found the element this time?" He gazed my direction. My lips pushed out in contemplation. "I have kept it hidden for over 343 years."

My mouth fell open. I knew he was old, but how old? Certain they didn't hand over an element to a baby, but to an elder. My brain stumbled on the math.

"Ravenna told you *she* hid me? Protecting me because only I knew the location of the element?" As I nodded again, he harrumphed, shaking his little head. "There is truth in that, I suppose." He crossed his ankles and scanned the woods. I waited.

"You see, I couldn't hide the element in a place. That was the mistake of my people." My eyebrow arched in surprise. "Ah, here we go."

He jumped off the branch, landing on the forest floor soundlessly. Before I could contest his actions, magic sliced through the air. Thunderous blasts sparked before me in shards of color. I recognized Rowan's voice immediately. As predicted by the little king, Rowan and Lorcan shifted through the trees below me in flashes of movement, light, and disastrous magic.

Trees exploded, sending bits of branches disintegrating through the air. Dirt flew as Rowan slammed Lorcan across the exposed, ragged terrain. Aeolus stood out of the way, watching the two men assault each other with bursts of magic. Neither noticed him.

"You will pay for what you did!" Rowan's voice rang out.

"I did what I was told! By the Council!" Lorcan tossed back while magic arched across in streaks of fiery light.

Rowan countered the magic with beautiful blasts of green, shattering the incoming attack. "The Council you work for!"

Lorcan threw up his hands and a flare of red flung out. I chose then to make my presence known, allowing myself to slide down from the branch. I landed between them, directly in line of the magic. My hands shot up, slamming the magic away. With a twist of my wrist, Air magic shoved Lorcan into a trunk of a pine and bits of bark whizzed across the clearing.

"It's not nice to fight." My words sliced the empty air, surprise strewn across both their faces. Wind began to cyclone around me, my dark cloak swirling in the air. I forced the whipping wind into Lorcan's face. "And you hurt my friend."

I clenched my hands into fists. Rain pelted all around us, watery daggers slicing into Lorcan, battering him. He struggled to use his arm to hide his face. I allowed the rage to slide back under my skin, and the magic feasted on my emotion immediately. Probably not my best idea, but I didn't care.

Aeolus's soft voice came from beside me. "You must let him go." His words cut through my magic, throwing me off guard.

"What? No!" I held the magic haphazardly while looking over at him. Flittering in the air, he put his small hand on my arm. Magic thrummed through me and my eyes darted to his.

How?

The element pulsated from his little hand and into mine. Confusion flashed through my eyes, and the magic holding Lorcan began to weaken. Distracted by the little king's large eyes in front of me, the presence of the element acute under my skin, Lorcan twisted out of my magical grasp.

Lorcan blasted me with his own magic, tossing me through the air. The ground exploded against my shoulder and I rolled into the base of a tree. Wincing, I tried to find my feet again as Rowan hurled a swirling ball of energy toward him.

My hand protectively holding my shoulder, I attempted to throw another ball of energy after Rowan's. Pain seared through me and I swore loudly. Whirling around the magic in impossible ways, Lorcan deftly avoided the magical blasts. A black swirl of energy formed at his fingertips and a malicious grin slid across his face. He pushed the magic through the air, slamming it into Aeolus.

The tiny king's body flew at impossible angles, landing with an unearthly thunk into the ground. The violent sound was much too loud for how small his body was. An indistinguishable roar issued from my mouth. I drove a force of magic toward Lorcan, but he disappeared. It pounded into a series of trees, sending bark flying through the forest.

Rowan came to me as I scrambled across the earth to reach Aeolus. His little body was shuddering, twisted and broken. His eyes, glassy and clear, made my heart ache.

"This was my purpose," he began, his voice hollow. "To hold the element until you could. 534 years was a long time to wait for my destiny to be fulfilled. You . . ." He took a trembling breath, then started again. "You are going to be a magnificent Keeper."

Stinging emotion pierced my eyes, and sounds murmured from my lips. Eyes heavy in desperation, I silently pleaded with Rowan, catching his gaze. There has to be *something. Can't we do something?* The words tumbled in my mind rather than out loud.

All this time, Aeolus had held the element within him. Tears welled on the edge of my lashes and tumbled down my cheeks. His little hand held mine, frail and marred.

I rested my other hand gently on his chest, feeling the shallow rise and fall as he took his last breaths. His eyes staring into mine, I watched the life slowly disappear. A sob stuck in my throat, my head dropped, and tears streamed out.

Beneath my hands, Aeolus' body began glowing an iridescent gold. The swirling marks embedded in his skin radiated against the golden light, shimmering brighter until the light concaved upon itself, becoming a ball of yellow. Gradually moving from his chest, it lifted upward and out of him. His once-yellow skin turned a dull ashen color.

The element held itself above his body, waiting. I cupped the golden orb, the power and strength of the ancient magic simmering within my grasp. My vision swimming in gold, I received Air, and with it came the lightness and freedom of the element. Shoulders shuddering, my throat tightened; the emotions were so vivid before me. The light dissolved into my hand and absorbed into the amulet hanging at my chest.

Silence hung heavily in the air. I glanced down to the king, running my hand over his eyes, closing them for the final time. Rowan reached across, trying to comfort me.

"It wasn't supposed to be like this. I was supposed to fight, to . . ." But the rest of my words would not come. My voice was empty and hollow.

38

"The little king outwitted me after all these years."

My head snapped up at Ravenna's voice. Her five-inch stilettos dug into the dirt, and streams of fury wrapped around her. We clambered to our feet, and Rowan stood behind me. He held magic at the ready in his hand, sparking with an unresolved fury. I brushed my fingertips across his arm, forcing him to wait. The amulet swung out from my shirt, shining brightly with yellow-golden light. The vampire swore viciously.

"I don't suppose you are going to hand that over?" Ravenna's lips curled into a sneer.

Is she serious? Yes, she was. *Awesome.* I brushed the dirt off the knees of my pants. "No. I don't suppose I am."

"I put up with that . . . *thing* for 253 years." Her icy cold words shot through the air. Rowan shifted his weight, edging his body in front of me. "Where was it? Hmm?"

Dark clouds pushed across the sky, casting odd shadows on the forest floor as thunder rumbled in the distance.

The vampire took a few slow steps toward us with her head cocked to one side.

"Not going to tell me?" She gazed down at the tiny body in disgust. "I suppose it doesn't matter. Perhaps I should be pleased."

"And why is that?" Rowan asked.

"Because that's one less thing I have to do." She slowly prowled closer, and in her vampire quickness, she reached for the amulet. It instantly blasted her back in a flood of magic, throwing her to the ground. *Ooh, that's a nice perk.* Shock filled her face, followed quickly by intense anger. Subconsciously, I took a small step back, really not in the market to piss off a vampire.

In rapid movement, she stood again, brushing her hands against one another. Her expression was calculative, her tongue gliding over sharp teeth as dark, soulless eyes penetrated mine.

"Fine. We will go about this another way, but you will give me the element." She disappeared.

The breath I held shuddered out of me. I had succeeded in letting a magical being die, obtaining an element, *and* pissing off a vampire in a matter of a few minutes. *Peachy.*

"What do you think she'll do?" I questioned Rowan.

"I have no idea." Rowan's voice was strained.

Then it occurred to me that Amy and Matthew were basically dangling bait at the cottage. *Shit!* Shrugging out of the cloak, I lifted Aeolus's tiny body and wrapped him within the dark material.

"Come on, we have to hurry!" I tucked him carefully against me, disappearing. Rowan followed.

An unnerving silence hovered in Riona's cottage. We

found the kitchen empty except for a piece of paper hanging in the center of the room. Swearing, I plucked it out of the air.

Should have just given me the element. Want to trade?

Ravenna

"Dammit!" I crumpled the corner of the note in my hand out of reflex. Rowan took the note and I checked the other room. Expecting no one, my head flipped back at the sight of Jax curled in a tight ball on the chair.

"What are you doing here?"

"Where else would I be?"

"Amy? Matthew?" I asked.

"Oh, she took them."

"You let her?" My voice hitched.

Lifting his head, eyes blinking heavily, he considered me for a moment. *"I was sleeping."* He blinked slowly. *"Besides, I'm a cat. What was I supposed to do?"*

I groaned. He was right, of course, but it didn't help.

"What is that?" Jax sniffed the air and the bundled cloak in my arms.

"Aeolus." My mouth set in a grimace. I wasn't sure of the traditions concerning burial in Hallervania, but I could not leave his body abandoned in the forest.

"That is very valiant of you. I think he would be grateful." My head cocked in the direction of the cat, unsure if he was being sarcastic or not.

"I think using the elements would be appropriate," Rowan said from behind me.

I bobbed my head as I regarded the body wrapped in my arms. Stepping outside, the sky was still heavy with clouds, murky and gray, which seemed to reflect my mood. With desperate care, I set the small bundle on the ground for a moment. The perimeter of the cottage held a plethora of medicinal plants and flowers, and I began pulling a mixture of everything. Rowan watched in silence before gathering sticks, branches, and leaves. Again, I worried about what was customary, but I knew what felt right to me.

A little place not too far from the house at the edge of the forest where the trees met the grass called to me. Kneeling on the ground, gathering the sticks and leaves, I created a pyre. With care, I removed Aeolus' small body from the cloak and set him down in his final resting place.

The sight of his frail, ashen body wrenched on my heart as I placed the delicate flowers around his body. Pinching my lips together and rubbing them against my teeth, I tried to restrain the emotion. Instead, I focused on the giant peonies in shades of pinks, roses bright yellow with fiery orange tips, and white carnations to fill in the spaces.

My face tingled with the threat of another round of tears, and I pushed my hands against my knees to stand, repelling the emotions away. At some point, Jax wandered outside, making his presence known by curling himself between my legs.

"He—" My voice cracked with the impending emotion. I paused and picked up Jax from the ground. "He was a pain in my ass, he really was, but he died for my destiny." I inhaled sharply, tightening my eyes, trying to hold my voice steady.

"He will not—" I bit my lip, pinching down, the pain superseding the lump in my throat. I tugged the sleeves of my shirt over my hands, fingers clenching to the material.

"He won't die in vain." My voice was almost a whisper. "I promise, Aeolus. I promise to reclaim all the elements."

Whiskers brushed my cheeks as Jax sniffed my face, following a tear as it crested over my lashes. In my right hand, I cupped a beautiful ball of swirling golden light. Closing my eyes, I focused my magic and the element of Air. The swirl fountained out of my hand, and the light cascaded down on his body in a shower of golden crystals.

Flecks of light rained down, turning Aeolus' body to dust. My chest tightened and I found myself biting my lip again. Hot, heavy tears traced down my cheeks and Jax rubbed his face against mine. Through wet lashes, I glanced at Rowan. The corners of his eyes were tight and downcast away from me. I could tell he was still wondering how many people would die for me, and for the elements. My thoughts settled back on Amy and Matthew.

Rowan turned toward me. "Aislynn, I . . ."

"We will get them back." My voice was constricted with heavy emotion.

"No, Aislynn . . . I just—"

"Rowan, we *will* get them back." I cut him off again. I wasn't sure why, but maybe it was because my nerves were sharp and exposed. Right now, I didn't want to hear anything that would break my conviction. He watched me for a moment, then he sighed, finally relinquishing his thought.

"Jax, any idea where they are?"

"Having their blood drained?"

"JAX!"

A chattered sound came from him in response. The thought of Ravenna hurting either of my friends sent fear trickling down my arms. Jaw tightening, I gazed down to the pile of ash at my feet and hoped Aeolus would be pleased. One last sigh and I walked back to the cottage, letting Jax leap out of my arms.

"Come on, let's go," I called back to Rowan.

"Where are we going? We don't know where they are."

"I don't need to know; I only have to listen." I could feel Rowan's questioning gaze from behind me.

Once inside the kitchen, I closed my eyes. I would use what Aeolus taught me and use the element to my advantage. I listened. Searching for Ravenna's sharp voice among the murmurs and whispers of voices coursing through my mind, I sharpened my intent.

I pulled through everything I heard, sifting and homing in on what I needed, and then . . . *there*. She was yelling at someone, but it wasn't quite clear. My eyes tightened as I fixated on her voice alone. *"I said now!"*

I tugged on her voice, thinking of it like a string to follow, to hold.

"I found her." I grabbed Rowan's arm, and we vanished.

The thread of her voice guided me like poison seeping through veins. I drew softly, trying to be careful because I didn't want her to know I was there. She seemed pretty occupied at the moment, though, as she raged at her minions.

We appeared in the murky shadows of a room, voices coming from the other side of the wall. A quick glance told me that we were close to the room where Aeolus had been kept, deep in the rocky hallways of the subterranean maze of Ravenna's home.

"Where are we?" Rowan whispered. I put my finger to my mouth to quiet him, listening to the two vampires talking. The voices were annoyed with Ravenna and her hasty choice to take Amy and Matthew. Apparently, Matthew bit one of them. *Score one for us.*

"No, Aislynn. You don't understand," Rowan demanded in a hushed voice. Hand clamping down on my arm, he teleported us out. We stood in the woods, the cloudy sky making the forest floor thick with darkness.

"Rowan! Amy and Matthew are back there!" I yelled. "I am going back."

"Aislynn! I know they are, but you can't just go bursting into a vampire lair without a plan," he pleaded. "I know you are upset with me, but Ravenna is *not* on our side anymore. She wouldn't think twice about killing you, Matthew, or Amy. Just because you haven't seen that side of her, do not underestimate the fact that she is a violent killer and she eats humans."

His arms fell to his sides. My shoulders slumped, knowing he was right; I wasn't thinking. Reaching out, Rowan grabbed my hand, his voice softening. "Aislynn, I am sorry. A lot has happened in a short period of time, and I need you to trust me. We need a plan." He watched my eyes for concession.

Averting my gaze, I blew out a breath. "Fine. You are right. And I am sorry, too. It's just . . ."

He squeezed my hand. "Let's get Amy and Matthew back."

"So how do you kill them? The traditional stake through the heart?" I asked, trying to divert my emotions.

"What?"

"You know, wooden stake?" My hands came together to move in a stabbing motion, but his eyebrows furrowed together. "Seriously? That isn't true either? Ugh, why can't any of our books get it right?" I said this more to myself than to him.

"They must have their heads severed from their bodies and the remains burned, which tends to be problematic because they move impossibly fast, as you have seen."

"Okay, some of them got it right," I relented. "Fire, I can handle, but the head thing? That's you."

He smiled with relief. I could tell he was pleased we were on the same page, and that smile also told me he wouldn't blink at the prospect of decapitating some blood-sucking monsters. "Remember, they have excellent hearing, Ravenna especially. Mind your thoughts." I nodded, well aware of this.

"Alright, this is my plan." Rowan gave me some ideas, but I wasn't certain we were much better off this time around. But what the hell?

We returned to the room in silence. Bellows cascaded through the walls, Ravenna's infuriated tone no longer in my head but booming everywhere. Rowan and I both cringed, sinking further against the uneven rock wall.

"They will be coming. Aislynn will not leave her friends in my hands." The vampire's voice had lost the control it usually held.

"How do you plan on getting the element?" I recognized Markus's voice.

"It doesn't matter what my plans are. You will do as you're told." Low guttural growling echoed out, followed by snapping teeth and barking. I inhaled sharply at the sound of Matthew.

"Shut up, dog," Ravenna snapped, then paused. "What is that I hear?"

Shit.

"Aislynn, come out, come out. I know you are here. I can hear your thudding heart!" Ravenna called through the walls.

Eyeing Rowan in the dim light, I transported us into the next room. Large looming walls of earth and stone surrounded us, lit by half-moon cauldrons of fire suspended into the rock.

One side appeared as a library of books, documents, and magical warfare. Opposite that was a torture chamber for the human variety. Chills ran up my legs as my brain slowly registered the vamp appurtenances: restraints hung neatly on the wall, and vials of blood were arranged in a system that was methodical and frightening.

I swallowed hard. This further defined the darker side of Ravenna; both seductive and deadly, her need for human blood became more obvious. I began to realize that she thoroughly enjoyed the way in which she prepared her dinner. My throat got hot and dry thinking of her victims and their last moments in this room.

Markus stood to Ravenna's right and two other vampires I recognized from earlier were to her left. Their menacing sneers grated the reality of standing against them rather than with. Behind them, Matthew was held in a cage and Amy tied to the bars. Sharp whines erupted from Matthew's throat and Amy's terrified eyes pleaded with mine. Then I saw the open bite wounds on her neck, and anger flooded my veins.

"You made a mistake, Ravenna." My words were unsteady.

She took long steps toward me, exaggerated by her long legs. She had exchanged the strappy stilettos for black leather boots rising over her knees. Ravenna brought her hand to her lips and her tongue glided across the tip of her finger.

"I am afraid I broke my promise." Her silky words were followed by a sultry laugh. "Amy is just irresistible. Her delicious blood was taunting me, and I needed to taste."

The words made me sick and my body shot forward, only to be held back by Rowan. Bile crept up the back of my throat. My eyes darted toward Amy.

"So. I have something you want, and you have something I want." Ravenna's words purred across the room. I wanted to attack, magic spurting from my fingertips, but Rowan held tight.

"Well, well . . . look at what we have here."

Everyone's attention shifted to the other side of the room where Daragon had appeared. Ravenna's groans of frustration filled the room, and Rowan's fingers tightened on my arm.

"I tried to warn you, Aislynn: you can't trust vampires. One minute, they're your friend; the next, they're eating you. Or in this case, your friends." His mouth pouted in fake concern.

"What are you doing here?" Ravenna rested her hands on her hips, resembling a sullen teenager.

"Well, one might say two birds, one stone?" He winked. "That's how the old saying goes, right, Aislynn?" He arched an eyebrow in my direction. "And I really can't resist an opportunity to kill vampires."

Daragon's eyes glittered as Ravenna assessed his threat. Her head ticked to the left, sending her minions to what I considered certain death.

In response, Daragon spiraled out a lasso of fire. A

spinning thread, aglow with licking flames, snapped across the room, slashing at the first vampire to approach. He scarcely escaped the flames flashing across his skin, but he was unable to escape the rebound slash.

The flames scarred across the vampire's body in a diagonal cut from shoulder to hip, burning and charring him in two. Ashes cascaded to the floor after the fiery consumption. The second vampire faltered for the quickest second, and that was all that was necessary for Daragon to lash the ribbon of fire at him. This time, the head of the vampire rolled across the floor, shock across its face, before burning to ash.

"And that, Aislynn, is how you kill vampires." A wicked smile crossed Daragon's lips. My face twisted in startled terror as I realized how much Daragon savored the brutal killings. Fire magic danced as the lasso swirled around him, flames licking and reaching for the next victim. I swallowed hard, reeling at the destructive dark magic.

"Should we continue? Or reevaluate, Ravenna?" Daragon asked.

Shifting my gaze to her, anger rippled off her limbs in shimmering rage. "Daragon." A conniving smile trickled across her face. "With the element, I can help you."

My body jolted at how quickly she shifted and switched sides, cold calculation rolling through her. As I watched Ravenna attempt to work Daragon into her ideas, I made a quick decision and snapped us next to Amy and Matthew.

Markus immediately shifted his attention from the exchange between Daragon and the Vampire Queen to us. Ignoring the impending attack, I put my attention on the ropes holding Amy. My fingers burned with piercing stings.

"They are wrapped in magic. You won't be able to

untie them," Rowan said over his shoulder, keeping his focus on Markus. A whirling ball of green bit across the room, but the vampire avoided the magic with deft precision.

"Get me out of here, Aislynn." Amy's eyes darted in desperation. Reaching behind her, I saw the piercing vampire bite on her neck, and the trail of blood that trickled to her shirt, where it dried into a congealed smear of deep red.

"I'm working on it." I threw an energy ball at the ropes, but it was deflected. A golden blaze radiated through her bonds.

"Ow!" Amy cried out, twisting her arms against the pain.

"Sorry!" I exclaimed, cringing against her reaction.

After a moment of reevaluation, I tossed fire out across the ropes, burning them away from the bars and Amy's arms. She instinctively rubbed and held her wrists, trying to soothe the pain. Clamping down on the side of my lip, I did the same to the unlock on the bars holding Matthew's cage.

"The magic wouldn't let him shift to another form—" Amy's words were cut off as the wolf careened across the room, slamming into Ravenna's back and knocking her off balance.

Matthew pinned her to the ground, snarling inches from her face. Sharp teeth snapping, threads of saliva spattered across her mouth as his paws dug into her chest. The vampire threw out her arms, shoving Matthew off and across the room.

In swift movement, she rocketed up to standing. Her fury raged as her face shifted, forcing everyone in the room to stop. Daragon was the only one who stood casually and unconcerned. Magic sat at the edge of Rowan's fingertips, and Amy stayed behind me. Matthew recovered and stood with guttural sounds emanating from deep in the wolf's body. The two vampires stood motionless, waiting.

"A short time ago, you fought together against me. Now look . . ." Daragon's mouth turned up with his own amusement. Ravenna pushed her hand across her face, rubbing away Matthew's wolf drool. She sent half a glance toward Markus. "Ravenna," Daragon added, "you just keep getting in my way."

Daragon reignited the fire lasso, swirling it around him and cracking it across the room. The movement blurred too fast to see, but I saw Markus narrowly miss the whip of flames. Fire seethed through the air, surrounding the vampire. A swirl of fiery threads spiraled around him, controlled by Daragon's arms. It constricted like a snake, closer and closer to Markus. Ravenna shrieked as she slammed into Daragon, teeth flashing ever-so-close to his exposed flesh.

Everything happened lightning fast, and I barely had time to react. I didn't particularly know if Markus was good or bad at this point, but I did know that he didn't deserve to die by a spiral of angry death flames. Without thinking, I spun my hands, engulfing Markus in a wall of water.

His eyes held silent gratitude as I gave him a small nod. I couldn't allow Daragon to kill anyone else. My hands opened at my sides, and I called upon Air. A violent thrust of wind pushed through the open space. The restraints on the wall clanked in defiance as the magical paraphernalia shivered in the cool, subterranean room.

For the first time, I fully embraced the magic of the element. It slid over my senses like a cool breeze on a summer day. A smile flickered across my face and a strange letting go happened as I rejoiced in the magic.

The air brushed across my skin and swirled at the edges of the room. My eyes closed as I focused only on the feeling of the magic trembling within. Then, I let it spin. The once-meticulous order became pandemonium as everything began to whirl through the air. The freedom of the element began to pull on me, finding anything in the room to draw from, including Daragon's magic.

Air drew from the lasso of fire magic, and my eyes shot open. *Oh, shit!* A frenzy of flames began to swirl around the room, sending Amy, Matthew, and Rowan for cover.

The air magic took control, feeding on the vortex of fire. It was out of my control, and I could feel Daragon trying to draw the magic back as I tried desperately to restrain the element. But Air and Fire combined to create a force neither of us could control. The flames wicked out, searching for anything to consume.

Ravenna's face was horror-struck as the fire poured from the cyclone. Air pushed the blaze across the ceiling in a sea of fire. Heat pulsed down into the room, and a hot wave pressed on my skin as panic flooded. I eyed the devouring blaze I couldn't stop.

Suddenly a flare plummeted down from the fiery sea above as if aware of the vampires below. Markus moved to protect Ravenna. He absorbed the inferno of flames, turning to ash and dust in seconds.

Crawling to me, Rowan stayed low, dangerously avoiding the licking flames, shouting my name across the roar of magic. I pulled on his presence and the magic residing within him. A cool earthy green energy helped me ground myself through the torment of elemental magic. I clamped my eyes shut and imagined roots digging deep into the earth, steadying my breath. With each exhale, I began the battle of dragging the element back into control. Teeth grinding, my muscles ached with the strain of fighting the magic. Eventually, the fire receded with gradual hesitation.

A vague awareness came over of me of Daragon doing the same, and his magic pulled back to the center. Glaring in his direction, I continued my labored effort and my open palms flashed into closed fists to close the magic. Breath heavy, I fell forward, resting my palms on my knees, resisting the urge to vomit.

"You might want to learn to control that," Daragon heaved out, as if this was my fault. Though he wasn't as winded as me, I could tell the magic had drained him. For the merest second, he seemed caught off guard by the lack of control he held over his own magic.

"Or you could just give it to me," he added with a sly grin. I knew he was trying to hide the unease sitting in his eyes. Curiosity burned over me.

Why is he really here? He had assisted me in killing vampires, and although he enjoyed it immensely, wouldn't it have been easier to possibly let me die? Something bothered me as I questioned his motives.

Ravenna, her face heavy with emotion, stood completely defeated, the only vampire left in the room. An awkward frown filled my face and I tried to convey my sorrow, but she merely sneered in response.

"I would take care of your friend," Daragon grimaced, pointing to his own neck as he implied Amy's wound. Mathew nudged Amy with his nose as she tried to stand in slow movements, her face paling with the effort.

"See you soon, Aislynn."

In a swirl of fiery light, Daragon disappeared. Discontentment flashed in Ravenna's eyes before her head dropped, conceding defeat. This clearly hadn't gone the way she desired. She left in a blur of movement, the door creaking as it fell back to closed.

Rowan let out a big breath, then teleported Amy and Matthew back to the cottage. Glancing across the room, I focused on the heaps of ashes that were once vampires now strewn across the floor, forgotten in the carnage caused by the sheer chaos of magic.

39

I returned to find Rowan inspecting Amy's neck. She barely registered my appearance, wincing under Rowan's investigating fingertips. Matthew nudged his nose under her hand with soft whines, trying to distract her.

"What did Daragon mean?" I asked.

"Vampire bites are poisonous," Jax explained with a yawn. He walked across the table and laid down, curling his paws beneath him.

"What?" My voice cut with abruptness, and Rowan glared at the cat.

"We need Riona," Matthew said. *"Do you know where she is or not?"*

Jax's ears twitched with annoyance. *"Yes."*

"What?" My patience with my cat was reaching new levels. Why hadn't he said anything before?

"Fiiiinnnee . . . I guess I will go. Since you are obviously impaired." Jax looked to Matthew in feigned disgust before disappearing.

"Explain poisonous." I demanded, pulling out the bench to sit next to Amy.

"Well, all vampire bites are venomous; the toxin of vampirism is in their teeth. All bites, scratches, nicks are dangerous. The severity of the bite, exposure, and the vampire involved all play a factor in the outcome." Rowan's fingers prodded as he examined down her neck.

"So, you are saying I'm screwed?" Amy cringed.

"No. I am not saying that." Rowan dismissed her remark, but underneath his words I could see the worry in his eyes.

"Aislynn, go to Riona's cupboard. Let's see if she has any antidotes." The cupboard was an entire wall of potions, herbs, and vials of ingredients. I was uncertain what I was looking for as the cure, since vampire bites hadn't been covered in my short magical education.

"Ow," Amy whined behind me.

Rowan hushed her. "I am just seeing if—"

"Seeing if what? My skin will peel off? Ow!" Amy pulled away from Rowan's harsh inspection with an uncanny quickness I witnessed from the corner of my eye. I hurried my inspection of the labeled bottles. For a moment, the only noise was the tinkling of glass on the shelves.

"Would you guys shut up?" Amy spat at us.

I turned abruptly at her tone. "No one said anything."

Her hazy dark eyes bored into mine. I knew enough about vampires in my Realm to realize this was a bad sign. *Freaking hell. Please don't let my friend turn into a vampire.* With shaking hands, I resumed my search.

"I don't even know what I am looking for!" I exclaimed, exasperated.

"Something labeled Starlight, or anything Ragwort or Blood-root. She will have it." Matthew's voice was heavy with emotion in my head. A vial fell over, followed by a waterfall of bottles. Groaning, I checked the labels as I stood them upright.

"Calm down, Aislynn," Rowan said.

Sure, calm down. *My friend will not be a vampire.* The thought stayed on auto repeat, hoping to believe myself each time. *What is taking Jax so long?*

"Jax do this, Jax do that." He peered down at me, reappearing on the top shelf. Sitting, he began to lick his paw, chewing in between his tiny toe beans.

"Where is Riona?" I asked, looking around.

"Yeah . . . she couldn't come."

"What?" I yelled. Amy cringed, glaring at me with dark and edgy eyes. Her usual blue eyes were gone, and instead her gaze held a predatory gleam.

The cat couldn't physically shrug, but he wanted to, I could tell. Matthew barked in harsh tones at him in a conversation that could not be heard with my ears.

Amy slammed her hands down on the bench. "Shut up!" she roared. Everyone stopped to stare. "You. Need. To. Stop. Talking! All of you!"

"Amy, calm down. Breathe," Rowan tried to soothe, and reached out to touch her with hesitation. In response, she slapped at him with a quick, ferocious movement that surprised all of us. Standing, breath heaving from her chest, she glared. I moved slowly toward her, putting my hands up as innocently as possible.

"Amy, it's okay. It is going to be okay." My words sounded as empty as they felt.

"Does this look okay?" she replied, her words biting.

"Well, no. But it will be. I promise," I said. Her eyes narrowing, I pointed at the cabinet behind me. "I am going to keep looking, okay? Rowan, a little help here?"

Rowan dipped his head and searched the shelves with me. Nipping the corner of Amy's shirt, gentle and soft, Matthew pulled her back down on the bench. A new determination sent us scavenging the shelves.

"We will stop the vampirism," Rowan said in my head.

"We freaking better." Squatting, I searched the bottom shelves, frustration rolling over me as I investigated each jar and bottle. Heart sinking, I wished for Ailianna's help. She would know exactly what to do. Ramming into the thought was adding another person to this fiasco—I should never have brought Amy here in the first place. About to teleport to Ailianna, desperate for any help, Rowan interrupted.

"Here we go." Rowan gathered several jars, holding some of them in the crook of his arm. "Grab that mortar and pestle." He pointed at the shelf next to me.

With ingredients scattered across the table, he began concocting a mixture, pouring and shaking everything into the mortar. I observed him with student-like intensity while giving cautious glances toward Amy.

Using the pestle, he smashed the ingredients together, combining everything into a thick paste. A pungent, acrid smell emanated from the bowl as he decimated the herbs, breaking free the oils. Then a strange hissing sound came from Amy as her lip curled, continuing to mutter her disdain.

"That smells awful. Get that away from me!" Her body recoiled away from us and the table.

"The poison of the vampire venom is going to fight this," Rowan said to me in a whisper. "It's not going to be easy."

"What are you going to do?" I asked as Amy sneered our direction.

"I think you should just let her change."

"Jax!"

"What?"

"We might have to hold her down," Rowan said.

"How do you propose we do that?"

The vehemence in Amy's eyes grew. She stood from the bench and took several steps back. Rowan, in unspoken words with Matthew, agreed upon something. Matthew jumped out at Amy, knocking her to the floor. He pinned her much like he had Ravenna, falling hard as Amy's head bounced on the hardwood floor.

Regret gathered in Matthew's eyes as he dug his paws into her chest, whining above her as Amy hissed. Sharp vampire teeth began to form as she struggled beneath his massive wolf form. Moving near the top of her head, I held her wrists to the ground as Rowan slathered the paste across her bite.

Amy writhed and twisted under our grasp. I grimaced as her fangs descended, snapping close to Rowan's skin. He shoved the paste in her mouth, trying his best to keep his fingers away from her sharp teeth as Amy thrashed with garbled sounds.

Pieces of the paste flew from her mouth in gooey, wet chunks. Emotions stung the edges of my eyes as I watched her suffer beneath the three of us. My throat tightened, and I made sure to keep my grip steady on her arms.

I should have never let her come here or go to Ravenna's. The thought intruded again. Amy's pupils dilated to the very rim of her irises as shock filled her face. Her chest began to convulse under Matthew's paws. The movement was slow at first, rolling into horrific, sporadic jerks next.

Instinctively, I knew what came next; letting go of her arms, I turned her head as she vomited. Deep, dry heaving thrusts racked her body as we rolled her to her side. Tracing my hand in small circles across her back, guilt tromped over me.

This is my fault.

Amy's shirt was cold with sweat underneath my touch as minutes went by. Then the convulsing stopped as quickly as it started.

"Oh my God! Amy! Is she dead?" My eyes wildly searched Rowan's, my fingertips searching for a pulse in her neck.

"Aislynn, she's okay." Rowan reached his hand out, trying to ease my panic.

"'Okay' is being generous. She is transitioning," Jax remarked.

"Transitioning?" I repeated, my voice rising to a scream. "I thought that was supposed to stop it!"

"I don't know if it will stop the transition. It was our best chance. We have to give her time," Rowan confessed.

Matthew nudged his dark nose against Amy's cheek, a soft whimper puffing out of his muzzle. I pushed strands of hair off her damp, clammy forehead.

Rowan reached down to scoop up Amy off the kitchen floor. He brought her into the other room, laying her gently on the couch and covering her with a light knit blanket. From my place on the floor, I watched his gentle touch and sharp concern. My head dropped, guilt stampeding my thoughts.

Fur pushed against my face, tickling my neck and ear. My mouth set in a deep frown, I rubbed the thick fur of Matthew's chest. He stayed for a moment like that, leaning against me as I rubbed him, both of us comforting one another in complete silence.

Back in the kitchen, Rowan put on the teapot. While waiting for the water to boil, he corked bottles and cleaned the mortar and pestle. Matthew let his tongue loll over the side of my cheek, then bounded out of the room.

Resting my chin on my arm, I glued my gaze to Amy, checking for movement. Silent and seemingly lifeless, the blanket faintly moved with her shallow breaths. Rowan made two cups without asking, knowing I wouldn't turn down tea. Pausing to set the mug on the table, he reached down to pull me up from the floor. Begrudgingly, I took his offer. He pulled me into a hug, murmuring something above my head.

"Hmm?"

"I am sorry for before, and this." He squeezed tighter. I nodded against him. There wasn't anything either of us could change, and fighting certainly wouldn't help. Releasing me, he stretched for the tea and handed me the mug.

Surprise rolled over me when I walked in the living room and saw Matthew in human form on the couch with Amy's head in his lap. His shaggy sable hair obscured his worry stricken hazel eyes. Kneeling in front of the fireplace, I stacked wood into the hearth, concentrating on the magic inside me. I drew my hands together, channeling fire across the layers of wood, igniting the room with a warm, orange glow.

The controlled, purposeful fire gave me satisfaction after seeing how fast it could morph into devastation. Picking up my tea, I curled myself into the chair as Matthew caressed Amy's face with a gentle touch. At that moment, I realized he was falling in love with her. *I wonder if he knows it yet.*

We sat for hours, waiting for Amy to return to consciousness. Rowan added more wood to the fire and our vigil continued through fitful naps. In Riona's absence, I wondered if we should have taken her to my sisters'. Perhaps they could have provided more help instead of sitting here, waiting. I regretted not instantly teleporting Amy and considered the weird tension between us, as well as the mess with the Council. Things had spiraled so out of my control, and I wanted to believe Ailianna would have helped.

Sometime late into the night, our fireside watch was interrupted.

"How is she?" Riona's soft voice sang from over my shoulder.

"Much the same. We gave her the antidote, but she is still unconscious." Matthew's voice was rough as gravel as he spoke. Riona nodded. She knelt beside the couch, turning the back of her hand against Amy's forehead.

"Where have you been?" I demanded. "We needed your help earlier when everything went to shit. Jax said you wouldn't come." I couldn't help myself, all the frustration of our situation seething out I my words.

"I could not come. I was engaged elsewhere, preparing for you to retrieve Water." Her answer dismissive, she turned her attention back to Amy. Before I could reply about the element, she continued. "Stopping the transition is not a simple task," Riona said inspecting the bite wound. "And we may still need Ravenna."

"Ravenna? Why?" I stuttered, lifting my head.

"Only she can truly stop the transformation." Riona glanced over her shoulder toward me. "Vampirism is a choice. A choice of vampire and human. Amy has a choice. Now, locked in her mind, she is deciding."

I peered at Amy and her shallow breathing. Behind those closed eyes, an internal battle took place. *Amy wouldn't choose to be a vampire, would she?* As a powerless human, she could transform into a seductive, compelling being with magical abilities. The only trade-off, of course, was the consumption of blood. Violence. Death.

No. Amy wouldn't choose that. My thoughts jumped to Ravenna, and I knew she would not help me or Amy. Not after what happened in the room. I understood her enough to know that. There had to be another way.

"So, what if she chooses not to be a vampire? If she chooses not to transform completely? Then what?" Desperation crept through my words.

"Then she will be a Halfling. Half vampire, half human. It would not be an easy decision, but there are some who live in this state." Riona's mouth was heavy with a frown. My stomach twisted with the mere thought of it and a newfound determination to save her overtook me.

"Time shall tell." Standing, she smoothed wrinkles from her cloak.

Rowan gave a short nod, but I wondered how he felt. Perhaps, if Riona had been here, Amy would have better chances. Dragging his knuckles across his chin, the worry seemed to consume his thoughts as it did mine.

"Wait, wait. Water?" I asked, hardly able to think about the next element, my mind consumed with Amy transitioning into a vampire. "I can't go after Water. Not until

Amy is okay." My demands were met with Riona's pursed lips.

The witch was out of her mind if she thought I would leave Amy; I *needed* her. Shifting uncomfortably in the chair, I reaffirmed my plan in my mind. Amy needed to be there as a crucial part. Maybe not *the plan* per se, but she was crucial to me being brave enough to reach through dimensions of freaking magic to retrieve the element. The distraction of Air, Aeolus, and vampires had officially ended.

"Well, then we must wait. You should all rest; you are going to need it," Riona said as her gaze landed on me in finality. In defiance, I pulled the quilt off the back of the chair and laid my head on the armrest.

"Aislynn, you should go to bed. Matthew will stay with Amy," Rowan tried.

"Yeah, I don't think so. I am not moving until she wakes up." I dug myself into the chair further, and he realized any attempts to make me move were pointless.

In the end, Riona was the only one to leave the room. A sentry of three waited.

❧

Sunlight cut through the room. Although my eyes were closed, the brightness pushed on me. Groaning, I tried to move, but the blankets were heavy with cat. Jax stretched his paw out, tapping my face.

"No move. More sleep."

Sleep had come in fits and spurts in odd positions on the chair. Eyes fluttering open, I glanced down at Jax as he twisted himself upside down, mouth opening in an exasperating yawn followed by a squeak. His paw batted me in the mouth. With furrowed brows, I reluctantly dug out my hand and scratched underneath his chin.

I turned from the mouthful of paw and saw Rowan face down on the couch, one arm behind him and the other hanging off the side. With his face smashed into the cushion at such an odd angle, I knew his neck would be sore.

Matthew appeared worse off, his head straight back, mouth gaping open, snoring. One of his hands was on top of Amy's head and the other rested carefully over her heart. I turned away from the affection between them and ran my hand down Jax. Small noises from the kitchen made me kiss Jax on the forehead and leave him in the blanket pile. Riona, the source of the sounds, and a bowl of sweet rolls on the center of the table beckoned me.

"There is a God," I muttered, tearing off a piece to shove in my mouth.

"There are many, but you know this." She smiled. "I believe Amy will wake today. More importantly, I have the spell to separate the dimensions of magic." She slid a paper across the table.

I rubbed my fingers together to lessen the stickiness before picking up the paper. Savoring my roll, I swallowed.

"I thought we had a spell."

"This one is better," she said. My eyes narrowed on the language I didn't know and glanced up at her in question. "You will need to learn the words."

Of course I will. My grip tightened on the paper as I held back my frustration. Not only would I have to separate layers of magic, but now learn another language. *Peachy.* She handed me a cup of steaming tea and I picked up another roll. Magic vibrated through the unknown words. The spell *was* better; I could feel it as I worked through the words.

"Tristan is ready. I have been working with him." She slid on the bench with tea in her hands.

"That is what you've been doing? Helping Tristan?"

With the mug at her face, she took a sip, an arched brow her only response. Rowan came into the kitchen, stretching his neck and groaning with the movement. He joined me on the bench, then grabbed a roll while glancing at the paper in front of me with a grunt.

A loud crash sounded from the living room, followed by grumbling. With wide eyes, Rowan and I scooted out the bench from under us, hurrying to the other room. Peering over the couch, we found Amy on the floor, rubbing her hip, mumbling in pain.

"Amy!" I rushed to her. "You're alive!" My eyes darted over her face, looking for anything vampirish.

"Of course I am." Her mouth turned in a grimace. "Are you afraid I am going to bite you? Because I am not." She pulled herself up from the floor, a long chunk of bangs swooping over one eye.

"Would you guys stop staring at me like I have three heads?" She shoved the hair behind her ear.

"We just want to be sure you are okay," Matthew said with tenderness as he reached out for her hand. Amy's eyes softened, and a small smile crossed her lips, I couldn't hold back any longer and I threw myself into her arms.

"Aislynn," Amy coughed out. "You're choking me." I relinquished my death grip.

"How are you feeling?" Riona asked from the edge of the room.

"I'm fine." Amy's voice held a slight snip. Riona's lips twisted before she nodded and turned back to the kitchen.

"Are those sweet rolls I smell?" Amy asked.

Wanting food must be a good sign.

Settling around the table, we devoured the remaining rolls as Riona slid a cup of tea toward Amy. I cherished the light citrus flavor of the rolls and wondered if I begged Amy enough upon our return, whether she would recreate the sweet bread.

Amy sipped her tea and garbled into an awful choking cough, spurting hot liquid across the table. Her body wrenched into a spasm of gurgling coughs. Trying to control her throat, Amy glared at Riona.

"What was in the tea?" I demanded.

"Nothing that can harm her," Riona replied.

"You put Bloodroot in it." Matthew's voice was accusing.

"If she had processed the vampire venom, she wouldn't have had a response." Riona tapped her fingers across the table.

"You tried to poison me?" Amy squeaked through more coughing.

"Hardly." Riona dismissed her comment. "It was a simple test to see if the venom was still in your system. It is, and now I will work accordingly."

"What the hell does that mean?" Amy spat, her throat finally relaxing.

"It means I am not taking any chances. I have a purpose: to help Aislynn fulfill her destiny. I will not let a transitioning vampire get in the way of that."

"Hey!" I protested. "That 'transitioning vampire' is my friend, and you will not give her anymore roots, or eyeballs, or anything else!"

Riona blinked repeatedly before exhaling. "As you wish."

Matthew covered Amy's hands in his own, mouthing "Are you okay?" Rowan and I exchanged glances. Scraping wood grunted beneath me as I pushed my corner of the bench out. I grabbed Riona's arm and pulled her outside. Once the back door closed behind her, I folded my arms across my chest. The cold air was just as biting as my attitude.

"What gives?" I asked.

"Exactly as I have said. She is a variable I was not accounting for." I could tell Riona was trying to be polite.

"She won't interfere with what we are doing."

"Aislynn, do not forget that your grandmother and I planned all of this carefully, trying to foresee every possible contingency. Amy was not one of them. We did not at any point see you bringing a human here who would turn into a Halfling, possibly a vampire. It impacts your destiny in ways you can't imagine or foresee."

I pulled my lips against my teeth. There was truth within her words, but I didn't want to believe Amy could harm me or affect my destiny in a negative way.

Riona's eyes grew soft. "Aislynn, it is the ones we love and trust that have the most calamitous impact on our lives. We rarely make good decisions when our emotions are involved."

Amy was visible through the window, smiling and talking with Matthew and Rowan. Would I allow danger to come to them? Would they impact my choices? Of course they would . . . every time.

But I refused to let my concern for my friends be a bad thing. Riona would just have to deal with it. It was too bad if Amy or anyone else didn't fit into her plans.

40

The spell raced through my mind again, still feeling foreign on my tongue, but I crammed the words in there with repetition. I tried to focus and visualize everyone's place, but the little cottage was overflowing with thoughts, worries, and incessant chatter. A building pressure swarmed around me, burning at the edges of my resolve. Unable to handle a second more, I slipped outside, drawing myself away from the chaotic noise.

I followed the trail along the tree line before weaving myself into the pines. An extreme calm washed over me with the massive trees looming above. Thick moss blanketed the bark and broken branches, giving each of my steps a soft, almost noiseless sound. Wandering deeper into the woods, ducking under fallen limbs, I eventually found an open clearing. I moved myself to the center, glancing up at the towering pines. The canopy above was so thick that the afternoon sun barely broke through the needles and branches.

The quiet centered me. I held out my hands, allowing

the tingle of magic to rush underneath me as I concentrated on the spell. Ancient words streamed through my thoughts. The pulsing of the elements was easy to feel, and a crackle of magic flowed from my hands, surrounding me in a circle of green fiery light. It drew through the air like a ribbon around the clearing. As I focused on each element, streaks of colors, shades of reds, blues, purples, and golden yellows twisted through the trees.

My emotions burned through the air and I used magic to soothe my heart and ease the tension in my core. I weaved the ribbons of magic around with eyes closed, focusing on the thrumming inside me. A sphere of pulsing light swirled like an Aurora Borealis, whipping trails of colorful magic.

"Pretty, but can you control it?"

Daragon leaned against a tree, arms crossed as he observed my magic. My concentration faltered in the slightest bit, causing my sphere to spit spurts of light. Gritting my teeth, I reigned the magic under control.

His eyes tracked every movement of my hands, and held a curiosity burning within them I hadn't seen before. I thrust my hands forward, pushing the magic toward him. It held him against the tree, and the colors of the elements coursed around him. His lips twitched in discomfort.

"Why are you here?" I inquired, holding the magic against him.

"Just waiting on you." His chin jutted out, and he stared a moment longer. Then he disappeared.

"Dammit," I swore at no one, letting the magic drop. Daragon had been watching all this time, waiting for me to retrieve Water, which meant he wouldn't be far behind.

A subtle whine came from behind me, and I turned at

the sound. Hazel wolf eyes pierced mine, and Matthew whimpered again. Kneeling in front of him, I rubbed behind his ears.

"Are you okay?"

"Yeah, I am fine. I just needed to be alone for a minute, ya know?" I continued my gentle massage.

"And Daragon?"

"Ugh. Who knows, with him? He can't separate the dimensions of magic, so he needs me to do it. I am sure he plans to take Water from me." Matthew pushed his face into my chest. "What are you doing out here?"

"Getting lunch. Sweet rolls don't really satiate my predatory needs."

"Ew." I grimaced. "Sometimes I really don't want to think about that."

He wanted to shrug, and I tried to not think about the bunny or other cute woodland creature who wouldn't be going home to his little family. My stomach twisted and we started walking back to the cottage.

"How's Amy?" I asked. Matthew sniffed the ground before turning to me.

"Okay, I think. It's difficult to tell right now, with the vampire venom."

"Is there anything I need to be aware of? Say, when I take her back to our Realm?"

"No blood, obviously."

I winced. "Right."

"The process takes three full days before the venom is 'cleared.' You either wait it out or feed, transitioning to full vampire. Which we would like to avoid."

"Yes, cutting Amy's head off isn't listed in the friend manual."

The wolf sneezed and huffed a laugh at me.

"I suppose it wouldn't be, and I kind of like her, so I would prefer you didn't."

I grinned slyly. "Kind of?" A sharp, playful bark sounded in response as he broke off into a full tucked butt run, careening through the woods. My laughter followed.

Upon returning to the cottage, I heard stern voices on the other side of the door. I paused with my hand on the knob, listening to the not-quite shouting match. As I pushed the door open, I was surprised to see Aila on one side of the kitchen, arguing with Riona.

"You can't let her do this!" Aila insisted. Riona huffed out an exhausted breath.

"Aila, what are you doing here?" I questioned, and they both jumped at my sudden appearance.

"It's too dangerous," Aila said without introduction or explanation, her green eyes pleaded with me.

"I know, but I don't have a choice," I replied honestly. After all, she had no idea what I'd been through since I last saw her; I was in this fight 100 percent, danger and all. "If I don't go after Water," I added, "Daragon will do something to force me, and that would be worse." I took a tentative step forward, the door creaking behind me.

"I just . . ." Aila's gaze drifted across the room, and I watched her look over all my new friends. "I don't want anyone to get hurt. You're putting everyone at risk." Her words ripped at my already shaky confidence.

"Aila, this is real magic, not what you have been exposed to all your life. You can't suppress it or hold it back to keep your unrealistic ideology of our Realm," Riona snapped at her.

Aila twitched as though she had been slapped. "And

what are you going to do when she rips a hole in her Realm and the element destroys the world she knows?" She crossed her arms in defiance. Keen cuts into my resolve made me chew the inside of my lip.

"She won't," Amy interjected. "She doesn't have it within her to fail or let anyone be intentionally hurt. If you knew her at all, you would know this." She took a few steps into the room, forcing herself and her opinion on Aila. Aila's eyes cut toward Amy, recoiling in shock.

"Oh my God! Yes, I was bitten by a damn vampire. Get over it!" Amy growled in Aila's direction.

"Aislynn," Aila's voice dropped. "You cannot be serious. An ostracized witch, a disloyal Council member, a shapeshifter, and a transitioning Halfling? Human, nonetheless?" Her words bit with acute asperity.

"You left out the time manipulator, but that is neither here nor there," Riona said.

Aila opened her mouth and closed it again. "Well, you should at least take me, then." She cocked a hip out, crossing her arms.

"Aila, it's too dangerous." I realized I was repeating what she'd just thrown at me minutes ago.

Aila instantly scoffed, rolling her eyes.

"I am serious. I have a plan, and not everyone is going. You need to stay. If anything, you need to protect your sister, and everyone else here. You know, in case I tear a hole in my Realm and all hell breaks loose." I offered a small smile, walking to her. "Please? Promise me you will stay?"

Her eyes flickered for a moment, mossy green in the shadowed light. Pursing her lips, she finally nodded. The clenching around my heart eased enough to breathe, trusting she would stay loyal to her words.

41

When I arrived lakeside at the cabin, unexpected heat blasted me in the face. Instantly, my mind reeled in confusion, and I looked around. Trees full of leaves and green cattails waving in the shallows clearly gave way to the season of late spring. Time had passed. *How is that possible?* And not just a little time; *months* had gone by. *Something is seriously wrong.*

My thoughts jumped to the conversation Rowan and I had about time and magic working together in balance. What happened when they weren't in balance?

Worry raged as I gripped the log railing, sun-warmed under my hand. The surface triggered memories as I raced up the worn steps to the cabin door. My mind's eye flashed backward in time, and I saw my grandma coming out the door yelling for me to come in for lunch as I played at the water's edge. The memory alive played out before me, like the damn Mirror of Memnosyne. *What the hell?* It was as if the element being sealed here, hidden in the dimensions of magic, was cracking the foundation of the Realms.

As soon as I shook off the memory, another blasted over me. Overlapping in quick succession, I saw all the summers I spent here as a child. I saw my grandmother and I walking up and down the shore looking for agates in the sand on a fast-paced loop. Those precious uninterrupted weeks with my grandmother were some of my favorite childhood moments. But having them play out in rapid motion created a wave of nausea.

Exhaling, I turned back to the heavy wood door of the cabin, trying to shake off whatever magic was gripping me. I focused on the Air element, whisking away the cycle of memories. *I need to hurry.*

With a small wave of my hand over the lock, it clicked open. *Who has time for keys?* The beautiful polished pine beams of the cabin's framing creaked and groaned with the wind. Each strong gust settled a deeper reverberation into the room, like a warning, whispering through its creaks. It was as if the air sensed the impending magic as it shifted around the property.

We didn't have much time to prepare, well-aware that Daragon would be close behind. There were some disagreements as I left Riona's cottage, but I stood my ground: this was my responsibility, my destiny. For now, I would begin this crucial step alone.

I can do this.

I tossed down my bag and gathered the crystal towers. The spacious open foyer in the entryway showcased the massive wooden joists, and it seemed fitting as I placed the crystals in the direction of the elements. Placing them with intention, the magic began to hum.

This place was aware of its destiny, created all those years ago when I was a child. My grandmother had been setting the stage for a grand moment. Now, standing in the northern top of the circle, the ancient words thrummed over my lips after countless hours of practice.

"*Aldeena, oona ta meritoona ah sona mayenta,*" I intoned, then followed in my native English: "I call forth my ancient magic as Keeper of Elements and reclaimer of Light. I call upon Earth, Air, Fire, and Water to make your presence known to reclaim Water to the Tree of Elements." The power shimmered, built, and a shift rippled through the air.

I winced, waiting for repercussions of some kind, but Riona's spell worked. The first step of the spell was to expose the dimensions. They shivered in my sight, wavering in layers around me. Hardwood floors appeared and disappeared, then bare trees contrasted full green willows as the world around me shifted. Worry and anxiety seized my heart, and I prayed Tristan would be able to maintain his freeze of time magic across the five dimensions. *There is so much to control.*

Pushing my worry aside, I focused on finishing the spell.

"I call upon the Aurora Towers to bring forth those to help me. Rowan, Amy, Tristan, come to me now through the power of Light." I thought of each of them, and my arms raised to contain the magic within the circle. They appeared in the center of the circle, and my heart sighed, settling just the slightest. We were one step closer.

"Are we safe?" Rowan asked, glancing around the cabin.

"We are good. He isn't here yet. But he's close . . . I can feel him." Daragon's magic was building in the distance, ripples of his dark energy cascading toward me. I knew that he didn't believe he would lose another element. I could feel his plan to steal Water as I opened the dimensions. I was just his key to a locked door and a mere annoyance.

"But we have another problem," I added.

Everyone's questioning eyes met mine as my flailing arm encompassed the wide window behind me.

"It's almost summer."

Amy's body rushed forward, face almost smashing into the glass as she took in the scene before her. "But I thought you said time didn't pass? When you came to get me, only days had passed in the middle of a snowstorm. This is months!" Her mouth gaped. "Aislynn. My job! My rent!" Her voice hitched higher.

It figured Amy would be concerned with her earthly responsibilities when we had far bigger problems on our hands, including her being a transitioning Halfling.

"What does this mean, Rowan?" I asked, nerves on edge. Rowan peered outside, frowning as his fingers settled on the window.

"Time is breaking down. Remember when I told you how time and magic work together?" He glanced over his shoulder at me, concern filling his eyes. "I imagine the magic holding Water is failing." Rowan confirmed my suspicions. "We need to hurry," he said. Fingerprints smeared the glass as he turned to me.

"Is this going to work?" Amy asked as she slung down her backpack, retrieving the books.

"I freaking hope so." Uneasiness penetrated my mind again. If months had passed in my Realm, would my plan to use Tristan still work? If time was breaking down, would he still be able to control it in our Realm? Was this too much for his abilities? What about the magic of the element? What if it was too explosive for me to handle? The time we had spent the last few months coming up with a plan may have all been a false sense of security.

The skies darkened as the clouds formed. Thick and furious, they pushed across the lake, sending shadows over the cabin floor. The air tingled. I could sense the elemental magic building to a breaking point. Through the window, white caps built as the wind cut sharp across the water. Although thunderstorms were common in the summer, the rapid shift let me know this was magically aggravated.

Amy's concern rippled over me and I began to worry about the feat before me. I also couldn't help worrying about my job at home, and my family. Everyone would be worried. Did they think I was dead? Were they looking for me? Tightness expanded across my chest as the mixture of real-life worries fused with the task of retrieving the element, compounding into a solid mass of anxiety.

"You can do this, Aislynn. It is within you." Tristan's soft voice came from behind me as he rested his hand on my shoulder. Soothing tingles brushed my anxiety. "As can I." An unsure smile crossed my mouth. It didn't matter if I thought I could or not, I *had* to do this. The time concern would have to wait. All the preparation, the practice had come to this moment.

We rushed down the steps to arrange the circle on the patch of grass adjacent to the shoreline. Riona's spell to separate the dimensions of magic screamed in my mind, along with her warning: control the magic, or the Elements would be lost forever and Water would be released upon the Realms. But I shoved those words aside.

The willows surrounding the property, danced in violence, whips reaching out to me as I placed the crystals once again on the ground. Distracted by the lake and the impending, waiting magic, Rowan's hair blew wildly. I knew that he never liked my plan, and his silhouette told me he still didn't. Amy and Tristan focused on creating the circle as the wind cycled through trees in fierce gusts. Droplets of water, cold and hard, hit my skin as I walked into the center of the circle.

"Aislynn, are you sure about this?" Amy half yelled, doubt scattering in her words. I nodded as Tristan came to stand across from me.

"Are you ready to make history?" I asked with an arched brow. Clasping my hands, he nodded. Behind him, Rowan and Amy stood together, Amy shielding her eyes from the stinging wind. Tristan's hands were warm in mine as rain pelted harder, and Riona's words careened through my head. *Invoke. Separate. Call forth.*

"*Incanta ashana lorotto,*" I called out. "I invoke the powers of Ancient Elemental magic. From the beginnings of time and creation of Light, I call forth the powers that be." White light whipped around us in a perfect circle, encompassing me and Tristan. "For the power of Light, I call forth the magic created here."

The earth trembled below our feet and white light shimmered brightly as the wind whipped, creating a blur of magic. A crack sounded through the air and the ground dropped out beneath our feet. Everything shifted. Amy and Rowan disappeared as Tristan and I were blasted apart.

"Tristan!" Dirt flew as he tumbled. Forcing myself to my feet, the waves lashed the rocky shore, and lightning blazed across the sky in shards of light. The landscape shifted to something completely different: before us now were barren trees and dark earth that stripped the land of life.

"This wasn't supposed to happen! We were supposed to bring the dimension to us, not us to the dimension!" I shouted to Tristan, but the air rumbled too loud to hear myself. Separated from Amy and Rowan, we were most definitely screwed. I needed them to monitor my control.

"It's okay, Aislynn!" Tristan cried over the noise of the wind. "Keep going! Hurry, before Daragon gets here."

Opening my mouth to respond, a mass of magic slammed into my shoulder, sending me backward. *Daragon.*

"You have zero idea what you are doing, Aislynn. You are playing with magic you do not understand!" Daragon's voice carried through the storm's noise. Another ball of fiery energy sat in his hand, and I pulled myself off the ground, again. The red swirl of light flew toward me, but my hands instantly deflected the magic with ease.

"Air was handed to you!" he snapped. "This won't be so easy!"

"You need to start the spell!" Tristan called. Swirling his hands, he flashed them to an abrupt stop, pausing time around us. Abrupt silence fell as the storm itself held still in Tristan's magic. "It won't hold him for long."

For the shortest second, I stood in wonder. Tristan was holding the dimensions of magic in perfect stillness. *He did it.*

Daragon was already trying to push through Tristan's magic, in jerky, slow movements beneath the magical freeze. I turned my attention back to the spell.

"*Incanto inroro divinus invocito!*" My words carried across the stillness, the roaring still pounding in my head. The separation of dimensions began gliding together again. There was a shift as the two worlds combined and separated like fragmented images sliding against each other. Both worlds slipped in and out of my vision. In one, Tristan held the magic in utter silence, and in the other Rowan and Amy howled while the storm raged. I kept going, holding the spell before it fell completely out of my control.

"The ancient elemental powers that be, I call upon Water, its deafening roar, the power it holds within." The lake roared behind me, waves spilling and rolling over the shoreline as thick droplets cascaded from the sky. Each molecule of water held an unforeseen force rippling through my core. Understanding washed over me, along with a snap of clarity.

Water, the source of life.

A brilliant azure orb burst from the depths of the lake, rising above the surface, hanging in the air. Glimmering in between the dimensions, Water moved toward me. The elements' power within the universe called to me. As it unraveled its unknowing, it compelled me forward. Consuming like a hurricane, it demanded my command.

Daragon finally freed himself from Tristan's grasp as the dimensions slid against one another. From the corner of my eye in the shimmers of magic, Aila appeared. Seeing her there so suddenly almost made me lose my concentration. I renewed my grip on the dimensions, and the beautiful azure orb begging my attention.

"Aislynn! You can't control it!" Her voice slid through to me.

What is she doing here? She had promised to stay. I should have known. Eyes pinching closed, I tried to focus, but my mind was splitting in too many directions. Aila, meanwhile, pulled back her bow string.

Shit.

She aimed the arrow on Daragon, now freed from the

time magic. I tracked the arrow to Daragon and watched the magic he created in response. A mass of thick black swirled in front of him, then everything slowed. The arrow streamed toward him. Magic building, he threw a hand at the arrow, reversing Aila's spelled shot.

Tristan's magic reached across the dimensions, trying to stop the calamity as Aila's attack flew back toward her. Daragon's black streamed to me, and Tristan's blue careened through both of them.

Riona's spell apexed in a stunning crescendo and the silver blue of the Water element rushed through me. The ancient magic thrummed into the amulet. The wild chaos of the element swam in my eyes.

Pandemonium.

I couldn't protect everyone as everything happened at once. The dimensions slammed into one. Aila's magic smashed back into her with pieces of Daragon's spell blasting her to the ground in a ghastly sound. Daragon's mass of dark magic was inches from hitting me when Tristan's light shot through the sky, halting everything.

"Daragon!" My anger sliced through the air. I had no idea if Aila was okay. Amy and Rowan were petrified in midmotion, running toward her. Daragon's magic hung in violent tendrils, reaching out for their target: me.

"Tricky to bring a time manipulator, but I'm afraid it won't work." His chin jutted out.

The magic of Water thrummed, coursing through my veins, driving my thoughts. He didn't understand. Not in the slightest. Though he had known the general whereabouts of the element, he had never possessed its magic, never felt a glimpse of what now rushed over me, sliding into my soul like a glass of cool fresh water.

Daragon was small, insignificant. Heat filled my face as I pitied his existence. The dimensions separated again, and more clarity ripped through me, like when Neo became amused once he understood the simplicity of the Matrix.

Oh, God. Did I just create a parallel between that movie and my life? I will need so much therapy after this. Head ticking to the side, pure awareness of my thoughts sauntered in with clear, crisp precision.

So much time.

My hand shot out, feeling foreign as it cupped the empty air. Even though Daragon was more than ten feet in front of me, my magic instantly created a vice grip around his throat as if he was next to me. Swirling water around his neck, I constricted it tighter against him. His hands flailed at his throat, trying to reach through the element holding him, his toes pawing for the ground they couldn't touch.

His dark eyes widened, darted around with panic, then met mine. Desperation washed over his face as he gasped for air. Captivated, I watched as his skin rolled through shades of reds then into deep purples as he struggled for oxygen.

I marveled at the difference of this element compared to Air. Water was wild, and an unleashing of compressed energy waited impatiently. It coursed through me, begging to be used, to facilitate, to create. To destroy.

I didn't need Tristan's magic to hold anything now, and I twisted my other hand to free everyone from their places. Tristan collapsed to the ground in exhaustion, head hanging between his legs. Rowan and Amy continued their sprint to Aila's rescue. I could feel Rowan shift his attention to me as he stopped midstride to stare at me. The rush of noise returned, although I paid no attention. For me, everything was quiet, slow, and still.

Somewhere, I was aware that Rowan shouted my name. My head turned slowly toward him, and he flinched backward, face full of alarm.

"Aislynn!" he yelled.

Why is he yelling?

"You need to control the magic! You are letting it control you!" His words slid across me with little significance. I turned back to Daragon and let the magic squeeze harder. Calmly, I watched his eyes bulge as he gasped uncontrollably. A smirk crept over my lips.

"AISLYNN!" From the corner of my eye, Rowan moved to me. Head turning again, I used my other hand to stream water straight up, creating a wall between us. His fists pounded against the water, and he continued to holler my name, but now the sound was muffled.

That's nice. Oh . . . what to do with my friend?

Regrettably, Daragon was beginning to run out of air. *Sad.* And it was somewhat disappointing. Tristan's screaming, too, added to the chorus of Rowan's muffled protests. Picking apart his words, I became aware that Tristan was calling to Rowan, something about the magic taking over, I couldn't control it, blah, blah, blah.

I was fine, obviously. *Eye roll.* Didn't they see I had perfect control? The smugness Daragon held in my dreams so long ago rolled over me, becoming an emotion all my own now. It was my turn to have the upper hand. Ultimate control. I caught movement at the edges of my vision. Amy scrambled to the backpack, yelling at Tristan, and there was more shouting. It became mind-numbing background noise.

Annoying. Tick tock. For me, everything was a slow wave of movement, every thought rolling into endless minutes. Time cascaded in front of me as an infinite source. *This must be how Tristan feels.*

Aila hadn't moved since her deadly thunk against the hard earth. I presumed she was dead. My attention went back to my friend. That meant he deserved to die. Besides making my life miserable for months, now he had probably killed my magical sister. Yeah, Daragon absolutely needed to die. All I needed to do was squeeze the little bit of life remaining in him. There wasn't much left. It was so incredibly simple to just *squeeze.*

Rowan circled around my encased wall of water, moving behind Daragon. I assumed he wanted to see my face, since I had stopped looking at him long ago.

"Water has possessed you!" he shouted, pounding against the suspended liquid, throwing his body against it, trying to find a way through my magic. Tristan tried freezing me and failed as well. Their pathetic attempts were somewhat entertaining.

There was less air now.

Tick tock. Tick tock.

Rowan came barreling through the water, charging at me. Somehow, he'd transported himself into my bubble. Momentum carried him into me and slammed us both to the ground.

"Aislynn!" Holding my head in his hands, he searched my eyes. What was he looking for? Although I was on the ground, the elemental magic still held Daragon dangling in a tourniquet of water. "You have to control it! Control the water!"

Aren't I? Everything moved in slow motion. An edge

of the magic ran through me, my awareness moved, and suddenly fear trickled over my skin. He was right: I was not in control. Magic—more precisely, *Water*—held control. Deep in my thoughts, Riona's warnings rattled me along with images of the White Witch burning villages.

Ah, shit.

"Come on. You have to hold it, contain it, push it down." Rowan rested his body on top of me. A push from the element told me to flip him off, like a gnat. *No.* I needed to push back. The magic prodded again. *Daragon. He killed your sister. Use me. Use me to make things right again.* An internal battle waged inside me, two ferocious forces pushing against one another, searching for the other's weakness.

"Aislynn!" Rowan shook my shoulders. A slow un-winding began as the magic unfurled itself from a deep coil twisted in my soul. I became aware of Daragon and the magic holding him, then released it in disgust. Daragon plummeted to the ground in a heap, struggling to breathe, no longer a threat to any of us.

Rowan pulled me into his arms, holding me in tense desperation. "Aislynn." Utter relief washed through his voice as he held my head against his chest. Breath heaved from both our bodies, his reprieve and mine exhaustion. "I thought I lost you."

"What the freaking hell?" Amy stomped toward us. "Dude, not cool!" Her finger shook in frustration. "Do you know what that was like? Seriously? Do you have any idea?" Her arms flailed as her voice pitched higher with each question. I couldn't stop the smile from creeping onto my mouth.

Rowan's eyes darted back and forth over mine, exam-ining me. My eyebrow arched in question.

"Oh, uh-uh, missy. Not cool. Do you have any idea what your eyes looked like?" She stood above us, a heap of limbs on the ground.

"My eyes?" I rolled my lips inward, glancing up from Rowan's arms. Awareness of the events and my lack of control darted around my conscience.

"Yes! Your eyes!"

"They looked as if the entire ocean dwelled within them and you were lost," Rowan whispered. His blue eyes searched mine, still holding traces of fear. He ran his thumb across my cheek.

Amy's mouth opened to speak again, but then she averted her gaze, walking over to Tristan instead.

Rowan tucked back the stray chunk of hair that fell across my forehead. "I thought the magic was going to consume you."

A thrumming rose within me, pounding through my body, and I swallowed with force. His forehead dropped, meeting mine, and the amulet swung between us. Catching it on the swing, I cupped it in my hand. A blue pulse emanated from inside, and a small smile passed Rowan's lips.

"You succeeded." My smile matched his. His lips pressed against my forehead with the lightest touch. The kiss brought shivers through my already thrumming body. "But please, can we not follow your plans anymore?" He stood, holding out his hands to help me to my feet. A flood of joy pressed into my heart, and I wanted to kiss him, trickles of magic still pulsing.

"What? My plans are genius." But then my smile faded as I remembered: "Aila!" The magic had been so powerful, so in control, I almost forgot.

Rowan's face told me everything, but I refused to

believe it. "Nooo! No. No. *No!*" The word ran together, becoming a stream of one heartbroken sound. My elation shattered driving me forward in horror. He held my body back as I tried to get to her, to escape his grasp. I had to . . . no. This couldn't be. No. Magic. No. Magic had taken her. Magic could bring her back. No. No no no.

"Aislynn." Rowan's voice was gentle, my head shaking in his hands. "Shh . . . she's gone. She's gone." He pulled me close, holding me against him. The dam imploded and my body heaved against his. *I let this happen.* I did this. Aila, my sister of magic . . . I killed her.

Her death ripped through me, leaving tattered, sharp edges. My body sunk to the earth, and Rowan's hold followed me down. *This is my fault.* Guilt and grief flooded, consuming my being. They were right, after all. *I couldn't control the magic.*

"No, Aislynn. This isn't your fault." Rowan lifted my chin toward him. The guilt was so overpowering I didn't care that he hopped on my thought train. "This is not your fault. Aila chose to come here. She chose to interfere. You are capable of handling the magic; it's your destiny. You were born to hold the elements, to control them. Aila couldn't believe you were capable of your destiny; and this was hers."

My eyes filled, blinking heavily and tossing the tears down my cheeks. "But . . ." Searching his eyes, I tried to find my guilt, my pain, and the loss, but I could see Rowan chose to hold it all for me.

It was unfair; it was mine to have and to feel. But I also realized I didn't have the energy to begin to process the loss. I cried against him, sobs heaving my body as he held on tight. He held, he shushed, he cooed, and he let me cry.

42

Awareness forced itself on me, but I was unsure how much time had passed. It seemed like days, but in reality, it was probably only hours. Huddled in Rowan's arms, cycling between crying and disjointed sleep. My vision was full of water, magic, and death. My body was heavy with exhaustion from the emotional pain and the tremendous magic I accomplished.

"Here, Rowan," Amy said in whispered tones. The aroma of tea slashed my nose. "Aislynn, too, if you think she will take it." Rowan shifted to take the mugs. A hand caressed my hair, trying to wake me.

Sluggish movement brought me upright, and I ran my hands over my face, dragging my fingertips under my eyes. I was positive smears of black mascara were brushed on my skin like a pitiful version of a deranged trash panda. My gaze drifted around, and I realized we were in my apartment. I pulled my feet under me, perching on a couch with my arms wrapped tightly around my knees. Rowan offered me the tea, and with a noncommittal shrug, I held out my hand.

The mug, heavy in my grip, mirrored my thoughts. *I let Aila die.* And as if that wasn't enough, I almost choked my mortal enemy to death. I blocked my friends from helping and I allowed magic to take control. People died. *Again.* The thoughts barreled in before I could stop them, and the heaviness wrapped itself in incomprehensible darkness.

My body tipped toward Rowan, letting my shoulder rest against him. His magic tried to penetrate my ball of shitty feelings, trying to find a way to project light within the dark. But my form on the couch was a direct representation of my energy; everything was wrapped rigidly as I internalized my guilt in the form of self-punishment.

This is my fault.

The tea tasted bitter in my mouth and I swallowed with force. Somewhere, I recognized it wasn't the tea, but my throat was thick with emotion. There had been a lot of crying. *Ugly crying.* I cringed at the thought. I shifted my thoughts. Where was Daragon? Were we safe here in my apartment? All my things stared back at me, my belongings which identified me up until a few months ago. Did any of it serve a purpose now? Did any of it have meaning?

"You really need to stop with this self-defeating crap."

Jax stared at me from the coffee table. *"This serves no one, including yourself. Exhaustion, yes. Sadness, yes. But 'Oh, poor Aislynn'? No."*

I glared at my cat. He seriously was an asshole. My gaze deviated, staring into a void of nothing.

"Jax, perhaps we should be gentler." Rowan moved forward, resting his elbows on his knees, mug in his hands.

"No, perhaps we shouldn't."

"You know, Rowan, as much as I hate to admit this,

the asshat cat is right." Amy sat on the edge of the coffee table.

"Has Hell frozen over?"

"Shut it, fur-face. We know Aislynn. She is a pro at falling into a self-deprecating pit of ugly, and if we don't pull her out now, she will take up permanent residence."

Fully aware of their conversation, I contemplated being angry, but I just didn't care. Amy had pulled me from several depressions over the years. I continued my glare of nothing, ignoring them and snuggling into my pit of dark reflections.

"Aislynn . . ." Rowan's voice was tender, and I knew he didn't approve of their harsh approach. The gentle protectiveness was a mistake, of course.

"People die all the time."

My head took a sharp turn, meeting my cat's sapphire eyes with gritting teeth. "It was *my* fault, Jax." I shoved my head back into my knees, choosing to embrace the darkness I created with my body.

"This was her destiny." He said the words as if they should make me feel better.

They didn't.

"Aislynn." Amy reached out and touched my knee. "He's . . . somewhat right. This isn't your fault."

"You think that, but it is," I murmured from beneath my knees.

"How in the world is this your fault?" Rowan asked.

"I couldn't control it."

"Uh, you held back five dimensions of magic, something that hasn't been done in centuries, managed to secure the element, left Daragon completely useless, and—" Amy stopped her words.

"And didn't kill anyone?" My words bit as I finished for her. "I think Aila would disagree."

"Amy, Jax, would you excuse us for a minute?" Rowan asked. I heard Jax squeak as Amy must have picked him up, not sure where they were going to go, but they tucked themselves out of my sight.

"Aislynn . . ."

I stopped him before he started: "You don't understand, Rowan. You are all in danger; I realize this now more than ever. I don't know what I was thinking, believing I could do this!" My arms flailed out, and I held up the amulet to make my point.

"What do you mean?" Frustration edged into his eyebrows. "You have accomplished so much. You already reclaimed two elements."

"But I can't control them!" I snapped.

"We warned you. Hole of ugly."

"Shut up, Jax!" we both shouted.

"At least she is angry now." His comment seemed to be directed toward Amy.

"You have controlled the magic."

"You don't know," I insisted and curled my arms back around my legs.

Rowan glanced over my head to Amy standing in the kitchen, searching for answers. I watched her raise her eyebrows with her hands in the air.

My gaze shifted into nothingness again. Rowan waited for me to say anything. The silence was deafening. Minutes passed, and I knew he wouldn't give in until I shared what was haunting my mind.

"It happened a long time ago." Grumbling, I held tighter. He patiently waited for more.

Huffing out my breath, I focused on the secret I had held this entire time. I was fearful of their reaction, their thoughts, and their opinions of me, but I realized they wouldn't let this go. *Insufferable friends.*

"When I was little, maybe seven? It was summer, and we were having a party, something my mother planned. I think the big event was when my dad made partner at the firm," I said, slipping back to the old memory.

"I didn't want to be there, because I had a friend's birthday on the same day, but Mom wouldn't let me go. Something about previous obligations, she said. This was in our old house, a catered event by the pool, and there were people everywhere. And I was mad. I didn't understand why I needed to be at an adult party. My mom kept getting frustrated with me, mostly because I was being a spoiled brat, but I didn't want to be there, and my attitude reflected that.

"Being an embarrassment to her is not tolerated, and at one point, she pulled me into the bathroom off the patio. Yelling at me, she told me I better shape up and change my attitude or I would regret it. She was angry, and looking back, I don't blame her. I was a bratty kid who wanted her way, I get it. I mean, not then, but I do now. I got mad, I stormed out of the bathroom, and tore across the yard up into my tree house. I was *so* mad." I gathered my breath to finish the story.

Amy slowly made her way back into the room, sitting on the barstool. Her frustration with my mother, who wasn't her favorite person in the first place, sat in her jaw, the muscles grinding back and forth. Rowan nudged me to continue. Rubbing my hands over my face and hair, I exhaled forcefully.

"So, in my tree house stewing, like little kids do, I kept thinking, 'If only her party ended, I could go to the other party that mattered to me.' The thought just rolled through my head, and from the window, the partly cloudy sky stared back at me. I remember thinking, 'If it rained, then everyone would have to go home. If only it would rain.'" Taking a moment, I rested my head on my knees.

"A storm filled my mind, blowing all the people away. Then my mom wouldn't be mad at me anymore. It was stupid, I realize that now. But the skies darkened, the clouds built, rolling into ominous thunderheads. I just wanted the people to go away." My voice was sullen and distant with memory.

"I remember my mom yelling as the wind kicked up to cover the food and bring things inside. She tried to keep the party going. I could hear her calm voice, even her laughter, and she said, 'You never know what the weather will do!' I sat on the platform, begging for the rain. Big, fat raindrops started falling, and everyone ran indoors. The wind really kicked up, tables blew over, and things flew into the pool.

"It was absolute chaos, and my mom forgot about me. Branches started breaking in the trees, and I remembered screaming out. The sky took on the eerie, murky green color it gets right before a tornado, and I curled into a ball. The tree house wasn't high up, but the branches were scraping the roof and the wind blew the rain through the windows.

"Then the awful screeching of the tornado sirens sounded across the cities, and a part of me understood I was responsible. I had started this, and now it was out of control. I was seven, and I'm not sure how I knew, but I did. Somewhere deep inside of me where the magic lives, hidden unbeknownst to me, I knew.

"About then, my dad began searching for me. I could hear him calling, but I was too afraid to move. The sirens were deafening, and I was petrified. My wish had come true; the storm came, and I couldn't stop it. Eventually, my dad came tearing across the lawn, screaming my name with his hands covering his head as debris whipped across the yard.

"When he found me, he scooped me up, gripping me to his chest, and ran back to the house. We waited in the basement for the storm to pass, with all the people from the party. I couldn't stop crying. I remember telling my dad it was my fault, and he assured me I was wrong. Of course, he had no idea."

As if the entire incident wasn't bad enough, I needed to finish. Both Amy and Rowan wanted to speak, much like my dad had done all those years ago, to assure me I hadn't been responsible. But they didn't understand. Not yet, anyway.

"After the storm passed and everyone went home, we spent the night cleaning up and, of course, watching the news. A tornado had touched down not far from us, about ten miles west in a little town called Victoria. Two people died." I let the words hang.

Their reactions smothered me, and I felt myself flinching back. They were sorry for the little girl I had been and the responsibility weighing on me now. But I didn't want their sorrow or pity; I only wanted them to understand why I couldn't allow them to be part of this anymore. More people would get hurt.

"Aislynn," Rowan began, his tone soft and deep with understanding. He reached out, wrapping his arm around my shoulders, pulling me into him. My body allowed itself to sink into him, and his cheek rested across my head.

"I am so sorry this happened to you. What a terrifying experience as a child." He held me as tears tumbled out of my eyes. Soon, I would need to control myself, but I was too exhausted to stop the emotion.

"I understand why you feel the way you do," he continued, his hand soothing as it ran down my arm. I allowed myself, for a moment, to absorb his unrelenting comfort and sympathy. A part of me, deeply hidden, yearned for someone to understand.

"But, Aislynn, it's just not true." He paused. "No, I take that back. I will honor your feelings. However, they are misconstrued; you are responding from old emotions, childhood, and fearful memories. They have no place here. You are intelligent and, more importantly, profoundly magical. You know you are capable of this, otherwise you wouldn't be here." He turned me to face him, piercing me with his intense blue eyes. His words echoed with a veracity that took hold of my heart.

"What happened all those years ago is an awful, terrible thing. The responsibility you must have felt at that age and carried since is incomprehensible. But you need to believe there is purpose in all things, including that event, and the ones since, and what happened today. We will all mourn the loss of Aila. I promise we will do whatever is necessary for you to move through this, but now is not the time to turn your back on your destiny, nor to push us away. This is the time to be strong and persevere. I won't give up on you, so please don't give up on me."

I stared, dumbfounded and speechless. Emotions flooded me, and my eyes filled again.

"Amy, you should start a slow clap. I would, but with my paws, well . . . it wouldn't be as inspiring."

Laughter sputtered from Amy's lips in a combination of weird sounds. "You are such an asshole."

Unable to stop them, my own half smile and gurgle of laughter followed. Rowan gave a smile, gently running his thumb across my bottom lip. Amy must have seen the look in Rowan's eyes as she reached down to scoop up Jax, who protested loudly with a mewl and they left the room.

Rowan's focus was on me. And my mouth.

"Aislynn, you were born for this." My eyes never left his. He held an absolute faith in me, a force that was infallible in spite of all we'd faced. The bleak part of me was growing smaller by the moment, but it tried to claw its way back.

"Push it away," Rowan said, his voice soft. "Be here."

My mouth inched closer to his. Hope, fleeting, yet growing by the second, pulsed in my belly. His magic and mine twirled together, and our lips touched. *Oh. Oh, this.* His tongue was against mine, his hand holding my cheek. Why didn't I realize this existed?

He pulled back, resting his forehead on mine. "I . . ."

My finger on his lips stopped his words. He pulled me into his lap, and I allowed my body to fill the space, laying my head on his chest. Beneath my ear, his heartbeat settled my own. Deep, restful sleep finally found me.

43

My throbbing bladder woke me, the dark room giving away the ungodly hour. As my eyes adjusted, I found Amy burrowed in my bed, covered in a heap of blankets. Rowan was beneath me, a pile of limbs embedded in the couch. Carefully, I peeled myself off him, trying not to disturb his sleep.

Stepping as quietly as possible, I eased the squeaky bathroom door closed before flipping on the light, instantly repulsed by the bright white. Squinting against the harshness, I caught a glance of myself in the mirror. I edged forward for closer inspection of the disaster before me.

Dark hair stuck to my forehead from sweat, tears, and God knew what else, and in the back, it stood on end, praying for help. As expected, mascara swept across my face in smears of dark at odd angles. In contrast, my eyes were swollen and red.

I assessed and concluded that I was akin to a dumpster fire. A freaking hot mess. Then I remembered Rowan kissed me, and mostly got sad *for* him. Even though it was almost four in the morning, I was awake after sleeping most of yesterday. A shower became my only necessity.

Halfway through conditioning my hair, I heard a certain set of paws push against the door. Worried about the light spilling into the hallway, I peered around the edge of the shower curtain and gave the cat a dirty look. Jax sat on the toilet, slowly blinking at me.

"Uh, hello? Naked here!" I whispered, annoyed.

"And? You never minded before."

"That was before I knew you could talk, and were, like . . ." I slid back behind the curtain.

He yawned. *"You do realize it's barely four in the morning."*

"Um, yeah, but I feel gross. And *awake.*"

"Does this mean I can have my space food early?"

I smiled beneath the stream of water. "Maybe."

"So."

I waited for the rest. Nothing.

"Yes?"

"You and Rowan."

This time, it was my turn to be quiet. Turning off the water, I reached my hand out, pulling the towel off the rack, drying myself off behind the curtain. Perverse cat. With the towel wrapped around me, I stepped out, giving the cat raised eyebrows.

"Yeah, I guess so."

"Personally, I think that took entirely too long. However, I approve."

Mouth gaping, I had no words. Grabbing my robe off the back of the door, I stared at the cat. He blinked. *Fine.* Rolling my eyes, I turned my back and slipped into the robe. In the mirror again, I blew out my breath with trepidation.

Here goes nothing. I began my limited makeup routine, figuring Rowan deserved a little effort after last night.

"I am so glad you approve." I gave him a half glance as I flipped the mascara wand over my lashes.

"You should be."

Avoiding his speculative glare, I changed gears. "Hey, I have a concern, now that I am a functioning human again. We have a problem."

Cat ears twitched, and he waited.

"This time issue. It has been months, Jax. My parents? My job?" I left the questions hanging.

Before answering, he curled his front legs underneath him into a black loaf of cat. *"Yes, that is a concern."*

"A concern? It will be a concern when I don't have a job or money to buy you space food." I smeared gloss across my lips.

"Magic is . . . transitioning."

"Transitioning? What the hell does that mean?" I shoved the gloss back in the bag.

"You'll see. What about Rowan?"

I groaned, and with a quick zip of my makeup bag, I threw it in the drawer. "I really don't think that will *be* anything. I mean, it might just have been a moment of heightened emotions." Jax stared, not buying my crap. "I am serious."

I leaned against the counter, folding my arms. "I am!"

He gave me another slow blink.

"I'm going to get coffee for everyone. My creamer is so old it has its own GPS location in Google Maps."

"The holy place does not open until five."

As I crept out the door as quietly as possible, I wondered if I should be concerned that my cat knew the hours to Starbucks.

The handle clicked closed and I noticed the note taped to the door. *Shit.* My mailbox downstairs was full. *I need to empty that.* Then I realized it was a good thing that my bills were all auto-withdrawal; otherwise, there might have been an eviction notice as well. Traveling the Realms and time made adulting even harder.

I locked my apartment door behind me and wondered why I bothered. Daragon wouldn't need a key. My fears had completely transformed after my time in a magical Realm.

Oh, the days of concerning myself with theft or safety. Perhaps they hadn't changed; they'd only shifted to bigger, scarier monsters.

After taking the elevator down, I pushed open the doors to my building, the crisp cool air of a spring morning hitting me in the face. The sky was beginning to shift at the edges of the horizon from dark blue to dusky orange. It eased my mind, like a twisted form of purging.

I revisited my moment with Rowan on the couch. Aside from my ugly heavy emotional grossness, the kiss had been . . . magic. And the fact he accepted me and all my failures melted the tension in my heart. He didn't need me to be anything other than me. This arrived as a new clarity I never received in past relationships.

Rowan made me feel safe. *Loved.* The sun broke over the horizon, cascading a brightness across the city, illuminating the glass on the buildings. Everything would be okay. For the first time, in a long time, I believed it. I darted across the street and made my way to the skyway level.

The early hour made the skyway quiet, but people were

still heading into work. Men, women, old, and young, all walked with a silent determination of their path in this world. Their biggest worry might be a project due today, their child's baseball game after school, or their dying mother in the hospital down the street.

Then there was me. Powerful, elemental bad ass, the amulet swinging at my chest holding half the cosmic magical power gifted to our world . . . and no one knew. No one had a freaking clue.

I wondered what would happen if they did know.

"They couldn't handle it, not really."

Startled, I turned to find the source of the voice. The White Witch.

"Um, hello?" My mind was in hyperdrive as I glanced around.

"No. I shouldn't be here," she said, answering the question I'd yet to formulate. "I am because it is deemed so." Her voice was clear and loud.

A girl walking nearby peered from the corner of her eye, giving us a strange look. The White Witch's appearance *was* odd in my Realm, let alone in downtown Minneapolis. She wore her white velvet cloak draped across her shoulders, held tight by a broach of red fire stones. The silver dress beneath hung to her feet, which were bare. At least she didn't have the hood of the cloak over her head, but people were still staring, mostly because the witch was stunning.

"Special privileges, you might say," she answered again before I asked. Her face was inquisitive as she admired her surroundings.

"First time?"

"To this Realm? Yes. It is very strange." Her eyebrows furrowed together, making me want to laugh. I could relate. A man scrolling on his phone nearly ran into the witch.

"Excuse me," he snipped, giving only a half glance up until he caught her eyes. He stumbled to a stop, dumbfounded before her, mouth slightly agape. "I . . ."

Rolling my eyes, I tugged on her arm, pulling her past him. As I peered back, he watched us with the same stupid expression on his face, and I shook my head in annoyance.

"What an odd man."

"You have no idea. Come on, Starbucks is just up here."

"Star . . . bucks?"

Rapidly blinking at her, I had to savor my greatest moment so far: the all-knowing White Witch was stumped over Starbucks. I evil-eyed the one person in line ahead of us while the witch stood in awe, gawking at the black board hanging from the ceiling and the complicated espresso machines.

"What in the heavens . . . ?" she began.

"Oh wait, it *is* heaven," I said with a smile. She gave me an odd look. Then Margo, my cheerful barista friend, saw me and her eyes widened.

"Aislynn! Where on earth have you been?" Her hands slapped down on the countertop.

"She has been in another Realm, of course," the witch replied before I could. Margo, taken aback by the witch's appearance, investigated with curious eyes.

"I thought you died. It's been months."

My teeth grabbed the bottom of my lip. *Oh yeah. Time. Biting me in the ass again.* Time tended to be annoying when you didn't participate in it and your friends might be concerned. The thought of my parents raced through my mind, yet again. I needed to make sure they knew I was okay and not dead in a ditch. "Yeah, I was out of town for a while. Then a work trip . . . and then some family stuff came up." I sounded like an evasive asshat.

"Oh. Well, I am glad you're back." She smiled, and her hair shivered with enthusiasm. It was pink now, a bright, bubblegum pink. She'd probably consumed five or six shots already. "What can I get for you and your . . . friend?"

My mouth pulled at the corners. "Well, two double shot vanilla lattes. One's for Amy, so you know how she likes it. A caramel macchiato for my friend here, and for me . . . something strong. I think it's a Revolver kind of day."

Margo tilted her head as she added to my order, eyebrow raised at my devil coffee. She, of course, had no idea how much I'd earned the damn drink.

"All Venti?"

I nodded.

"You got it, darling!" I handed her my card, which drew more odd glances from the witch. Leaving the counter, I sat at one of the small tables.

"We have to wait?" she asked.

"Well, yeah. They need to make them." Her eyes digested this new information. "Unfortunately, we can't snap our fingers here and make things happen."

"This is uncomfortable," she said, pulling out a chair to sit.

I snorted a half laugh. "Why are you here?"

"Well, to set up a meeting." Her mouth turned upward, and my eyebrows followed. "Fire. The next element."

No rest for the wicked.

"Hey, do you mind if we get a picture?" Two guys interrupted our conversation at the edge of our table, one with his phone out. He stared at the witch, his eyes pleading.

"What?" I turned, taking in their colorful chucks, zip hoodies, and ogling eyes.

"Yeah. I mean, she's perfect. You guys going to Comicon? I mean, dude. She looks just like her," rambled the one not holding the phone.

I peered up. What was on his t-shirt? *Yup*. A teddy bear with a pompom coming out of his head.

"Did you just call me *dude*?" I asked. My question was disregarded over the witch's response.

"Look like who, my darling?" Her sing-song voice of distant Realms danced through the air.

"The White Mage in Final Fantasy XIV. Seriously, *just* like her!" His head bobbed in excitement. This one's bright red shirt had a large skinny chicken on it.

My eyebrows traveled deep into the creases of my forehead. I would never understand the gaming world. Ever. The witch seemed entertained.

"And what is a picture?"

"Yeah, yeah, I want to post it on my Instagram. We are headed over to the convention center later. This is bomb!" They hovered closer, moving around her shoulders, chicken t-shirt holding his phone out in traditional selfie standards.

"You've got to be kidding me," I muttered under my breath.

The witch was intrigued upon seeing her reflection in the camera. Her ice blue eyes shimmered, and I wondered how they would show up in the picture. The guys probably assumed she wore contacts. I hoped.

"This . . . White Mage? Who is she?" she asked them.

They blinked, unsure how to answer. If we were weirding out the gamers, we were walking a dangerous road.

"She's kidding!" I insisted, cutting the awkwardness with a half laugh. Laughter bubbled out of them, and I let out a sigh of relief.

"Thanks! You're the best! You look great, by the way." They walked off, their faces glued to the phone, a certain giddiness in their step.

"What is . . . Instagram?" she asked. Taking a moment to answer, I acknowledged everyone around us glued to their phones, focused on their games and social media apps. I was one of those people consumed by the absurd nonreality of the internet. A fleeting thought of posting a picture of the amulet passed through my mind. #halfway-there #onlytwomoretogo #keeperofelements

I tried to hold back my laughter as Margo handed us our coffees, setting the carrier of lattes on the table.

"It's good to see you," she said with another coffee-enhanced grin. "And I am glad you are still alive! See you later. Oh, and tell Amy hey!" Margo's hand settled on my shoulder as I nodded at her. Was it bad my friends were constantly concerned about my health and safety? And she had no idea of the imminent danger I always found myself in.

The witch picked up her cup, bringing it to her nose for a speculative smell, the question of Instagram forgotten. Eyes sparkling with her inhale, I grinned in return, urging her to drink. She took a tentative sip and her face told me I had transcended the Realms with the gift of coffee.

"Oh, this is . . . delightful! And well worth the un-earthly wait." Satisfaction melted down her face. I took several gulps of my Revolver, savoring the bittersweet love of six shots of espresso. Pushing out of my chair, I began the walk back to my apartment.

"I have a question," I began, glancing over at the beautiful being beside me. "Time has passed, and a lot of it. I asked Jax, but he was evasive." My words tumbled over each other.

"Yes. As I told you, elemental magic has been waning for some time. These are some of the repercussions." The witch eyed me.

The ever-present need to hurry rushed through me. Two more elements were waiting.

"So, Fire?"

"Mm-hmm," she murmured as we walked over Lyndale Avenue, still savoring the warm cup between her hands.

"I don't suppose you know the location?"

"It's never that simple, is it?"

Shaking my head, my bangs shifted over my eye. I shoved them behind my ear. How long had it been since my last haircut? I had lost all sense of time. Sympathy for my grandmother grew by the day.

"Fire has been long kept by Dark, as I told you before." I nodded, listening. "They chose to keep it hidden, for the most part. However, that is difficult now that you have Air and Water."

"Why would that matter?"

"Well, the elements are four pieces of a whole and are drawn to each other. Especially now, as they are un-covered."

This made sense. After everything I had gone through, I was weary of her intentions, remembering Aila's bitter feelings about this witch. A deep sinking struck the moment I thought of Aila and the magic which took her life.

Chewing on the side of my lip, I focused on pushing down the emotions I still hadn't come to terms with. The witch's stare was apparent, and I concentrated on the tile in front of me.

I realized then that I had used getting coffee to further procrastinate something that had been on my mind since waking in my apartment: I had to tell Ailianna. Maybe there was some kind of magical connection between the sisters and she already knew, not to mention her considerable powers as a Seer. But I had an obligation to tell her the details to her face . . . as soon as I had the courage.

"I can help you to the location," the White Witch offered in reverence. My eyes immediately jumped to hers. "I can take you there. But you must follow my instructions explicitly."

Once again, I found myself placing forced blind trust into someone. She snapped her fingers and a piece of paper appeared. The heavy cardstock, stiff and folded, sat in between her long fingers. She handed it to me.

"Read this later." Her words were sharp. "They are always watching."

"Who?" I asked, stuffing the paper in my back pocket. A blanket of magic shimmered around me.

"You shall see soon, Aislynn."

Then she disappeared. In the middle of the skyway. Thankfully, it seemed no one noticed, and if they did, what would they say? A heaviness filled me as I continued my walk.

44

Fumbling my keys, I tried to balance the coffees, chastising myself for locking the door after all. Finally, pushing the door open with my foot, I managed to get inside, only to almost trip over Jax as he swirled between my legs. *I should've teleported.*

"That took long enough."

"Yeah, well, you are about to be covered in vanilla latte, cat." I pushed the coffee under my chin, balancing the cups in one hand, trying to shut the door. I realized I made quite a lot of noise when Amy's head popped out of the covers.

"What the hell are you doing?" she grumbled, rubbing her hands over her eyes and flattening the hair standing straight off her head. I set down the carrier, and she grabbed hers as I held it out.

"Your Elixir of Life, Madam."

Amy was not a morning person. She was likely to maim and kill before her coffee, if one wasn't careful. Grunts were the only sound she made as she consumed the beverage with fervor.

The heap of blankets on the couch appeared to be void of Rowan, and the bathroom door was open with the light off.

"Oh, Margo is a goddess." Amy finally spoke. "Thank you."

Grabbing my coffee, I sat on the end of the bed in the mess of covers and gestured toward the couch. "Any idea where he went?"

Amy shook her head, taking several more swallows. I was sure it was half-gone already.

"How are you feeling?" she asked in between gulps.

My lips puffed out with my breath. "Like crap?" Her eyebrows arched in response. "However . . . the White Witch got coffee with me."

"Wait, *the* White Witch? I thought she couldn't travel the Realms or something." Amy's brain was still trying to process on limited caffeine, trying to connect all the pieces of information I had given her.

"Yeah. Well, exceptions to rules, I guess." I dug the paper out of my pocket. "She gave me this. Oh, you would've died! Some gamers took pics and totally geeked out over her at Starbucks."

"Oh, jeez. If they had any idea this shit actually existed, they'd pee themselves and beg for their mommies."

A burst of laughter came streaming out of me. Amy always made me laugh with her absurd comments. She took the paper, examining the front then the back. "It's blank."

"Oh, for hell's sake." I looked at it myself, and sure enough both sides of the worn heavy paper were blank. "She said something about being watched. Who knows? I am getting tired of this mystery crap."

"Dude." Her eyes, still heavy with sleep, glared. "I am beyond done with this. After almost being eaten by vampires . . . oh, wait! That's not enough: I am half one, or turning, or something. I was done with this." She swirled her hands in front of her in dramatics. "But here we are."

Several gulps of coffee later, I grimaced my agreement.

"So now what?" She shook the remaining bit of her coffee.

"I guess we go back. I'll need to tell Ailianna . . . you know. And figure out what the hell this says." I held up the note. Bile crept up my throat when I thought of Ailianna and again I wondered if she already knew. Amy set her empty cup on the table and agreed to get in the shower.

Finishing the last of my coffee, I put my attention on my apartment, which required an entire cleaning team. Instead, the actions of folding blankets, making my bed, and loading the dishwasher gave my body the distraction it desperately needed.

But, unfortunately, not my mind. My thoughts flooded with everything that happened on a vicious cycle of repeat. In despair, I shoved my earbuds in and turned on my music to an ear damaging level. As I was wiping down the counters and stove, I turned around to find Rowan sitting at the counter watching me. Half screaming and jumping out of my skin, I ripped out my headphones.

"Freaking Frack! You really should give a girl warning."

"Sorry, I didn't mean to scare you," he said.

"Amy is about ready. We should probably head back to Hallervania." I put the cleaning products back under the sink. "Where were you?"

"I wanted to check something, back at the lake." The

evasiveness in his eyes was not lost on me. I waited for a moment, then decided to let it go.

"Had coffee with the White Witch," I offered instead. I pushed his very cold coffee across the counter toward him.

"In the public? That must have been interesting."

"Pshh, you have no idea. Anyway, she implied she is helping with Fire."

"We are going to need it."

Chewing on my lip, my hand hesitated before racking my knuckles against the heavy door of my sister's home. My chest tightened with apprehension when Ailianna answered. Her eyes were red, and her face was wrecked with grief, twisting the knife in my heart.

"Oh, Aislynn . . ." She reached out, grasping me in anguish. I held as she sobbed against me.

"I am so sorry. This is all my fault." My words were broken with tears. We stood holding one another in the doorway, her grief and my guilt wrapping into one mass of emotion. Everything I held back tumbled out.

"This isn't your fault," she murmured against me. "This wasn't you." Her voice was stern as she pulled back, eyes darting back and forth between mine. My head shook in refusal. She glanced up to Rowan and Amy.

"Come, let us go in." She pulled us in, closing the door behind us. In a fuzzy haze, I followed her into the kitchen where she began to make tea.

"I'm Amy, Aislynn's friend from the Earthy Realm," Amy offered.

"I have *seen* you. Aislynn is lucky to have you." Ailianna gave Amy a small smile. Slightly bewildered and unaccustomed to Seer life, Amy arched a brow my direction.

"Aislynn, you must know I am not upset with you."

These were not the words I expected. "What?" My face scrunched. "This was my fault." I took responsibility, again.

"No. It wasn't. As Rowan told you, it was her destiny." She nodded at him. I tried not to be bothered by the creepiness. *How does she know what Rowan told me?* She set out mugs, scooping tea for each of us, her lavender chamomile blend filling the air. Soothing us with her herbs was her innate magic. She remained quiet while pouring the water.

"I saw it many years ago as a child," Ailianna explained as she handed me a cup.

"That must have been awful," Amy responded before I had the opportunity. I shuddered, thinking about the ramifications of seeing the death of my own family members.

"Indeed. I pleaded with my mother that day. I did not want my gifts; they must have been wrong. I would not allow my sister to die." She took a careful sip.

"You knew all this time." Regret saturated my voice as she nodded.

"And I also knew that there was nothing I could do to change her destiny. Aila would do as she believed right." A soft smile filled Ailianna's mouth as she placed her hand over mine with a gentle squeeze.

"You take so much, Aislynn, which is not yours to hold."

Amy pulled her lips together, and I could see her attempting to hold back a response. Ailianna tilted her head. "See? Even your friend knows of what you do."

"I wanted you to be angry with me," I confessed.

She sipped her tea thoughtfully. "It is hard to anger a Seer."

I recognized then that she wouldn't relent. Her tears were not angry. Her grief was just that: grief, over the loss of a sister, of a friend. And it was completely out of her control.

"May I see what she gave you?" Ailianna held out her hand. I didn't bother to be surprised she knew of the White Witch's visit. I dug out the folded parchment and slid it across the table. As I did, markings and symbols became visible across the paper.

"What the!" Amy exclaimed as Ailianna smiled at her.

"She spelled it before entering your Realm." She unfolded the paper. The markings began to move within the paper. In inky streams, they danced off the paper and created a scene before our eyes. My eyes widened as the image before us became the Tree of Elements. Dark lines swirled upward. The lines moved, changing as they shifted again. Now, The Orchard appeared with figures walking through the trees. Shifting again, it dropped back to the paper.

"Oookay," Amy remarked in confusion.

"Hmm." Ailianna touched the paper with her fingertips, her eyes swirling into a sea of turquoise as she began to "see." Amy's eyes went wide. The room was quiet except for the occasional cracking and popping of wood in the fire.

"She has chosen to reclaim her destiny," Ailianna said with a whisper of voice not her own. Moments passed, her eyes continuing to swim with the color of the Caribbean Sea.

"I am sorry, what did you say?" Rowan stretched forward, touching Ailianna's arm, pulling her from the vision. Her eyes shifted back to their normal appearance.

"She . . ." Ailianna paused, glancing at the three of us. "I'm sorry. I don't know. I don't understand what it means." She pushed the paper back to me. My brows met in contemplation as I inspected her eyes and the fear held within them.

"Ailianna, what did you see?" I pleaded with her. She shook her head in response, and a piece of her long curls came unfurled from the pins holding them back. Her lips twitched with emotion, matching the trepidation written across her face. "Please."

She stood from the table, taking her tea to the sink, a clear distraction to my pleading. With her back to us, Ailianna hung her head. She gripped the sink, trying to steady what seemed to be trembling arms. Eventually, she turned back to us.

"I can't." Tears raced down her cheeks, leaving the three of us speechless.

❧

We teleported to Riona's cottage, leaving Ailianna as she asked. Because she was so tormented by whatever she had seen and what she refused to tell us, there was nothing we could do. We couldn't force her. My insides gnawed at me, thinking about her response. The unknown ate away at the little resolve I had left. *Did she see my death? Her own? Everyone's?*

"You're back!" Tristan exclaimed, standing from the

couch. Concern bled through his eyes as he hugged me. "I am sorry, Aislynn. For Aila."

Rowan shed the bags he carried to the floor, pushing them into the corner of the room. I tossed my bag to the pile after hugging Tristan.

"Riona and Matthew will be back," he added, indicating the empty home around him. "She knew you were on your way. Something about the White Witch . . . ?"

"Yeah." I glanced around the room. There was something distinctly different about this space since I'd last been here. I couldn't place it, and an odd tickle touched the corners of my mind.

My hand ran across the back of the sofa and the quilt folded on top, searching. I pulled the inside of my cheek with my teeth, staring at the room, seeking the source of what rattled my subconscious.

"What?" Amy asked, observing my odd behavior with her own curiosity.

"Something . . . I don't know." I faded off as I continued to search for what bothered me. Amy shrugged, then Riona and Matthew appeared, breaking the cobweb of frustration I was trying to unravel.

"Congratulations, Aislynn. You are halfway." Riona's words teemed with pride.

I swallowed the sentiments with equal parts bitterness and anguish. So far, there had been a severe cost to reclaiming each of the elements. Worry seeped in as I wondered if each would require some sort of sacrifice. The amulet pulsed at my chest in acknowledgment.

"The White Witch gave you something?" Riona prompted, breaking my concentration yet again.

"Yeah, she did." I pulled out the parchment. Riona placed it on the table, much like Ailianna did. Once again, it followed through the production of figures, shapes, and images. Riona observed the magic from multiple angles, turning her head this way and that. Murmuring sounds of interest escaped her lips while viewing the rigmarole.

"Would you like to elaborate? Because Ailianna's response wasn't much better," Amy said with a slight snip in her voice.

"Ailianna saw this?" Riona's head was still at an awkward angle as she watched the images transform.

"Yeah, we went there. Well, you know . . ." My voice was heavy.

"I see." The witch stood upright, and her finger tapped her lips in contemplation.

Goosebumps flashed up my spine, and I whipped around to look behind me. Although empty, I sensed a presence there, as if someone stood in front of me. A hot flash ran across my arms as I stared, searching for the source of my unease. Rowan caught my action, his eyebrow arching up in question. With a slight shake of my head, I turned back to Riona.

"This is a request to meet her in The Orchard," Riona said with apprehension, and it was obvious she left something out. Amy waved her hand in small circles, coaxing more words from Riona. "I will need to check a few things."

Amy's head arched back in an exaggerated eye roll as Riona disappeared. I may have laughed if I hadn't felt so unsettled. Whatever strange vibes I noticed went unchecked by Amy, who curled herself into the corner of the couch, one leg tucked under the other. Tristan disappeared with a hasty goodbye and a promise to return later with Riona.

"I am not impressed by the reactions we are receiving," Amy said, implying the note.

"Yeah. Me either." I plopped on the opposite side of the couch, choosing to reject the creepy vibes. Rowan crouched behind the sofa, chin resting on crossed arms. His cautious blue eyes met mine.

"Are you okay?" he questioned.

"Yeah," I said, and a half smile formed. Amy glanced toward the cold fireplace, feigning discomfort. I knew better; inside she gooed over what might be between me and Rowan.

"Well, I am going to grab a few things real quick," Rowan said. I nodded as he rubbed his hand over my arm before disappearing. Amy wriggled her eyebrows at me.

"Stop!" I snorted with a half laugh.

"What?" she asked. I smirked, shaking my head. "Seriously, though. What was with before?

"I don't know." I searched the room again. "Just something seemed off." Amy cocked a brow. "Yeah, yeah," I added. "All of this is . . . off."

"You said it, not me. However, what do you make of the White Witch?"

I blew out a breath. Glancing at the empty fireplace, I threw a ball of fire on the dry wood, igniting flames several feet which slowly reduced to a warm glow.

"That is just freaking cool." Amy was enamored by the dancing flames.

"I think that Aila was right all along." I rested my head on my hands. "She didn't trust her; in fact, she downright despised her, if I'm honest. But I feel like . . ."

"You are constantly getting screwed over?" Amy answered for me. I allowed my eyebrows to raise in agreement.

"I am tired of people underestimating me and manipulating me. They keep twisting me into doing what they want me to do." I vomited the words at her.

"So, what are you going to do about it?"

I sat for a moment, watching the fire. Flames twisted out, reaching for an unknown force, without a care where they went. No one had control over them. An idea tickled at the edge of my mind, and I wondered if I could get away with it.

"Screw up their plans."

"How are you going to do that?" She peeked at me with one eye.

A coy grin slid across my mouth. "By doing what they don't want me to do."

45

*S*crew *everyone and their excessive planning. I'm over that shit.* I trudged through wet snow in The Orchard. Snow. Freaking snow. Why? How? I didn't know, but it started late into the night and piled up across the valley. I thought I escaped this crap, but here I was wading through it like the old ball pits at Chuck E. Cheese. *Dammit.*

Wrapping the heavy cloak tighter around me, I tried to keep in the little warmth radiating from my body. The snow seemed directly connected to my decision to leave for The Orchard. Late last night, Riona had informed me the message from the White Witch was also a request to accompany me to retrieve Fire. Tired of the clandestine messages, I didn't trust the witch. Though I was certain the snow was a bad sign, I left before anyone came back to stop me. At least Amy would stay put; no one could force her from the cottage in this awful white evilness.

"Where are you going?" The White Witch appeared nearby and called out to me. The hood of her blood red cloak sat low on her forehead, meeting her brow against the discontentment which sat firmly on her face.

"To get Fire," I responded, pulling back the hood off my head.

"I was trying to help you with that." She folded her hands together in front of her.

"Were you?" My eyebrow arched in doubt.

Her lip twitched holding back a response, deliberating. Finally, she shrugged. "I have been waiting a long time for this moment." A harshness spilled into her voice that I hadn't detected before.

"Well, I appreciate your help, but I am going to do what I need to do."

"I gave you explicit instructions," she argued. "I am going with you."

"Explicit? Um. Your weirdo paper movie message didn't make any sense and no, you aren't." The thought occurred to me that she would not relent, so I concocted a backup plan. I squeezed the Aurora Towers I held deep in the pockets of the cloak.

Waving her hand to the side, a ball of fire ignited in midair, opening into a roaring loop. Flames swirled in orange and red, giving way to an inky blackness in the center.

"Fire is captivating, isn't it?" the White Witch said. "For the longest time, I cursed my magical gift and my affinity for fire because it destroyed everything good in my life. It destroyed *me*." Her eyes were leaden with the sadness I had seen long ago in my dreams. Behind the sadness resided something else, in a brief flash that was almost indiscernible.

Holding the towers, I focused on them surrounding

the witch to hold her here, locking her in place. Her head ticked to the side as if reading my mind, then she flipped her hand and knocked me off my feet.

"What the hell?" Recovering fast, I made a quick decision and ran toward the Fire loop. The witch cried out against my movement, grasping after me.

We fell into the fiery loop simultaneously, and immediately we were seized into traveling. Both of us twisted and turned blindly in the air. Eventually, we were thrown out of the portal and tossed across hard ground. Dark rock bit and scraped me as I rolled. *Ow!* I peeled myself off the ground, feeling like I had been skipped across asphalt naked. To my right, the White Witch did the same, her appearance rough unlike her usual polished self. My lips pursed with triumphant smugness. She shouldn't have followed me.

"Where are we?" I asked, brushing off my black skinny jeans.

"The Caves of Lasaironia." A tenseness washed over the witch as she tried to obtain her normal, cool confidence.

I felt like the small word *cave* didn't quite capture the sheer walls that towered hundreds of feet above us, glowing in firelight. Craning my neck upward at the expansive, open space left me with a wave of dizziness. The entire city of Minneapolis could fit inside this cave with room to spare. An eerie, muted silence filled the air and the walls of stone looming around us left me with a sense of apprehension eating at my skin.

"Come on, this way." The witch pulled the red velvet over her head, stepping silently across the slab of stone beneath our feet. I followed her through a channel of rock that made up a labyrinth inside the cave. Weaving our way deeper, the pathway narrowed, and I wondered if we were crawling into the belly of a massive beast, never to be found again. Shaking off the foreboding feeling, we came to a stop behind a wall jutting out in front of us. The witch silenced me with a finger to her lip.

We peered around the corner of the jagged wall, which led to a larger cavern of open space. In the center of the cavern sat a large cauldron of flames that licked twenty-five feet high toward the ceiling hundreds of feet above. The flames danced as if with purpose, casting shadows of fiery light shimmering on the inky black walls.

Without thinking, my body moved toward the edge of the wall in a hypnotic dance before my hand was wrenched back by the witch. Shaking her head in silence, fear trickled over her face. I almost asked her a question when a booming voice reached through the cavern.

"Aislynn! Come, come!" The thunderous voice held a cheerful tone while the witch pinched her lips together and ripples of magic cascaded from her body. I wondered then if I could follow through with my plan. *Send her back.* The crystal towers were ready in my pocket, waiting for my magic to hold her in place. Before I could decide, the voice spoke again.

"Ah, Seraphina. You must join us!"

Seraphina? Is that the White Witch's name? My face was full of distrust when I looked at her, and she slowly shook her head from side to side. Tired of the confusion, I tugged my hand from her grip and walked out into uncertainty. Probably not my most intelligent move.

The booming voice belonged to a man standing opposite the cauldron of open flames. He stood over six feet tall with long, black hair, silver strewn throughout. His face was covered in trimmed facial hair dark as night. I took cautious steps forward. Dressed in black pants and a shirt fitted over his lean frame, he shifted his weight with a refined confidence.

"Aislynn. Finally, we meet," he declared, interrupting my assessment. The man eyed me like some sort of decadent dessert. We stood across from one another, the flames dancing between us. Closer now, I discovered it wasn't a cauldron but an open hole into the earth reaching uncertain depths. I peered downward, afraid to get too close as the heat of the fire pressed on my skin.

"I am surprised you have come alone. Well, besides Seraphina. But you weren't planning on letting her stay, were you?" A coyness in his voice brought a smirk to his lips.

My chin jutted as I crossed my arms. *How the hell does he know my plans?*

"Who the hell are you?" My words came out more attacking than I expected.

"Ahh . . . as I thought, she didn't tell you." He glanced toward the White Witch. "Tsk tsk, Seraphina." Disappointment settled in his eyes as he reprimanded her.

Glaring between the two of them, Seraphina clenched her jaw. With her mouth set in a grim line, she folded her hands underneath her cloak.

"Well, my sweet Seraphina, aren't you going to tell her?" His voice was cold and scolding. He tapped his foot, clasping his hands together, index fingers held in a point.

The witch heaved out a breath, clenching her teeth. A moment passed before she spat his name.

"Viego."

Viego? My mind raced. I knew the name. *Where did I know the name from?* At last, it came to me: I remembered the story the White Witch or Seraphina told me the first time we met. My head snapped toward him. *How is that possible?* That had been some two thousand years ago.

"But . . ." My brain couldn't form cohesive thoughts.

"But? How am I here? Why didn't she tell you? So many questions. So little time for answers," he quipped, his tone scolding. "You have been quite the little nuisance, Aislynn." His mouth tilted into a frown.

Viego snapped his fingers, and Daragon appeared before us with a look of surprise on his face. He quickly assessed his surroundings, and traces of fear leeched onto his face after his gaze landed on Viego.

Whipping his hands in a spiraling motion, Viego encased Daragon in a chain of flames. "You will stay right there, my friend."

His magic awed me. The fluidity of energy from him was enamoring. Something old and ancient flooded through his hands as the magic extended out as if it were a part of him.

"Now, Daragon. You have allowed two elements to slip from your fingers." Anger seething through Viego's words. "You are telling me that this tiny little human outmaneuvered you, not once, but twice?" Viego swirled his hands again, and the fire chains glowed a searing red orange, tightening closer to Daragon's body. His eyes widened as he looked to Viego then me. I thought about how I had strangled him with Water and swallowed hard.

"Master, I—"

Viego's dark, shimmering eyes flipped the chains tighter yet again.

"No more excuses. You have cost me dearly. Mostly because you have given this poor girl hope. And hope can

ignite one to believe they are capable of the impossible."
His words were vicious poison pouring from his mouth as
anger burned in his eyes.

I watched Viego scold and torture Daragon, knowing
full well that Daragon had brought me so much discontentment, including killing Aila. But some part of me was
sickened by Viego's controlled cruel behavior. A malice
coiled within him, twisted by centuries of Dark magic.

Realization trickled over me then: I knew I couldn't
win against Viego. Daragon had been a servant ordered in
front of me as a test, with Viego pulling the strings like a
puppet master.

Fear bloomed in my chest, sinking to my abdomen and
stewing like rancid meat. Seraphina had known Viego was
the true enemy and allowed me to come here unprepared
and alone. My body took a hesitant step back, without my
control, adrenaline assessing the situation. *I absolutely made a
massive mistake.*

"Ah, my sweet girl. No, no. You will not be leaving us
yet." Viego's hands shot out. He twisted them in a pattern
that reminded me of Tristan. My last thought before my
body was frozen in place was: *Time magic.*

Within my frozen stillness, I was capable of thought. I
could still see everything going on around me but was
powerless to react. *Shit.* Several things occurred to me at
once. One: I was totally and utterly screwed. Two: this was
how Viego had stayed alive for more than two thousand
years. He had used time magic.

Three: I was so freaking screwed.

"Now. My Seraphina, what to do with you?" Viego's
head cocked to the side. From the corner of my eye, I
realized he had frozen her as well.

Why hadn't I told anyone where I had gone? What I was doing? The ramifications of my choices pounded into my mind. No one would know where to find me, particularly not in the depths of these caves. Fear marched over me, snowballing my thoughts into garbled chaos. *Think.*

"You stole what was not yours to take." Seraphina somehow managed to force out words through the time magic. "You took everything." Centuries of pent up fury rolled through her. She had been waiting for this moment, when she would face her greatest enemy.

"I stole?" he scoffed. "No. I only took what you willingly gave up." He took slow, methodical steps toward her, hands folded behind his back. With how close he was now, I saw that despite how tall the White Witch was, Viego still towered above her. With eyes cast down, he whispered something in her ear. The witch struggled beneath the magic holding her, a viper needing to strike.

"Use the Elements."

A voice sounded desperately in my head, and my eyes shot to Daragon. *"Use them!"* My eyes darted from Daragon to Viego and back again. I was curious why he would help me, but I closed my eyes and focused on the magic. Even inside my time lock, it pulsed stronger than my own heartbeat, just a thought away. Reaching out with my mind, I drew from the ground and up the cave walls for the magic that waited to be called upon.

Air flickered within the amulet. Bringing the magic to a fine point, I blasted it, escaping from my magical lockdown. A shot of air reverberated through the cave, throwing everyone to the ground. Shock flew into Viego's eyes as he righted himself and threw his hands toward the earth. A slow tremble rolled through the ground. Gritting my teeth, I steadied myself.

"Free me."

Daragon's voice again filled my head. I chanced a quick glance in his direction, not wanting to distract my gaze from Viego. Daragon's black eyes pleaded with me. The trembling under my feet grew stronger as a rainfall of pebbles cascaded down the walls.

"Please, Aislynn."

The decision wavered in my mind. Could I free him? After everything he had done? *Why does he want to help?* Or was it his own skin he wanted to save? Before I could decide, my vision went black. Blinking rapidly against the darkness, I tried to reach out, to reestablish my awareness and sense of balance. Then, crying sounded in the distance. The sound was far away at first, muffled, but as I focused, the voice became clearer. It was a voice I knew better than my own.

Mitch.

"Why the hell are you crying like this?" he shouted down to me. The memory from two years ago slid in front of me, real and vivid. My throat turned hot and dry. I pushed that night away. *No. This can't be real. Mitch can't be here.*

I pushed back with my mind, forcing his demeaning tone out of my space. The image before me shifted and faded until my parents' home took shape. Their kitchen appeared destroyed, the windows blown out. Rubble lay everywhere. I took a small step forward. Glass crunched under my feet as I reached out, my hands trembling in front of me.

"Mom?" I cried out. "Dad?" I followed the trail of debris through the front living room. More destruction was spread across their beautiful house. A leg protruded from underneath what had once been an antique wood coffee table.

I flew to the ground, heaving off wood and bits of furniture to uncover my mom's unconscious body. She lay facedown, her clothes ripped and tattered. Blood pooled down the side of her head.

No. No, this can't be. Blood coagulated in her thin blonde hair, and I pushed it off her face, the strands sticky under my touch. A long gash revealed itself along her temple, and her skin was cold beneath my touch. A garbled scream escaped me. My eyes searched the room frantically for my dad.

"AISLYNN!" A muffled shout came to me from far away. My head cocked, I listened, trying to hear my father. *"AISLYNN!"*

That wasn't my father. Daragon. Had he done this? Confusion trampled like a thousand pinpricks at once, overriding my panic.

"It isn't real."

Not real? What wasn't real? My parents' house suddenly disappeared. A pool of terror sunk to the pit of my stomach. My parents! I needed to get back to them. Slamming my eyes shut, I thought of them, trying to find them. Blackness filled my vision.

It isn't real.

The thought persisted. *Viego.* Had he created an illusion? But the vision of my parents' house held such validity in my mind. Panic dove deep under my skin. I desperately tried to find any basis of reality to grasp onto as fear devoured me. I felt trapped within my mind, descending into a fragile lunacy. *The caves,* I thought. *I am in the caves.* I focused on my feet, feeling the floor underneath me and remembering the cliffs of stone reaching up around me.

Forcing my eyes open, I struggled through the magical fog which held me in its grasp. Finally, I pushed through. The cavern took shape, and I was out of breath from the effort.

Brain melt. Check.

"Aislynn." Viego's eyes tightened. Was that admiration in this voice? Or irritation that appeared in his eyes? A little of both, perhaps.

"You are quite the challenge. Maybe I should not be so hard on Daragon after all." He sent a nod in the direction of Daragon, still wrapped tightly in fire chains.

Seraphina was held in a sphere of magic that hung in the air. She appeared translucent, almost unseen as she wavered in the magic that seemed too ancient to be real. Her body was suspended, her back arched, her cloak cascading downward in folds of red velvet. Her body hung peacefully like an aerialist dancer entwined in silks, except for the horror that filled her face.

Cringing inwardly at her tortured, blank stare, I swallowed hard. My eyes traced back to Viego's. Their piercing black voids met mine, and I kept my focus on him as I sent thoughts to Daragon.

"Why are you helping me?"

"Helping you is helping me. I don't particularly want to die. Not at the hands of him." Even in the grips of death, his sarcastic cadence took aim.

"You killed Aila."

Silence filled the air. Viego kept watch with curiosity,

one eye squinting in calculation. He shot a glance toward Daragon.

"Oh, what to do with the two of you?" he mused, glancing back and forth. "Ah, I know."

Whipping his hands, the fire chains unwound themselves from Daragon. Another flip, and Daragon stood frozen. Viego's right hand squeezed the invisible air and sent Daragon into a fit of ear curdling screams. The sound echoed off the walls and I shuddered at the terror in Daragon's voice. Goosebumps pricked my skin as I wondered what sort of mental torture he was subjecting Daragon to. Then the screams stopped as quickly as they started.

"Now, Daragon. Let us see if you can redeem yourself." A wicked grin spread across Viego's face. "Take back the elements from her. Or you will suffer even greater consequences." The words were sharp, and when he looked to me, an evilness slid over his entire face, twisting it into a demented form of delight.

"Good luck." Viego winked while crossing his arms, malicious laughter escaping from his mouth.

"Aislynn, I am sorry." Daragon's voice chimed in my head as he whipped a fire lasso across the space.

He apologizes followed by attacking me. What an asshole.

With a newfound strength, I grasped my magic and streamed a span of water toward the ripples of fire. I spun around, taking my left hand across the floor, building magic and cycling it toward Daragon. The blast of water blew him across the stone with the force of dynamite, crashing into the wall. He recovered in haste, or fear, I wasn't sure which.

For the first time, I thought about Fire. Viego requested Daragon to take the two I had, but Fire possibly resided within these very caves. Gnawing on the inside of my cheek, I focused on the element. To my left, the crater of flames ignited, propelling upward. I clenched my hand, twisting the flames and drawing them toward Daragon. The two of us fought fire with fire, and oppressive heat seared down. Eating the space between him and Fire, I pushed sizzling flames up his lasso. Daragon whipped himself around, trying to escape what might be certain death.

The earth trembled again, and I snapped my teeth against one another. Of course Viego would intercede. Pushing water under my feet, I sent a wave rushing toward him.

"Hope is a real bitch, isn't it?" The massive wave crashed down, rapping his body against the floor. I swirled Air and locked him into a tornado of wind. I reeled in my hope. Whipping the fire lasso back toward Daragon, I snapped him back in chains.

Realization struck when I stopped and caught my breath, observing the magical beings that were now all at my mercy. All three of them had deceived me in one form or another. They had each used and manipulated me to their own desires.

Resentment slid into me, an old friend that clenched my heart. Magic slammed through the caves. Air, Water, and Fire ate away within me, fueling each other into magical retaliation.

They all deserve to burn. Seraphina fell to the floor, the bubble of magic holding her disintegrating. I wanted to see them burn and writhe in misery for everything they had done. Wrenching my hands closed, my audience of three began to choke.

I heard a combination of gasping sounds that were desperate for air that wouldn't come. Fear settled across their eyes staring back at me. Viego pulled at his throat, twisting his hands to try and use time magic. Instead, I blasted his hands back and held them with tourniquets of water.

Viego closed his eyes, reigning in his fear. Upon opening them, he revealed swirling masses of black. He had centuries of time to learn magic that I hadn't conceived of, and I didn't especially enjoy the nightmare illusion he produced before. Not wanting a repeat, I swooped my hand across the air, whipping him off balance and tossing his lean body into the sheer wall behind him.

The elements burned inside of me, edging themselves forward to push me over the brink of insanity. A ring of fire burned around the edge of the pit at the center of the room, glowing an iridescent orange. It began to ooze through the cracks and crevices of the rocky floor.

Awareness trickled over me as the orange glow expanded outward that it was molten lava bubbling up from the open earth. A surge of white-hot fire burst from the center of the gaping hole like a rocket of jet flames issuing from the depths of hell.

The sound rocketed through the open space above, sending my audience writhing in pain. The three of them shrugged their shoulders to try and cover their ears for relief. The magic flooded through me, etching itself into every cell of my body, digging into the marrow of my bones.

Fire shot toward the ceiling, reaching for the unseen sky above. The consumption was uncontrolled; there was no one to pull me back now, and their shrieks rang through my ears, hitting nerves like an out of tune piano. Using air, I muffled the sound. Now I only saw them writhing in pain. *Much better.*

"*Ais . . . lynn . . . pl—*"

Daragon's choked voice tried to reach through the magic. Barely giving him a glance, I reveled in the magic burning through my veins. Viego appeared as if he was in a serene sleep, unaware of his predicament. Irritation sparked, and when I cocked my head, I set a blaze at his feet and watched the fire dance upward. Fire, Water, and Air bled together in a bond too strong to ignore. They enticed me with their pulsing, asking to consume everything.

These three used you. They took advantage. Show them your vengeance.

A small, distant part of me screamed to control it. *Push it back, Aislynn.* A part of me knew my eyes were swimming with Fire, consumed by the elements. Seraphina's face filled with fear, and I knew that she knew better than anyone how perilously close I was to losing control.

This time, only I could save myself.

But anger rolled and seethed. *They are monsters. They deserve to be tortured. To die.*

A flash of magic erupted from Viego. He hadn't re-signed to his place against the jagged wall of rock at all, but was in fact calculating, plotting, and seeking. A brilliant white light ignited the caves and magic exploded from the walls, throwing me to the ground. The earth splitting beneath me created a chasm through the stone. My nails dug across the earth, reaching for anything as I tumbled. Jagged rock dug into my back and legs before I slid to a stop, dangerously close to the edge.

Magic drove me upwards, and I observed deep cracks running through the rock as the lava bled upward from below. I blasted fire at Viego. His hands flew up, slowed the flames, and froze them from further movement. Then he slammed his hands down toward the ground, and shards of the rocky wall cascaded down upon us.

The White Witch was thrown to the ground, pummeled with heavy stone. Seraphina's body twisted in inhuman ways. Viego turned on Daragon, tossing him across the ground with a flip of his hand.

"I have had enough!" he yelled. Another twist, and I was frozen. He stepped around the open fissures, stalking toward me. His eyes were steady on the amulet. Screams stuck in my throat, unable to move. My mind frantically tried to come up with ideas, anything to save myself. Part of me even felt like I should have killed him when I had the chance, but . . .

Viego stopped inches from me, and looming, dark magic tendrils slithered forth, eating at my resolve. Fear blossoming, I realized I was a lamb at slaughter, completely at Viego's mercy. His hand reached for the amulet.

His eyes, dark pools of evil, flickered behind me. I wanted to turn, but magic kept me locked in place. Instead, I focused on what I could feel: there was a presence behind me, and a familiar tickling of my senses. More magic began to build. But who's magic? Viego's eyes were processing a conversation I could not hear, and frustration built within me.

Past Viego, Daragon's hand moved, his foot dragging itself against the hard stone ground. Methodically, he tried to pull himself to his feet, one arm held across his abdomen, face full of pain.

Everything went to shit then. Magic exploded across the caves. Another flash of bright incandescent light enveloped us. Too bright to comprehend, it sizzled the air. Daragon appeared before me, then a blast of magic flew from Viego.

Daragon's face caught in a twist of horror as his shriek rang out against the cavernous walls. We both tumbled to the ground, Daragon's heavy, unmoving body on mine. His weight crushed down upon me, and when I turned my head, eyes lost to death stared back at me.

I was going to die, too. This would be my end. Past Daragon's dead eyes and leaden weight, Seraphina's hand twisted beneath the rocks.

It was the last thing I saw.

46

Stinging pain registered first, then my eyes flickered open and found nothing. Disoriented, I realized I was face down in the snow. The cold left my skin tingling, and I wondered how long I had been lying here.

When I tried to push myself to my hands, pain shot down my spine, and I immediately retreated to my prone position. *There. No pain. I'll just stay here, lying on my bed of white suck for . . . forever.*

"Well, you screwed that up," spoke a voice I didn't recognize. Turning my head, I tried to look, but pain seared, sending stars across my vision, and blackness crept in. A dreadful groan escaped as my response.

"Now two more people are dead, and you didn't even retrieve Fire."

Vicious swear words ran through my mind. Whoever this was really sucked. The more aware I became, the more my pain sensors ticked their disapproval. There was something incredibly wrong with my ankle, and my right elbow wasn't super pleased, either. Indistinguishable sounds racked my body as I moaned into the cold, wet snow.

"Why would Daragon choose to save you?" the voice asked.

Daragon saved me? I tried to remember the last few moments in the cave. Daragon had appeared in front of me before being blasted with magic. *He saved me.* Why, indeed, would he do that? I contemplated this with my face still planted in the snow.

"You are pathetic," the voice chided.

Seriously? I decided rolling would be best, but it happened reluctantly. I was determined to look my judgment-throwing accuser in the face . . . well, from the ground, anyway. My movement was delayed and pain ridden, and though I gathered my snarky comments, I found no one to hurl them at.

"Dammit!" I said aloud to an empty field of white. Mind-numbing cold bit into my exposed skin, and I refused to move. The mystery voice had a point. I had totally screwed up. Daragon was dead. Seraphina probably was, too.

Gingerly, I held up the amulet. Air and Water were swirling before me, but no Fire. I groaned, and more swear words flew out of my mouth as flakes of snow started falling from the sky.

In my delusional state, I tried to place the voice and came up empty. Perhaps the voice belonged to whoever Viego had been communicating with in the caves and in the cottage when my creepy vibes went off.

My conclusion was clear: it had to be the same person. *A rude person.* Cold burning encased me now, and when I tried to move again, the agony lessened. Or maybe it just became more ignorable.

The flakes got heavier and bigger as they drifted down. I pushed myself to an upright position, my ankle screaming with the weight. *Great.* Brushing the thick flakes off me, I teleported back to the caves.

Destruction enveloped the landscape. Sheer cuts ran through the looming walls, and crevasses jutted across the floor in haphazard formations. The once fire pit was now an open hole of inky void to the hells beneath. Teleporting across the space from one piece of stone to the next, I searched for where Seraphina had been buried under stone.

Memories forced to the forefront of my mind: I remembered Seraphina's hand twisting with magic before being knocked unconscious and thrown out in the snow. Finally, finding her hand, I saw that her fingertips were still twisted as if throwing out magic.

Minding my ankle, I kneeled carefully until pain shouted disapproval and I ended up on my hip instead. Edges of her white-blonde hair peeked out from behind bits of rock, and my heart ached.

What was I doing? I extended my left leg to ease the torture from my ankle, my mouth twitching with emotion. The pain. Seraphina. Everyone else who had been hurt. I reached out a hand to touch the edge of her fingertips.

"I am so sorry." My voice was soft and choked. My gaze darted across the open cavern to see Daragon's lifeless body. Why had he saved me? How had I been booted from the caves? Unanswered questions lingered in the silence.

Holding Seraphina's cold fingertips, my eyes began swimming in fiery red. Suddenly, my mind's eye was thrown backward, and visions whipped through my mind. Flashes of light showed Seraphina as a young witch, and her wedding to her lost love. Emotions pummeled me as I was forced through the White Witch's memories.

Scenes from my dreams played out before me again, and I watched as she scoured the villages with fire magic. The anger and the burning fed her desire to destroy. Next was her punishment. For years and years, she roamed the planes without magic. A new feeling took over: revenge. I saw her search for Viego, observing him over the years, using the elements to his advantage.

A serene location faded into existence then: a warm sunny beach spanned out in front of me, and I saw Viego laughing while watching a young girl play in the edge of the surf. She had long dark hair, and dark eyes that stared tentatively at the waves.

The girl, about eight or nine years old, looked to Viego for security and safety with careful eyes. A wave crashed, almost knocking her over. Wet, salty hair stuck to her face as she grinned mischievously at him.

The memory ended and flashed forward. The girl was now a few years older, and her hands rested on a sphere of crystal, her dark eyes swimming in colors.

She's a Seer. I recognized the actions, so similar to Ailianna. Viego encouraged her to continue. The crystal ball flashed images of magic, and I struggled for a better view, but the memory held me locked into one angle.

Again, another image burst forth. The girl was sixteen, stunning and beautiful. Her long hair twisted in braids tied with feathers and trinkets, full of pops of pinks and purples. Her fingers were covered in ornate rings with crystals and symbols of magic embedded within the metals.

Chains of gold draped across her forehead with a center crystal hanging over her third eye. She was mesmerizing as she stood in a clearing, magic pouring from her hands. Viego watched from the sidelines like a proud parent, encouraging the magic with sheer will. She twisted arcs of color, vibrant blues and greens swirling.

"There is much more you do not know."

I heard Seraphina's voice. The rampage of visions stopped, but the girl swirling in magic wouldn't leave my mind.

Blinking, the caves came back into focus and I found myself on my back, again. The hard ground bit at my already tender body. A swarm of energy rode through the desolate cavern. The pebbles and rocks all around me vibrated, bouncing on the ground next to me.

The sound echoing off the cave walls made me want to slam my hands to my ears. A loud pop of magic sizzled across the air. Sitting up, my fingers reached for Seraphina's. Instead, I found empty stone. My head darted, searching for her body.

"What the . . . ?"

"You didn't really think I was dead?" Seraphina asked.

Craning my neck around, the witch stood with perfect hair, cloak, and a snide smile. I turned back to the pile of rock and pulled myself upright.

"Well, yeah. Kind of." I avoided putting weight on my left foot.

"That is ridiculous. I was punished by the Gods, re-member? I am like your friend Jaxon, only I have unlimited lives." She smirked.

My mouth popped open, begging to ask about the nine lives bit, but she interrupted.

"He did save you, you know." She gestured toward Daragon's body.

"Why?"

The witch only shrugged. "I'm not a mind reader." Seraphina shifted her hands beneath the cloak. "Well, I'm not. However, I suspect he began to question his role in Viego's quest."

My gaze went to Daragon's body, and I nodded. *That would explain a few things.*

"Had Viego's magic touched you . . . well, I would be waiting another thousand years for a new Keeper. Frankly, I do not have the desire to wait. I needed to intercede."

Throat tightening at the closeness of my mortality, I realized that it was Seraphina who had tossed me out into the cold snow, saving my life.

"And the girl?" I asked, still seeing images from the visions in my mind.

"Mm. Well, that is a bit trickier." She opened her hands, and a sphere of magic encompassed us. I gave her a questioning glance.

"To block any listening ears," she explained. "Believe me, they are there."

"I felt her here, in the caves and before at Riona's."

"I know," the White Witch replied.

We walked through the cavern, me slowly limping beside her. The sphere of ruby light bounced along with us as we made our way to the center where the fire had teemed up from unknown depths. Now, it had broken edges and made an odd uneven circle.

"Fire has been moved," she said.

I peered down the walls of rock into cold murky darkness. Shame assaulted me. I had my chance, and I blew it. Failure trickled through my veins, settling itself in my chest.

"Not necessarily," she offered, following my inner dialogue.

"What do you mean?"

"Well, I brought you here not thinking you would actually retrieve Fire but to show you what you were up against."

I stared at her, grinding my teeth. "You're kidding, right?" Anger snapped through my words. She shrugged, turning away from the cold empty pit. "No, don't turn away from me," I snapped. "You just said I would have died! You risked my life to show me I am up against someone who is the very essence of evil and Dark magic?" My yells echoed off the stone.

"Some things can't simply be told." Her voice was cool as she arched a brow. "You needed to see what you are up against. You need to plot, conspire, and use everything you learn to finish reclaiming the elements. There are no second chances. Not for you, anyway." She turned, walking away from me.

The reality of her statement slammed into me, stopping me in place. The magic sphere stretched and elongated, trying to encompass both of us.

"Come. I still have a few tricks up my sleeve." The witch glanced back. I followed, limping toward her as the magic tightened once again.

"The memories you saw?" Seraphina asked. "Let me show you." Waving her hand in a sweeping motion, the scenery changed.

My senses distorted as we appeared on a white sandy beach, and I recognized it as where the little girl had played in the surf. The sun shining brightly, I took a deep breath of humid, salty air and the tension around my heart eased. After the oppression of the dark caves, the open expanse of the sea became a welcomed change. My ankle no longer hurt either, thank God.

Woohoo to weirdo visions.

"The girl?" I inquired as the waves crashed with subtle softness.

"Viego molded her, creating another version of himself. He thinks of her as his own child."

"But she's not?" I asked, horrified.

"No. But even that has darkness splattered through it. You already know of her."

"I do?" I raised my hand to shield the sun from my eyes, glancing over at the witch.

"Yes. Rowan told you the story not so long ago." A wave crashed, sending a rush of warm water over our feet.

Everything clicked in my mind as the pieces came together: Zarah. The girl was Zarah. She was the one Rowan had been looking for, the one Eirnin had taken.

"Viego took her? He used the council, and killed her parents and family? Then he raised her as his own child, or some sick, twisted version of it?" Dread poured through my words with each question, part of me hoping I was wrong. But the witch nodded, her own face riddled with uneasy emotions.

I halted, my feet sinking a bit in the wet sand. "That's screwed up!" I protested.

Seraphina arched a brow in agreement.

"So the memories," I continued, glancing out at the

blue horizon, "of her growing? Learning to use magic, her powers? She is a Seer, right? At the core of it, that is her gift?"

"She is."

"Then, all this time, that was how Viego watched what we were doing." It explained why Daragon always knew my location, what was happening, and when to intercede.

"This has all been under his control," the White Witch confirmed.

Things began to make sense. I started to see why my grandmother kept everything hidden and a constant puzzle, including Seraphina with her hidden messages. Piece by piece slid into place as a perfect picture formed.

"There must be a way to stay hidden from her, right?" I questioned.

"There are ways. Like secret paper movie messages." She arched a brow my direction and I immediately winced. Perhaps I shouldn't have been judgy on the witch's efforts.

We began walking again, in silence as the water lapped at the sand. Palm fronds twisted against one another in the warm breeze. Seraphina's face glowed in the sunlight. I thought about how lonely she must be, even in places as beautiful as this. She had no one.

Eventually, my thoughts went back to Zarah and her disturbing childhood. Did she remember her parents were killed? Did Viego twist that as well?

"Her soul is riddled with the darkest magic. She has been raised to think with Dark magic, to embrace every thread of dark and to *be* evil. She knows no other way; Viego distorted her reality." Seraphina's lips pursed together, then she continued, "Viego only sees you as an annoyance. He does not believe he will lose. The fact that you acquired two elements is mere fun for him. This is only something to entertain him at this moment, which will end for you, not him."

"Then I have the upper hand."

"How so, my child?"

"Because, I have hope. Remember?" I winked with a wicked grin.

A smile pierced the corners of her mouth. I wondered if she realized she was as jaded as Viego.

"You have more than that." Her eyes twinkled with mystery. "One last gift from your grandmother."

I snapped my attention to Seraphina as she mentioned my grandmother.

"You have one more box."

My eyes widened, remembering the larger box I still held in my possession. "But . . ."

"I know. It simply was not time. There is order and balance to all things, remember," she told me. "Abigail was determined not to let you fail. To do so, she wanted to give you a pure magic. It is an ancient power, and something Viego would not suspect. Of course, helping her was helping myself." She turned to me, her eyes pleading for me to understand. "Your grandmother was a very brave woman," she continued, and now her voice was unsteady. "I've never met anyone so willing to lose everything for her purpose in helping you."

Tears stung the edge of my eyes as I glanced away, pushing my hair behind my ears.

"Securing such a magic wasn't easy, nor was finding someone to help her. I agreed to do so. Looking back, with

everything I know now, I am not sure I would do it again."
Her voice was heavy with despair, and I met her eyes once
again.

"I am so sorry, Aislynn. The magic was too much for
her to hold, and our plan did not work. It was my fault your
grandmother lost her life that day. This is why Riona hates
me so. She blames me. But I promise you, your grandmother would have it no other way. Her last words were
making me vow I would help you succeed. I swore to her
that you would be given the Astra Flaris, no matter the
consequence." Her hands grasped my shoulders, ice blue
eyes settling on mine. "And I will keep my word."

A tear slid down my cheek.

"The magic which so long ago started with me will
soon be balanced." Her mouth set in a firm promise.

"I—" My words cut off because I was suddenly
traveling.

When I appeared in a grassy clearing, five pairs of eyes
glared at me, four human and one pissed off cat. Riona
stood in front of me, and to the left Matthew and Rowan
completed the circle. Amy and Jax watched from outside
the perimeter.

"What the hell?" My hands flew up in frustration. The
sky darkening with the setting sun gave away the late hour.
I had been gone too long.

"You are alright!"

"Thank the Goddess!"

Several different exclamations burst out at once and
everyone came toward me.

"Yeah, I am alright! But you have to send me back!" I insisted.

"Where were you?"

"Why?"

"What do you mean?"

More questions layered over each other.

"I was with Seraphina! I need to go back," I barked at them.

"Who the hell is Seraphina?" Amy asked, stepping into the circle. Riona's mouth set in an angry frown as she tapped her staff against the ground.

"Quiet!" A snap of magic brought silence.

Rowan took two long steps toward me. His hand tentatively landed on my shoulder, and a tenderness trembled through me along with his concern. "We were worried about you. We would have never pulled you with a teleportation spell if we thought you were okay." His voice was soft.

"Sorry." A sheepish look settled on Amy's face. "They made me tell them! We tried to give you time, but when you didn't return . . ." She shrugged in a half apology.

"It's okay. But I wasn't aware you could teleport someone to you." I shot a questioning look at Riona, distracted by the magic that brought me here.

"The magic is not looked upon kindly, for obvious reasons. It is for emergency situations only and frowned upon for regular use. Which is why it takes more than two to accomplish the spell," Riona explained with hair blowing in the breeze. She gestured Matthew and Rowan forward. "Come, you must tell us what happened."

Riona walked past us, heading toward her cottage down the hill.

"Can it involve food, please? I am starving," I said to her back. As I turned to follow, my ankle collapsed beneath me. My cries of pain were littered with swear words. Rowan caught me before I fell on my ass.

"Are you okay?"

"Yeah, well, I forgot about that. Actually, I hoped it would magically get better." My eyes narrowed as I met his and grumbled to myself.

Jax's laughter could be heard as he sauntered off in front of us, long black tail twitching in the grass.

"Magically get better'... that's a good one!"

"Asshat," I muttered. Rowan let me lean on him as we three-legged walked down the trail. Each step sent immense pain shooting through the joint, and I knew Rowan was aware of my wincing under his grasp.

"You know, I am supposed to be the klutzy one," Amy said from behind us.

I could hear the smirk in her voice and glanced over my shoulder to glare. Instead, my eyes focused on Matthew and Amy holding hands, causing me to stumble over my own steps. Apparently, a lot happened while I was gone.

"Enough of this," Rowan said as he twisted us into traveling back to the cottage.

He set me gently on the couch.

"I can walk, you know." A playful smile crossed my mouth. Rowan arched his brow as he put a pillow on the table, carefully placing my ankle on top.

"There is no need to suffer." He left to raid Riona's magical medicine cabinets. Everyone gathered around, Amy bringing me a bowl of soup and rolls, Rowan returned with a magical arsenal of healing herbs and pastes to heal my swollen ankle.

Magic soothed under his gentle touch, but I wrinkled my nose at the smell of the herbs. Instead, I pulled the bowl of soup under my nose to focus on the aroma of stew, digging the spoon into the bowl. In between spoonfuls I told them everything that happened in the caves, they interrupted what seemed like a thousand times to ask questions that demanded answers that then required more questions.

"So after, she took me to this beach, where the girl had been in the memories," I said.

"Who was it?" Matthew asked as I slid my spoon into the bowl, capturing the last bite of soup.

"I . . ."

Rowan's face caught my attention. His fierce, watchful eyes searched mine, almost as if he knew. I spooned slowly, using the time to think.

"I . . . I don't know. We don't know," I lied. I wasn't sure why, but I did. I couldn't see Rowan hurt; if he was aware that all these years, she had been raised by Viego, he would blame himself. It would tear at his heart, and I couldn't force myself to tell him.

Then I realized something else: even if I had the heart, I couldn't tell them about the magic, nor about Zarah . . . not any of it. Seraphina told me everything within a magical bubble to protect us from Zarah and her visions. If I told them about the magic my grandmother found, Zarah would instantly know.

The Astra Whatever was my only advantage left, and I wouldn't dare give that away. I shifted uncomfortably on the couch, looking at each of my friends. They were the ones who supported me, who got me to this point, and I just lied to them all.

I needed to. My grandmother's game of secret mysteries became clear. Everything she had arranged, all of the twisted truths could only be perfectly revealed without prying Seer eyes nearby. This was a game I hadn't thought through. I swallowed hard.

"That's why I need to go back." My words became rushed. "I need to ask her what she knows."

More lies poured out of my mouth. This would protect them. It was the only way. I scratched at my shoulder as an irritation sparked on my skin. Even my body was physically rejecting the lies.

I averted my eyes from Rowan to Amy, then the floor as I shifted again. I was a terrible liar, and Amy knew it. I had to be better. Forcing my eyes to each of them, with a new determination, I spoke again. "I need to talk to her." My words were strong and clear. *There. I must be believable.*

Rowan's eyes narrowed, searching for the tidbits I left out. In response, I pushed up a wall. *He must believe me.* I didn't want to hide from him, magically or otherwise, but it was the only way to keep him safe. I had to keep them all safe.

"Are you certain you can trust the White Witch?" Riona asked. She raised an eyebrow as contention sat in her mouth.

"Seraphina? Of course. She pulled me out of the caves. She saved me as much as Daragon did." I put my bowl down and pulled my foot off the table. Testing Rowan's healing skills, I rolled and pointed my ankle, finding it completely pain free.

"Thank you, Rowan." Guilt pierced my thoughts as I met his gaze.

"I think you should be careful trusting the White Witch," Riona cut in, refusing to use Seraphina's name.

Amy took my bowl into the kitchen with Matthew following her. There was a distinct energy between them I could easily see: the lust, the excitement, the small smiles between them. The two of them had fallen to a place excluding them from the Darkness.

"We need to use more protective energy, to shield us from Viego and whoever else he may be using." Leaning forward on my knees, I glanced at Rowan next to me, then Riona in the chair.

"I have kept us well protected thus far." Riona snipped her words, crossing one leg over the other, adjusting her cloak around her.

"I know, I just think we need to be more careful than ever. I saw his magic. He would take out any of us without second thought."

At least that was the truth.

47

The magic of the Astra Flaris burned a hole in my curiosity. I nervously picked at the skin on my thumb, contemplating the moment I could leave without anyone being aware. With the sleeves of my hoodie pulled over my hands to stop my obsessive behavior, I held my bag against my body as I feigned sleep in the dark room.

Using Air to listen for the shift into sleep, I waited for heavy, slow breaths throughout the house. As I solidified my plan in my mind, I realized the more they knew, the more danger they were in. I wouldn't allow anyone else to get hurt.

One advantage I had was Amy had fallen down the rabbit hole of love, keeping her well distracted from my pitiful lies. Any other time she would have been on to me faster than a snow cone melted in hell.

Rowan was more difficult to read, as he had watched me meticulously all night. I didn't know if he realized I had made my own devious plans without his knowledge. Leading up to everyone going to bed, he had continuously pestered me with his magic, trying to pry at my shields.

Magic pulsed inside of me as I listened again through each of the rooms. Slow heartbeats thrummed, and I knew it was finally time. Sitting up, the bed creaked under the shift of my weight. Wincing, I shrouded myself in a shadow of protective magic.

Quickly, I teleported myself to a clearing deep in the forest, expanding my shield to encompass the open space. Relaxing a little, I blew out my breath, dropping my bag in front of me. Certain someone would follow, I expected Rowan or Riona to appear just behind me, but silence permeated the forest.

Unzipping the bag, I pulled out the wooden box, tracing the carvings across the top with my finger. The box, previously residing in the storage unit in Minnesota, began to glow a vibrant cobalt blue. A hazy light seeped into the clearing.

I wondered how or why it hadn't been more protected. There must have been magical protection spells that I hadn't been aware of, which explained why Daragon's guys had attacked us. More of Zarah's watching, I presumed.

Did she know what it was, or only that it was important? A part of me was aware that it didn't really matter; I would continue to keep it as hidden as possible. Anxious feelings rippled through me as I pondered opening the box. Maybe I should confer with Seraphina first.

"It doesn't matter," Seraphina said from outside my defensive spell. "It's your magic." Dressed in a black velvet cloak, the sides of her face and blue eyes appeared inky in the faint blue light. "May I?" Her hand gestured to the shield in front of her. I nodded, and she stepped through the magic.

"The Astra Flaris is protected by several layers of magic, which is why you were unable to open the box, especially without knowing the contents. Abigail made sure of that one thing."

"What is it?" I asked, still holding the box. A part of me wanted preparation for the magic within my grasp.

"An ancient magic, forged in the Astra Ice Fields, created with Fire and Ice." She peered at the box, a wave of tentative energy flooding from her cloaked form, hesitant to move too close.

"The Gods and Goddesses created the Flaris as a balance to Light and Dark . . . for one cannot exist without the other." She held her hands out in front of her like scales. "But when one has ruled over the other for an extended time period, the Astra Flaris seeks the balance for the good of all." She dropped one hand, then evened them again.

"That is not an answer."

The witch shrugged. "But it is. And this is the only magic that will save you and our realms."

"So, don't screw it up?" I asked. *Shit.* "Anything else I need to know?"

"Yes. Zarah is watching." Her eyes darted over my shoulder.

"What?" I followed her stare as I flipped around, trying to make out anything in the dark empty woods.

Seraphina huffed a small laugh. "She can't hear us. You have done well with your protection, although she is displeased." Seraphina's thin lips curved in a small smirk. "You have come a long way, Aislynn, from the girl in Minneapolis."

She disappeared before I could respond. An ominous quiet left in her wake, and I listened for a moment to the groans of the pines twisting in the wind above. My eyes were drawn upward to the dark sky.

Sitting, I balanced the box on my knees. Checking my shields, I pulled them in tighter before hovering my hands over the box. *Well, here goes nothing.*

Cobalt-blue light seared my eyes as it streamed upward. Beams of brilliant blue shot in every direction, creating daylight in the dark night. The magic burst from the box, slamming me on my back.

Oh, shit!

That was my last thought before darkness interceded.

Somewhere awareness trickled in, my fingertips touching the damp earth beneath me. A pulse thrummed upward like tiny threads connecting me to the ground. Opening my eyes, vibrant blue fibers traveled out to the trees and beyond. Much like an intricate root system, the threads continued past the clearing to each tree as small animals scurried to the underbrush.

A timid rabbit, heart racing as his nose twitched. It sniffed the empty air as it led me to another strand, following an owl soaring above, sharp eyes scouring for his next meal. Farther out, I became aware of the cottage, Rowan, Amy, and Matthew. Threads linked them to each other, and to me. A web of beautiful light overlapped all things.

The layers within the realms became visible. *This would have been helpful with Water.* My realm was woven with this one and several others I hadn't been aware of until now.

Each layer, each strand, contained its own song. I heard a beautiful reverence of notes strung together, placing everything perfectly within the web. Each soul was a bright light tucked in the layers, joining in intricate ways almost impossible to see.

How was this possible? How could I not be aware of this? Suddenly, floating hundreds of miles in the sky, a vibrant blue network became visible, binding everything and everyone together.

Overcome by a sense of harmony, I was aware of the union of all things as one. Pleasure rippled through my body as I followed each fiber like a note of a song coming together during the crescendo of a masterful piece of music.

The feeling abruptly ended when I came upon several dark threads disintegrating into a void of nothing. The absence of the beautiful web brought me a sense of nauseating disease. The murky black void lured me toward it, and my own fear sent me hurling even faster.

As I got closer, realization struck me. An inner acknowledgment informed me what this absence of nothing was. Sick dread filled me, and I consciously pulled myself to the forest floor.

Vomit came rushing from my mouth as I sat up, rendering myself to all fours. In utter exhaustion, I laid back down, sweat prickling my brow as the cool evening air settled across my skin. Deep breaths helped calm the intense nausea and I vowed not to throw up again. Closing my eyes, I rested my hands on my forehead. I heard a soft crunching sound in the distance until paws stepped across my body.

"Is there a reason you are on—Ew. Is that . . . vomit?" Jax

sniffed the air and a horrified, disgusted look filled his cat face.

"Do you mind not stepping on me?" I groaned as he took a few more pointed steps before getting off me.

"So, the Astra Flaris."

Surprise made me fly up to my elbows so fast intense nausea delayed me from communicating. I put my hand to my mouth, then took a few uneven breaths.

"Do not vomit on me," the cat demanded. I wanted to roll my eyes at him, but I didn't have the energy.

"How do you know about the Astra Flaris?" I managed in between breaths.

"I know everything, remember? I just can't tell you about it." He picked up a paw and began licking it and drawing it over his ear.

"What? Please tell me you are kidding me right now." I sat forward, yelling at the cat.

He blinked slowly. *"I have told you this."*

"But . . . but this . . . you could've told me—"

"No," he said, exasperated. *"I have clear rules."*

"Rules?" Irritation prickled my voice as I pulled my knees up. "Astra Flaris. Speak now, fur-face," I demanded through clenched teeth.

"Sheesh." He rubbed his paw over his ear again. *"Your grandmother retrieved the Astra Flaris as a fail-safe for you. An ace in the hole, if you will."*

My eyes tightened. "So far, all it has created is vomit."

"You understand, then? What it is?"

"I . . ." Fading off, I thought for a moment. Did I understand? Swallowing hard, I nodded. This didn't mean I knew how to use it, but none of this had come with an instruction manual.

"Then let's go get Fire." Jax stood, turning away from me.

"Wait, what?" I scrambled to my feet, nausea rolling over me.

"We need to hurry."

"Where are we going?"

"Back to the cottage, of course. You need Rowan's help."

Grumbling a litany of dirty, mean words at my cat as he disappeared, I realized my plan just got shot to hell and I was sure no one cared.

Back at the cottage, an uproar ensued about me leaving the house unattended. During the arguing, Jax reminded me not to share anything about the Astra Flaris. Jaw clenched, I crossed my arms, glaring at the little douche nugget.

"We must leave now. Rowan, Aislynn. Now. There are some time constraints."

More arguments were made from Riona, but the questions were interrupted by a light knock on the door.

"What on earth? Who would be here now?" I exclaimed, taking note of the hour. When I cautiously opened the door, I was greeted by a deep-sea-colored cloak covering long blonde hair.

"Oh good, I am not too late." Ailianna stepped in past me, my face an open fish mouth.

"I am so sorry for my late visit." She slid the hood around her shoulders before wrapping her hands under the cloak. "But, Aislynn, it is my vision. You must go, as Jax insisted. This is the only opportunity if you want to secure the element." Ailianna's eyes were soft, and her discomfort was palpable.

"I would have never come if it wasn't important." Her pleading gaze met mine, then drifted to Riona.

"Of course," I relented, giving her a small hug, realizing how much I missed her gentle presence.

Finally, everyone came to an agreement. Riona, Ailianna, and Amy would stay. Matthew, Rowan and I would go. Jax, well . . . who knew what the hell he would do? I refused to talk to him. *The little asshole.* Before leaving, Amy gave me a nod and pulled me into the hallway.

"My bad juju senses are pinging like the slot machine that keeps paying out." Amy's eyes narrowed. "Be careful. Like . . . don't trust anyone."

My eyes questioned her as my hands turned up.

"I don't freaking know! I am just telling you. Something is . . . wrong," Amy insisted in an agitated whisper. Over the years of our friendship, I had learned to trust her instincts more than my own. Of course, nothing could be simple, and I groaned. We hugged, promising I would kick ass.

48

It was strange to see an image which had only been described previously play out before me live. White velvet shrouded Seraphina paced in the snow. The bare orchard trees' wet bark stood out in contrast to all the stark white. Worry enveloped the waiting witch.

"You made it," she called to us once we were closer, relief washing over her face.

"Why didn't you just tell me?" I asked. My question received a knowing frown. "Never mind, never mind." My hand went up to stop any tirade about how she wasn't allowed.

Matthew nosed the snow in front of him. When he lifted his head, flakes of snow stuck to his nose. I pulled my arms inside my cloak to protect them from the bitter cold.

"Well?" Rowan demanded.

"As Fire was mine to hold all those years ago and that right was stolen from me, I feel it is my moral obligation to correct this wrong. Over the years I have waited, searching for ways to do so, and with you, Aislynn, I can be free at last." Seraphina's eyes closed and magic beamed. An iridescent glow opened next to her, reminding me of the fire loop.

"This portal will take you to the Realm of Hidden Shadows, where Fire is being kept. Please hurry. I cannot keep it open for very long." Her face was straining with the magic.

"The Realm of Hidden Shadows is not somewhere we should go," Rowan persisted in my head as Matthew whimpered next to him.

"We don't have a choice. Fire isn't going to come to us." I walked to the portal. The smashing sounds of energy balls suddenly sounded from behind us. *Freaking hell.* The magic pummeled Seraphina's shield. Her eyes were pleading as I grabbed Rowan's arm and threw us through the portal.

We slammed across rough ground, landing in a heap of limbs, human, and wolf. Recovering, we stood slowly, Matthew giving a full body shake of his silver fur. My eyes adjusted to the dim light giving way to the murky landscape.

The earth was rocky and dark, appearing like a barren lava field, but without a blue sky to showcase its beauty it felt desolate. A sinking swam through me, leaving my skin tingly. Rowan tossed a small ball of light above us, casting a white haze across the bleak terrain.

"We must be quick about this, Aislynn. The longer we are here, the more danger we are in," Rowan said in a quiet whisper. "The creatures who choose to reside in this realm are not ones we want to meet." He took my hand, pulling me forward. Rowan's fear was palpable, but I stalled, glancing at the dark surroundings.

"Creatures?" I squeaked. This place reminded me of the Upside Down in *Stranger Things*. An eerie flooding reached through every crevice of my being. "This place is giving me the creeps."

"Not so eager now, are we?" A whine puffed from Matthew's cheeks.

"What kind of creatures are we talking about?" I whispered, squeezing Rowan's hand. The small orb bobbed as we walked, keeping the pathway illuminated in shadowed light. "And what is this place?"

"The Realm of Hidden Shadows is between Hallervania and your realm, for those who choose to live in the in-between." Rowan's hand was warm in mine as he explained. "They are bound to no rules on this plane."

A disturbing crunching sounded to the right, sending Matthew's nose to the air as he sniffed cautiously. Guttural moans succumbed to silence, followed by thrashing through the brush. I pulled myself closer to Rowan.

"There is no Light here. Only Dark resides, the deepest of Dark magic, and those who bare their soul before it."

"What a shit hole. Why would anyone choose this?" The bleak surroundings scratched at my fear.

"They would say the same of you." Rowan's face was tight and wary as he met my gaze.

"How the hell are we going to find Fire in here?" I asked. Soft whispers in my ear sent my head darting to the left to the source of the sound. Strange words that didn't make sense poured into my head, and I strained to see through the murky shadows in front of me.

A silhouette moved through the trees and the shape of a woman emerged. Her pale skin and ebony hair contrasted one another in hideous opposition. She was frail at first glance, with an overly thin and bony body. Her eyes sunk deep into her face, which appeared slightly off kilter. Dark fragments of clothing hung over her awkward body, but her motion was silky and serene.

"You must take it." Her voice was a scratchy whisper.

Rowan shot out a hand to stop me from moving closer to her. "Who are you?" he questioned.

"It doesn't matter. You don't belong here. It doesn't belong here." She slithered closer in nonhuman movements.

"The element? Fire?" I asked, pushing past Rowan's arm. "Can you tell me where it is?" My head tilted, asking my questions in whispered tones. More deafening crashes and crunching could be heard in the distance, causing me to tremble before her.

"They will show you. Follow them." She pointed to the ground, which abruptly cascaded into movement. Squinting into the dim light, I tried to see what was on the ground.

Hundreds of black fuzzy creatures moved around us. Each one was the size of a baseball, round and fluffy. They shifted across the rocky terrain in waves of motion. I became torn between being creeped out and amused by their adorableness.

Bending down for a better look, one turned to me with giant woeful eyes, and I reached out my finger to touch it. The creature began a shivering and shaking as I got closer, trembling as its oversized eyes blinked. Rowan grabbed my hand with such fierceness I swung around behind him. He kicked the fuzzy little creature, sending it bouncing across the rocks.

"What the hell?" I roared as the woman grimaced in the shadows. "Why did you do that?"

"Do not touch the Cuddlers," Rowan warned.

"Cuddlers?"

I watched in horror as the black mass swarmed the harmed Cuddler, piling all around it. With impossible quickness, they ripped the body apart, consuming every trace of the small creature. My eyes went wide with shock. Rowan sighed in relief as the flurry of movement began again.

"Cuddlers are deceiving, appearing as everything they are not. They will look cute, cuddly or whatever else, when in reality they burrow into your body, consuming your very essence." He met my eyes with a sideways glance.

"Why the hell would you call them Cuddlers, then?" I snapped.

Rowan shrugged as Matthew growled at the creepy creatures. The tall, willowy woman pointed as the Cuddlers moved down the trail.

"Why can't we follow kittens? Or little tiny unicorns?" I muttered to myself. Rowan shook his head and pulled me forward to follow.

I tried to focus on their rhythm and how it reminded me of a swarm of birds traveling together as one entity. But their legs crawling and wiggling over each other made me tremble and shattered my beautiful bird illusion. The woman slithered back into the darkness, disappearing from view. The light bobbed along with the horde of Cuddlers. We followed the black mass in silence across the rough terrain, listening to the odd, sporadic sounds enveloping the darkness around us.

A soft tickle brushed against my arm, prompting alarm in my body then again across my face like silky spider threads ensnaring me into a web.

"Gahhh!" I rubbed and slapped at my skin to lessen the disturbing feeling as I freaked out in sporadic motion.

"Shhh!" Rowan hissed, then halted with his head cocked.

"What?" I said louder than I should, trying to calm the creepy heebie-jeebies feeling I had.

"It sounded like we were being followed." Rowan scanned our surroundings. Matthew sniffed, trailing where we had just walked, intermittent growls heaving from his frame. Eventually he padded back to us, and we resumed our terrifying trek. We walked for some time, the constant hum of whispers and crunches emanating from the surrounding darkness.

"What did you say?" Rowan asked.

"Me? I didn't say anything." I responded.

"No, not you. Matthew."

Matthew responded with a growl in a conversation I wasn't privy to. Rowan stopped and turned. Gleaming wolf eyes narrowed on Rowan. Matthew's shoulders dropped, and one paw padded forward as if to attack.

"What the hell is going on with you two?" Stepping between them, I put my hands up.

"He knows," Rowan said in my head.

"Knows what?" I wasn't about to have a secret conversation in a creepy realm of bullshit when soul-sucking black balls surrounded us.

"That I was there that night."

The words processed slowly, and I realized Rowan was referring to the night Matthew's family had been attacked. *Shit.*

"Matthew," I began, and dropped to my knees, wary of the Cuddlers. "I know, too. And I am sorry, but it isn't what you think. This place is bad news! It wants there to be discourse among us, but we can't fight now." His eyes met mine and his snout dropped. "You can chew off his arm later, okay?"

"Excuse me?" Rowan asked. My head flipped around with a glare as Matthew whined.

"We need to keep moving, before those little creep balls eat our faces." I gestured down at the poofs. "Can we keep going? Please?"

The two of them seemed to come to some sort of agreement as Matthew turned and continued our journey down the path, the Cuddlers resuming their blaze of movement.

Finally, the wave of creepy creatures flooded to a stop surrounding a tree. It reminded me of the Tree of Elements, but its form was inverted and more dead, if that was possible. An ear-piercing scream rang out, and my hands clamped over my ears. The sound was a deafening tone that made my brain tremble.

"Another benefit of the Cuddlers!" Rowan yelled in my head over the high pitch noise. *"The element must be here!"*

Matthew howled, as if trying to drown out the awful sound. My face contorted in an ugly grimace against the sound as I allowed my hands to fall away from my ears, trying to reach for elemental magic. Focusing on the hum in my fingers instead of the sound, I pulled the tethers of Air magic swirling through the trees. The magic finally quieted the sound.

A deep howling from behind sent us swirling around searching for the source. Beady crimson eyes glowed in the distance, revealing a black frame of fur that resembled a wolf. It raised wet lips to unveil angular, jagged teeth while snapping unusually large jaws.

My magic sputtered to a stop in response to the hideous beast before us, my focus interrupted by fear. Rowan nudged me to continue in spite of the horrific sight staring us down. My fingertips strained to reconnect to the magic, smearing throughout the murky realm. I kept my attention on the Cuddlers and the wolf-monster-thing.

The massive beast charged forward, and Rowan threw an energy ball at it, sending Matthew in a fit of ferocious barks and snarls. The rocky earth trembled beneath our feet, and crevices broke open around us. Fissures cracked with thunderous booms as the terrain separated further apart.

Heat ripples began rising from the splintering earth, separating each of us onto our own islands of Hell. There was but darkness on all sides of me, and the dead tree at my back. The wolf leapt across, throwing Rowan to the ground. Matthew followed in a flash of silver fur, attacking the wolf from behind.

The noise was unbearable, and I considered using magic to stop the attack, but I couldn't risk hitting Rowan or Matthew by mistake. Fire roared, surrounding me in a wall of flames, the ear pinching screeches of the Cuddlers grating on my resolve.

The black wolf careened through the fiery wall landing, in front of me. I stumbled several steps backward, toward the edge of the jagged rock. Dropping its abnormal head, the wolf stalked nearer with terrifying snaps of its teeth. Rowan shouted through the roar of flames, and I sent a fiery blast of air to push the wolf backward.

Flames pulsed upward again, and the magic swirled through the air, slamming into me. Flying back, I landed against the dead tree which the Cuddlers surrounded. Groans escaped me, and pain settled in my limbs. My eyes darted, watching for the wolf and his inevitable attack. Instead, a black swarm of Cuddlers gravitated toward me.

Ah, shit. The Cuddlers are going to suck out my soul. The creepy mass of black inched closer in a commotion of movement, and I scrambled to stand, blasting them with a wave of water magic. Cuddlers bounced backward in the surge of water. A sickening sound filled the air as they burned through the flames. Their ear-curdling screams rang out, making me cringe. Fire magic streamed, and I allowed it to surge through me.

Every nerve sizzled with fire, sending ripples of magic coursing over the desolate landscape. The darkness flared with bright ribbons of red, illuminating the invisible world of barren trees and jutted rocks in flashes.

Red tendrils of light scoured through the fissures, creating a misty radiance. It drew toward me as the element settled into the amulet. Fire couldn't be contained in this dark chaotic realm, the magic here too depleted to sustain its vitality. It needed life. Something to thrive within.

Already familiar with my presence, it easily flowed to me. Gradually, the murky red dimmed, and the wicked darkness resumed.

In retaliation, the wolf shot through the flames, landing among the wave of Cuddlers. It snarled and snapped its uneven jaws, grabbing several Cuddlers at once. The wolf pierced them with its massive teeth and tossed them to the side. The remaining Cuddlers began to tremble, instantly engrossing the wolf in a fury of black motion.

The piercing screams of the monster wolf shredded my courage as I watched the horrific scene in front of me. The Cuddlers finished their consumption, and I feared they would continue with me. Instead, they disappeared into the crevices of rock in a flurry of sinking black.

Magic dissipated, leaving the land cold and barren and through the dim light I turned to see Matthew nudging Rowan's unmoving body. *Shit!*

A weak whine melted in Matthew's throat as he looked to me. Leaping across the broken shards of rock, the skin on my palms ripped open as I skidded across the sharp surface. On some level, I was aware of my jeans being torn at the knees. I scrambled to Rowan's side, fingers shaking as I palpated for a pulse. There was nothing. I moved my fingers again, searching.

There. The thready beat under my fingertips sent relief rushing over me.

"He's going to be okay," I said aloud to Matthew and myself. I put a hand on Rowan's shoulder and one on Matthew. Without a thought, I pulled us into traveling through the dimensions.

49

We landed in a heap on Riona's floor. The groaning that issued from each of us made me realize I really needed to be better at this teleporting other people business. Riona, Ailianna, and Amy fell to our sides with questions.

"We were in the Realm of Hidden Shadows," I explained quickly. "He's hurt, I think by the wolf, but I don't know. There were Cuddlers, too." I looked pleadingly at Riona as shock filled her eyes.

"Hidden Shadows?" Riona mumbled and prodded at Rowan before moving to her cabinet of magical remedies. Ailianna was quietly shrouded in worry.

"What the hell are Cuddlers?" Amy questioned.

"Demented Furbies from Hell in a barren wasteland," I said.

Matthew bounded out of the room, I assumed to shift back into being human. He had gotten weird about doing it in front of Amy.

Riona began her magic healing, moving around Rowan, lifting his shirt to reveal deep gashes across his abdomen. I noticed her try to disguise the shock from her expression. Drawing myself closer to him, the amulet swung out, filled with yellow, blue, and red swirls of color. Ailianna sighed with relief.

"At least you retrieved the element," Riona said, turning back to Rowan's unconscious body.

"Barely." I resumed my gaze upon Rowan's body, taking his hand in mine. My heart raged to a place I wasn't prepared for, and it occurred to me I wouldn't be able to bury my feelings much longer. The elements weren't worth this . . . losing anyone else. Losing him.

"Aislynn, your hands are bleeding," Amy said. She reached down, pulling my hands into hers.

"Oh." I didn't want to take my eyes off Rowan.

"Come on, let me clean this up." Amy helped me off the floor. "Geez, your knees, too?"

Amy sat me on the bench and gathered supplies. I busied myself with assessing my shredded hands. Skin peeled back and black goo seeped from the edges of the wounds. I assumed that was an after effect of being in a realm of Dark evilness. I was brought back to reality by Amy dragging warm towels over the open sores on my knees, wiping away bits of debris. A new level of wincing occurred when she reached my hands.

"Alright, Nurse Ratchet! That freaking hurts!" I tried tugging my hands away from her tight grip.

Mumbles spurted from Rowan's mouth, sending me to the floor in a rush. Amy swore as I ripped my hands out of hers.

"Are you okay?" I asked Rowan.

"Mm," he groaned as he sat up in slow movements.

"Did you get the element?" His voice was dry and scratchy. My eyes lit up as I pulled up the amulet, the colors glinting in the light.

"Good." He winced as he touched his abdomen with supreme gentleness.

"I am not done yet, but you will be fine," Riona said. Rowan nodded, carefully making his way to his feet.

"The wolf was Viego's work." Rowan sat on the bench, pulling me with him. "Let Amy finish." He flinched as Riona continued her magic and pushed me toward Amy and her mean fingers.

"Aislynn, you are not going to like this, but you must go again." Ailianna stood, her voice all but a whisper.

"What? Why?" I asked as Amy scraped the raw skin on my hands.

"She can't! She needs to be healed first," Amy sneered.

"She must." Ailianna folded her hands in front of her, eyes begging.

"What do you know?" I huffed out my breath.

"Viego and—"

Ailianna's voice cut off, implying the name she would not say aloud. *She knows about Zarah.* Right now, there were two Seers trying to out-see each other. I let my head fall to the table in frustration.

"I have seen things, Aislynn. Things that cannot happen." Ailianna's voice was full of distress in my head. Images flooded through my mind, again, reminding me of what Aeolus had shown me:

Burnt mountains, devastation through the lands, and this time my attention settled on many bodies. I saw the lifeless forms Amy, Matthew, Riona, and Rowan. All of them. Everyone.

My eyes flew open, landing on Ailianna. Her face was solemn under the weight of the visions.

Shit.

"You must stop him, Aislynn." Ailianna's words were a mere whimper now.

I looked around the room at my friends. I couldn't let them die. I had the Astra Flaris. That meant I had to hold on to the hope of an ancient magic that came with no instructions.

My hand rested at my forehead to shield the bright light. I stood, waiting. The lame plan I had, one in which I insisted on being bait, was not my brightest moment. I assumed Zarah would be watching, so I thought I should expose myself and wait. It would only be a matter of time, as Viego had diligently trained her to be tuned to my magic.

Any second now. I gazed across the grove of aspens. I had teleported myself several mountain ranges away from Riona's cottage.

Viego appeared down the hill from me.

"Aislynn." His mouth twitched, settling into a frown. "You are becoming quite the enigma, always surprising me. Perhaps I shouldn't have been hard on Daragon." He folded his arms behind him as he casually weaved his way through the trees. My eyes narrowed watching him.

"Come on," I snipped. "This is all just fun and games for you, isn't it? After two thousand years, this must be exciting," I taunted. He responded with a warm smile and nod, as if we were talking of the weather and not the future of magic for all kind.

Point for the crazy folk.

"Perhaps," he replied, his voice contemplative. "But I do have objectives, and you seem to continue to complicate them." He barely glanced up as he walked closer. "I will have to take the elements back, you know." Disappointment settled across his mouth.

"Uh. Yeah. That's not going to happen." I shook my head in a gentle movement as a grimace formed and my teeth slid across each other.

Head tilted, he looked up slowing, his pace casual. With an intense stare, his hand flew up, two fingers flipping the air. A horrid cracking from afar erupted as an entire pine tree, roots torn and full of dirt, flew through the trees toward me.

My hands shot up, pushing the tree away. It landed with a deafening crash, the aspen closest to me taking the hit. A stream of fire raged toward me next, and I shielded myself with a bubble of water. The earth below me scarred black with ash as I walked through the fire unharmed.

"You have improved." Pleasure rippled through Viego's face, and it made me sick. I tried to steady my bouncing foot, waiting for him to move closer before giving the sign. He paused as if he knew the steps of our plan.

Come on, I insisted, trying to coax him with my thoughts. A smile, gross and irritating, beamed at me. I wanted to punch him.

"Is it"—he looked around—"about here"—he took a few more steps—"that you want me?"

An endless stream of bad language flooded my thoughts. *So much for that plan.* Everything happened quickly as Rowan materialized behind him, and Viego nodded with a knowing smile. Then Zarah appeared.

Standing among the trees with the sun behind her, she seemed to glow before us. Her long hair was held in braids, which were twisted and knotted into a large bun. She wore tight pants and sturdy boots paired with a tank top, but what I found most odd were the sunglasses perched on her nose. Zarah looked as though she had been plucked right from my realm.

My steps faltered with the thought, and she swirled her hand, producing a ribbon of blue energy that shot toward me. She smirked as the whip of light trailed millimeters from my skin.

Rowan stumbled a half step toward her. "Zarah?" His voice was unsteady as recognition overcame him. Viego's eyes bounced from him to me.

"Ah . . . you didn't tell him," Viego said to me in feigned shock. "I am not sure that was a wise choice." He clucked his tongue, scolding me.

Rowan's gaze shifted from me to Zarah, and I could feel his heart breaking as he realized what she'd become because he never saved her.

Shit.

Viego took advantage of the moment by throwing magic at Rowan, a dark spear of certain death hurling at him. I responded with my hands shifting the magic away from Rowan before he had the opportunity to do the same. He stumbled awkward steps toward Zarah, consumed by her presence. Concern rippled through me as he reached out hesitantly, even though he was still ten feet away.

"Zarah, I am so sorry. I tried to save you, to look for you after they took you." His clear blue eyes pleaded with the little girl he tried to save all those years ago.

Zarah's eyebrows shot upward, her face contorting

into disgust. "Are you kidding me?" She pulled her sunglasses down, revealing deep lavender eyes. The distance between them shortened. "I should be thanking you, shouldn't I?" Her voice was sharp, full of knives. She twisted magic in her fingertips as laughter reached the edges of her eyes.

She's completely batshit crazy. My attention cut to Viego, and I noticed a green glimmer at his neck. A necklace, much like mine, but shorter and smaller, sat at the hollow of his throat. My heart sunk when I realized he held the Earth element. *Dammit. Dammit. Dammit.* Our plan officially became screwed.

Apparently, Viego had given up hiding the elements and resorted to personally holding Earth. Perhaps this was a sign; maybe he believed me a more formidable enemy after all. My lips pulled to one side as I considered my next move. On a whim, I allowed elemental magic to sing through me. Air, Fire, and Water wrapped together as a familiar friend, and I embraced Plan B.

The clouds began to build above us, wind cutting across the top of the trees as the sky darkened and rain drove to the earth in hard pellets.

"Rowan!" I shouted in his head. *"Get over here. Forget about Zarah!"* I needed him helping me, not worrying about her crazy ass. He gave one last hopeful glance toward her before teleporting next to me. *Thank God.* Mostly I didn't want him to get hurt, and I certainly didn't trust her.

The dark clouds rolled off the mountain tops, and much like when I was seven, I focused on them building. The fear was absent this time. Instead, the control that resonated through me made my mouth twitch in satisfaction. Hands flying up toward the sky, I pulled down a cyclone of air. A tornado twisted through the trees, devastation assaulting the earth.

"Aislynn . . ." Rowan's voice was hesitant as his arm reached for mine.

"It's fine, I have it." Confident, I rolled my hand in a fluid motion, moving the tornado toward Viego and Zarah.

With a watchful eye, Viego turned his hands, rolling the earth under him. I widened my stance to hold balance through the earthquake movement, gritting my teeth to control all the magic. The tornado edged closer to them, wind whipping through the grass. I managed a glance in their direction and was caught off guard by the amusement I found on their faces. There wasn't a trickle of fear within either of them.

My confidence was shattered into little pieces as my body tried to hold the weight of intense magic in my hands. Zarah pushed her hand out in front, then swirled it over her head, creating a bubble of protection around the two of them. She smirked again as one eyebrow cocked upward.

Viego's casual stance allowed his pride to be visible once again. Deep pools of black pierced my eyes before he squinted at Rowan. Worry invaded my senses and Rowan dropped to his knees with gut wrenching screams.

As my attention switched back to Rowan, I released the magic. The tornado immediately dissipated back to the sky above. Tortured by whatever hell Rowan was being subjected to, I focused the magic back on Viego.

How can I break through Zarah's bubble of protection and her twisted form of Dark magic?

An idea slipped into my mind. Using Rowan's tortured screams as my source of determination, I whipped magic in my grasp. Concentrating on Zarah's bubble and the ground beneath them, I accumulated moisture from the ground, pulling it from the trees and the earth. A tiger took shape behind them. I leaned down, pretending to help Rowan, but my attention was only on the tiger.

"Stay with me, Rowan," I whispered through gritted teeth. Twisting the magic, the massive beast of water slashed out, cutting the magic with an unexpected fury.

As a result, Rowan was instantly released from the magical hell and slumped to the ground, gulping huge breaths of air. Water enveloped Zarah and Viego in a tourniquet, squeezing the air away from them.

Shock drizzled over Zarah's face as her mouth bobbed open and closed, searching for the air that didn't exist. Her lavender eyes filled with panic as she struggled against the magic. With my attention on Viego, I used water to pull the necklace away from him.

A whirlpool of water spun and levitated the element off his throat. His hands remained locked at his sides, unable to help him. Without warning, Rowan rushed through the magical sphere of water, throwing Zarah to the ground.

"What are you doing?" My scream was garbled into groans when his glassy, cool eyes met mine. *Ah, hell. He's been bewitched by Crazy Pants.* Elemental necklace forgotten, I shifted the magic back toward them.

"Aislynn, don't hurt her!" Rowan propelled himself in front of her, extending his arm. "She is not a threat to us."

Behind him, Zarah smiled nastily. Rowan glanced back to her, and her expression shifted into one of fear and uncertainty. *Oh, for hell's sake.*

"Please!" he called to me again.

Anger sliced its way into me. Zarah was a lying piece of shit, and I knew it. Rowan, however, didn't, obviously under some spell of hers. *I hope.* Or perhaps he believed he could save her, which was asinine. *There is no saving that.*

"Please, help me." Zarah's words trembled, her voice a mere whimper. Magic roared through me as she spewed her lies. Everything Rowan embodied, the warrior and protector, stood defending the wrong side.

"She is evil, Rowan! Can't you see?" My jaw pulsated as my teeth hammered against each other. I continued to hold Viego in water magic.

"She is only a child," Rowan's body jolted forward, generating distance between her and I, as if I was the bad one. How could he not see?

No child existed in the girl standing behind him. I saw the deception glimmering in her eyes as she cowered. Rowan's betrayal was an acute slash to my being as I watched him protect the very one who had led every attack we managed to live through.

Was there something else going on? Something I was not aware of? An onslaught of questions raced through my mind. Zarah grasped Rowan's arm in fear. *Fear of me.* In my mind, his hand clasped around her fingertips, affection, care, concern enveloping between them. *Does he love her?* He cared so much for her, and after all these years trying to find her, at last he had.

My head slowly shook, protesting the thoughts. *He doesn't love her; he doesn't even know her. She's a child.* Confusion pummeled my mind as I tried to keep hold of the elemental magic in my grip.

The two of them morphed in front of me, Zarah now older. Her head rested on Rowan's shoulder, love radiating around them as her icy glare held. Passion swarmed as she reached up, kissing him. I blinked against the image, forcing it from my view. Then, once again, the cowering girl whimpered behind Rowan.

"I don't need you." Rowan's voice cut through my mind like a knife. Without warning, my stomach knotted, leaving sick panic in its wake. My magic faltered, seeping away from me as I processed the images. Zarah laughed, deep and sultry, as she held Rowan.

"She is pathetic. You don't want her." Zarah's hand slid down his face and he smiled at her. Kissing again, their hands roaming, I turned away. I didn't want to see this. I couldn't. I—

Jealousy and anger rolled into a coiled snake within me and magic spurted out. Streams of fire shot unexpectedly from my fingertips, searing the earth below me in jagged streaks of black.

"Aislynn! What are you doing?" Rowan's disgust grated my emotions and more fire bolted out. As rage boiled over my skin, I met his gaze. Worried, fearful eyes met mine. Rapidly blinking, reality transformed before me. No longer did I see Rowan making out with Zarah, but Rowan's concern and confusion with my actions.

Viego.

This was his magic. Mental mind games and illusions had created false realities inside my mind. *Fuck.* The rage seethed, and I tilted my head to the side as I focused on him. Finally, clarity rolled through. He used my fears and my emotions against me, playing me like some pawn. *Again.*

Fury rocked me, and my hands trembled at my sides. Something broke. I felt the crack, a slow fissure at first, but then it careened open like a burst dam. An imaginary line I had created so long ago out of fear, the line that held me back, kept me and magic in check, disintegrated.

My arms came up on their own accord and streamed toward Viego. Water rippled across, forming a siphon of energy, lifting and pulling the element hanging at his neck. *I want the element.*

Wrenching with magic, the chain broke as it strained against him and came flying to me. Simply taking what was mine to have, Earth was finally in my grasp. This time when the ground rolled beneath us, it was by my hand.

A version of shock cascaded down Viego's face. In complete disbelief at losing the Earth element, he reached for the now-empty space at his throat. Flipping two fingers in front of me, a beautiful aspen ripped from the earth. It flew in front of him, landing at his feet. I moved closer to him.

"No more games." I didn't recognize my voice. It now held a tone that chewed through bone.

"Aislynn!" Rowan called from behind me. "The elements—" But he broke off.

It was useless to continue.

50

You will pay for everything you have done." My voice resonated through the trees. All four elements ultimately together in the amulet melded into a harmonic tone, bleeding ancient magic through my bones.

And I welcomed it.

I sauntered down the hill toward Viego, my fingers trailing to the sides and whipping the wind. The forest floor darkened as the clouds above shifted into heavy lead sinking down on us. The elements danced through my eyes in colorful swirls of magic. I disregarded Rowan's incessant screaming and filtered the sound to the edges of my mind.

Viego's face shifted. I saw his new strategies already forming, still believing he held the upper hand. The wind thrashed the trees around me, flexing to the magic I held. The power sang as the earth readjusted to the presence of ancient elemental magic, whole once again.

Viego moved, disappearing before my eyes.

Turning quickly to Rowan and Zarah behind me, a blur of movement raced through the trees. Rowan's eyes met mine for the quickest moment before the magic hit him. His body skidded across the ground, contorting in impossible ways before coming to a sudden stop. Throat clenching closed, I screamed.

"ROWAN!" His name was drawn out in a frantic cry, my own voice unrecognizable once again. With all the power I held, Viego found my weakest link and simply cut.

A small smirk flitted across Viego's mouth, and he disappeared. Zarah watched as I fell to Rowan's side.

"You just keep disappointing me. I keep wanting more from you, a formidable enemy, but you are pathetic," she snipped, repulsed by my presence.

Anger flooded me, and I blasted magic at her, sending her tumbling through the trees. Checking Rowan, I feared the worst. This time when I placed my fingers on his neck, I could not find a pulse. Mouth dry, my throat burned as dread sunk down to my belly. Fingers shaking, I searched again. My lip quivered under my teeth's grasp and my heart tore at my chest wall.

Touching his shoulder, with gut wrenching hope, I sent his body to Riona, praying she would save him. Certain Rowan arriving in a heap on the floor would freak them out, I could almost hear Amy's screaming. But I saved my focus for Viego.

Prying myself to stand, aware he wasn't far, I searched the mountain valleys. At the crest of a small peak, his silhouette was just visible. Clenching my teeth, I disappeared. Reappearing on the opposite crest, a valley of trees between us, I summoned the magic within me.

"Back again for more?" Viego's voice trailed through my mind.

A stream of green light arched across the valley, reaching for Viego. It met a flash of vivid black, cracking the air like a whip. Sparks of black exploded like fireworks, illuminating the cloudy, dark sky. I shielded myself with a barrier of water and the sparks singed to the ground in fiery embers.

Magic engulfed the open space in shards of color and thunderous sound. Each of us cascaded constant spells over the terrain. Trees ripped from their roots flew down the ravine, leaving gouges in the forest floor. Viego disappeared again, reappearing lower down the mountain, and I followed, finding him at the edge of a lake nestled between the trees.

A surge of water formed behind him, and I imagined a tidal wave smashing down on top of him, crushing his soul. But before the wave solidified, he threw a sphere of indigo light burning into my shoulder. The force of his magic whipped my body around. My scream tore through the air as I collapsed in pain. The water, waiting my instruction, crashed down and flooded the shores.

"Aislynn, you have been entertaining, but nothing more." The water trickled away from him as he stepped toward me. Zarah emerged behind him, and he glanced back with a satisfied smile.

"Perhaps we will find you a new toy, my darling." He spoke to Zarah with regret as she crossed her arms, contempt sitting in a snide line across her face.

Agony ripped through my arm as I pushed myself back to my feet, sloshing in muddy water. I would stand to face my death, as that would be what came next. Daring to glance down at my shoulder, I expected charred black skin, but I found nothing. My shirt was torn, but there were no marks, burns, or anything else.

Eyebrows furrowed, I flexed and extended my wrist, elbow, and moved my shoulder. The pain was almost gone. *What the hell?*

My attention shot to Viego, expecting another blow. The magic was sitting within his fingertips, but everything slowed as my thoughts rampaged.

Viego had lived two thousand years, elongating his life with his family magic, living beyond his capacity because he used time magic illegitimately. Just like at the lake house, magic and time were falling out of sync. Seraphina's words burned into my mind.

Balance.

Then there was Tristan's answer to my bizarre question: *Could you freeze something forever?*

No. Magic has a limit; time must always continue. Catch up, if you will.

With the elements now stripped from his possession, his magic was failing. Time was failing.

And he didn't have a clue.

The inky black cloud of magic drove toward me in relentless destruction. Its only objective was to consume and eliminate. I could see it, feel it, as the magic moved toward me. Perhaps I would die. I was certain it was possible, if I allowed that Dark consumption to slide through me. Instead, my arms jutted out to my sides as the cloud rolled over me.

From the outside, it probably appeared as if I was a complete goner, but instead I resided through his magic. From my place at its heart, I began to pick it apart. The evilness, the ruthlessness, and the vile decay of Viego's magic flooded past. A part of me grieved for him, and what he had done to himself.

A *very* small part.

The four elements swirling, the ancient magic merging together for Light, the amulet throbbed at my solar plexus. Pulsating magic through me and I made the decision.

The moment to embrace my last secret. My skin flushed, sending a surge of tingles through my extremities, preparation for what was to come. I had no idea if it would work, what would happen, but his nauseating Dark magic swarmed around me. And I had a choice.

Die within his evil abhorrent magic. Or embrace the unknown.

Inhaling, I used it then. My final gift from my grandmother. I embraced *love*.

The Astra Flaris rushed into me, transcending every singular emotion or life experience I ever had until this precise moment. A pure enlightened awareness struck like lightning. Every choice my grandmother had made, I made, Viego made, brought us to this place. There was no escaping destiny.

A beautiful dance leading to this moment. The luminous cobalt light of the Astra Flaris sent his dark vile magic back to the earth. I could have been stunning from the outside, I believed, but I stood gleaming within the magic. Bright color filled my consciousness and I understood the Astra Flaris then.

The beautiful, blue flame was not a magic to wield. It wasn't a sword, a stone, or a weapon. *It's knowledge.* It was the pure awareness of all things. The truth. The reason. Our purpose.

Viego's mouth slackened as his thoughts spilled through my mind. *How has she escaped my magic? What is this?*

How can this be? His hands dropped, and he stared at his open palms with empty disillusion.

"You don't understand any of this, Viego. Not the elements. Not the magic." I took slow steps toward him. The earth was uneven below my feet where his magic had left an ugly trail.

Viego's head shook in disbelief. He didn't understand how I stood before him; his magic intended to kill, to destroy. His mind was wild and chaotic, just as the earth around him. It was scarred with magical destruction, trees uprooted, with deep, ragged trenches dug through the ground, mimicking his soul. The damage was visible for anyone to see if they only looked. They merely had to remove themselves from the fear he projected.

"You have misused magic from the beginning, and there must be balance. Magic is not yours for the taking. Everything you have done shall be returned."

Close to him now, I could see my eyes reflected in his. Vibrant purple swirled, and behind the reflection, fear settled in his own gaze. The thoughts barreling through his mind gnarled into black, soulless magic.

I touched him then, my index finger meeting the center of his chest with the smallest, slightest pressure. The Astra Flaris plunged into him.

Viego's face distorted into a mixture of shock and horror as magic feasted on him to find balance. His screams were almost unbearable, but I stood watching as his body contorted before me. Zarah's screams melded and harmonized with his in a nefarious song of terror.

Viego's face aged before us, years and years of time magic catching up and seeking revenge. Deep wrinkles and sagging skin caressed his face. His hair turned from inky onyx to a deep gray, and finally faded rapidly to vibrant white before disintegrating on his head. The skin around his mouth opened into a gaping hole of cloudy darkness. It began tearing at the corners, becoming wider as a plume of black shot upward.

Viego's body tightened, shriveling upon itself as his skin turned colorless, then translucent as it constricted against his bones. The terror continued as his body turned as hard as granite, wrenching him into a deformed, twisted shape. A tortured statue of what was once Viego crumbled into ash, falling to the earth in a heap of gray dust.

51

A sharp sizzling crackled the air. Zarah's magic burst from her fingertips in furious rage. Bolts of lightning struck the ground around us and I tried not to outwardly cringe at the electrical charge. Arms trembling, her face twisted into a distorted form as emotions cycled through her body.

"You destroyed everything!" Vehemence pounded each of her words.

Viego had radiated a Darkness and everything it encompassed, but after thousands of years, his ego led him astray. He didn't believe anyone was capable of stopping him, and that led to his demise. Zarah was different; I could see it now as her eyes shimmered a wickedness Viego never touched.

"Magic has no place in our world. It destroys everything." The wind whipped her braids across her body, like snakes striking empty air. The thought occurred to me that she didn't mind using the very magic she objected to. Perhaps she couldn't control it; she just needed to feed the darkness coiled inside her. My thoughts were interrupted by a loud hissing on the ground next me. Jax.

"Hey, you're still alive."

"Seriously?" I snapped back. *"Is Rowan okay?"*

His response was just another angry hiss, and the avoidance concerned me. Silence rippled as Zarah stared at Jax. Apparently, they were having a conversation to which I was not privy. Jax's tail whipped in a thrashing movement.

"You may have recovered the elements and restored magic for Light as intended," Zarah said with disdain. "But there is something your Goddesses, Gods, and that damn *cat* of yours didn't see." She took several long strides in our direction. "Me." She brought her finger to her chest, eyes defiant and dark.

"Oookay." My voice held every ounce of snark it owned. It probably wasn't the best idea to further piss off crazy pants, but I couldn't help myself. Besides, I was glowing in a high of ancient magic.

"You know nothing, Aislynn. You have been blind, manipulated, and used from the beginning to do their bidding. *His* bidding." Her head jutted toward Jax.

What the hell does that mean?

Zarah's eyes glinted as she watched me process her words. "I will change everything."

A guttural growl escaped Jax's small, furry body, followed by a violent spitting hiss.

"Don't, *cat,*" she spat.

The exchange confused me and set my nerves on edge. I pointed back and forth between the two of them. "What are you talking about?"

Zarah's mouth sat in a firm line, anger grinding on her teeth as she glared at my cat. Contemplative, she swirled her hands around her body. Purple trails of magic arched through the air and images slammed through my mind.

I saw the Earth Realm, my home, destroyed. Minneapolis was devastated, and other large cities I instantly recognized were burning, disheveled ruins. Magic was being abused and utilized openly to cause complete ruin.

My stomach rolled as the visions came faster than I could handle, overwhelming me with a relentless stream of destruction. Fear and desolation trailed, then Zarah finally gave back my sight.

Lurching forward, my hands landing on my knees, I tried to breathe through vomiting. *I refuse to vomit, yet again.* Tired of being used as a magical pin cushion, I blasted my hands out, throwing magic at Zarah. The result was only a slight stumble of imbalance, which irritated me further.

"I will end it all." Her voice grated in eerie tones, echoing her promise. She held a steady gaze until she vanished.

"Whatever, crazy ass!" Jax snarked after she disappeared.

Palms pressing on the tops of my legs, again, I took several uneven breaths. Zarah scared the shit out of me; she had been a level of psycho I wasn't adequately prepared for. Jax caught my eye, making me wonder what his real story was.

He sat licking his paw, completely unaware. Or was he? I didn't know. The amulet hung down against my chest, glistening with swirling color. I did it. I reclaimed the elements for Light. Slowly standing, I realized it was about time to find out if Rowan was dead. My stomach knotted at the thought.

Silence greeted me at the cottage when I arrived. Magical ingredients were strewn across the kitchen, and black smudges scarred the wood planks, magnifying the sinking feeling the quietness created. Tracing my fingertips across the table, my voice stuttered as I called out.

"Hello?"

The floor creaked under my next step. *Maybe they had to leave for help.* But where would they go? I thought of Ailianna and disappeared. The same deafening silence met my ears when I arrived at her home.

Shit. Pushing open the door, I glanced around, yelling and waiting for a response. I stalked around the house, then past the circle as wind rustled the leaves and rippled air across the grass. No one was to be found.

"They are waiting for you."

Turning quickly, I saw Seraphina standing behind me, a smile on her lips.

She turned away. "Come."

Following her down the trail, I soon realized we were traveling. Before I knew it, we appeared before the Tree of Elements. Magic hummed across the field, the sun shimmering in the distance.

The massive tree stood before me, its decaying branches reaching for the earth. Their dry and brittle forms reminded me of myself, before I was shoved down this path. My eyes tightened and I chewed on the edge of my lip. I had been incredibly closed and disconnected. To everyone. I kept myself locked in a bubble of my own making, protecting everyone from myself and the magic I couldn't control.

Walking to the tree, I let my hand settle on the trunk. The rough bark began to pulse. My eyes closed, and I thought of the Astra Flaris and the elements sitting at my solar plexus.

This journey had brought an incredible amount of loss, but my mind infused itself with the things I had gained. Myself. I'd found a belief in myself and my power, and the strength of who I could be when I believed in both. But I also learned to trust others, and to keep faith in their trust of me. That was something I had never allowed before.

The tear fell before I could stop it, and the elements pulsing in the amulet began to thrum, cascading life in a stream of colors throughout the tree. Overcome with emotion, I allowed the flood to surge.

Beneath my hand, the magic streamed upward. New growth soared up and out toward the sky as the elements shattered through the branches. An electric purple illuminated shards of light to the tips of the branches and deep into the root system below. Leaves unfurled in impossible quickness, teeming with elemental colors shimmering on the limbs.

The Tree of Elements blossomed before me. Earth radiated in a green spiral. Air shot upward in sparks of yellows and golds. Fire flamed out in a dance of reds and oranges, followed by the wave of blue and Water that descended the branches.

The elements were alive once again within the tree, and all the while the amulet still pulsed, glowing in elemental tones. I knew they were both inside the tree and yet held by me as Keeper of Elements.

The tree unified the elements with the Realms, layering the magic into existence.

Magic projected from the top of the tree, reflecting in prismatic hues across the sky. The spark of energy and colors rippled, and the layers of dimensions became visible to me. Magic permeated the Realms, saturating every layer, blazing into every creature and being.

Like the web within the Astra Flaris, each soul ignited with a new energy, a colorful light spraying along with their own distinct personal song of color. Impossible tones shattered across the sky, whipping trails of orchid, peacock green, and a thousand others that I couldn't name. Slammed by the sheer power of the magic before me, I stood awed and speechless.

The expanse of beauty caused the smallest amount of fear to trickle into my thoughts. I hadn't expected this. *But what did I expect?* I didn't have the answer. Of course, all of this was right and necessary, saving magic for Light, restoring what had been lost. I shook off the oppressive thoughts, choosing to be moved by the brilliant display of magic transforming before me.

The Tree of Elements shot further into the sky, looming above me, embellished in colorful arcs of magic and light. The crescendo of magic came to an end, leaving me breathless. This. A vibration fluttering through me became a zinging feeling alive within my body. Still in my state of blissful shock, my body was suddenly knocked off balance by an intense hug.

Amy.

"You freaking did it!" As her body slammed into mine, the intensity of which I perceived Amy shocked me. There was more to her. I watched a sudden bubbling of light and color that visibly streaked and smeared around her.

Well, that's new. My movements slowed as I registered this new version of Amy. Lilac burst off her shoulders, and

I wanted to reach out and touch the strange fluff of color. My eyes tracked to the rest of my tribe of magic do-gooders, eventually landing on Rowan. My heart tugged.

He's alive.

Surveying every inch of him, I found his right arm held in a makeshift sling and could tell he wasn't putting weight on his right leg. Spurts of color bounced off him as well. Shards of reds melted off his right side, and greens and blues cascaded on his left. *What in the world?* Leaving Amy, my gaze solely on Rowan, I made my way to him.

"You're okay."

He pulled me into his chest from his left and rested his chin on the top of my head. Eruptions of purple strings issued from his chest. Enveloped in his grasp, I reached my hand up to touch one of them, hoping I didn't look like an insane person. The ribbon moved beneath my finger, and my own melted pink thread met his. I jerked my hand back, tucking into his chest, trying to focus on anything but the colorful smears.

"I'm so sorry, Rowan," I began. "For before. Viego, he . . ."

"Shhh. It's okay. I know." Using his left arm, he squeezed me closer. Something in his voice made me wonder what atrocities he had endured with Viego.

A soft sound behind us made me turn. Seraphina, still wearing the white velvet cloak, appeared insignificant standing underneath the beauty of the Tree of Elements. Stunned again by the splendid array of colors and the majesty of the tree in full form, I tried to keep my focus on Seraphina.

"Aislynn, you fulfilled your destiny. And now I am finally free of my own." Her voice softened. "Remember, the world of magic is one of unpredictability and consequence. There is much you aren't aware of, and I wish you the best."

A shower of red cascaded down upon the witch, encapsulating her in light. Then she was gone.

"Well, way to be a Debbie Downer." Amy peered over her shoulder with an arched brow. I tried to smile in return, but it felt flat.

Riona's staff tapped the ground, sending sparks into the air. "We shall celebrate!" Her voice was jubilant, singing across the air as fireworks exploded across the sky. The enthusiasm she invoked finally reached me and a smile slid across my face.

I did it. A sputter of laughter jumped from my throat and allowed my heart to relax as I leaned into Rowan. A tug on my arm revealed Ailianna.

"Aislynn, congratulations." Underneath her joy, I found her eyes restrained. "I am going to go, though." She glanced at everyone happily laughing, and my heart sunk. "But I want you to know, Aila would have loved this. She believed in you. Even though you didn't see that, she did."

The tears came, and I couldn't stop them. Ailianna had become one of the most authentic, genuine people I had ever met, and my heart ached for her. We celebrated saving magic while she still mourned the loss of her sister. I didn't blame her for wanting to leave.

Her mouth turned up in a small smile. "I hope to see you again soon. You are welcome anytime."

I embraced her in a full hug and sparks of turquoise fluttered out in waves. The vibrant stain of color surrounded her, and I tried to ignore it while simultaneously wondering if anyone else saw the snaps of color.

"Thank you, Ailianna. For everything." I released her and she vanished.

"I feel terrible," I said to Rowan.

"She will be okay. Ailianna is strong." He winced against pain in his shoulder.

"Are you going to be okay?"

"I'm strong, too." He winked. "You should probably go talk to her." He pointed to Riona.

Chewing on my lip, I nodded as I watched Riona laughing with Matthew and Amy. The smears of colors were fluid and flowing around the three of them. The bizarre images gave me pause, then I thought perhaps it was only the overflow of magic from the tree.

"Aislynn," Riona embraced and released me, holding the sides of my arms. "Your grandmother would be so proud of you right now." Tears prickled my eyes again. "We can continue your elemental training whenever you are ready."

Training? Seriously? Hadn't I completed my destiny? I turned, staring hard at the tree and the magic dancing freely upon the leaves. "I was kind of hoping I could go back and be a normal human being again." Saying the words out loud brought a lightness to my chest.

The witch's face twisted into confusion. "Why?"

"Because it's normal?" I half laughed. An extreme need to decompress on every level flourished.

"I see." Her mouth set in a line. "Perhaps a break would be good. I will be waiting. As Witch of the Ancient Keepers, it is my duty."

"Thank you." I smiled, glancing back to Riona. "For everything. I couldn't have done any of this without your help."

Riona turned to face the tree. "A truly magnificent sight. You did well, Aislynn." Her hands rested atop of her staff.

"It is. The colors are incredible."

"Colors?" Riona questioned.

So she doesn't see them. Interesting. Shaking my head, I pushed the question away.

"Well, Aislynn, I will see you soon." She tapped the staff to the ground and with a thunderous clap she disappeared, leaving Amy, Matthew, Rowan, and me standing in the expansive field.

I turned my gaze back to the tree, still rippling a kaleidoscope of colors into the sky. I wondered why no one else could see the vivid display. Perhaps, it was a Keeper thing. A part of me wanted to ask Rowan, but my mouth clammed shut and the only thing I could focus on was the strange tension between us.

Zarah rattled into my mind, and the memories of Rowan and her kissing in Viego's mind-melt land gnawed on my self-esteem. I wanted to kiss him, but the thought of her exploded again.

"This is going to be difficult for them." Rowan interrupted my thoughts, gesturing toward Matthew and Amy.

"The Halfling–shapeshifter part? Or the maintaining a relationship across Realms part?" I joked, watching them walk hand in hand by the tree. Greens and pinks shimmered and melded, saturating them in the emotion of love.

"Ha!" Rowan shook his head at me. "Both, I suppose." He glanced down and away shifting in his makeshift sling. "You will have to keep her away from blood, though. The last thing you need is a changing vampire on the loose in your Realm."

"Ugh. Yeah, no thanks."

"I heard you say you are going back?" he asked.

"Um. Yeah. I thought, maybe, I should just be a plain ole human for a while. You know, normalcy?" I gave him half a glance and sparks of red and black jumped off Rowan's abdomen. *Because that certainly is not normal.* Emotion ripped at me; leaving here meant leaving Rowan.

"Understandable. It has been an intense couple of months." A flat smile filled his face. "Plain ole graphic design and tall buildings, then?"

"Yup! And I won't even complain this time." I grinned thinking about the evening we first met. "What about you? What are you going to do?"

"Figure out the Council, I guess." He transferred his weight to move from pain. "Reevaluate its existence now that magic has been restored and Dark flushed out." He rubbed his hand across his jaw.

"Yeah, with Viego gone, his followers should scamper off back to their caves of stupidity," I said.

Rowan gave me a sideways glance. "I will miss those witty remarks, you know."

This is the part I wanted to avoid.

Feelings.

Shit.

Threads of pinks and deep emerald green swirled from Rowan's chest, and my heart pounded against my ribs. "I'm sure." An odd burst of laughter accompanied my words.

Oh, dear God, Aislynn! Don't be lame. Why was I so terrible at this stuff? Emotion throttled itself in my throat, and I couldn't think, like some sixteen-year-old dim-witted teenager.

"Rowan—"

"Aislynn—"

We both spoked in unison, followed by uncomfortable smiles.

"You first," Rowan said.

"Thank you, for everything. For helping me do this." I waved my hand at the tree. "And saving my life on multiple occasions."

"Of course," he said, and a smile passed his lips. "It is my duty."

Laughing, I fell into his left side again, being careful of his injury and allowing Rowan to hold me one last time. I wanted to share how I felt, but the words stuck, unable to free themselves. I would see him again. This wasn't a forever goodbye. Maybe, after more time and recovering from everything we had been through, I would be able to find the right words. For now, I let myself be embraced in the swirls of stunning color.

He rested his cheek on my head, and a softness enveloped us. The threads of greens emitted in zings of emotion as he kissed the top of my crown. Time seemed to slow as the vibration of love cascaded down through me.

Maybe it was enough for now.

52

"There you are!" I said, walking out of my bathroom, finishing the text to my parents. The text was a well-devised spell to secure the timeline as well as remove my absence from their memories. They now believed I had been in England for a conference. *Nifty.*

I focused back on my cat, surprised to find Jax curled in the middle of my bed. I hadn't seen the furry bastard for over a week.

"Yeah, I needed a long nap after all that. It was a lot of work." With a squeak, his face opened into a wide yawn.

"Seriously? You have some explaining to do!" I slung my messenger bag across my chest. It was almost time to leave.

"Explaining? Explain what?" He glanced up, slowly blinking his brilliant blue eyes as his tail twitched wildly against the blankets.

"Like, uh . . . Seraphina mentioning she's like you, punished by the gods? Except she has more than nine lives." I folded my arms.

"*Oh, that.*" Jax lifted his paw, proceeding to lick the back of his leg.

"AHEM!"

"*What?*"

"Answers!"

"*Well, I thought it was obvious.*"

"What? That you were punished by the Gods?" My foot tapped against the carpet in irritation.

"*Well, yeah.*"

"What? Why didn't you tell me?"

"*It's not obvious I am an asshole?*"

"I thought you were just a cat!"

"*That's fair. Cats are assholes. Probably why this form was chosen.*" He resumed his licking, moving closer to his butt.

"So, wait? You are not a cat?"

"*Well, I mean, no.*" He paused, ears pricking forward.

"What?"

"*I mean, this furry little body is convenient at times, but it's not what I would choose.*"

"I . . . uh . . ." I stumbled over finding the right words. "Why are you even here?"

"*Punished. Helloooo?*"

"Are you freaking kidding me, *cat?* Or . . . whatever you are?"

He resumed licking his ass.

"I am going to work! To be a normal *human*. When I get home, you will be explaining this shit to me and where the hell you have been."

"*Uh-huh.*" He continued wet slurps of his fur.

"Arrrggghhh!" I spun on the spot, disappearing. I needed coffee to deal with this crap, and I reconsidered my decision on being human. After a quick stop for Starbucks, I teleported to Amy's living room.

"Aims, you ready to go?" I called out to her.

"Yeah, yeah," she yelled from the bathroom. "I am . . . just . . . pudding on yip goss." Poking her head out into the hall, she smeared lip gloss across her lips, making weird air sucking sounds. Meeting her in the hallway, I handed her the coffee.

"Oooh, thanks." She took a sip. "This teleporting shit is awesome!"

"Ha! I know, right?" I laughed, taking several swallows of my own coffee.

"And it will cut down on my commuting expenses!" Keeping Amy off the metro transit buses was the best possible solution for humanity, and I deemed it my new destiny.

"Are you ready?" I asked.

She nodded, and I teleported us to an empty elevator close to our buildings. With my new abilities, I found it easy to sense empty places to travel. We walked in relative silence, stopping in the middle of the skyway that hung above Nicolette Mall.

We peered down on the city. Sunlight cut sharply across the concrete, creating odd shadows through the street. It was all such a stark contrast from the beauty of Hallervania. Sipping our coffees, we watched the sun gradually rise with the new day.

"So, we just go back to being graphic designers?" Amy asked, peering out the glass. I was aware she yearned for the place beyond our Realm. Leaving Matthew in Hallervania had been a difficult choice for them, but it was best for the time being.

"I guess." I shrugged.

My entire life had shifted. Everything that had once been important changed into entirely new things. Now, I was aware of things that mattered: connection. Truth. Magic. People. People mattered. All of them, all around me, walking by, down on the streets on their phones going about their morning, they mattered. Their presence in this Realm mattered.

Before, humanity frustrated me. Coworkers, work, and my family all agitated against my sense of happiness. But each person here and in the magical Realm held their own story, their contribution to the whole.

Rowan had been right all those months ago when he asked me about a bigger purpose. We each had to find our own place in the grand design and believe in one thing. We had to find our purpose. Our divine story in this precious journey.

The colors had remained, although subdued in my Realm. I could still see the ripples and arcs bouncing off of each person. I hadn't told Amy, though I am sure she would have some great insight regarding auras or some other magical crap. I didn't want to think about it. A part of me feared the meaning behind the vivid span of colors that had filled my vision ever since the Tree of Elements was restored.

"When are you going to see Rowan again?" Amy peered at me over her coffee.

"I don't know. Soon, maybe?" The corners of my lips rose as a flush of color spread.

"Ha. I knew it. I like him. He's good for you," Amy said.

I tried not to roll my eyes as I half smiled, and my heart tugged at the thought of him. "What about our jobs? Isn't that going to be a problem? You know, since we haven't been there?" she asked, pulling me from my thoughts.

"I took care of it. A little magic in our Realm never hurt anyone." I winked at her, and she gave a half laugh. A little bit of magic was exactly what started this disaster. Riona shared with me a simple spell to weave our presence in the timeline of our Realm. No one would realize we hadn't been there. Like a fuzzy dream, they would convince themselves they had merely forgotten. As well as our families, they wouldn't remember we had been missing for months.

"But we are freaking amazing!" Amy snarked, and I realized she was stalling. "We did unbelievable things." Her eyes sparkled as if I hadn't been there with her the entire time. I sipped, nodding. "And we don't even get to tell anyone." Bittersweet sadness trailed through her words.

"Nope." I shook my head.

"Dammit."

"Mm-hmm. Imagine if we could, though." I grinned. She paused for a moment, sipping her own coffee, both of us sharing wicked smiles.

"I'd tell them we are motherfucking sorceresses." A fierceness exuded through her words which made me burst into laughter.

"Cheers to that." We tipped our coffees together and magic crackled the air, sending sparks of yellow over the cups. A few people turned at the sound, but with the sun behind us, we appeared as shadowed silhouettes, the magic hidden by the light of the sun.

&PILOGUE

Clearfield, Utah

Ten-year-old Riley sat in his room, frustrated. He hadn't meant to lie, not really. He had planned to do the chore later; he just wanted to keep playing his game. And now he couldn't play anything for a week! The phone sat in jail, nestled in Mom's back pocket.

Upset with him, she had gone outside to water the plants. His guy hadn't been moved to safety, and he was going to lose all the stuff he'd earned. Riley punched his pillow. If Mom had let him save his spot, he wouldn't have been so mad. *I need to save my guy.*

But there was nothing he could do now, so he stomped off to the bathroom. It was too bad he couldn't make stuff magically appear. Then he would make his phone be on his bed when he came back. That would be cool.

While washing his hands, he thought about his phone being back on his bed, like a little present. He pushed open his door of his bedroom, and his phone was there! In the middle of the bed!

What? Had Mom forgiven him? He checked out his window and saw her spraying the flowers. *But . . . ?* He tentatively picked it up and tapped to open his game. *Cool!* Adjusting his pillow, he made himself comfortable and began to work on saving his guy and all his stuff.

"Riley! Where are you?" Mom yelled not long after.

"I'm in my room!" she shouted back.

"I told you, you are grounded from that phone!" She hollered up the stairs.

"But you gave it back!" he cried out.

"What?" She opened his door, holding her hand out for the phone. "No. How did you get it? It was in my pocket!"

"But I came out of the bathroom and it was on my bed. I swear, Mom. It was on my bed." Hand shaking, he handed the phone back to his mom.

"But how is that possible?"

Tears pricked the little boy's eyes as he shook his head.

Manchester, Connecticut

Bekki's phone chirped, causing her to jump at her desk. Sliding away the notification from the FollowPeeps app, her stomach lurched to her throat. Paul was leaving his office. Even though she knew because Charlotte had told her, she didn't want to believe it was true. But there, the blinking blue light showed Paul leaving.

She stared at her phone, watching the blue circle track further away.

Her husband was cheating on her.

The signs had been there all along, staring her in the face, but she ignored them. Paul kept hiding his phone, had late evening appointments, and missed many dinners. She couldn't handle him leaving her. She couldn't go through a divorce; what would she tell her family? Slowly, Bekki moved from her desk, shutting her office door with an audible click. She sat back in her chair.

The blue dot mocked her as it drew closer to its destination: *her* house. The Mistress.

The tears came before she could stop them. The idea of him with someone else shattered her heart into a thousand pieces. Sobbing sounds erupted from her chest and she hoped no one would hear.

Jaw muscles writhing as Bekki's teeth clenched, she imagined what she would say to them if she walked in on them, proving she wasn't the stupid one. Again. She envisioned them in bed, ripping off the covers. The thoughts barreled, unstoppable, in her head. Closing her eyes, she fought against the now unwelcome images.

Then she opened her eyes.

She stood in *her* house. The bedroom door was right in front of her. This couldn't be real. How could she be inside her husband's lover's home? A shaking hand reached for the knob, cold under her grasp. She turned and pushed open the door.

Paul, in the middle of taking off his pants, stopped at the sight of his wife.

"Bekki?" he stammered.

Anger rolled through Bekki, eating away at her resolve. *How can he do this to me?* A fire seethed from within her, raging to escape. Her fisted hands shook at her sides.

"What are you doing here? Get out!" the mistress screamed.

How dare she tell me what to do! Bekki's hands flashed open. Flames poured out of her palms, igniting the wood floors.

"Bekki!" Paul shouted as the flames engulfed the room.

Sacile, Italy

Five-year-old Thea let her hand settle across the water in the fountain as she ran around the edge. Her mom wouldn't let her go too far, so she tried to stay close. The water cool under her touch tingled the tips of her fingers. She drew her hand up, pulling the water upward and back down again. The water wanted to play with her; she could hear its pretty song in her mind.

"Thea, come here, please! Don't play in the water," Thea's mom called. Dragging her hand in the water, she moved closer to her mom. Thea looked up at the sparks of color that filled the sky. Splashes of greens and pinks filtered through the air.

"Look at the colors, Mamma!" Thea exclaimed and pointed to the sky. Her mom turned, following the direction of her daughter's finger.

"What colors, love?" She looked but didn't see what Thea meant.

"They're everywhere." Thea put both hands out and the colors poured through her hands. Twists of blues and turquoises danced across her body, making her laugh.

"You are silly!" her mom said, turning to pack up the lunch they shared. "Come on. It's time to go back home." She smiled at her daughter.

"Okay, Mamma. The colors come too, okay?" Thea dragged sparks of light behind her, and she blew a kiss at the fountain water. Turning back to her mom, Thea didn't see the water bubble up and spray farther out of the fountain than normal.

Dingle, Ireland

Aiden slipped out of the pub for a quick walk into town. His brother could manage the lunch shift without him. He needed some air; something about the afternoon had made him edgy. The clouds dropped, sitting heavy in the sky, promising rain, adding to his already uneasy mood.

Up ahead, he watched a couple teenagers laughing on their phones, pushing and messing around like typical boys. Aiden shook his head. He and his brother had spent their afternoons in fistfights, not staring into phones. The thought made him smile until he registered the little red car coming down the lane, swerving to miss a dog running across the road. *Mr. Grady's Collie is loose again.* The car headed straight for the teenagers.

Aiden's heart hammered in his chest as everything seemed to move in slow motion. The car barreled toward the kids who weren't paying attention. His hands shot up, and he screamed for them to move when everything unexpectedly stopped.

Still.

The car halted midmotion. One teenager was glancing at him, with the other looking behind at the car. Everything and everyone was frozen.

What in the heavens? How? Aiden stood shocked by the pub's entrance for a moment before running toward the teenagers. He shoved them out of harm's way, then everything began to move again. Yelling and screeching tires filled the air. The world was alive again.

The car barely missed the boys and Aiden. The teenagers, swearing, gestured toward the driver. Aiden didn't move, eyes full of confusion. A loud crack of thunder sounded, and the rain fell in sheets. The downpour sent the teenagers tearing off into the coffee shop, leaving Aiden standing in the wet.

Ruth Gorge, Denali National Forest, Alaska

The ice is warm today, Gabe thought when he slammed his ice ax into the wall. Checking the hold, he shoved the crampon of his right toe into a small space. Ice climbing had become his escape from thinking about Jen after they broke up a couple months ago.

Pulling himself over, he reached into his bag for an ice screw. Gabe held steady into his feet, then screwed into the ice. A loud popping radiated as the ice cracked, breaking underneath the screw. *Dammit.* Fingers searching for another spot, he screwed again as water dripped down the wall.

He probably shouldn't be climbing today. The conditions were subpar at best, but he couldn't resist the temptation the ice held. Testing the screw, he clamped the carabiner, tugged, and the ice groaned in protest. The screw wasn't secure. *Third time's a charm.* Changing his position, he settled a little farther down, finding a better hold for the screw.

There. Gabe clipped, tugged, and chipped at the ice under the screw so the quick draw hung clean. Setting his feet, he jammed the ax into the wall. A thrumming deep in the wall came forward as the sheet slipped. The ice screw popped, sending him hurling down on his rope. The weight of gravity pulled the next screw and the next as he fell downward.

Gabe's brain went through a thousand thoughts in seconds as he sailed through empty air. *Is this really the end?* Fear ate away as he knew he didn't *want* to die. Though he used the climbing as a way to move through his pain, he didn't want to die. *Just scare myself shitless, maybe.* Suddenly, the rope went taut and stopped. His body bounced as the screws further down the wall held him. *Thank God.*

He swung back to the wall, and another loud pop sounded. *SHIT.* Down he went again. This time it was a rhythmic sound of continuous popping as he dropped. *Mom is going to bring me back from the dead and kill me again.*

Time passed in such slowness as he fell. There was nothing to stop him this time except the ground below. And then something shifted. Gabe felt a weird tingling, strange and foreign. He stopped falling, and somehow, he moved upward. Eyes laser sharp, he scanned below him. Screaming out, the squawk of an eagle pierced his ears.

What is happening? This must be death. But he wasn't dead; he was soaring.

Wings replaced his hands, and he flew. He soared above where he had been climbing as chunks of ice fell to the earth.

Sydney, Australia

Claire set her glasses on the bathroom counter while she waited for the water to warm. The arthritis screaming in her hands this morning made her wince. *Getting old is a real witch.*

She'd do anything to have her twenty-year-old body back. Hell, she would take the forty-year-old one. Stepping into the shower, she held her aching hands under the hot spray as it rained down, rubbing at the wrinkles and age spots as she thought about being younger.

With her cupped hands, she scooped the water over her face, imagining the "old" being washed away. *Ah, if it were only that simple.* Carefully turning her back to the spray, Claire envisioned the water running down her spine, building new bones and new discs between the joints, invigorating her body. She learned long ago that visualization was a helpful tool, but in this case, she wished it could actually work.

But, alas, the human body must go through its own cycle.

After the heat loosened her joints, she resorted to leaving the shower and wrapped herself in a towel. Steam saturated the small bathroom and helped ease her pain more. The morning was getting late and Bruce would be up here soon nagging at her.

She wiped her hand across the mirror, revealing a smeared version of her face. She jolted closer to the mirror. Wrinkles . . . where were her wrinkles? Immediately, her hands went to her face in shock as she pulled on her skin.

"Claire, are you ready yet?" Bruce asked as he came around the corner.

"I . . ."

Bruce's face said everything. The familiar lines and creases moved into bewilderment.

"Claire?" His hand reached out in shaky uncertainty.

Turning to the mirror once again, Claire looked at herself. Her reflection revealed a firm, young, twenty-five-year-old face.

"I don't know what is happening." She stuttered over the words.

ACKNOWLEDGMENTS

First, you. My reader. Thank you. I want to extend my deepest gratitude to you for taking precious moments of your life and spending them with me and my magical world. In these crazy and uncertain times, it means more than ever, as we have all come to recognize the preciousness of our moments. I truly hope you found an escape from the chaos and perhaps, along the way, discovered an awakening of the magic that exists within you.

This book was delayed in so many ways from my internal timeline and expectations, but I have come to realize everything happens in divine timing, and this is the moment *Awakening* was meant to be shared with the world.

My Chick Peas. Oh, what would I do without you? Probably cry in a corner. Amy, Lo, Kristine. Thank you for keeping me laughing in this insane world. I can't wait for our writing adventure together.

Hannah. My magical word goddess. The words "Thank You" are neither grand nor magnificent enough for your editing prowess. You made me see each of my characters differently, digging into the deepest corners to find the beautiful threads that needed to be melded together. Thank you for traversing this world with me.

Tod, please expect the truckload of chocolates soon. Ha. Seriously, thank you for your formatting genius. Your precision and eye for your work makes my little OCD heart happy. You made the inside of this book stunning.

Jayelle, my hero. You are a divine goddess. Thank you for being my lifesaver. The cover you created proves magic is real.

My ARC readers: Tess, Jess, Sarah S., Megan, Natalie, Sarah F.W., Tina, and Patricia. Your love for this story created a strength and belief in myself to bring Aislynn and Jax to the world. Oh, and Rowan; we can't forget Rowan. My gratitude for each of you is bigger than you know.

Daria, oh Daria. I am sorry again about Daragon. I will make it up to you. Thank you for being my saving grace in IG land. Thank you for always making me laugh hysterically and being such an amazing friend.

Tessa, my magic sister, your constant presence and support is invaluable to me. Thank you for being my earthy balance when I need it most.

Amy and Matt, thanks for letting me make you into magical creatures. I promise not to be too mean.

To my boys. I love you. Thank you for always being patient with me, especially when it's "let me finish this one last thing!" and all my crazy antics. I am so thankful you will create characters with me. Those soul-sucking Cuddlers are all yours, boys!

Caleb, my human, thank you for supporting my dreams and always wanting to hear my stories. Even though you are pissed when I read you half-finished shoddy versions. Your belief in me as an author defies logic and reasoning, and I love you for it.

To my grandma—your phone calls as you read meant the world to me. Your excitement for a genre absolutely outside your normal reading reminds me that I can bring light to anything, anywhere.

About the Author

Amazon best-selling author Finn O'Malley is an elemental goddess who loves writing, crystals, and daydreaming about her next meal. She lives in Northern Utah with her human husband, two lovable teenagers, and two cat overlords on the hunt for adventure, world domination, and wet food. When she is not in her garden growing human-sized bushels of herbs, you can find Finn sitting on a mountaintop practicing yoga or penning witty urban fantasy adventures for humans who need a break from reality.

Finn's short story "Fire Dance" is featured in *Dragons Within: Guarding Her Own*, which was an award-winning Finalist in the Fiction: Anthologies category of the 2020 Best Book Awards sponsored by American Book Fest.

You can follow Finn on social media at:

www.finnomalley.com
www.facebook.com/FinnOMalleyauthor
Instagram @finn.omalley.author
www.amazon.com/author/finnomalley